CW00762661

An Elephant for Aristotle

An Elephant for Aristotle

L. Sprague de Camp

an imprint of

Rockville, Maryland

An Elephant for Aristotle © **1958 by L. Sprague de Camp.** All rights reserved. This book may not be copied or reproduced, in whole or in part, by any means, electronic, mechanical or otherwise without written permission from the publisher except by a reviewer who may quote brief passages in a review.

This is a work of fiction. Any resemblance to any actual persons, events or localities is purely coincidental and beyond the intent of the author and publisher.

Tarikian, TARK Classic Fiction, Arc Manor, Arc Manor Classic Reprints, Phoenix Pick, Phoenix Science Fiction Classics, Phoenix Rider, The Stellar Guild Series, Manor Thrift and logos associated with those imprints are trademarks or registered trademarks of Arc Manor, LLC, Rockville, Maryland. All other trademarks and trademarked names are properties of their respective owners.

This book is presented as is, without any warranties (implied or otherwise) as to the accuracy of the production, text or translation.

ISBN: 978-1-61242-127-8

www.PhoenixPick.com
Great Science Fiction & Fantasy
Free Ebook Every Month

Published by Phoenix Pick
an imprint of Arc Manor
P. O. Box 10339
Rockville, MD 20849-0339
www.ArcManor.com

To Howard and Marianne Annin

in memory of many pleasant times
and in gratitude for many favors

Contents

Introduction

Harry Turtledove

AN ELEPHANT FOR ARISTOTLE was L. Sprague de Camp's first straight historical novel. In many ways, it's still one of his best. The genesis of the novel was pretty straightforward. A French scholar noted that Aristotle wrote about elephants as if he had seen one with his own eyes. Spotting that set de Camp wondering how Aristotle might have seen an elephant. Perhaps Alexander the Great sent his old tutor one from India, whose western fringes he conquered.

Even today, you can't FedEx an elephant. Back in the fourth century BC, you *really* couldn't FedEx an elephant. It's about 2,000 miles from the banks of the Indus to the Acropolis of Athens. Somebody had to take charge of that elephant and bring it across those 2,000 miles through Alexander's often imperfectly conquered empire to the philosopher. That somebody would have had to keep the elephant alive. He would have had to keep it fed. He would have had to keep himself and whoever he had with him alive and fed and unrobbed. The roads would have been bad, when there were roads at all—a lot of the time, there wouldn't have been. The people through whose country he was bringing this monster would not always be friendly, which is putting things mildly.

De Camp realized the real story there was not that Aristotle saw, or may have seen, an elephant. The real story was how the elephant got from the banks of the Indus to Athens alive and in one piece. And that is the story of *An Elephant for Aristotle*.

The (fictional) officer responsible for bringing the (possibly fictional) elephant west is Leon of Atrax, a town in the northern Greek region of Thessaly. Under his command, along with the Indian elephant-keeper and his assistant, are a troop of Thessalian cavalrymen he commanded in Alexander's furious push to and past the borders of the world previously known to the Greeks. Also traveling with him is the (real) Greek skeptical philosopher, Pyrron. The troop has with it other specimens from India as well as the elephant, and a large, heavy sum of money (no credit cards or even banknotes back then, either) to pay for supplies, to give the cavalrymen their wages—and to give a sizable gift to Xenokrates, Aristotle's leading rival. This, de Camp speculates, was Alexander's little (well, not so little) joke. Aristotle would have the elephant, which would promptly start eating him out of house and home. Xenokrates would have plenty of cash to buy fodder for it, but would sooner throw his silver into the sea than let his intellectual antagonist use it.

The problem with all this, of course, is that Leon of Atrax is only a junior officer and has only a troop of horsemen under his command. Somehow, he has to get not only the elephant but all that lovely money past the swarms of greedy generals and civilian officials between India and Greece. How he does it, whether he can do it…That's the substance of the novel, and I won't spoil it for you here.

I will note that, as always, de Camp's people are realistic and his research is impeccable. He has gone through Aristotle, the historian Herodotus, and the geographer Strabo with gun and camera, as well as using modern scholarly works, travel accounts, and reports from archeologists. Till someone comes up with a time machine, we can't know for sure what this stretch of the Near East was like more than 2,300 years ago. Reading *An Elephant for Aristotle* will get you about as close as anything, though.

In making his people feel real, de Camp pulls what I think is a very cool stunt. Ancient Greek, like the modern English of England and Scotland (not so much like the modern English of the United States), was a language of strongly marked dialects. As soon as people opened their mouths, you could tell where they came from. You could pretty much make out what someone who used a different dialect was saying, but you wouldn't always be sure about every word or turn of phrase.

De Camp's characters reproduce this in their dialogue in the novel. Leon and the other Thessalians, who come from the far north of Greece, are made to speak with a Scots burr and with vocabulary to match. Ionian Greeks did not use rough breathings at the start of words; they are made to talk like Cockneys, who also drop their h's. Attic Greek is closely related to Ionic, and Athens was the cultural center of Greece the way London is in England. In An Elephant for Aristotle, then, Athenians sound as if they might be auditioning for the BBC. And Spartans and other Greeks who used the southerly Doric dialect are given a drawl in the book. It's a nice way to keep the reader clued in on who comes from where and what that means when he's dealing with a person from somewhere else.

Incidentally, lest you think *An Elephant for Aristotle* is not just fiction but fantasy, and the events it describes fall totally beyond the realm of the possible, you should know that, in the early fifteenth century of our era, the young Mamluk Sultan Faraj sent a giraffe as a gift to the court of his fellow Sultan Timur (also known as Tamerlane). Faraj ruled in Egypt; Timur's capital was in Samarkand, in Central Asia. The distance between the two courts was something over 3,000 miles. That giraffe walked every step of the way. Spanish ambassadors, also on their way to Timur's capital, saw the beast on its journey in Azerbaijan. One of them, Ruy Gonzalez de Clavijo, left behind one of the earliest European descriptions of the giraffe. So, in this case, fiction is not stranger than truth. As best I can tell, they walk each other to a dead heat.

Prologos

MANY HAVE TOLD of Alexander's conquests. Howsomever, such was the vastness of this revolution in the affairs of mankind that, I think, not even minor events of Alexander's career should be suffered to perish from memory. Therefore I, Leon son of Aristos, of Atrax in Thessalia, have written the history of certain happenings in which I took part during the divine Alexander's reign, nigh unto thirty years ago.

Some may deem my account a paltry thing. For, so far was I from commanding ten thousand men, like Xenophon, that my force at no time exceeded a hundred. Nevertheless, the work I performed for King Alexander was in many ways so singular that fain would I not die without recording it. And if I be guilty of insolence in presenting an account that is mainly a tale of my own adventures, I trust that the gods will indulge me.

I have sought to write foreign names in forms as close to the originals as can be done with Greek letters, except for some, like "Xerxes," whereof long usage has sanctified a Hellenized form. However, most Persian and Indian men's names end in the nominative either in vowels, or in hissing and breathing sounds that we do not have in Greek. Therefore I have ended such names with the letter *s* to make them seem less strange to my readers.

BOOK ONE

India

MY STORY BEGINS at the end of the tenth year of the reign of Alexander, son of Philip, when Hegemon was archon of Athens. In the great battle in which Alexander vanquished Poros, the giant Indian warrior king, I, in my twenty-seventh year, fought as troop closer in the Thessalian Troop of Demetrios' cavalry regiment. We were the last Thessalians in the army. The rest of the levy, which at one time numbered two thousand, had been sent home from Media and Baktria.

In this dreadful struggle, I took an Indian spear through the calf of my leg. I bound up the wound and fought on as acting troop leader, after our troop leader fell before a javelin cast by Poros himself from the back of his towering elephant.

We fought till our javelins all were spent and we could hardly hold our swords for sweat and blood. Unhurt men were falling from thirst and exhaustion when at last I heard cheers from other parts of the field. The rest of our army had forced a crossing of the Hydaspes and were coming to help us.

The Indians, who had fought with the greatest fury though half surrounded, saw them also and began to fall back. Many elephant drivers had been slain, and the animals wheeled about and started for home. Soon the whole Indian army crumbled into a mass of fugitives. King Poros was one of the last to leave the field.

I sought out our squadron leader, a Macedonian named Eriguios, and asked for orders.

"Let Krateros' fresh horse handle the pursuit," said he, wiping blood from his face. "We shall wind-break our beasts if we push them further. Rally your troop and fetch back those who have gone off after the Indians."

I grieved not to miss the pursuit. Not only was I too weary to kill anything stronger than a rabbit, but also I do not like thrusting fleeing foes in the back. It seems a mean and unworthy thing to do, even to foreigners.

I rode back to where our troop had collected and sent our aide around the battlefield to rally stragglers. When he came back, several men were still not accounted for. I left one of the flank guards in command and rode off with the aide to look for the missing men. We picked our way among the bodies of hundreds of Indian foot soldiers slaughtered in flight. Happy the horseman, who has a good chance to escape if his side be defeated!

A few furlongs away I came on a curious sight. Poros' huge elephant stood with arrows projecting out from him like spines from a hedgehog. The drapes that hung from his sides were tattered and splashed with mud and blood. On the elephant's neck sat the driver, protected by white, quilted robes of Indian tree wool, which grows on a bush instead of a beast.

In the booth on the elephant's back sat Poros, poising a javelin. He was the largest man I have ever seen. He wore a gold-inlaid helmet encircled with gleaming gems, and a coat of silvered scale mail. His beard was dyed green. His right arm hung limp and was covered with blood from a shoulder wound.

Some of our horsemen stood by, though at a prudent distance, for they had seen what this colossal king could do with his darts. Among these onlookers I saw most of my missing men.

King Poros was carrying on a lively dispute with one of our allied Indian kings, who sat on his steed near the elephant and shouted up at his fellow monarch. Though I could not understand them, I gathered that our Indian was trying to persuade Poros to give himself up.

Then the elephant settled matters by kneeling down, so abruptly that Poros was almost shaken out of his booth. I suppose Poros took this as a sign that his deities wished him to yield, for he climbed stiffly down from his mount. The other king dismounted to help him. They turned back toward the battlefield. Poros walked slowly with his left arm around the other king's neck and wept at the sight of all the dead Indians.

"Ē! Hither, all Thessalians!" I called in a husky croak, for my tongue was so swollen with thirst I could hardly speak. "Come on, lads, back to the troop!"

We had started off beside Poros when we met Alexander and his staff. Alexander drew rein a few paces from the two Indian kings. His famous charger, Ox-head, had fallen dead in the battle, so he rode another horse.

"Silence!" cried the heralds. Poros drew himself up and stared haughtily at Alexander.

There were two interpreters, one translating from Greek to Persian and one from Persian to Indian. Alexander said to the Graeco-Persian interpreter: "Ask him how he expects to be used."

The interpreters passed the message along. I could follow the Persian part, having learnt a smattering of that tongue from Hyovis, my Persian concubine. She, alas! perished of snakebite a little before the battle.

Poros rumbled something in Indian. After a pause for translation, the first interpreter said: "He says: 'Why, as a king, to be sure!'"

Alexander cocked his head and smiled. He said: "That is a right royal answer. Tell him I shall do that anyway, for my own honor. Now ask him if there be aught he would especially like for his own sake."

When the interpreters and Poros had spoken again, the Greek-speaking one said: "He says that to use him as a king includes all."

Alexander laughed, dismounted, and stepped forward. The seven-foot Poros, who towered over the little Alexander, closed his eyes and swayed. He would have fallen had not Alexander and the other Indian king caught him. Alexander's staff closed in around them so I could not see, but I heard Alexander's high voice calling for water, bandages, and medicines. Alexander fancied himself as a physician and liked a chance to practice his medical skill. Belike I owe my life to the fact that he never had occasion to employ it on me.

Soon Alexander commanded his folk to stand back. He had helped Poros out of his mail coat and put his wounded arm in a sling. His staff made a litter of spears and a cloak, on which they carried the giant.

I led my men back to where I had left Eriguios. The Thessalian Troop, which numbered seventy-four at the start of the battle, had come through it with seven slain, and ten or twelve others gravely but not fatally hurt. I had but one wound, in my leg, though I had traded handstrokes with several Indians. Golden, my Baktrian mare, had several cuts but nothing crippling.

As we were all half dead from thirst, Eriguios led the squadron to the margin of the Hydaspes for water. I dismounted, fell in a heap, and swooned from loss of blood.

I came to my senses in the new sick quarters. The slaves and camp followers had arrived with tents and provisions from our old camp on the west side of the Hydaspes. The camp surveyors were pacing off distances and ordering people to their proper places. Grooms set up horse lines and took our beasts away to care for them, while the mercy killers cut the throats of the fatally wounded, and the scavengers stripped and dragged off the slain. It was dark before a physician got around to cleansing my wound and tying it up again.

I spent several unhappy days in sick quarters. My wound swelled and ached. The slaves who cared for the sick were slow and slack, and too few. The rain pattered on the tent for days at a time, for in India the rains fall in summer instead of in winter as in Hellas. The tent leaked, dripping on me and soaking my pallet.

At this time I was much alone, having no slave of my own. My concubine was dead and, not being a southern Hellene, I had no bent toward love affairs with men. Hence, I had no one to trouble over me, though this did not fret me so much as it would some folk.

At least once a day somebody came to visit. Betimes it was King Alexander himself, speaking a few words to each man in sick quarters. He looked at their wounds and spoke with the physicians about treatments and chances of healing. The first time he came to my tent he said:

"Rejoice, O Leon! How goes it?"

I murmured respectfully. He knew me well by sight, though we had never been intimate. Alexander was a short man, broad of shoulder and mighty of thew, with many scars lining his fine-featured face and muscular limbs. At close view one could see that he was no longer the young demigod who had left Macedonia eight years before. The ruddy gold of his hair was turning dull, with streaks of gray. The winter winds of Baktria had roughened his skin and filled it with little red veins.

The man who now looked godlike was Alexander's secretary, Eumenes of Kardia. He stood, smooth and ruddy, at the king's elbow with a tablet on which to note any divine thoughts that Alexander might utter. But then, Eumenes had been writing letters to kings and adding up the army's payroll during all those years when the rest of us were out in all weathers, chasing the wild Sakai across their boundless plains.

"You shall soon heal," said Alexander, smiling, "if I must issue a decree to that effect. You did well in the battle. It has been told me how you rallied your troop when Poros attacked them on his elephant. What can I do for you?"

I decided to hammer while the iron was red. "O King, seems it not strange to you that after seven years' service, including three great battles and many skirmishes, my rank should be only that of troop closer?"

Alexander laughed and said to Eumenes: "Hermes attend us! Does it not beat all how men at death's door still think of promotion?" He clapped me lightly on the shoulder. "Present your plea to Eriguios, who will pass it on through proper channels. Alexander will do you justice, whether it be what you expect or not. Farewell for now!"

As he went out, I was tempted to call after him, pursuing the matter of promotion. But I knew the king's uncertain temper too well. When he chose to unbend he could be the most charming of men, but a soldier who presumed too far on his affability might find the king turned suddenly haughty, and receive a tongue-lashing or worse.

So I kept my peace. Learn to profit from the follies of others, as we say in Thessalia.

Other regular visitors were Eriguios the squadron leader and the flank guards of my troop, Gration of Trikka and Sthenelos of Athens. Eriguios, more bookish than most soldiers, brought over the books he carried and read them to me. I enjoyed especially Aineias' *On Tactics*, Simon's *On Horsemanship*, and Xenophon's *The Cavalry Commander*. Xenophon was my favorite author, being the only philosopher I knew of who applied his mind to matters of practical use in everyday life.

Then my wound began to heal. One day Eriguios found me hobbling about on a stick. I said:

"As you see, I shall soon be back in my command. I have some promotions to propose."

"Say on," he said.

"First, I think I should be confirmed as troop leader."

"It pleases. I will recommend the promotion to Demetrios."

"Then I would fain have Gration made troop closer in my place; Sthenelos moved from left flank guard to right flank guard; and Thyestes of Pharsala made left flank guard."

"I like not Sthenelos' affected ways," said Eriguios, waving his fingers languidly in mimicry of the Athenian.

"Belike, but he's a fell fighter and quick of wit."

"So be it, then. Thyestes is that little red-faced fellow, is he not?"

"Aye. He's a double-pay trooper the now."

"But is he a man of any family?"

"Nay, no birth at all. He's the bastard son of a soldier and a miller's daughter. But he's a daredevil horseman, and I think he has the makings of an able officer. Which carries the greater weight?"

The next day the rain stopped long enough for the king to order the long-deferred celebration of victory. During the games there was a stir in the camp as Phratapharnas, viceroy of Parthia, rode in. He led a squadron of Thracian horse which the king had left with him in Persia to put down rebels. Phratapharnas could have sent the Thracians under someone else, but I suppose he wished to ingratiate himself with Alexander and see some new country. Persians think nought of taking horse for ten thousand furlongs, for no more compelling reasons.

On the following day Alexander founded a new city, Nikaia, near our camp. He traced out the walls by riding slowly round the circuit in a chariot and sprinkling barley meal out of a sack. When birds flew down to eat the meal, Aristandros, the chief soothsayer, prophesied that, as these birds gathered, so should a mighty multitude gather to make this city a metropolis. Aristandros was rightly called a great soothsayer because he ever contrived that the omens came out as Alexander wished.

I was watching Alexander walk back to his tent, talking in lively fashion to the crowd of Indian kings, Macedonian generals, Greek poets and philosophers, and other notables, when Eriguios joined me, saying:

"I have been looking for you, Leon. The king assents to all your proposals for the troop but one."

"Which?" I said.

Eriguios grinned. "The one about yourself."

My jaw dropped. I clenched my fists. "By the Dog of Egypt! Of all the unjust—"

I caught a warning glance from Eriguios and mastered myself. Time had been in the Macedonian army when men spoke their feelings boldly, as one would expect free Hellenes to do. But, since the king had acquired foreign ideas of imperial power, courtly etiquette, and divine attributes, wise men did not complain too loudly where he or his sycophants might hear.

"What's the matter?" I said.

"Do not look as though you would murder me; I but jested. He has picked a Macedonian to lead the troop, to be sure; but that is nought in your disfavor. He has another task for you, at which you will have a troop leader's rank and pay."

"Another task? What sort?"

"I know not. He sent word by Demetrios that you should visit the royal tent this afternoon."

After the noonday meal, I put on my uniform, limped over to the royal tent, and gave my name to Ptolemaios the Companion, now king of Egypt. He greeted me pleasantly and bade me wait. I sat on a log between a stinking, sheepskin-clad Massagete, wearing a Scythian necklace of bear claws and amber, and an Indian bedecked with jingling ornaments of silver and turquoise. There was the usual coming and going: bejeweled envoys from Indian states, messengers from Persia, Hellas, and other western lands, as well as officers of our own army.

Finally; at Ptolemaios' signal, I hobbled into the tent between a pair of shaggy Sakan guards. The king, wearing a long yellow Persian robe, sat among his people at a table littered with scrolls and maps.

Besides the ever-present Eumenes, I recognized some of the learned Hellenes—the philosophers Anaxarchos and Pyrron and the geographer Polykleitos. This was a great thrill for me. I had long wished to meet these scholars but as a soldier had neither the occasion to do so nor the temerity to invent one.

I took off my helmet, cried: "Rejoice, O King!" and started to prostrate myself, albeit awkwardly because of my wounded leg.

The king, with his usual quickness, saw what troubled me. "Never mind the foreign antics, dear Leon," quoth he. "We are old friends and comrades-in-arms. Sit down. How is your wound? Mending fast, I trust? I have told my historians to make special note of the valor of the Thessalian Troop in the battle of the Hydaspes. Now, speaking of the troop, I hear my few remaining Thessalians wish to go home. That is true, is it not?"

This was, meseemed, a day when one need not take Alexander's godhood too much to heart. I said: "O King, none denies that to serve you is the greatest boon that can fall to the lot of mortal man. Nevertheless, we have been seven or eight years from home—"

He stopped me with a wave. "Forget the rhetoric, old fellow. You are weary of adventures, are you not? Now that the Thracians have come, I can spare you, especially if you make yourself useful to me on your way home. I trust you will not mind going by way of Athens?"

"On the contrary, King, I should rejoice. Ere I was called to your service, I planned to go to Athens to study under the philosophers."

"Know you Aristoteles son of Nikomachos?"

"The philosopher who once tutored you and now teaches in Athens? Aye, I've heard of him."

The king said: "Aristoteles stands less high in my esteem than he did before his great-nephew turned traitor. Still, I promised to send him specimens from far lands I visited, and if Alexander keep not his promises, how shall common mortals do so? I have here a chest of notable things of India. Show them, Pyrron."

Pyrron of Elis, a tall, slender, handsome man somewhat older than I, opened the chest and took out several objects. There were skins of the tiger, the leopard, the crocodile, a lizard as long as a man, and a serpent twelve cubits in length. There were skulls of animals, the horn of the unicorn (a great piglike beast with a single horn on its nose), the shell of a large tortoise, a piece of Indian tree grass, a specimen of tree wool, and other things.

"Besides," said the king, "Aristoteles was always curious about the elephant. Once he told me he would die happy could he but scrutinize one of these creatures himself. Now, I happen to have the finest elephant in the world. When King Poros submitted to me, he gave me his personal war elephant."

"The one he rode in the battle?" I said with a hollow feeling.

"Yes. The beast sustained some wounds but will soon recover. You, my dear Leon, shall take this elephant to Aristoteles."

"But—but Great King!" I cried. "How shall I get this monster to Athens? Hellas is myriads of furlongs from here, beyond towering mountains, parching deserts, and stormy seas. Zeus! How shall I feed it? How—"

The king's look turned to ice and he struck the table with his fist so hard that the scrolls on it bounced. "By the Dog, when Alexander commands an officer, he expects him to leap to the task and not bother him with details. If you know not how to do any of these things, find out! Do you understand, Thessalian?"

"Aye, King."

"You shall be hipparch, with the rank of troop leader. Learn what you will need in men and money and supplies, and take the matter up with Eumenes. He will go as far as he can toward meeting reasonable needs.

"Now, another matter. Aristoteles is not the only philosopher. Many deem his rival Xenokrates the deeper thinker. Therefore, to prove my divine impartiality," (he winked at the philosophers sitting with him) "I shall give you, besides advance pay for yourself and your men, the equal of fifty talents of silver. This money you shall deliver intact to Xenokrates in Athens. You shall send me a receipt from him for the full amount."

The king looked hard at me, as if to say he knew what sometimes befell large sums sent far away, and would take revenge on anybody who stole his gifts.

"However," he went on, "they tell me you are an earnest and trusty young man." Alexander turned a boyish grin on Eumenes. "That will teach old Spindleshanks!"

I grasped his plan. It was a kind of kingly joke. He would send the elephant to Aristoteles, as promised, but no money for the up-keep of the brute. Aristoteles would be beggared buying food for it. At the same time, Alexander would send a princely sum to Aristoteles' greatest rival. This money, though ample to support the elephant, would never be used for that purpose because of the hostility between the two philosophers.

Eumenes said: "Have Xenokrates write out that receipt in triplicate, Leon. Send one copy to me and one to Harpalos in Tarsos, and keep one yourself."

"Furthermore," said the king, "Pyrron will go with you. And, moreover, I shall give you letters to Aristoteles and Xenokrates." He handed me two unsealed sheets of papyrus. "Read them, so if they be lost you can still deliver the gist of my message. You read and write, do you not?"

The first letter had the following directions on the outside: "To Aristoteles Nikomachou of Stageira, at the Lykeion at Athens." Unfolding the sheet, I read:

ALEXANDROS PHILIPPOU, KING OF MACEDONIA AND ASIA, WISHES ARISTOTELES WELL

You were wrong to send me forth with the belief that I should treat Hellenes alone as comrades and all foreigners as slaves. In Egypt the priest Psammon taught me a wiser rule, that all men are brethren under the gods, that the basic division among them is between the good and the bad, and that no tribe or race is either all good or all evil. The Persians have taught me that one can be a gentleman whether one wear kilt or trousers. And for myself I have learned that, to rule the world, one must use all subjects with equity, whatever their speech and customs. The gods made many nations, each with something to contribute to the world's welfare. I shall devote my life to choosing the best from each and promoting its adoption by all.

Perhaps you have not heard of the fate of your great-nephew Kallisthenes. He became so envious of my glory that he stirred up my own pages against me. When I learned of this plot, I put Kallisthenes in prison to await a trial by the full council upon my return to Persia. But recently I was informed he had died of natural causes.

However, as I do not suppose that you wantonly inspired Kallisthenes to these treasons, I send you this letter by Leon of Atrax, together with an elephant and some natural specimens from India. Thus Alexander shows he has not forgotten our early friendship and the many useful things you have taught me. Still, before you dogmatize about any nation of foreigners again, it were wise to live among them, as I have done, and come to know them on a man-to-man basis.

The other letter, much shorter, merely stated that Alexander was sending Xenokrates the money in view of his contributions to philosophy.

Eumenes said: "Read them until you can recite them from memory and then bring them to me to be sealed."

"I will," I said. "Shall I withdraw now, King Alexander?"

"One thing more," said the king. "Someday, when I have conquered all of India, I shall return to the West. When I do, I mean to bring some elephants. It will amuse me to see the proud Carthaginians run from them. Hence it is my wish to know which routes are practical for elephants.

"I would also keep in touch with the provinces of my empire, not only through official reports, but also through private correspondence. Therefore, my dear Leon, I expect regular letters telling of the state of things along your road. Note the condition of the route and listen for remarks about the government, either good or bad. Follow the post roads and write at least once every ten-day. Eumenes will give you a seal that will command the Persian couriers to take your letters.

"Eumenes will see to further details. Draw your plans with care, and do not leave until your wound is better. Remember that the people you meet on the way, though their customs be strange, are as much my subjects as you. Therefore, use them with justice and moderation. There shall be no robbing or raping or bullying; and you shall pay for everything you take."

"Everything, O King?" said I, a little aghast. "D'you mean food and lodging and all, as if we were but private travelers?"

"That is right. It has long been the wont of the folk of this empire to run whenever they saw a party of the king's men approaching, for fear of being plundered. Now shall begin a new age of justice and righteousness. The official and the countryman shall look upon one another as father to son, instead of as wolf to sheep. Again, Alexander thanks you for your noble work in the battle. Now you may go. Rejoice!"

I left the king's tent with my head in a whirl. On one hand, the prospect of meeting and knowing famous philosophers stirred me. On the other, the size of the task appalled me. I was proud of the king's trust, but also more frightened of the onus laid upon me than I had been by Poros' elephants in the battle.

As far as I knew, no one had ever taken an elephant west of the Taurus Mountains. How would the creature abide the cold? How would it be fed? How could it be carried by water from Asia to Europe? Must I, like Xerxes, build a bridge of boats across the Hellespont? How did I know that all the lands the king had left behind him remained loyal? Any province might have revolted and so be impassable. Nor could I slip through by wearing the dress of a countryman and making myself inconspicuous. Anything less inconspicuous than a beast the size of a small mountain would be hard to conceive.

Well, I thought, it is a rough road that leads to glory. Deciding I ought to know my new charge, I walked to the side of the camp where the elephant lines were. It was a long walk, and I arrived sweating and limping.

Here were scores of elephants which either belonged to the allied Indian kings or had been given by them to Alexander. They stood in long lines, swaying, flapping their ears, tossing their trunks,

26

and giving those shrill squeals that sound so silly from so large a beast. Each elephant was tethered to a massive stake by a chain about its foreleg, but keepers unchained their elephants to take them down to the river to bathe, so there was a constant coming and going. Keepers fed their beasts, renewed the designs painted on them, shoveled dung, or lay about talking and sleeping. The place smelled pungently of elephant. The beasts ate hay, greens of all kinds, and, as a special treat, a kind of cane or reed with a marvelously sweet honeylike flavor.

Being unable to pick out Poros' elephant by sight, I spoke to some of the keepers in Persian; but they only smiled, waved their hands, and answered in Indian. All the Indian I knew were the few phrases any soldier needs in a land he is invading, such as: "Where is the army?" "I want food," "Give me your valuables," and "Obey or you will be killed."

When it was plain that neither party could understand the other, one keeper dashed off toward the Indians' tents. Soon he came back, accompanied by a tall Indian with a blue-dyed beard. I introduced myself in Persian. The man placed his palms together and bowed his head over them, replying in broken Persian:

"I Kanadas of Paurava, master of Poros' elephants."

Like most Indians, Kanadas wore only a piece of gauzy cloth of Indian tree wool wrapped around his loins and a long strip of the same stuff wound about his head and tied with a knot as complicated as that which the king smote with his sword at Gordion. Kanadas' upper body was bare but for necklaces with dangling amulets.

I said: "May I see the elephant that Poros gave King Alexander?"

"Yes," he said, and led me hither and yon until we stopped in front of the monster. The animal's paint had been washed off and not replaced. Several wounds could still be seen, but they seemed to be healing. The elephant's keeper lay curled up asleep between his pet's forefeet.

As soon as the elephant got a good look at me, however, he threw up his trunk, screamed, lunged forward to the limits of his chain, and reached out for me.

I started, backed into the rear of another elephant in the next line, jumped in surprise, slipped in the mud, and fell into a pile of

27

dung. All the keepers, who had formed a small crowd around us, burst into laughter.

A man need not be oversensitive about his dignity to be annoyed by such a thing. I got up and wiped myself off, scowling at the Indians. Their smiles disappeared, for my thick black eyebrows give me a fearsome frown. Some of them frowned back and muttered words I do not think were meant as compliments.

The elephant was still making hostile sounds, despite the efforts of his keeper to soothe him. Kanadas said: "He no like Greek helmet."

After so many men wearing tall horsehair crests had hurt the beast, he would hardly feel friendly toward men so clad. I laid my helmet down several paces away and came back. The elephant quieted but still grumbled suspiciously. I kept out of reach of his trunk.

"What is he called?" I asked.

Kanadas said: "*Mahankal*—Great Death. Is named for one of our gods, Siva the Destroyer."

I said: "Have you heard that Mahankal is going to Hellas? The king has so commanded."

"What is Hellas?" asked Kanadas.

"My country, far to the west."

"Oh. How far this land? One day travel? Two?"

"Farther."

"Ten day? Month?"

"Much farther than that! It may take us a year."

"What?" Kanadas seemed puzzled. As I explained, his face took on a look of horror. He spoke in Indian to the keeper. The two shouted excitedly, and Kanadas ran off toward the main camp.

Soon Kanadas returned with tears cascading down his raisin-brown face. He spoke to the keeper. Both wept, hugging and kissing the forelegs and trunk of the elephant, who shifted his weight and gurgled as if he sensed that something was wrong. The other keepers gathered round. When they heard the news they, too, wept, casting hostile looks upon me.

"Blame me not," I said to Kanadas. "I only brought the news. I am not the king, merely one of his servants."

But they only wept and lamented the more. At last I gave up and went back to the officers' tents of my troop. Here I found Gration honing his sword and Sthenelos writing a letter. I told them about my speech with the king.

Sthenelos looked grave. "*Pfeu*, poor dear Leon!" he said. "I warned you against gorging. The king has at last taken pity on your nag and shifted you to a beast big enough to bear all that beef."

"But seriously, lads, what in Hera's name shall I do?" I said. "How does a body get such a monster halfway across the world?"

Sthenelos said: "Your best chance, blessed one, is to go north through the lands of the Sakai till you come to the country of the one-eyed Arimaspians who war against the gold-guarding gryphons. Catch a team of eagle-winged gryphons and break them to harness and build a wagon big enough to hold the elephant—"

"Na, na, that's too fancy," said Gration. "An elephant that big can ford the Aegean Sea."

"It's too deep," said Sthenelos. "It were easier to train the elephant to fly by flapping its ears."

"It is no too deep," said Gration. "Gif the sea be over the elephant's head, it can stretch its trunk up to the surface to breathe. Have you no seen them here walking on the river's bottom?"

"Oh, bugger you two knaves!" I said, and went back to sick quarters. It seemed I must needs rely on my own wits to solve my problems.

My dear father Aristos, who taught me many canny stratagems for getting through the battle of life, used to say: "Little by little does the task." He explained that when a problem looks so big as to be overwhelming, one should break it down into smaller problems and solve them one by one. In my tent I sat and thought about my elephant problem. I broke it down into several parts, thus:

First, there were the questions of what route I should follow and how long the journey would take. For this, I needed to know how long the routes were and how fast a party with an elephant could travel. The people to help me in this matter were the Greek surveyors of Alexander's technical staff, who measured each day's march and entered the distances on their maps.

Second, I could not get the monster over this route by myself. I knew not how to drive an elephant, let alone control one if it became fractious. Therefore, I should have to take some Indian elephant men.

Third, in the deserts of Persia the elephant could not live off the land. There must needs be enough well-mounted men to scour the countryside for fodder. In turn, these men would need cooks, grooms, and other servants if they were to do their special tasks ably. Such a crowd of civilians would need more soldiers to guard them. By the time I finished, I was commanding a full troop of cavalry, sixty or seventy men, with an equal number of servants, interpreters, a physician, and a veterinarian. I even included a soothsayer. In my younger days I believed strongly in omens and portents. At the time of which I write, I had become aware that many, like those which Aristandros staged, were bits of simple trickery, but I had not yet come to the point of ignoring auguries and presages altogether. There might be something to them, and it were well to be on the safe side.

Fourth, this little army would need food and supplies. The Macedonian army got its food partly from local governors and allied rulers and partly from sutlers, who bought food in the neighborhood and sold it again to the soldiers. In hostile country we foraged, meaning that we stole everything edible within leagues of our line of march. But, as the elephant party's route would lie through Alexander's domains, we could not forage among supposedly friendly people. I would, therefore, hire a sutler on contract to procure food on a fixed wage instead of on the profit he could wring from the soldiers.

Fifth, as we should have to buy our food as we went, it behooved me to make sure we went off with plenty of money besides our advance pay. This in turn meant a careful reckoning of times and distances.

The first people to see, then, were those who could advise me on routes and rates of travel. I rose and limped over to the tents where the Greek technicians lived.

Polykleitos greeted me cordially and fetched Baiton, the surveyor. They spread out their maps.

"Where are we?" I asked.

"Here." Polykleitos showed a dot beside the wriggly line that stood for the Hydaspes, with the name "Nikaia" lettered near it. "This direction is north, this west, and so on. Here is Peukala. From Peukala you will ascend the Kophen by the same route you followed hither, through Paktuika to Kaboura—"

Baiton interrupted: "You'll need guides and interpreters through Gandaria. You can obtain them at Peukala."

Polykleitos continued: "At Kaboura, turn southwards to Gazaka and Kandacha; thence west to Phrada. You went over that route with the army on its way to Baktria. Do you think you can find your way back?"

"That was three and a half years ago," I said. "I misdoubt I shall recognize some places, but it were well to hire guides. What route shall we follow from Phrada?"

Polykleitos said: "You could retrace the king's route back, through Parthia and Hyrkania. But it might be shorter to proceed southwest from Phrada through Karmania into Persia. There's a post road through the Waterless Plain."

"A blithe-sounding place, that," I said.

"Yes indeed; you'll traverse some difficult desert. But, on the other hand, you wouldn't wish winter to overtake you in the northern mountains."

"How shall we manage for water in the desert?" I said.

"I suppose you'll hire camels to transport water. Baiton, could you estimate the quantity of water an elephant consumes each day?"

"I have no idea," said Baiton. "How should I?"

"Even approximately?"

"No. I suppose, though, we could ascertain by watering the elephant out of a bucket of known capacity for a fixed period. I'll see what I can do."

Polykleitos continued: "Once you reach Persepolis, the remainder should be smooth sailing."

"Speaking of sailing," I said, "whence shall I sail? Phoenicia, Ionia, Egypt, or what?"

Polykleitos shifted to another map that showed the eastern Mediterranean Sea and Hellas. He frowned over it and said: "Phoenicia is your next objective. From Sousa you must detour around to the north to avoid the Arabian desert." He swept his finger in an arc over the map.

"What shall I do for a ship?"

Polykleitos pondered. "Menes, governor of Syria, administers all maritime transportation from Phoenicia to the West. He might be in Damascus or in Tarsos or in some Phoenician port. Perhaps it were expedient to cut west from Sousa and inquire for him at the governmental offices in Babylon. It wouldn't do to plod all the way to Phoenicia to find that Menes was elsewhere. Procure a letter from Eumenes directing Menes to send you to Hellas by sea."

"How far can I march each day?" I asked.

Baiton said: "That depends. In Gandaria, inferior roads and steep grades will retard you, but elsewhere you can maintain a good speed."

"What's a good speed? Alone, I can ride two hundred and fifty furlongs a day without pressing, but with the elephant and its escort?"

Baiton said: "Persian postmen ride over three hundred furlongs a day, but they change horses at each stage. A party of horsemen and mule carts and an elephant would do well to attain half that distance. Also, we must allow stops at the larger towns to repair your equipment and rest your people and animals. Let me draw you up an itinerary as far as Babylon. How soon will you depart?"

"As soon as my cursed leg is better and I can gather the people and things. Let's say in another ten days."

"I'll have it for you tomorrow," he said.

Although he seemed willing, Baiton did not have my itinerary ready next day, nor yet the day after that. For three days I killed time. I moved from sick quarters back to my own tent and passed my time in gaming and reading. The Indians and Thracians danced and sang to celebrate events in their religious calendars.

The rain poured down. When it stopped, I watched my troop exercising under Gration's command. They maneuvered at a gallop and threw javelins at a shield hung from a tree. Alexander tried an experiment by making them carry the little leather bucklers of the heavy infantry. In those days Hellenic cavalry seldom bore shields, because the regular footman's shield is too heavy and leaves the rider but one hand for both reins and weapon. When King Philip adopted, for Macedonian infantry, the eight-cubit pike, which needs both hands, he devised this small shield that can be pushed up on the left arm to free the hand. His son had continued these experiments.

I skimmed through Eriguios' books to see if they had aught to teach me. Alas! None said a word about elephants, because no elephant had yet been seen in Hellas.

Xenophon, however, had a thought about horses that could be applied, meseemed, to other beasts. That is, if one would have a horse like something, one must see to it that this thing is always associated with the animal's eating and drinking. If I were to be with the elephant for months, the risks of the journey were deadly enough without having the beast watching ever and aye for a chance to kill me.

Now, India abounds in tasty melons. I sought out a sutler, a Syrian named Elisas, and bought a melon from him. I carried this melon over to the elephant lines, found Mahankal, and gave it to him. While the keeper looked on suspiciously, Mahankal took the melon in his trunk, stuffed it into his mouth, and crunched it up.

After three days of this, Mahankal squealed with delight when he saw me coming, even in my helmet. He rubbed his snout lovingly against me, which is like being rubbed by a live tree trunk. Even the keeper became friendly, though neither of us could understand the other. The keeper's philosophy was simple. Whomever his elephant loved, he loved.

News of the elephant project spread through the camp. Many asked me to arrange for them to go in the elephant's escort. Others came with letters to deliver in Hellas. I read Alexander's letters to Aristoteles and Xenokrates until I knew them by heart.

The third day after my interview with the king, I insisted on seeing Baiton. I found him in his tent, measuring off distances on his maps and writing them down.

"Come in, Troop Leader Leon," he said. "I'm working on your itinerary."

"Wherefore the delay, laddie?" I asked.

"A dispute among the king's advisers. We've been interviewing Indians about the territories to the east and south. As you perceive," (he made a small circle with his finger tip around the place where Nikaia appeared on the map) "we were under the impression that this was all there was to India. Here's the coast, with nothing beyond but ocean. However, it now transpires that India extends on in this direction hundreds of leagues." (He swept his fingers far out to sea.) "They tell us there are many cities, and myriads of people, and great kings with thousands of elephants. For instance, the capital of the Prasians is said to be more populous than Babylon. It stands on a river called the Ganges, mightier than the Indus."

"What says the king to that?"

Baiton chuckled. "The king has decided that India terminates a few days' march to the east, and nothing lies beyond but ocean. People who allege otherwise are craven rascals who seek to intimidate him into turning back when he has all but conquered the whole inhabited world. It were better not to dispute the matter with him."

"I won't," I said. "We shall go west, so it matters not how far India extends. Hurry that up, man."

The next day I had an audience with Eumenes. When he saw the lists of people and money that I had prepared, he threw up his hands.

"Why not demand the whole Macedonian army, Troop Leader?" he said. "That's far too ambitious."

"Then what should I ask for?" said I, abashed.

He frowned over my lists, making marks. He cut out this man and that man until he had my detachment down to a third of the size I had planned.

"Two can manage the elephant," he said. "One warrior to fight from the creature if you be attacked, and one keeper to feed and water it. Know you any of the Indians?"

I said: "Kanadas, Poros' elephantarch, would do for the warrior if Poros can spare him. He speaks a little Persian, so I could give him commands directly. As for the keeper, I'd take his present one, Siladites. Indian elephant keepers feel about their elephants the way most folk feel about their kin."

"It pleases. How about this sutler?"

"A Syrian named Elisas is willing. I think he'll cheat us no worse than the rest."

"That is good. Now, you don't need this vast corps of guides and interpreters. Through Gandaria you will hire local guides. For Persia, all you need is one able-bodied Persian who knows the main tongues of the empire. I have the very man for you. His mother's sick in Sousa, and he wishes to go home to see her."

34

"Aye, good sir. And, I pray, fail not to give me a letter to Menes, commanding him to provide us with a ship."

Then we had a lengthy wrangle over money. Eumenes was much more willing than I to assume that all would go well. Since he was far above me in rank, I could not argue so forcefully as I should have liked. I said:

"Suppose we meet with disaster, like an ambush or a landslide, and run out of money. Could you at least give me a draft on the treasury to get me the rest of the way?"

Eumenes laughed. "Perhaps the king should have chosen a leader with a less gloomy imagination, man of Thessalia. However, I'll give you a letter to Alexander's treasurer, Harpalos, authorizing an additional payment in case of disaster. But you'll have to account to him for all the money you start out with, and he is a shrewd reckoner. You'll find him in Babylon or, more likely, in Tarsos."

I went to see Elisas, who was delighted at the tidings. He said: "Is the king serious about paying for everything at the market price?"

"Of course he is, fellow."

Elisas gave me a sly look. "The villagers along the way will not have yet heard of this strange notion. If we did not tell them, there would be a goodly sum left over to divide between you and me."

"None of that! I have my orders, and I'll carry them out in spite of gods or men." I spoke in a blustering tone to hide the fact that I was sorely tempted to fall in with Elisas' proposal, as most of my comrades would have done without a second thought.

Then I sought out Kanadas, whom I found fussing over the elephant. When I explained that he was going with Mahankal to Hellas, Kanadas burst into tears again. So did Siladites when Kanadas broke the news to him.

"Come, come," I said. "It will not be so bad. There will be a strong escort, plenty to eat, and the sight of strange lands and peoples." It seemed ridiculous to be comforting a man who was not only older than I but also a full head taller.

"That is what is amiss," moaned Kanadas, tearing at his long blue beard. "I no want strange land. Strange folk eat me. Strange food defile me. I fall off edge of earth. Never see dear wives and children again."

35

"I thought you brave," I scoffed. "You drove an elephant through the great battle without fear, but now the thought of a little travel terrifies you."

"Of course I brave! No fear men. Kill many enemies. But what can man do against demon and monster that live in foreign land?"

"But think! You would not leave poor Mahankal in the hands of strangers, would you? They might not know how to care for him."

"Oh," he said. "That true. Could I bring family?"

"How much family have you?"

"Two wives, six children."

"Too many. You may bring at most one wife and two children."

"We see," said the Indian.

I went back to my tent, leaving Kanadas and Siladites at least half reconciled to their fate.

A few days later, Eumenes called a council of the officers of the expedition. He told us to sit and offered wine. Kanadas came in looking cheerful for a change. Last of all there appeared in the doorway a Persian, Vardanas of Sousa, whom I knew slightly. When he saw me he cried:

"Is *this* the man who will command the expedition?"

"Why, yes," said Eumenes. "What's the matter?"

"I will not serve under him! He hates Persians. He has insulted my honor!"

"What's this, Thessalian?" said Eumenes, turning to me.

"Oh, some of us were talking before the battle," I said. "We had too much wine, and unseemly words were passed."

What had happened was this. As I have said, my concubine, Hyovis, died of snakebite a few days before the battle. Although she was only a foreign woman, I grieved sincerely. She had taken good care of me; in fact, her cooking had put more weight on me than is good for a cavalryman to have. Forbye, she was a mettlesome steed in bed.

When I got over the first shock of grief, I found a Magos with a staff, wandering among the tents and looking for snakes to kill as part of his religious duties. I like not the Magian practice of exposing dead bodies for wild beasts to devour; but, as the lass had been a devout adherent of the Persian religion, I thought it only right to do what she would have liked.

When we had committed Hyovis' spirit to Auramasdas, I paid the Magos, who went off to find more snakes, and returned to my tent. Here I found the other officers of the troop: Diokles, the troop leader who fell in the battle; Gration, the right flank guard; and Sthenelos, the left flank guard. Sthenelos was no Thessalian, but neither were a third of the other men in the troop. They were leftovers from disbanded bodies of Greek horse, who had stayed on as mercenaries just as we Thessalians had. Sthenelos had brought a skin of the local wine.

"This slop isn't Chian," he said, "but if you shut your eyes and gulp you can get it down." He spoke in Attic, full of city slang, while the rest of us used our Thessalian dialect among ourselves.

I had liefer been let alone, even though my comrades deemed me a misanthrope. However, they thought they had to console me; and I did not wish to offend them. As for Sthenelos, no Athenian can bear to be alone for an instant, or to stop talking for an instant either. But then, he was an amusing lad, and the gift of wine was kindly meant.

"I grieve with you, old boy," he said. "Don't you even have a lover among the men?"

I had heard questions like this from southern Hellenes so often that I was used to them. "Nobody would love a great ugly lump like me," I said.

This was not false modesty, for I know my limitations. Though no more stupid or timid than the next man, I am no beauty, being a whin over medium height, with blunt features, and inclined to stoutness.

Sthenelos, who, like the king, shaved his face in the Egyptian manner to keep his boyish beauty, fluttered his eyelashes. "Dear Leon, you're not so unattractive as you make out. Why, even I might make the supreme sacrifice if properly courted!" When I only gave an embarrassed grunt, he added: "Unless you have one of these droll barbarian prejudices against manly love."

Diokles said: "Oh, fie upon you, fair Sthenelos! In our rustic wilds we dinna hold a man to be queer for preferring women."

"How beastly!" said Sthenelos. "But enlightenment will spread even into your land of Cimmerian darkness."

"O Herakles!" I said. "I'm finding the whole subject a bore. Make love to ilk other or to the baggage mules for aught I care. I'm for home the first chance I get."

"Have you had enough adventuring, then?" said Sthenelos.

"Aye, enough and to spare, laddie. Now Hyovis is dead there's nought to keep me, and I've seen my fill of strange lands. I ken the now that Indians neither build their houses of gold bricks nor pave their streets with pearls, whatever the stories say."

"I feels the same," said Gration. "There's no future here. A body canna rise to high rank, even, outen being a Macedonian."

"You maun put thoughts of going home out of your minds," said Diokles. "With a big battle coming, the king will need every man."

Sthenelos yawned. "No doubt, my good man, but the king can't go on forever. We keep hearing it's only a frog's hop to the end of the world, but the end of the world seems to flee before us like the end of a rainbow."

Gration said: "We can pray that either the end of the world or the end of the king's ambition will come soon. I sudna be sorry to go. This army grows more Persian and less Greek ilka day."

"True," said Sthenelos. "One would think they'd conquered us instead of the other way round."

This was always a good subject for complaints, as the army now had far more Asiatic than Hellenic horse. The other three squadrons of our own regiment, for instance, were made up of Persians, Baktrians, and Sakas.

For that matter, we Hellenes looked more Asiatic than Greek, because our original clothing had long since worn out and had been replaced by whatever we could get. Many of the younger Hellenes had taken to trousers during those horrible Baktrian winters. The older and more conservative ones clove to their tunics and kilts, preferring to freeze their thighs rather than give in to foreign fashions.

I said: "We drubbed these polluted Persians with spear and sword, and now they thrash us with fancy manners and spangled robes. Such is fate."

"Let's be just," said Diokles, always loyal to the king. "Some of these Asiatic horse are bonny soldiers when well led."

"They're dirty," said Sthenelos. "They never wash; they just sprinkle perfumes on themselves when they stink."

I said: "Aye, and they're so fearful of scratches they cover themselves all over with iron scales, and—"

"I heard that," said a voice in Greek with a mushy Persian accent.

The speaker was a Persian in the maroon and yellow uniform of King Dareios' horse guards, much faded and patched. He was about my age, but taller than I and less stout. He had a big hooked beak of a nose in a long swarthy face and a pale scar across his forehead. I felt I had seen him before, but all those Persians looked alike with their long hair and black beards and bucket-shaped felt bonnets. The man went on:

"Persia was not conquered by a horde of lying, faithless, boy-loving Greek robbers. It was overcome by one man—Alexander. He is half Persian. He will be all Persian when we teach him the right manly way of doing things."

For some reason, the man chose me to glower at. Either it was that I happened to face him, or that my gibes had bitten deepest, or that my somewhat forbidding appearance drew his glance. Albeit not given to brawls, I was full of pot-valor and sought a way to purge my grief in action. I picked up my scabbard and rose, saying:

"So one of the curs has bared his teeth at last, eh? Keep on, Persian, and you'll be a man before your mother."

The Persian put a hand to his hilt. "Remember, Hellene, it is not we Persians who are always wailing to go home. We were beaten when we had a weak and timid king. That might happen to any folk. Now that we have a great and doughty king, we shall conquer the world. If you treat us respectfully, we may throw you a few scraps from our table."

"Why, you saucy braggart—" I began, starting to draw. But Diokles leapt up and pushed me over.

"Stop or I'll arrest you all!" he said. "The king says the next time there's a fight atween a Hellene and a Persian, he'll crucify both. Persian, I apologize for my comrades' rude words, but perhaps you had better get back to your own squadron."

"I go," said the Persian. "But know that I am Vardanas of Sousa by name. I am flank guard in Chousraus' troop. So, if you would carry the discussion further, you know where to find me." He stalked off.

Sthenelos giggled. "What cheek! Why does he think any of us would wish to speak to him again? He's certainly no gentleman!"

"He was offering to fight," said Gration. "'Tis their code of honor that when insults have been passed, the rivals go out behind the barn and settle it with swords."

"How utterly quaint!" said Sthenelos, pouring himself another cup. "What's this lunacy about the king's being half Persian?"

Diokles explained: "The Persians think Alexander is really the son of a Persian princess and so a more-or-less legitimate heir to the Persian throne."

"They must be mad," said Sthenelos. "Everybody knows—"

Diokles stopped him. "I know what everybody knows, but this myth salves their self-love. If it make them fight better, why spoil their dreams? The Egyptians think he's half Egyptian, and no doubt the Indians will be finding he was begotten by one of their ten-armed gods."

Then Diokles scolded me sharply for showing bad temper before a foreigner and risking getting us all into trouble. He had me blubbering with drunken self-pity ere he finished. But the matter passed over, and I thought no more about Vardanas of Sousa until he appeared in the official tent at Eumenes' conference.

Eumenes, looking hard at me, said: "You know what the king said."

"Nought serious was meant," I said, "and after the battle nobody doubts the Persians' courage. If the lad come, I'll not strive with my yokefellow."

Vardanas stood silently for a while, chewing the ends of his mustache. Then he said: "I would not come except that I may not have another chance to see my mother. If Leon will swear to deal justly with me, I will forget our quarrel."

"I swear it by Zeus and all the gods," I said. "Now can we finish our plans?"

Vardanas sat down. I was vexed with him for putting me in the wrong with Eumenes. I hid my annoyance with an effort, as I am a plain blunt man who calls a fig a fig and a spade a spade. But the wise man does not defy necessity.

I had thought so much about the project that I had counted my chickens before they were hatched. I saw my name in the history books as the hero who first brought an elephant to Europe. Athens would make my day of arrival a yearly holiday, and Alexander would appoint me satrap of Bithynia or the like. Naturally, all this made me ardent to push the expedition through to success.

My final muster roll showed sixty-six persons. The officers were myself, Vardanas, Kanadas, and Thyestes of Pharsala from the troop. Thyestes was a typical soldier in that he thought of little outside his duties except wine, women, and loot.

Neither Gration nor Sthenelos came. Gration had taken up with Diokles' concubine Amytis and did not wish to cause a family scandal by bringing a foreign woman home to Thessalia. Sthenelos was wanted in his native Athens for murder, resulting from a quarrel with another man over the love of a boy.

In charge of the elephant were Kanadas the elephantarch and Siladites the keeper. Kanadas left his family behind because his jealous wives would not agree that either might go without the other. As Siladites was a childless widower, the problem did not arise with him.

Baiton had tried to measure the elephant's intake of food and water but had failed. The reason was that the Indians persisted in feeding and watering the beast when he was not around to weigh its aliment, and they could not understand why he got so excited over the matter.

The soldiers were eighteen Thessalians and four Sakan horse archers, of the Parnian tribe of the Dahan nation. Sakas are nomads from the plains north of the Persian Empire, in speech much like the Persians and in habits like the Scythians who live beyond the Istros in Europe. These four Dahas had begged to be suffered to leave India because, they said, the dampness was ruining their health as well as rotting their garments.

Then there were Pyrron the philosopher, Elisas the sutler, a cook, eight grooms, six camp men, five personal slaves, nine women (concubines of the Thessalians), and eight children.

Besides our advance pay, the king commanded Eumenes to give us a silver talent each as a discharge bonus. Eumenes gave me the money, with no very good grace, and warned me not to pay it out ere we reached our goal.

"If you do," he said, "they'll try to borrow against their bonuses in order to squander the money in lewd living in the cities. Then, when it is all gone, they'll desert."

Because so much silver would have been too heavy to carry so vast a distance, Eumenes gave me the equivalent in new golden staters. I made sure he gave us the current rate of exchange of twelve to one. But the abandoned Kardian cheated us anyway, by using Attic weight instead of Babylonian. You can understand why I wept not when I heard he had been strangled by orders of Antigonos in the wars of the Successors.

After much talk, debates over maps and routes, inspection of equipment, and changes of plan, my detachment drew up before sunrise on the twelfth of the month Hekatombaion. The king came out to see us off, together with several hundred soldiers and camp followers drawn by curiosity. The camp was astir anyway because the king had issued the order to prepare to march eastward against the farther Indian kingdoms.

Alexander led us in prayer. While the Hellenes prayed to Zeus, Apollon, and Herakles, Vardanas raised his hands to the rising sun and prayed to Auramasdas. The four Dahas stuck their swords and axes in the ground and prayed to the Sakan war god; the Indians bowed their heads to Ganesas, an elephant-headed Indian god. Aristandros and a Persian soothsayer took the omens and found them good, naturally.

The king stepped fearlessly up to Mahankal and cried: "O elephant, I, Alexander, rename you Aias, after the Achaian hero, and dedicate you to the sun! In honor of my kinsman Apollon, god of learning, I send you to the philosophers of Hellas for study. Be a faithful servant to those whom Alexander has placed over you!"

The king then made a short speech urging us to push ahead to our goal and let nought stop us. We cheered him, and Mahankal (or rather Aias), at a prod from Siladites, raised his trunk and trumpeted. Alexander and the other Hellenes blew a kiss to the rising sun, which flashed redly on helmets and weapons and on the golden bands on the elephant's tusks.

The giant King Poros hugged the elephant's trunk and bid the beast a tearful farewell. Gration and Sthenelos ran up to kiss me, followed by a score of men from the troop. I was so surprised to find that they loved me (since I considered myself a strict officer) that I shed a few tears with the rest.

At last I cried: "Prepare to mount! Mount! Left wheel by twos! Advance!"

With cries of "Get up!" off went my little hipparchia, hooves drumming and cart axles creaking while the onlookers cheered. I turned back to wave a final farewell. To my surprise, Pyrron of Elis, who had been standing by his horse and wearing a broad-brimmed black hat, still stood, bemusedly waving farewell with the other bystanders. I beckoned frantically. Pyrron came to himself, scrambled into his seat, and spurred his horse. The animal leapt forward so suddenly that the Eleian turned a back somersault over the horse's rump. It took a quarter hour to catch the beast and reunite it with its awkward rider. Despite the soothsayers' hopeful auguries, I could not help thinking that a bad beginning makes a bad ending, as we say in Thessalia.

On the other hand, it was a relief to get away from the scrutiny of the king. Despite his many godlike qualities—his military genius, his inspiring leadership, and his invincible charm—one could not help noting his growing haughtiness, hastiness, and immoderation in dealing with those in his power. During interviews the thought kept creeping into my mind: what if he fly into a passion and run me through as he did his old friend Kleitos the White? As the Persians say, a cut string can be joined again, but the knot remains for aye.

The camp smell of ordure, sweat, and garbage had hardly died out of our nostrils when the clouds closed in and the rain began again. It rained all the way to Taxasila.

BOOK TWO

Gandaria

AN ELEPHANT NEITHER TROTS NOR CANTERS. It single-foots, slowly or swiftly as the case may be. An easy speed for an elephant is that of a horse's trot, though it can attain the speed of a gallop when angry or frightened. Aias swung along for hours at a time, at a pace too fast for a walk. As no horseman can long trot with comfort, the rest of us cantered until the elephant was a few furlongs behind us, then walked until he caught up.

Our normal order of march was as follows: Vardanas and I rode in front, I on Golden, a hard-mouthed, hard-gaited animal who would bite if she could, but strong and tireless.

Then came the four Dahan horse archers, followed by the Thessalians. Next came the mule carts with the women, children, camp servants, and slaves; then the grooms riding some of the spare horses and leading the others; and lastly the elephant and one horse. Kanadas and Siladites took turns riding the elephant and this horse. The elephant carried a booth on its back, in which we had piled a part of the baggage. I named two strong and trustworthy Thessalians as guards of the chests of money and Indian specimens, which rode in our largest cart.

Vardanas and I, even though we rode together, spoke not much. We watched one another warily. He watched me to see if I should cast more slights upon his dignity; while I, sensing his grudge, watched him lest he cause trouble by stirring up quarrels or spreading false tales. I was sure that once we got into Persia he would desert us and gallop off homeward. When we did speak, it was with cold courtesy.

Vardanas no longer wore his iron-scaled leather gown or rode the giant Nisaian charger he had used in the battle. That horse belonged to the king. The Persian rode his own horse, Rakous, a big strong beast but no Median monster. He had packed away his mail coat and wore one of his shabby old imperial uniforms with maroon trousers and yellow Median coat embroidered with flowers.

On his back he slung his bow case, which held forty arrows and a thick double-curved Persian bow made of strips of wood and horn glued together. From his belt hung, besides a sword with an ornate hilt of silver and ivory, a horrid weapon: a stout bludgeon with short iron spikes affixed to the knob so that they stuck out in all directions. On his head was a crested Greek helmet, for many foreigners have taken to this kind of headgear. He had the indefinable look, alert yet easy, that marks the seasoned soldier.

I put Vardanas in command of the Dahas, as he was the only one who could talk with them. They were typical Sakas, big men with long filthy hair and beards, pointed caps, short coats, and trousers tucked into high boots. Although Vardanas, having been promoted to troop closer, was second to me in rank, it seemed better not to set him in direct command of Hellenes any more than emergencies required.

The first day we spent much time in stopping to shift loads and make minor repairs. Remembering Xenophon's advice, I had laid in a store of straps. Hence we were never held up for long by breakage of harness. By evening we had shaken down into a workable cavalcade.

I chose a camping place near a village and sent Elisas to the village for food. The camp men cut down a small tree for firewood; the cook grumbled as he strove to start a fire in the drizzle. I rushed about counting noses and inspecting equipment until Pyrron, speaking Attic (albeit with a noticeable Doric accent), said:

"Don't take life so hard, my boy. The too tautly strung bow is the first to break."

45

I began an angry retort, but thought better of it and laughed. "Aye, 'tis true I'm over-anxious, best one. This is my first independent command, and I'll have nought go awry with it."

"Worry enough and something probably will," he said. "You exhaust yourself seeking knots in bulrushes."

"Worry not at all, as you seem to do, and something will go agley, too," I said. "I've been looking forward to serious talks with you, O philosopher, but I have been over-busy with my duties."

"You'll be frightfully disappointed. I gnaw at people's basic assumptions, and most folk loathe having their basic assumptions disturbed."

"I fear no truth, however painful. Now tell me, what is Aristoteles like?"

"I have never encountered him. From what I hear, he knows much and thinks he knows much more. A clever man, but an incorrigible dogmatizer—why, what's wrong?" he said, observing my change of expression.

It had suddenly struck me that I did not remember packing the king's letters. I rushed to the chests and rummaged through them, but no letters did I find. I was still rummaging and looking stupidly over and over in the same places a quarter hour later when Pyrron wandered into the tent and asked:

"What are you seeking so frantically, old boy?"

"Those two letters from the king. This is terrible!"

"My word! Have you looked in your wallet?"

I looked into the pouch at my waist. Sure enough, there were the letters, along with my comb, spoon, loose money, a map, and an amulet.

I took a long breath of relief and asked: "Why gave the king these letters to me to deliver instead of to you? These philosophers are your colleagues."

"He said I was too absent-minded and would surely lose them, although perhaps I'm not the only one with that failing."

Abashed that Pyrron should have caught me without my dignity, I came out of the tent with the Eleian and brought up another subject. I pointed toward the stream, where Kanadas was cooking his own dinner over a small fire. His food was made up largely of an Indian grain called rice, lately raised also in Sousiana and Babylonia as well. This, when cooked, becomes a mess of little white lumps.

"What's that fellow up to?" I said.

Pyrron replied: "Kanadas is a *xatria* or member of the warrior caste. A high-caste Indian cannot eat with the rest of us, for religious reasons."

"What nonsense! I see his comrade eats everything he can lay his hands on."

"The other Indian belongs to the herding caste, much lower in the scale. So nobody cares what he eats. Anyway, why are their religious rules any more nonsensical than ours?"

I stared at him. "Are you daft, man? I'm a Hellene! I am civilized and these foreigners are not. Therefore, my customs must be right and theirs, as far as they differ, must be wrong."

"Who says so?"

"I do, of course. I mean, if all the great Hellenic thinkers agree that the Hellenes are the most civilized folk, it must be so."

"What do you expect them to say?" asked Pyrron.

"What mean you?"

"You wouldn't look for a Hellene to admit that other folk are superior even if they were, would you? Like everybody else, we think we are the best. So do the Persians: they hold the pure Persians to be the best of men; then come the other Arian races like the Medes; and lastly the rest of mankind, and the Indians feel the same about themselves."

I tried to be just. "I suppose 'tis natural for foreigners to grow up with such ignorant prejudices. They lack our advantages."

"Ah, but who determines which is prejudice and which is truth?"

Forgetting that even a fool can often pass for a wise man by holding his tongue, I barked: "I know there's something amiss with your argument, though I cannot quite see where the flaw lies. But I remember the Athenians killed Sokrates for questioning basic truths as you do. Take care the same befall not you. Now I must see to my men."

I went off gruffly to harass my little hipparchia. It was a stupidly discourteous way to treat Pyrron, especially after I had bragged of fearing no truth. Howsomever, I was young and unsure of my authority. Hence I felt that I had to snap at anybody I suspected of not taking it seriously. Luckily Pyrron, the most easy-tempered of men, took no offense.

After three days we forded the little Tabara and reached Taxasila, the capital of Alexander's ally, King Ombis. Taxasila is a town of good size, although no Babylon. The circuit of its mud-brick walls is about fourteen furlongs. The eastern approach is made unpleasing by the burial grounds, or rather unburial grounds, for many Taxasilans follow the Persian custom of exposing bodies for wild things to devour. We rode past, holding our noses, while vultures, kites, and jackals squabbled over the remains. On the other side of the road lie heaps of ashes where the Indians burn widows alive.

We camped outside the walls on the banks of the Tabara and ate our lunch. I decided we could do all our needful business during the afternoon and set forth the following morn. This announcement brought groans from the men, who were looking forward to several days of the pleasures of the city.

We had seen Taxasila before, when Alexander's army passed through on its way from the Indus to the Hydaspes. We had stopped for several days to rest and be entertained by King Ombis' musicians and dancing girls. After four years of seeing nought but the villages of Baktria and Gandaria, Taxasila had seemed like the capital of the world. Now the men wanted more of these joys.

I, on the other hand, was eager to be off. I thought the most dangerous parts of our journey would lie through the wilds of Gandaria and Arachotia. If any disaster befell us, it would be there. Hence I was anxious to put this part of the trip behind me. Sooner begun, sooner done, as we say in Thessalia.

In the city were traders from Persia and Syria, envoys from unheard-of kingdoms to the east and south, professors of Brachmanic theology lecturing their disciples, naked holy men, snake charmers and jugglers, and thousands of tall Indians with dyed beards. The town, like the older cities of Hellas, seems to have grown up in no particular order. The houses are placed at random and crowded together, making the streets extremely narrow and crooked. The houses are all made of brown mud brick, unadorned and graceless on the outside, though I am told that some have handsome interiors.

My first business was to seek out Philippos son of Machatas, Alexander's viceroy of Taxasila. I found him, a fat jolly-looking man, in a wing of King Ombis' palace, sitting over a table littered with muster rolls and bills of account, with a brace of Indian clerks to help him. For want of papyrus he used the local writing material made from palm fronds.

"So you propose to take this elephant west to Hellas, Hipparch?" he said. "Hermes attend us! That is a man-sized task. You must call upon my brother Harpalos, the treasurer. He will be overjoyed to see you, overjoyed."

"I shall probably have to wait upon the king's treasurer in any case," said I, "to replenish my funds. Where shall I find him—in Babylon?"

"He writes me that he spends most of the year in his new palace in Tarsos, where the principal mint now is. He only comes to Babylon for a few months each winter. So, if you reach Tarsos before the beginning of Poseidon, you will probably find him there. Give him my love."

"I will indeed convey your compliments, General," I said.

Philippos said: "He should entertain you in style." He winked at me. "If the treasurer of the empire cannot live well, who can? Let me give you a hint for dealing with my brother. If you desire to get favors from him, give him something lively in the female line. Harpalos has never been a physically strong man, and the only athletics he indulges in are of the horizontal kind. But he makes up for his other shortcomings by his prowess in these."

I arranged with the viceroy to draw on the government's local stores of fodder, as Eumenes had authorized. I also obtained the name of a trustworthy caster of omens for the next stage of our journey. As we parted, Philippos urged again:

"Be sure to call upon Harpalos for any help you need. I will write him that you are on your way."

Back at camp, I had finished dinner and was beginning the first of my reports to the king, when Thyestes said: "I ken the best whore in the city, Leon. Come along and you'll have a gallop to remember while crossing the deadly Persian deserts."

Pyrron said: "I'm for some Indian colleagues this evening. Why don't you come and listen to Indian philosophy?"

I wavered between the offers. I was young and healthy and had not mounted a woman for a month. Having no taste for carnal intercourse with men, I was finding my lusts bothersome in spite of the resolve I made after Hyovis' death, to live chastely like an Indian ascetic. As they say, though you drive Nature out with a spear, she will return.

On the other hand, I should like to have spent the evening with Pyrron. While I doubted if any foreigners like these Indians had much to say worth listening to, it might be worth a trial if Pyrron thought so.

In the end I declined both offers on the ground that I had to finish my letter to the king, thus salving my conscience and at the same time avoiding offense to either of my companions. Some would have neglected to send any reports to Alexander at all. But I was sure that the king, if he failed to hear from me, would send an order by the Persian post dismissing me and giving Thyestes or Vardanas the command. This bent, to run myself to death in trying to forestall every contingency, has cost me much pleasure in life but has probably saved me from some disasters too.

Next morning we struck camp early, for, as we say in Thessalia, the morn favors the traveler on his road. It was then I found Pyrron, Vardanas, and Kanadas missing. I rushed back to Taxasila. First I tried to question the guard at the gate, but he and I had no speech in common. It was the same with the others I met until I came upon an early rising Persian merchant. With his help, I got directions to a sacred grove on the western side of the city, where lived the Indian philosophers.

Here I found a dozen naked Indians pottering about with a morning meal, while my missing officers lay propped against the roots of trees, wrapped in their cloaks and snoring.

I shook them awake. Pyrron, when he had rubbed the sleep from his eyes, laughed at my wrath.

"These are the *rhamanai* whom Oneskritos and I interviewed last spring," he said. "We brought them some rice and barley and sat up conversing almost until dawn. Vardanas and Kanadas translated. I must expound their hypotheses of metempsychosis and divine justice—"

50

"We're on the king's business," I said. "Come along, and next time vanish not like that. For aught I knew you might have been murdered."

"I'm sorry, old fellow. You should have accompanied us."

I was sorry, too, though I would not then have admitted it. I have become sorrier since, for I have never been to India again. As Herakleitos said, one cannot step twice into the same stream.

In India food for the elephant was no problem. The rains had covered the bare brown plain with new grass and herbs, on which the animal grazed whenever we stopped.

We rode along a narrow river of brown mud between seas of grass on either side. Now and then we passed Indians afoot or riding asses and camels. Often the carts got stuck. When this befell, I boggled not at plunging into the mud to heave on the wheels with the rest. As my father always said, example is better than precept.

At least once a day a Persian postman galloped past. They leaned over their horses' necks, their faces half hidden by their headcloths, and swerved off the road just far enough to miss us. The first day out of Taxasila, a heavy downpour had halted our column when a postman flew past. A clod of mud from his hooves struck me fairly in the face.

I wiped off the mud and shouted after the courier: "Zeus cover your arse with boils!" By then he was out of sight behind the curtain of rain, and he would not have understood me anyway. I said to Pyrron:

"Does nought stop these lads?"

"Don't you know their motto?" he said. "'Neither snow, nor rain, nor heat, nor gloom of night shall stay us in the swift completion of the course assigned to us.' This Persian postal system is a wonderful invention; I don't see how any large empire could function without it."

I made him repeat the motto, and Vardanas confirmed it. We made a joke of it in the hipparchia. Every time a postman passed us, we all roared out in chorus: "Neither snow, nor rain..." and so on.

We crossed the Indus without mishap on a raft which some local Indians ran as a ferry. As we advanced into Gandaria, we entered higher and drier country. The daily downpours faded away to clear blue skies, and the mosquitoes that had assailed us in myriads were left behind. We had to begin scouting for food for the elephant. Aias ate a greater weight of food than all the human beings in the party together. He consumed over two hundred Babylonian pounds of hay and vegetables every day. I began to feel sorry for Aristoteles.

We found Peukala, the capital of Gandaria under the Persians, still half ruined from its sack by Hephaistion's division. Sangaios, an Indian whom Alexander had made governor of the town, was rebuilding it little by little. He found enough hay to feed Aias for several days and recommended a guide to see us to Kaboura. This was a Paktyan trader named Kavis, who covered most of Gandaria on his trading trips and knew the dialects. Sangaios said:

"This man is half Persian, so you can probably trust him."

Kavis, as soon as he joined us, said: "You had better keep double watches and scout the land ahead of you. The hill tribes of Gandaria are fierce and independent folk. They like not strangers who pass through their land with fire and sword."

This seemed good advice. Something about the mere sight of Gandaria makes one look for trouble. It is dry, rocky, and mountainous to a terrifying degree. We have stony hills in Hellas, but compared to the Gandarian mountains they are mere piles of pebbles. These mountains are carved into fantastic shapes, making one think of legendary giants turned to stone but likely to turn back any time and crush one like an insect.

There is little sign of life other than dry bushes and a few scrubby trees in the gullies, lizards scuttling over the stones, and birds of prey wheeling against the deep blue sky. Betimes a hare darts across the road, or a man with keen sight espies a troop of wild goats or sheep on a crag. The native huts of stone and mud so blend with the landscape that one sees them not until one is almost upon them. The traveler in Gandaria, however, soon learns that, however empty the landscape looks, somewhere a pair of sharp black eyes is glaring from behind a rock, and a dirty brown hand is whetting a knife.

I told Vardanas to take his Dahas and ride ahead, searching up side roads and valleys and bringing back tidings at each stage of our journey. They raced off happily in a whirl of dust, for the Dahas had recovered their spirits on getting back to an arid country.

My health improved also, oddly enough because of our cook's incompetence. I was no longer tempted to overeat, as I had been by Hyovis' delicious repasts. Had I not feared loss of dignity before my men, I should have taken over the cook's task, which I could have performed far better than he.

The stony roads of Gandaria reduced our speed by half. Had we gone more swiftly, we should have worn down our horses' hooves faster than they grew. To spare the animals, instead of alternately walking and cantering them as we had been doing, we alternately rode at a walk and led the horses on foot. I held hoof inspection twice a day and dreamt of walking on red-hot sword blades at night.

The elephant, also, disliked the sharp stones. He minced along, grumbling, and refused to be hastened. We had our first real trouble with him on the second day out of Peukala. It befell in this way.

Although the Kophen River runs from Kaboura to Peukala, it makes a far-flung loop to the north ere it reaches the latter place. Therefore travelers, instead of following the Kophen all the way, go by a smaller stream, the Chaibara. This river, which pierces the mountains by a deep narrow pass, had been a brown torrent when I rode through the pass in the early spring with Hephaistion's division. Now, however, its bed was dry.

One enters the pass eighty furlongs from Peukala. For over two hundred furlongs the road winds through the pass. In places the going is easy enough, but elsewhere the road is hewn from the sides of precipices. In such straits there is not room for two horsemen to pass each other.

When we came to a place where the narrow road overlooked a steep drop, Aias pressed himself against the cliff wall and huddled there, squealing with terror. Kanadas coaxed him and Siladites prodded him with his goad. Both shouted "*Malmal!*" but to no avail. Aias, misliking cliffs, refused to *malmal* for all they could do.

After a quarter hour's trying had failed to budge the brute, Kanadas said: "Must push him, Troop Leader. You help."

I told off two strong camp servants and led them, teetering on the edge of the precipice, past Aias' legs. Kanadas, the servants, and I put our shoulders against Aias' hind legs. We grunted and heaved, but might as well have pushed against a pair of ancient oaks.

I thrust back my helmet to wipe the sweat from my brow. Thyestes squeezed past the elephant's legs to say: "*Ea*, Leon! A trader with a string of asses and a party of Gandarians afoot have halted fornent our column. Fain would they know when yon great stirk will move so they can pass us."

I spread my hands. "He'll move when somebody thinks of a way of moving him."

"By Zeus, I can do that!" said Thyestes. He poked the elephant's haunch with his javelin, shouting: "Get up, son of a strumpet!"

Aias screamed angrily and shook his head, so that poor Siladites had much ado to keep his perch on the creature's neck. Kanadas yelled:

"You stop that! If you hurt him, he kill you someday!"

Thyestes stopped. He was brave enough, but Kanadas was twice his size and bore a huge two-handed Indian sword with a blade thirteen palms long, which could take off a head as easily as lopping a daisy.

Vardanas, who now joined us also, said: "If the elephant keeps on rubbing against the bank, he will start a slide of loose rock. Then we shall really be in a strait."

"*Papai!* What is your idea, then?" I asked Kanadas.

"If we put hay on road ahead of him, he get hungry and come forward to eat," he said.

"How long will it take for him to get hungry enough?"

"Two, maybe three days."

"Herakles! We cannot wait so long, man. This fornicating beast blocks the road like the stopper in a bottle."

I sat down with my feet dangling over the cliff and tried to think what Xenophon would have done. In a way he had things easy. He had only ten thousand men to lead, not a moody monster like Aias.

Kavis, too, came back from the front of the column. He said: "Hipparch, a lord of the Andakans waits up front with his chariot for us to pass on."

I gestured at the elephant. "Can you make him move? None of us seems able to."

"Could we hitch ropes to him and all pull at once?"

"And where shall we get so much rope? It would take enough rope to rig a ship."

"True," he said. "That is a flaw in the plan."

Voices and the tinkle of bells drew my regard back along the road to India. Around the nearest bend came a string of camels. When a score were in sight, the leader stopped, and the others jammed up behind with moaning and gurgling cries. A trousered Gandarian hastened up and spoke to Kanadas. After some words had passed back and forth, Kanadas roared an epithet and reached for his sword.

"Hold!" I cried. "What is it, Kanadas?"

"He say, make fire under elephant! Bad, wicked thing to say!"

The caravan leader smiled doubtfully and spoke in Persian: "No harm meant. But you halt my seventy-three camels. Must I then go back to Peukala?"

"He did but jest," I said to the still fuming Kanadas. "After all, you have not thought of a better way to shift this mountain of meat."

"If this melon head does not mean bad things, he should not say them," growled Kanadas.

"Melons!" I cried. I jumped to my feet and kissed Kanadas, which startled him. "You have solved our problem. Has anybody a melon? Elisas! A melon!"

The sutler sadly went back to his provision cart and got one of the remaining melons out of our stores. "I was saving it for—" he began.

I cut him off and returned to Aias, silently thanking Apollon that we did not have to send a man all the way back to Peukala for melons while traffic piled up for leagues on either side of the Chaibara Pass.

"Come, Mahankal!" I said, holding out the melon. (The king might give the elephant a new name, but teaching the beast to answer to it was another matter.) As Aias reached for the melon, I backed beyond the length of his trunk. "Come, laddie; come, body; that's my good-man! *Malmal!*"

Aias shuffled forward with tiny steps, scraping against the cliff-side and bringing down small showers of earth and stones. As he came, I backed, calling over my shoulder for the rest of the column to move on and clear the way. For the next few furlongs the party moved in this uncouth fashion.

Then the road widened. Aias caught up to me in one long stride. Trying to augment my speed backwards, I caught my heel on a stone and fell on my back. The next thing I knew, the elephant was right over me. I cried out and shut my eyes, expecting to be squashed as flat as a sheet of papyrus. When something wet struck my face, I thought I was on my way to join the shades in Hades.

Feeling no pain, I opened my eyes. Aias still stood over me. The wetness, however, was not my gore but melon juice that ran down from his chin as he ate.

I got up amidst general laughter. Even Kanadas, who seldom found anything funny in life, smiled. Betimes I thought that the gods took particular pleasure in wreaking indignities on me. I am naturally sober and dignified; but, whenever I try to present a noble front to the world, something like this melon farce occurs.

Still, it does no good to fret and fume. Instead, one must feign as much mirth as the rest. Therefore, I gave a hearty if not heartfelt laugh and set the column back in marching order.

We passed the trader with the asses, the Gandarians on foot, and the squire with the chariot, who had a pair of well-armed outriders. We drew ahead of the camel train.

I found that I knew not the form of the pass, save in a general way, for on my earlier passage I had been over-busied with keeping the troop in order to heed such matters. I therefore asked Kavis:

"How far is it to the end of the pass?"

He smiled. "Two leagues or a little more. We shall reach it by nightfall."

We plodded on for at least three leagues. Night fell, but there was no sign of the end of the pass.

"We shall get there early tomorrow," said Kavis. "It is not more than a league beyond this point. Set a strong watch, for the Chaibara Pass is a favored place for hillmen to rob travelers."

Next day we were up and moving before the sun. Aias balked several times, until it became a question of which gave out first, the pass or our supply of melons. At the top of the pass the gorge opened out into a saddle, from which I saw an immense distance. Wherever I looked, there was nought but this frightful wilderness of towering peaks and tumbled crags. Kavis kept telling me that the end of the pass was but a few furlongs further until I shouted:

"*Auramasdatai zata bia!*" which means "May God smite you." I added: "You are a dog-faced liar. According to your promises, we have already cleared the end of the pass a dozen times over!"

He spread his hands and smiled cheerfully. "But, lord, had I told you how long the pass really is, it would have made you sad and faint-hearted. As it is, you have marched joyfully, believing the end to be only beyond the next turn."

Not knowing whether to strike the impudent fellow or to laugh, I turned away. This, I found, is a habit of the Gandarians, when asked how far anything is. Either they have a misguided sense of politeness, or they know no distance accurately. I suspect the latter, for the Persian league is not a fixed length. It is, instead, the distance one can walk in one hour. Hence it may be any length from twenty-five to thirty-five furlongs, depending on the walker and on the ground. The only way to be sure of any distance in Asia is to measure it off oneself, as Baiton and his colleagues were doing.

We camped in the pass for a second night. Next morning we had more trouble with the elephant, but luckily our last melon got him through the last tight place. Then the pass opened out into a stony plain. There was a postal station like a little fort at the end of the pass, where relay horses were kept for the postmen. Behind the station stood a huddle of mud huts with a few mulberry trees.

While the hipparchia rested, I went into the postal station, made myself known to the postmaster, and wrote a letter to the king. I told Alexander this road was more suited to goats, or better yet eagles, than to elephants. Thereafter I tried to keep a few spare fruits for Aias in our stores whenever we traveled through mountains.

When I had signed and sealed my letter, I came out to find a group of Thessalians cutting up a fresh-killed sheep and preparing to cook it.

"What's this?" I said.

"We bought it in the village," said one of them, Polygonos of Iolkos. "You said we might rest for an hour."

The looks that the men gave each other made me wary. I said to Kavis: "Come with me."

In the village I found the headman and said to Kavis: "Translate my words with care. I wish to know how much was paid for that sheep my men are eating."

The headman broke into a stammering, stumbling spate of speech. Kavis said:

"It was not paid for. Two of your men threatened to kill a villager if they were not given it."

"I thought so! Tell him to come and point out the thieves."

The headman looked frightened. Kavis said: "He fears to do so, lest they return to slay him."

It took some persuasion to make the man come. Kavis said: "Do you really mean to punish these men, Lord Leon?"

"I shall carry out the king's orders."

Kavis shook his head. "Imras save me! Your king must indeed be a god, or else a little mad. In all the years of the Persian Empire, I do not think any official ever paid for what he took from a villager. I hoped to visit some of my old enemies and seize their goods as a king's man."

The headman pointed out Polygonos and one other man, Geres of Lapathos, whom I at once had seized and flogged. I gave the headman ten drachmai and dismissed him. Howsomever, for the rest of our stay he hovered as close to me as my own shadow, fearing that, if he got out of my sight, the Thessalians I had punished would kill him. Later that day, our road rejoined the Kophen. Here we halted to bathe, for our march through the pass had laid a thick layer of dust on our skins. That is, the Thessalians and their families bathed. As we stripped on the bank, I saw that Kavis, Vardanas, and the Dahas had not joined us. They stood apart with eyes averted, looking like men blushing for shame, though we were all burnt so brown that no blush could be seen.

"Will you no bathe, too?" I said. "It costs us nought."

"I pray you will excuse me, Troop Leader," said Vardanas. "To us, such an act seems highly immodest. Moreover, no Persian would bathe in running water. We hold rivers sacred and not to be defiled by human offscourings and waste."

"Suit yourselves," I said. "Stand guard over the rest of us, then."

Since Indians do not share the Asiatic superstition that it is indecent to appear naked in public, Kanadas plunged in with us. So did Siladites when Kanadas relieved him of the care of the elephant.

The road ran along the south side of the Kophen into Paktuika. Here the valley of the Kophen is a sandy desert, bare save where the Paktyans irrigate it to grow wheat and mulberry trees. Distant mountains hem the flatland like walls: the Indian Caucasus to the north, its high peaks snow-capped even in summer, and a smaller range to the south. We found the hot winds so oppressive that, on Kavis' advice, we slept through the heat of the day and marched in the early morn and late even instead.

Finding a camp site became a subject of hot dispute. It began the morning of the second day after we rejoined the Kophen. Thyestes said:

"Leon, yonder's a bonny place to camp. See the broken rock that runs halfway round it for a defense, and that little peak where the sentry can sit?"

"Aye, it pleases," I said, and gave the signal to halt.

Kanadas, riding the elephant, came up to the head of the column and loomed over me. He leaned down and said: "You stop here, Troop Leader?"

"Yes."

"No good."

"Why not, man?"

"No shade for elephant. He get hot in middle of day, get sick, fall down dead."

"By the!" said Thyestes. "What's the big black Kyklops havering anent the now?"

When I translated, Thyestes said: "Sunstroke, on a great beastie like that? The wight's daft; dinna heed him."

"He knows more about elephants nor you do, laddie, and our task is to get this one to Athens alive and hale."

"Our first duty," said Thyestes, "is to see our throats be not cut by wild highlanders."

"What he say?" said Kanadas. "He think it no matter if my beautiful Mahankal die of sun? Just wait till I get down—"

"Oh, bugger the surly sumph!" cried Thyestes. "He'll let us be for done to keep his pet cool—"

"Silence!" I shouted. "One more word and I'll take a fine out of your next pay. Now hear me. We must find a site both shady and defensible. You, Kanadas, shall ride beside Thyestes at the front of the column. When the twain of you agree on a place to camp, let us know."

Kanadas mounted the horse that Siladites had been riding and jogged beside Thyestes. They glared at each other, for they had been on bad terms ever since Thyestes speared the elephant in the Chaibara Pass.

The first result of my experiment was that we marched all day without stopping. Whichever pointed to a site, the other thought it worthless. Their collaboration was further hindered by the fact that they had about twenty words in common, and I refused to act as interpreter. Forbye, Thyestes followed the Greek habit of wagging his head for "yes" and tossing it for "no." As Kanadas' custom was the opposite, sign language only deepened the confusion. The rest of us roared with laughter to watch the pair struggling to carry on their feud in the face of these handicaps. It was suppertime when, weeping tears of rage, they at last agreed on a camp site.

Thereafter we learned to look for a grove or a sheltering cliff for each daytime halt. When it was a grove, Aias would spend his rest in tearing off branches and pulling them through his mouth, stripping them of leaves, till the oasis was spoilt for the next wayfarer. I had, however, enough concerns of my own, let abee taking on those of other travelers.

With practice, Kanadas' Persian became fluent, and he even picked up a few phrases of Greek. The man had a natural gift for languages, of which, however, he made little use, remaining aloof and distant. When not weeping for homesickness, he complained about the weather, the food, the road, and aught else that came to his mind.

His low-caste companion, Siladites, was the opposite: a cheerful, friendly man who could learn no foreign language, however hard he tried. He would memorize a word of a phrase and then next day weep with vexation to find he had forgotten it. Hence his communion with us was almost limited to signs.

On the twenty-fifth of Hekatombaion, we were jogging past the place where the Chavaspes flows into the Kophen from the north. Here the valley of the Kophen narrows and the mountains close in. Down the valley of the Chavaspes runs a crude road that crosses the Kophen by a ford. We were nearing this ford, and Vardanas was away scouting, when Pyrron rode up beside me and spoke. He had to speak twice to get my attention, because he had the habit of muttering and whispering to himself. This habit disconcerted his comrades until they learnt to ignore it and Pyrron, too.

"Oblige me by translating, old fellow," he said. "I would question the guide."

"Say on," I said, as Kavis came up on the other side.

Pyrron said: "Have you ever heard of a book on foreign countries by a man named Herodotos?"

"No, but go on."

"He said that in Paktuika live enormous ants, as big as dogs, which, in excavating their burrows, bring gold to the surface of the earth. He asserted, further, that the Paktyans approach these burrows in the heat of the day, when the ants are underground. They scoop up the gold and flee on fast camels before the ants can devour them. Now, inquire of Kavis if this be true. I missed Paktuika on my way east, being up north with the king, and have wondered about these ants."

I told the tale to Kavis in Persian. (My Persian was becoming fluent with practice, if not correct.) He laughed and said: "My ancestors invented that story to keep the Great King from stealing our gold. There is a little gold in the streams of Paktuika, which we get by swirling the gravel with water around in a bowl. As for the so-called ants, there are some of their burrows now!"

Kavis pointed to some little black dots at the base of a nearby hill. When I looked closely, I saw these to be the holes of the mountain mouse, an animal about the size and shape of a beaver but with a short bushy tail. There is nought in the least antlike about them.

The guide went on: "The tale was put abroad in the time of the first Dareios, and the Persians believed it for twenty or thirty years.

Then, in the reign of the first Artaxerxes, an agent of the Great King came upon some of our people washing gold from the streams. The sight aroused his suspicions, and he tarried long enough to settle the true nature of these 'ants.'

"When Artaxerxes learned the truth, he was wroth indeed. You see, the whole purpose of the Persian Empire was to grind the last bit of gold and silver out of poor folk like us. For years, the government had not been getting so much as they might, had they known the true state of affairs. So the Great King sent an army to take vengeance on us who had flouted him—"

I never learned the outcome, for there came an interruption. A horseman appeared, galloping toward us on the road along the Chavaspes.

This newcomer had been richly dressed in Indian garb. Now his clothes were tattered, and a bandage encircled his head. He plunged into the Kophen and cantered across the ford, throwing up fountains of spray. He stopped at the foot of the slope that separated us from the river and raised an arm, while his steed panted and blew foam.

"Are you King Alexander's men?" he shouted in bad Persian.

I said: "Yes. Who are you?"

"Sasigouptas, viceroy of Gandaria. The Assakenians have revolted and slain their governor. Some are after me." He pointed back along his tracks. "There they are!"

A group of horsemen came into sight far up the valley, riding hard. Sasigouptas continued:

"I ride for Peukala to send word to the king. You must hold these rebels. Fight to the last man!"

He raised his voice to a scream and spurred his horse. Away he went, torn cloak flapping and gravel flying.

"Imras preserve us!" said Kavis. "I will fight for you, but then you must pay me a bonus on our reckoning."

I was not much taken with the viceroy's order to stand and die while he fled to safety, though on reflection it was plain that somebody did have to carry word to Peukala. I watched the Indian grow small in the distance and disappear around a bend, while the Assakenians drew nearer. There was no sign of Vardanas and the Dahas.

My first thought was of flight, but then neither the mule carts nor the elephant could keep up with us, and they would be taken by the rebels. We faced a hard choice. I called the men to attention and said:

"Heely, lads! Rebel tribesmen are galloping down upon us. An we flee, we might get clean away, but the carts with our wives and bairns could no. An we stand, 'twill be a hard fight, as there's mae of them than of us. But we ken that Fortune helps the brave. Not only are Thessalians bonnier fighters than any mere foreigners, but also our weapons are muckle better. We have armor of bronze and leather and canvas; they have nought but the rags they wear. We have swords and spears of keen iron; they have but sharpened wooden poles. We have training and discipline; they are but rabble. Will we fight?"

The men looked at their families. One said "Fight!" and soon all were shouting: "Fight the thieving limmers! Screed them! Slay them!"

"That's my braw buckies," I said. "Arm, then, and hurry! Throw fear to the wind! *Iai* for Thessalia!"

The men swarmed about the carts in which they had piled their fighting gear. I saw I had erred in letting them disarm because of the heat, for their helmets and canvas corselets were all jumbled, and they wasted time scrambling for them. I feared they would have to fight half armed, thus giving our advantage in armament to the Assakenians. However, the clearness of the Gandarian air is deceptive; our foes were much farther away than they looked.

I talked over our plan of battle with Thyestes. "An we stand in line on the crest of this bank," I said, "we can shower those wights with javelins as they come up. They'll be slowed by the water and then by the slope. Later we can charge down and possibly turn them while they mill around."

Thyestes said: "What for no using our old lozenge formation? We could split the knaves into fragments."

"Na, there's no enough of us. The lozenge would have only four or five men on a side and be swallowed up."

"Well then," he said, "it would help gin the servants ran down ahint us with spears."

"What good can they do?"

"They can push in atween us and stab the foreigners' horses and pull the men from the saddle. We shall have a gey thin line."

I said: "The grooms shall form a second mounted line. I doubt the servants will do much serious fighting, but we have nought to lose by trying it. You!" I said to Pyrron, who sat with his traveling hat shading his face as if none of this concerned him. "How will you fight?"

"Who, me?" he said.

"Aye, you! Or did you no think they'd cut your throat as soon as the next man's?"

"Dear me," he said, "it never occurred to me. But I suppose I ought to do something."

"What weapons can you handle?"

"It were better if I fought on foot. I've had heavy-infantry training, since I was neither wealthy enough nor proficient enough a horseman to apply for the Eleian cavalry."

"Lead the servants, then," I said. "Take a javelin and one of those bucklers."

I armed Pyrron with misgivings, because, though a tall well-built man, he was so awkward and unhandy that he was likely to trip over his own feet and skewer himself. I turned to Kanadas. "You and Siladites don your quilts and get up on the elephant with plenty of javelins."

I told him our plan and added: "When we advance, Aias shall charge out from the right end of our line and circle round to take the Assakenians in flank."

I had to repeat everything, until at last he said: "Yes, I understand. I do that."

I kept looking up the Kophen for Vardanas and his horse archers. Probably, I thought with bitterness, if they did see us attacked they would run for home. But what could one expect of foreigners?

The men got their gear sorted out at last, and I drew them up. I gave each horseman three javelins instead of the usual two.

Now the Assakenians were close enough for me to make out what they were like. There were about eighty or ninety big men, most of them bareheaded and clad mainly in goatskins, and riding small horses. Their long black hair floated behind them. The man in the lead wore a plain bronzen helmet, but otherwise there was no sign of armor in the lot. The usual weapon was a wooden lance with the tip sharpened and fire-hardened, though they also had a few proper metal axes and spears.

As the clatter grew louder, I walked Golden up and down in front of my troop. A wise commander does this less to watch the enemy than to watch his own men, lest they steal quietly away and leave him to fight his battle alone. Not that my brave Thessalians would have done such a thing, but the camp servants and grooms might well have stolen off without my eye upon them. Pyrron stood among them, leaning on his dart with his usual look of vague good nature. I saw that Elisas, the sutler, had disappeared, but the rebels were too close to go hunting for him. I led the Thessalians in a short prayer to Ares.

When the Assakenians neared the ford, I took my place in the center of the line and poised a javelin. The enemy neither turned down the Kophen after Sasigouptas nor tried to parley. They galloped straight through the ford, yelling and screaming. Evidently the sight of our cockscomb crests was enough. The Assakenians, I heard later, had sworn undying enmity to all Hellenes because of Alexander's massacre of the men of Massaga.

I called: "Ready! Cast!" I was a little too quick, so that some of our first volley fell short.

"Ready! Cast!" This time we could not miss. There was disorder among the Assakenians as men and horses fell into the stream. Our horses fidgeted with excitement.

I shifted my remaining javelin to my right hand and cried: "Charge!" I spurred, swearing to kill Vardanas someday for his desertion.

The men shouted: "*Eleleleu!*" Down we rushed, one thin line of twenty horsemen, followed by the eight grooms and then by the servants afoot.

Kanadas sent the elephant shuffling down the bank toward the flank of the foe, as planned. However, the nearest Assakenian, seeing the monster looming over him, threw his lance. He aimed for the eye but missed. The point pierced the elephant's cheek and wounded his tongue. The elephant screamed, wheeled, and ran off down the river, despite the efforts of Siladites to turn him by beating him over the head with the elephant goad.

Now that we were bereft of our flanking force, there was nought to do but try to turn the attackers by sheer mettle. I aimed for the leader in the helmet and he for me. We met. I knocked the point of his spear aside with my buckler, while he avoided the thrust of my javelin by a sudden movement. As his spear went to my left and mine to his, we found ourselves in close embrace. The horses plunged on past each other, with the result that the twain of us, still clutching each other, slid off over their tails.

The next thing I knew, the hostile leader and I were grappling knee-deep in water. Each of us dropped his spear and tried to draw his sword, while the other strove to prevent him.

By a quick catch of his heel, the Assakenian tripped me. I fell backwards, lost my grip on his sword arm, and went under. When I got my face above water again, the Assakenian was already swinging his sword in its fatal arc. All around us, horses' legs were stamping and men were struggling and screaming. The Assakenians shouted "*Gis! Gis!*"

I tried to scramble away and draw my own sword, but I was hours too slow. I caught the chief's first blow on my shield, but the impact, helped by the clutch of the stream on my legs, knocked me off my feet again.

The Assakenian lunged, reaching for my beard with his left hand. Then he twisted, showed his teeth in a grimace of pain, and fell on me.

When I found my footing again, I saw Pyrron thrusting a javelin into the submerged body of the Assakenian leader. As he jerked the weapon out he drove the butt into my midriff. Although my corselet saved me from serious hurt, the blow took my breath away.

The forest of horses' legs had gone from around us. The mass of fighters moved back across the ford, and soon the Assakenians fled back up the road by which they had come. The servants, who had run forward under Pyrron's leadership, were left behind and now went about spearing wounded rebels. The water was rust-colored with mud and blood.

"What—what befell?" I asked when I stopped coughing.

Pyrron pointed to a half-submerged body with a Sakan arrow sticking in its back. "Our friends opportunely returned," he said.

I looked toward the pursuers and saw the pointed caps of our Dahas. Thyestes blew the recall, and our men collected by twos and threes. There was Vardanas with a broad smile and brains dripping from his spiked club. From down the river came the elephant. Aias had pulled the spear out of his face with his trunk and returned at a slow walk, moaning and drooling blood.

Pyrron told me: "The Persian and the Dahas returned while you were hoofing around in the stream. They halted a few paces from the Assakenians and began shooting. The foreigners flinched away from the tempest of arrows, and that started the whole lot retreating. That, and the demise of their leader."

As he spoke, he waved his javelin with enthusiasm. I had to duck to avoid getting the point in my face. I said:

"O Pyrron, you have saved my life, and I'm grateful. Now please put that thing back in the cart ere you slay me with it." As Vardanas rode up I said: "That was a timely arrival, laddie. I feared you had left us."

Vardanas pursed his lips angrily. He replied: "I gave you my word, did I not?"

"Are you saying that when you Persians talk of keeping your word of honor, you really mean it?"

"Be not more Greek than you can help! Of course we mean it. At least I do."

Well, as we say at home, it is better to learn late than never. I said: "My friend, I was wrong and you are right. You are a gentleman and a warrior, and I'm proud to know you. I would fain clasp your hand in the Persian manner to pledge our friendship."

He smiled and gripped my hand.

Eight Assakenians lay dead. We had many wounds, but only one man dead and one likely to die. The dead man was a camp servant whose head had been split by an Assakenian ax as he tried to pull the foreigner from his horse. The sorely wounded was a Thessalian, Zethos of Larissa, pierced through corselet and chest by a wooden lance. His comrades helped him to the bank, where he lay, coughing up bloody foam. As usual, the losing side had lost out of proportion, because men slightly disabled were caught and finished off when their comrades fled.

I said to Thyestes: "See that all wounds are cleansed and bound, and send men to pick up the fallen weapons. I'm going to look for our braw sutler."

"*Ea!* D'you mean the cowardly coof has fled? Give me the slitting of his throat!"

I found Elisas behind a rock not thirty paces from the bank. When he saw my look, he ran. Because of his slight build he drew ahead of me until a Thessalian threw a javelin whirling against his legs and tripped him. I caught his arm as he got up, and began to beat him.

"Mercy, great lord!" he screamed. "I am no warrior! Not hired to fight!"

"Hold him, lads," I said. "He jerks so I canna get a good swing at him."

Two Thessalians held him while I swung my javelin with both hands until I was tired and Elisas hung limply. When they dropped him, he crept off moaning and half fell down the bank of the river. He doffed his tunic and bathed the welts on his back, still weeping and muttering Syrian curses.

"Next time, dung man," I said, "obey." I turned to Kavis, who was binding a small leg wound. "How far to Kasipapoura?"

"Less than a league. If you do not mind marching in the heat, we can reach it by noon."

"Is this another of your Gandarian leagues, that stretches and shrinks like a lump of warm pitch?"

He laughed. "No indeed; we can almost see my city from here."

I ordered the men to place Zethos in one of the carts and make him easy.

"His lung is pierced," said Thyestes. "Aweel! I misdoubt he'll die."

"That's up to Fate." I said. "Let's be off, ere another rebel army come upon us."

Kasipapoura lies a few furlongs west of the junction of the Kophen with the Chavaspes. I first saw it over the orchards and wheat fields that the Paktyans grow by a far-reaching system of irrigation ditches. Kavis said:

"Yonder is a good place to camp, by the river. While you set up your tents, I shall ride home to ready a feast for you and your officers.

You, Hipparch, shall stay the night at my house. I would invite all, were my place big enough. Is it well?"

"It is well," I said. Off went Kavis at a gallop. I sent the sullen Elisas after him on a mule to buy food for our people and beasts.

We set up our tents and crawled into them. I was just falling asleep when a sentry roused me.

"Troop Leader!" he said. "A man asks to speak to you."

The man was fat, ill-favored, and jingling with turquoise ornaments. He was, he said, Toragas, the leading man of Kasipapoura. When I could not understand his scraps of Persian, Vardanas crawled out of his tent to help. At length Vardanas said:

"He says Kavis is an evildoer, a very *daiva*. Kavis, he avers, has lured us hither so his men can fall upon us and slay us. For ten talents of silver he will protect us from the wicked Kavis. Nay more, he will entertain us at his palace. There we shall enjoy the pleasures of Bishta, the Gandarian paradise."

Even had the fellow's tale been true, the amount he asked was absurd. I said: "Say we thank him but can take care of ourselves."

The man spoke again, in tones of menace. Vardanas said: "He warns us we had better pay him for protection. There are many all-daring rogues among the Paktyans who would cut our throats for nought but our weapons, let alone for our treasure."

"What treasure? He knows nought of what we have. Tell him to begone."

The man went. I tried to sleep again but could not for worry over Toragas' warning. Kavis had done well for us, but one could never be sure with foreigners.

Two or three hours later, as I was falling asleep for the second time, Kavis came back. "All is ready," he cried. "Follow me. You too, Kanadas."

Kanadas said: "You no angry if I no eat?"

"The more fool you; but come anyway. Bring some grooms to hold your horses outside the city, Hipparch, as our streets are too narrow for riding."

Kavis led Kanadas, Vardanas, Pyrron, and me to the city. Thyestes had to stay with the detachment. Kavis led us through the gate, exclaiming: "Is this not the most beautiful city in the world?"

Compared to Babylon, or even Taxasila, Kasipapoura was a mere huddle of hovels, made even less winsome by heat, dust, and flies. Howsomever, I forbore to wound our host by untimely candor.

"It is indeed beautiful," I said.

"What a dreadful hole!" said Pyrron in Greek.

"He, too, thinks it beautiful," I said. Vardanas caught my eye and burst into a fit of coughing.

"I rejoice that you know true beauty," said Kavis. "Here is our dancing stage, where we dance and vote on tribal matters...." He went on to tell of their democratic government.

"In fact," he said, "all that keeps Kasipapoura from being a paradise on earth is my foe Toragas, who lives on the other side of town. My family has been at feud with his for generations."

I was about to mention Toragas' visit when Kavis said: "Here we are. Enter and use my house as your own."

Like the other larger houses in Kasipapoura, Kavis' house was built like a small fortress. We entered through a gate that looked as if it would keep out elephants and found ourselves in a courtyard decked with a rose garden. Kavis proudly showed off his roses, though compared to the gardens of the lordly houses of Persia it was a dismal little show. We sat down on a rug in the courtyard.

There were two other men, the headman of Kasipapoura, Outamer, and the commandant of the Greek garrison, Laomedon of Keos. Alexander had left thousands of such Greek mercenaries in garrisons on his march to India. Kavis also presented us to his two wives and three daughters.

I told Laomedon of Zethos' plight and asked: "Have you decent quarters where I could leave him?"

"Let's see," said Laomedon. "You carry this man's advance pay, do you not?"

"Aye." I thought it better to say nought of Zethos' discharge bonus.

"If you leave his pay with him, he'll be welcome. If he live, we shall need him, in case the Assakenians come hither. My command is no larger than yours, though I am supposed to rule the most insolent, truculent race on earth. Whereas if he die..." Laomedon cocked an eyebrow at me, as if to say that then the money would be put to good use. "However, we'll take good care of him. We have no physicians, but, with a lung wound, prayer is as good as aught they can do."

Kavis' wives and slaves passed the wine. Soon we all felt at ease. Laomedon and the headman insisted on the story of the battle. I told my version, and then they asked Vardanas for his. The silly man shamed me by giving the true numbers of the Assakenians, which I had swollen for the sake of the tale—not much, only to double their true size. These Persians, who spoil a good story for the sake of a few facts!

I forgave Vardanas, though, when he praised my generalship. "In truth," he said, "it was the plan that Arsites used at the Granikos. He was an able general, too."

I said: "You puzzle me, Vardanas. Did not Arsites lose the battle of the Granikos? I missed it, because I joined Alexander later, at Gordion. But I've heard many tales of this fight."

"I was in the thick of it," said Vardanas. "True, Arsites lost, but only because he fought against the genius of Alexander and the will of Auramasdas."

"How so?"

"Like this," said Vardanas, taking a handful of coins from his wallet and setting them on the rug to denote the units at the Granikos. "Let this dareikos be Arsites; let this golden stater Alexander be. Arsites' plan was to stand on this high bank, as you did, and ply the foe with darts as they came. One charge we turned back with heavy loss. Then Alexander led the next charge." He moved his coins.

"Foreseeing this, Arsites had told his officers that, if all else failed, they must stop the Macedonian invasion by killing Alexander. Therefore, when our remaining javelins failed to halt the attack, Arsites led his officers straight at the Macedonian, to slay him or die trying.

"Well, you know what happened. All the Persian generals but Arsites himself perished in the hacking and stabbing around Alexander. And this is why I say the gods took a hand. For Alexander sustained blows that would have slain any mortal. They were dealt by mighty warriors who had fought from the sands of Egypt to the snows of Sogdia. Yet Alexander came through with nought but a few scratches.

Not that Alexander is not a doughty fighter, small though he be. But no man could have withstood the onset of so many brave and well-armed foemen at once without divine help."

"The way I heard it," said Laomedon, "the Persian horse deserted their Greek mercenary foot and fled before the battle was decided."

"You heard wrong," said Vardanas. "We withdrew when all our leaders were slain or wounded, and the Macedonian foot assailed our flanks with their long pikes, and Memnon's Hellenes failed to aid us. If there was any deserting, it was the other way round."

Laomedon asked: "Why did Arsites put his Hellenes behind the horse, where they could do little?"

"He trusted Memnon not," said Vardanas. "And later I suppose he was too busy fighting to send an order to Memnon. But Memnon should have advanced on his own."

"I ken the answer to that," I said. "Alexander ordered his raiding parties not to touch Memnon's estates. Naturally, the Persians thought there must be an understanding between them."

Vardanas sighed. "Against such subtlety, what could we simple, straightforward Persians do?"

"Anyway it was a good fight," said Laomedon. "Let us drink to the shades of all who fell in it, Greek or Persian."

Kavis' household set wooden platters in front of us. Thereon they placed big slabs of Gandarian bread. These look like round pieces of leather but are better by far than the bread our cook made, which was either soggy or iron-hard. On the bread they put cuts of mutton, with side dishes of cucumbers and dates. We finished with melons and a kind of cake the Paktyans make of mashed mulberries.

When the twilight faded, Kavis' other guests reeled off into the dark, singing and shouting. All, that is, but Kanadas. Having drunk little and eaten nought, the Indian remained as dour and grave as always. Kavis showed me to my chamber, where a bird in a cage squawked once at me and then went back to sleep.

I was falling asleep when a racket brought me up again. I donned my shirt and went out. In the courtyard stood Kanadas, Vardanas, and Pyrron, Vardanas holding his head and Pyrron nursing an arm wound. Kanadas held, by its long black hair, a Gandarian head. Kavis bent to examine the face of the head by torchlight.

"It is Viden, one of Toragas' horse boys," said Kavis.

"Men attacked us in a dark street," said Pyrron. "Kanadas routed them. Help me with this bandage."

"I see," I said, and told of Toragas' visit to our camp.

"Why did you not tell me before?" cried Kavis. "I should have known the *drouz* would try something."

"I meant to, but other things came up and I forgot. I suppose he hoped, by killing my men, to make me give in to his demands."

"Partly. But he is also wroth because I got the task of guiding this noble party and have guested a friend of the great king. This gives me honor and will help to re-elect Outamer, my family's candidate for mayor. Therefore, Toragas tries to shame me by harming you while you are under my protection. If you will fetch your soldiers while I arm my household, we will storm Toragas' house and put all in it to the sword."

"No, thank you," I said. "Much as I should like to kill Toragas, duty comes before pleasure. I shall go back to camp with my men this time, to make sure they meet no more ambuscades. But it would oblige me if you sent some men with torches."

Kavis not only sent two of his men, but also came himself with another torch. This time there were no alarums. Pyrron told me the story:

"We left Outamer and Laomedon at their homes and set out for the gate. But, ah—'inflaming wine, pernicious to mankind' had rendered us unsteady. Without a moon, we got lost in these irregular streets, and six or eight men assaulted us with knives and clubs. Vardanas received a knock from a cudgel. My sword got tangled in my cloak, and an attacker dealt me this flesh wound—"

"You dealt it to yourself, you left-hander!" said Vardanas.

"Be that as it may, the sober Kanadas, like 'mighty Aias, a host all by himself,' brought out his great sword and rushed roaring upon the foe. He sheared through their clubs like straws. He severed the head from one and an arm from another. When a third was cut half through at the waist, the rest made off."

Vardanas said: "Let us take up Kavis' offer, to storm Toragas' house. Our honor demands it."

"Nay," I said. "With two or three of them dead, against but a couple of trivial hurts on our side—"

"Trivial hurts, *phy!*" said Vardanas, fingering the lump on his skull.

Zethos lingered, neither mending nor dying, until I left him at the house that Laomedon had turned into a barrack. I asked the others to withdraw while I bade him farewell.

"Do you hear and understand, laddie?" I said softly.

Zethos opened his eyes and wagged his head in affirmation.

"Then hearken. I have your bonus, but I shall take it with me. An I leave it here the now, Laomedon might slit your weasand to possess it. D'you ken what I mean?"

Again he gave a faint shake of his head.

"When you get back to Hellas, seek me out and I'll pay you. An I be not in Atrax, my kin will know whither I've gone."

Zethos smiled faintly. I kissed him and said: "*Pheu*, lad, it gars me greit to leave you, but 'tis your best chance. Fare you well!"

I kept his talent separate from my own funds for years, but Zethos never came to claim it. I know not what befell him: whether he died in Kasipapoura, or perished in the treacherous massacre of the homeward-bound Hellenes by Peithon's Macedonians after Alexander's death, or suffered some other doom.

The valley of the Kophen remained narrow for our first day's march from Kasipapoura. Then the valley opened out again. A new moon appeared, marking the onset of the month of Metageitnion.

At Thyestes' suggestion, I raised a Thessalian to double-pay trooper so that he could act as Thyestes' deputy. This was Klonios of Skotoussa, a mature old war horse who had fought well at the Chavaspes.

On the third of the new month we reached Kaboura, the Orthospana of the Persians. This town stands in a corner of a plain, above the fork of the Kophen, where spurs come down from neighboring mountains on either hand.

As we passed through the gate, a crowd of idlers and beggars gathered. The loafers gauped at the elephant and the beggars cried their one Greek word: *argyrion*,[1] which they pronounced, *"Giroun! Giroun!"*

I asked Kavis: "Where shall we find the commandant?"

Kavis pointed to a castle that loomed over the town from a nearby crag. "There the king put his garrison. And now I have kept my bargain. When you have paid me I shall leave you. Do not forget the help I gave in the battle!"

I counted out his money, with a liberal bonus. He said: "May you never tire!" and trotted off with a wave.

The rest of us threaded our way through the narrow streets toward the castle. When the crowd became so thick as to hinder us, Siladites prodded the elephant so that Aias raised his trunk and trumpeted. The throng gave back, falling over one another in their haste.

At the foot of the crag I found a path leading up to the stronghold, barred by a pair of heavy-armed Hellenes in full panoply. When I stated my business, one of them plodded up the path, craning his head back to look until he almost fell off the cliffside. Soon the commandant came clanking down.

"Hegias of Corinth am I," he said. "By the Dog! What will go through here next? A train of dragons and gryphons?"

I told him our problems. He directed me to a camping place and added: "Lay in plentiful supplies, Troop Leader, for there is no town of decent size till you reach Gazaka. As for a guide, I'll do what I can, though I trust no Gandarians."

We rested for a day, mended our gear, and scoured Kaboura for shoes for ourselves and food for Aias. The beast had lost some of the plump look he had at the start of the journey. Gathering whole talents of straw and leaves had become our heaviest chore. Kanadas said:

"He is not well. Needs good meal of elephant bread."

"You mean they feed bread to elephants?" I said.

"Yes. In Sindou, make special bread, big loaves like this." Kanadas held his hands a cubit apart.

---

1   Money

In the late afternoon I was writing the king and thinking of the dinner to which Hegias had bidden me, when Thyestes and three Thessalians appeared, running from the town. As they came, I saw that the troopers bore armfuls of foliage. After them came a crowd of Gandarians with staves and knives.

I seized the trumpet and blew the alert. Thanks to my earlier drilling, the soldiers sprang to their war gear as if the demons of the waste were upon them. By the time the fugitives arrived, we had a line of mounted men, with the river in our rear and the Dahas at the ends of the line with arrows nocked.

The Gandarians stopped a score of paces away and milled, shouting.

"What say they?" I asked Vardanas.

"I do not know their speech. They shout something about Monis, a Gandarian god."

Thyestes gasped: "We were looking for foliage for the polluted elephant. We cut a puckle boughs from a wee tree, not knowing it stood by one of their wretched shrines—nought but a pedestal of rough timber with a great stone abune it. The loons began to waul, so we came away."

I had noticed these shrines before in Gandaria. Usually they had poles at the corners topped by human skulls and other trophies of raids. Without an interpreter, however, we could not explain our innocent intentions to the Kabourans, even supposing they would listen.

For most of an hour they churned about, coming as close as they dared, to scream, shake fists, and spit. More kept coming from the town until the throng far outnumbered us. Some of the newcomers bore spears and other weapons. Clods and stones began to fly. Our horses danced and reared as the missiles struck them. My men growled.

"Hold your rank!" I said. "Dinna cast even an insult at yon dog-faces afore I give the word!" But the men were getting so angry that I foresaw trouble in holding them.

Then a line of crested helmets and bronzen breastplates appeared behind the mob. Hegias' garrison marched into them from the rear, smiting and jabbing with spear butts. Panic seized the Gandarians, who fled off to the sides to avoid being surrounded.

The throng broke into small groups and single men, who drifted away, pausing to shout parting curses. Hegias strode forward.

"What does this mean, Troop Leader?" he said. "Not seeing you when I expected and hearing a clamor, I turned out my men."

When I told about the tree, he burst out: "As if I hadn't enough grief with these murderous knaves, one of your lackwits has to tamper with a sacred grove! I ought to tell the barbarians to go ahead and slaughter you!"

After he had fumed for a while, he calmed down and even fed the sacred branches to the elephant. By the time I had climbed up to his crag, he was in a good humor once more. After dinner a Gandarian came in, a thin, stoop-shouldered man with a twitching eyelid, and a head shaven all over but for a scalp lock two palms long.

"This is Niliras," said Hegias. "He'll guide you to Alexandreia Arachotion."

"May you never tire!" said Niliras in broken Persian. "I great guide. Know all countries in world. Know all nations and tongues. You lucky to get me."

"What's that jabber?" said Hegias.

I translated, adding: "If this modest chappie be as good as that, he's a demigod in disguise."

Hegias snorted. "More likely he'll lead you over the edge of a cliff or into an ambuscade. But that's your worry, Hipparch."

"Is he then the best you could find?"

"What matters it? There's no point in seeking a better, for these ready-for-aughts are all like that. Can you be off tomorrow? After today's riot, it were foolish to stay longer than you must."

BOOK THREE

Arachotia

BY TURNING EVERYBODY TO, I got my hipparchia on the road again before the following noon. We followed the south branch of the Kophen, traversing narrow gorges and crossing many tributaries. Ever we climbed and bore southward. We entered Thatagous, the name of which, according to Vardanas, means "Land of a Hundred Cows." In reality, we saw few kine, and those were little scrubby beasts that a Thessalian yeoman would sneer at.

As we passed the shoulder of a hill, Niliras pointed up and said: "There I ambushed an Andakan and slew him with a single arrow."

A little later, as we wound through an area of tumbled boulders, he said: "Here I killed four Assakenians in sleep. Two men, one woman, one child. Am I not wonderful?"

Still later, as we crossed the dry bed of an affluent, he said: "Here my brother and I caught Arachotian merchant apart from caravan. *Ch-ch!*" He drew his finger across his throat, grinning.

"Meseems you have slain many," I said.

"Oh yes, I mighty slayer! Best in my tribe!"

"How many have you murdered altogether?"

Frowning, Niliras counted on his fingers. "Man and woman in Gazaka—man north of Kaboura—man on west branch of Kophen—

78

three men in Kapisa—woman and baby in Gorva—should I count baby, think you?"

"By all means."

"Then I have slain sixteen or seventeen; cannot remember which. I mighty hero, yes?"

"No doubt of it," I said, glancing at my sword to make sure it was handy.

"My father killed thirty-three before some dirty murderer slew him. Some day I beat his record. You lucky to have me for friend. Everybody not my friend, I kill."

"I will try to keep on your good side," I said.

"That easy. Pay me more money."

"We agreed on a certain amount, and that you shall have."

"You pay too little! Slave's pay for great hero like me! You pay more, or watch yourself!"

"To Zozouka with you!" I said, naming the Gandarian Tartaros.

Niliras screamed curses in his native tongue. Some Thessalians looked at him and hefted their darts. I laughed, and Niliras calmed down.

The sun was setting behind the western peaks when I ordered a halt, near another dry stream bed. Niliras rode forward and shouted that this would be the place to camp.

"See soft sand!" he cried. "Good for sleeping."

"Do not camp in the stream bed," said Vardanas. "A sudden storm might send a torrent down the bed and sweep us away."

"Stupid Persian!" said Niliras. "No rain this season!"

"I still think you had better camp out of the stream bed," said Vardanas. "Know you not the proverb: 'He who stops to tie his shoe in a dry river bed is lost'?"

As between a Persian gentleman and an all-abandoned Gandarian who boasted of his many murders, I chose the former's advice. Niliras sulked. Then he approached me, again demanding money. I became wroth.

"Get out!" I said. "I have given my answer. At the next word about pay, I will knock your teeth out."

"Then give me what you owe me now."

"Here." I handed him the two and a half oboloi I owed him for the day's work. I could have held back his pay till we reached Gazaka, but I was weary and wished to be rid of him.

Niliras snatched the coins, ran off a few paces, spat back at me, and shouted: "Ious take you, foreign dog! I fetch my tribe, kill you all and take treasure!"

He capered and shook his fists. I snatched a javelin and hurled it. The Gandarian avoided the cast by leaping aside. He ran after the dart, picked it up, and waved it.

"Now you lose spear too!" he screamed. "Stupid foreign slave, *ia-ia-ia*!" He ran up the hillside.

We all shouted. I ran after Niliras with my sword; some hurled javelins; a Daha got off a brace of arrows. But the Gandarian leapt up the rocks like a goat, bounding hither and yon so that all our shots missed. I chased him up the mountain but was soon halted by my pounding heart and puffing lungs. Niliras, now far above us, made an indecent parting gesture of defiance and vanished.

We kept a double guard at night thereafter but saw no more of Niliras.

The valley opened out into a broad plain, with little villages surrounded by crops. The post road to Gazaka was plain enough; we were in no danger of getting lost. The traffic, which had been light in the Kophen Valley, waxed thicker. Gandarian traders put their camels out to pasture in the spring and summer, and work them autumn and winter. They were now rounding up their beasts and making up their caravans.

Our difficulty was that, without a guide, we could not tell the villagers that we would pay for food and fodder. Hence the natives, seeing the glitter of our arms, feared that we should plunder them, as officials and soldiers everywhere are wont to do. The larger, walled towns slammed their gates and prepared for defense; while the people of the smaller, open hamlets fled to the hills, driving their little flocks before them.

Thus, when we found a village deserted, we helped ourselves to what food we could find, and I left a few small coins on the doorstep of the largest house for what we deemed fair payment. One day I found, after leaving such a village, that I had forgotten my knife in the square where we had eaten. I rode back and, on recovering my knife, discovered that the money I had left for the food had vanished. Someone in my party had taken it. After that I made sure of being the last to leave each village.

Another trouble was with shoes. As the stony roads had compelled us to wend afoot a deal of the time, so the walking had quickly worn through the soles of our thin riding shoes. As nobody in this part of the world makes a proper walking shoe, let alone an Iphikratean marching boot, my poor men had been reduced to patching their soles with any odd bits of leather, or wrapping their feet in rags. The horny-footed natives go barefoot in summer. In winter they wear a huge felt snow boot, which, as I found out by trial, is useless for a march like ours. And we had not stayed in Kaboura long enough to get ourselves decently shod.

To keep Aias from shrinking further, we cut more boughs from trees. I tried to spare fruit trees and trees near shrines but did not always succeed. In this arid land we often marched for hours without seeing a single tree.

The hills closed in again and the road ascended, until I found that exertion made me weak and dizzy. We crossed a broad saddle and started down the other side into the land of Arachotia. The Arachotians are smaller and darker than the Gandarians, but are much like them in their ways.

Nine days from Kaboura we reached Gazaka, a strong-walled city on a high, dusty tableland. Alexander renamed it Alexandreia Arachotion when he made it the new capital of Arachotia, but he named so many places "Alexandreia" or "Alexandropolis" that I think it will confuse my readers less if I use the native names, however uncouth they sound.

The main range of the Indian Caucasus, which runs north of the Kophen, bends around and sends a long branch southwestwards, west of Gazaka and Kaboura. The citadel of Gazaka is perched on the final hump of a spur of hills thrust out from this branch.

I asked for Menon, the viceroy of Arachotia, but learned that he was in Kandacha. Therefore I sought out the Greek commandant and got from him not only help, but also another guide. This was a pleasant-looking youth named Barmoukas. If a fair exterior be a silent recommendation, I thought, I should have less trouble with him. We also managed to buy a few pairs of wearable shoes.

When we set out from Gazaka, I took Barmoukas aside. "Some folk," I said, "think it clever to take on guide work at a pay agreed upon and then demand more as soon as they are out of sight of home. Now, I have been all through this and will not abide it. The first word I hear of higher pay, you had better start running, for I shall be after you to beat you to a pulp."

"Yes, yes, I know," quoth he, all smiles. "Fear nought. I am soul of honor."

"So said your predecessor of himself. Mark well my words, fellow."

From Gazaka we wended south again along the bed of an intermittent stream. Albeit this stream was now dry, we could always strike water by digging into the stream bed. However, the heat waxed torrid as we descended from the heights of Gazaka until it became unbearable. We Hellenes went nude in the heat of the day, heedless of the shock to Asiatic modesty.

Now the stream we followed began to have water in it, so we took to the post road along the bank. Then we came to Lake Arachotis, fifty furlongs wide. On the west side of the lake stood a deserted city. One meets many such nameless ruins in Persia. Often they are the result of raids.

Whenever a nomadic tribe has a bad season, or simply gets bored with tending their flocks and crops, they plan a raid, as do the Aitolians in Hellas. They often travel vast distances in the course of such a raid. If they raided a nearby neighbor, there would be war; but, by raiding afar off, they hope to avoid retribution. The stronger Persian kings kept a curb on raiding, but under the weaker it always revived. At the time of my story there was much raiding and confusion in the empire, because many of Alexander's governors proved unworthy, and many evil folk supposed the king would march on eastward forever and never return to punish their crimes.

When the people of a Persian city have been wiped out or driven away by raiders, the city soon crumbles. The Persians, while vigorous builders, have little interest in keeping up a structure once built, and the winter rains soon eat away their mud-brick houses.

That night we slept in crumbling mud houses and next day followed the road into the valley of the east branch of the Arachotos River. Thence the road runs straight and clear for more than a thousand furlongs down this river.

Hitherto Barmoukas had guided us without complaint. Now, however, trouble arose. At the first camp after we had crossed the Arachotos, as I was inspecting the tents, I heard an uproar. I hastened to the edge of the river to find Barmoukas and Vardanas shouting and shaking fists, while the former held up his trousers with one hand.

"This filthy savage," said Vardanas, "was about to relieve himself in the river!"

"What difference, you stupid foreigner?" screamed Barmoukas. "It will all be washed away. Are you mad?"

"Rivers are sacred!" yelled Vardanas. "It is an offense against the gods to defile one!"

"Go on up the bank, well away from the river," I said to Barmoukas. Then I said to Vardanas: "Next time, be not so hasty to berate these fellows without speaking first to me."

The quarrel passed over, but thereafter Barmoukas' mien became sullen and sorrowful. At length I inquired:

"What ails you, man?"

"Working for a wage that would shame a slave," he said. "I am poor! I have three wives to support! I must have more money!"

I sighed and said to Thyestes: "Oblige me by fetching a mule whip. I have a beating to give."

"No! No!" cried Barmoukas. "I did but jest."

Next day he again began hinting at higher pay. I silenced him with an oath.

The day following he did it again. I dealt him a buffet that hurled him from his seat. He dragged himself back on his horse looking like Ious, the chief Gandarian demon, in an evil mood. Thereafter he muttered and scowled but said no more of a greater stipend.

The next day, when the sun was sinking behind the Indian Caucasus, we came to a town on a rocky shoulder that rises a plethron and a half from the side of the Arachotos. As with most cities in this land, the houses were arranged in an oblong, placed side by side so their mud-and-timber outer walls formed a continuous barrier, unpierced save by the gates and by loopholes. Two wooden spy towers rose from opposite corners of the oblong. The place looked like a hard one to take. I said to the guide:

"Is that not Haravatis?"

"It is," he said.

This, then, was the former capital of Arachotia under the Persians, who called both the province and its chief city Haravatis. As I use the Greek form for the province, I shall use the Persian word for the city to keep them distinct.

When we had crossed a small tributary, we met three women with water jars on their heads, coming down the path from the town on their way to the river. They stepped off the road to let us pass and stood, havering and pointing, until the elephant appeared around the shoulder. Then they dropped their pots and ran screaming back up the road to Haravatis.

"Come," I said to Barmoukas, and spurred after them. As I arrived at the top of the slope, before the front gate of the town, the whole population boiled out like bees from a hive. They began to crowd out the back gate and run for the hills.

One oldster with a missing foot could not keep up with the rest, though he hobbled along at a lively pace on his crutch. I rode after the throng out the rear gate and drew up before the cripple.

"Tell him to stop," I said. "Tell him we mean him no harm and will pay for food and fodder."

They talked. Barmoukas said: "They fear the great gray beast with two tails."

I bethought me that we were getting into lands that had seldom seen elephants. "The animal is harmless," I said. "We will pay those who gather straw and leaves to feed him."

I calmed the old man's fears by handing him a copper. Barmoukas said: "They would not have run had not most of their men been away on a raid."

"Tell him to fetch his folk back," I said, for I could see the heads of the Haravatians peeping out from behind rocks and shrubs.

The man stumped off. An hour later the townsfolk straggled back. Soon they began bringing fodder to Aias. At first they were almost reluctant to take their pay. Methinks they had never known an official to use them thus and feared some trick. Once they grasped the idea, however, they began shouting for more. The most exasperating thing about the Arachotians was that they were not used to coined money. Among themselves they trade by barter or by weighing out lumps of metal. Therefore, they insisted on weighing every coin. This in turn led to sharp disputes over scales and weights, further embittered by the fact that we could not speak directly to one another.

We had just settled ourselves when a new alarum arose. Shouts heralded the return of the raiders, trailing down the valley of the tributary in single file in the dusk. As they drew near, a great wailing and keening arose. I learned that fifty men had gone up the valley to raid another village, but they had been ambushed and lost three men without getting any loot. This return was hence a tragic occasion.

Soon the whole town was aboil. The kin of the slain men capered, screamed, beat their breasts, tore their hair, and banged their heads against the wall. The rest of the people shuffled and stamped in a war dance, crying on Gis for vengeance. Barmoukas said:

"The *outas*—what you call priest—says the funeral will be tonight. You stay; very interesting."

I was doubtful of this, as the Haravatians seemed a scowling, un-friendly lot. But Barmoukas urged me, and I thought it unwise to show any fear of these folk. Also, I have enough of the true traveler's spirit so that I hate to miss any kind of show, even at my own peril.

"I shall be back after dinner," I said, and went off to the camp for a meal of bread and roast goat.

An hour later I came back to Haravatis with most of my party. We took places around the edge of the market place and watched. It was nearly dark, with no moon. A small bonfire blazed. The outas orated and gestured in front of a platform on which stood three round things the size of melons. When my eyes grew accustomed to the dark I saw they were human heads. Barmoukas explained:

"No, not heads of enemy, but of men of this city who were killed. When raiders cannot bring back the whole body, they fetch head for funeral."

The outas, weeping, made an endless speech extolling the virtues of the dead. Presently the whole town began dancing around the square, weeping, chanting, and posturing to the tap of a set of tiny drums and some reed pipes that gave two or three feeble notes. The people had smeared dirt on their faces and donned their most ragged garments. The women, wearing horned caps bedight with beads and bits of bronze, danced in a separate circle.

I began to feel that all was not going well. As they passed, dancers slowed down to glower at me, as if to mark me for trouble. A few shouted in menacing tones. I sidled around the square till I found Thyestes and told him of my feeling.

"By Zeus, 'tis the same with me, Leon," he said. "Something's agley. Yon brandlings do but wait a signal to assail us."

"Then take the lads, one at a time, and tell them to slip back to camp and arm."

Thyestes moved slowly round the square, whispering in each man's ear. One by one the men faded away.

There were but a few left when the outas suddenly pointed at me and screamed: "*O-o-orr!*"

With deafening yells of "*I-i-iamash!*" the townsfolk rushed upon me. I drew my sword but, before I could strike, they seized my arms. I went down under a press of bodies.

I kicked and punched and bit, but the Haravatians fastened on each of my limbs like leeches. When the crowd opened out again, they dragged me toward the central fire. They had seized two other Thessalians, while a third lay on the ground. Those not holding me tried to kick or strike me but got in each other's way. Hence they delivered but few solid blows.

Putting forth all my strength, I jerked my right arm free and knocked over one of my captors with a hammer blow of my fist. The others loosened their grip long enough for me to kick myself loose. For an instant I was almost free. I shouted: "*Ē!* Thessalians!" ere I went down again.

Then screams of fear arose all around, mingled with Thessalian cries of "*Iai! Eleleleu!*" The townsfolk dropped and trampled me as they fled in many directions. In a trice the square was clear but for corpses.

I crawled out from under a ruckle of bodies. Thyestes had led the Thessalians in a charge afoot, with sword and buckler, across the square. My men had struck down a score of townsfolk, and slew several more as they fled. They also caught several women but had the discretion to drag them out of my sight before raping them. From what I heard later, the women were glad to get off so lightly. One, in fact, declared her passionate love for her ravisher and would have joined us had not even my hard-bitten troopers found her too dirty to tolerate.

I had a bloody nose and many bruises, but no broken bones. One Thessalian, Sosikles of Pherai, had been stabbed at the start of the fracas and was dead when we picked him up.

Thyestes and another dragged forth the outas, bleeding from a scalp cut. Thyestes asked the man in Greek: "What means this?" When the outas did not answer, Thyestes shouted at him and struck him.

"Let me try," said Vardanas. He spoke slowly in Arachotian, of which he knew a little. At first the priest feigned not to understand, but a burning brand against his bare foot sharpened his wits remarkably.

After a long and halting dialogue, Vardanas said: "His tale, if I understand him aright, is that Barmoukas told him we planned to surprise and slay them all and feed them to the elephant. Barmoukas—where is the vagabond, by the way?"

We looked but found no sign of the guide.

"Barmoukas," Vardanas went on, "also told him we had a vast treasure and urged him to attack us and seize it before we assailed them. So they planned to capture us all and sacrifice us to their war god, Gis. They thought Gis was wroth with them for neglect and had therefore caused the raid to fail."

Although I never let anybody see inside the chests, the mere fact of guarding them closely would soon betray the fact that they held things of value.

"He also says," continued Vardanas, "that your king wronged them by changing the capital of the province to Gazaka. This ruined their prosperity, so they feel entitled to vengeance on all Hellenes."

I was about to order the outas' head stricken off when a thought came to me. We could not kill all the Haravatians, as they had fled

87

into the hills. But, if we slew the outas, they would simply come back after we had gone and try the same trick on their next Greek guests.

"Tell him," I said, "that Alexander will post some soldiers near here, and the next time the Haravatians molest harmless travelers they will be utterly destroyed."

Some Thessalians murmured at my leniency. But I, remembering the king's lecture to me, insisted.

"I will try," said Vardanas. "He will probably not believe me even if he understand. These folk are such liars that they think all other men are, too. For my part, I had rather bind him between boards and saw him in halves, as the three-headed serpent-king Dahax did to Zamas the Radiant."

As if the loss of a good soldier in this wretched village were not enough, we picked up some sickness that ran through the whole hipparchia, with fevers and fluxes. We crept down the Arachotos, with many halts to gather our feeble strength. Some of the men reported prophetic dreams of doom; others read disaster in the flight of birds. One old vulture—at least, I think it was the same bird—followed us hopefully for days, circling over us just out of bowshot. Vardanas and the Dahas, though splendid archers, missed the carrion eater several times until they decided it was no mortal bird, but a *drouz* or evil spirit seeking to tempt them to waste all their arrows.

Luckily, considering how weak we now were, news of our slaughter of the Haravatians spread ahead of us, so that the villagers along the way either fled before our coming or used us with utmost respect. While kindness and affability are often useful in getting strangers to treat one well, the ability to avenge any wrong tenfold is more effective yet.

When I found a man named Arakon, who could understand Vardanas' Arachotian, I hired him as a guide to Kandacha. But fortune is never satisfied with a single calamity. The second night, a Thessalian, Pelias, came to me saying:

"That whipworthy guide has run off with my purse! Let's slay all these thieving skellums!"

A search of the camp showed Pelias to be right. I dashed my helmet to the ground, crying: "I swear by Zeus the king and all the gods to flay this branded knave gif ever I catch him! How long sin he's been seen?"

It turned out that Arakon must have slipped away just after dinner on the pretense of a call of nature. Therefore, he had a start of over an hour.

"The Dahas and I might scour the neighborhood mounted," said Vardanas.

I pondered, then said: "Na, na, laddie. 'Tis over-dark, and the risk of a fall is too great. I'll no have my force whittled down yet further for the sake of a few oboloi."

"A few oboloi, forsooth!" said Pelias. "There were twenty-six drachmai and two bonny dareikoi in that purse!"

Later, as we sat about the fire listening to the yelp of jackals and making the best of things with a skin of wine, I said: "By the deathless gods, the Hegias was right when he said never to trust these villains. The king should have wiped them out."

"Oh, come," said Pyrron. "They may have virtues of which we are not cognizant."

"Name one," said Thyestes.

"How about it, Vardanas?" said Pyrron. "Do you know of any virtues in these Eastern hillmen?"

"True, they are brave to the point of folly," said Vardanas, who was sewing another patch on his coat. "And they are kind to their beasts, though they care nought for human life."

"You see?" said Pyrron. "Moreover, they, no doubt, consider us altogether as obnoxious as we regard them. People present their worst aspects to foreigners."

"'Tis easy for you to talk," said Thyestes. "You've no been robbed."

"No, I pronounce but the truth. After all..." Here Pyrron cleared his throat, which meant a lecture. "After all, we are all good friends here who have saved each other's lives, though we come of several nations. Yet I'll wager that each—Hellene or Persian or Indian—finds some customs of the other two nations strange and horrible."

"Foreigners find *my* ways offensive?" said Thyestes. "I believes it no. I'm but a simple professional soldier; there's nought strange and horrible about me. Any wight who thinks so maun be daft."

"Everybody thinks those who disapprove of him are mad," said Pyrron. "Come now, will you keep your temper if the Persian and the Indian tell us their honest opinion of Hellenic habits?"

"Aye, that I will."

"Well then," said Pyrron, "let Vardanas expound what he thinks are the most objectionable Greek customs."

"Without meaning offense," said Vardanas, "we find Hellenes the most grasping, lying, treacherous race on earth."

"By the gods! How say you that?" said Thyestes.

"Your own poets say so. Who wrote: 'Put faith in no Hellene,' Pyrron?"

"Euripides, I think," said Pyrron.

"And know you not your own history? How about Pausanias' betrayal of the Plataians? How about the great Demosthenes, whom everybody knows was long in the pay of the Persian kings? How about—"

"Na, na," said Thyestes. "No scholar am I. I've heard these men's names but dinna ken the fine points of their history. I admits that some of my countrymen are a whin less careful of their plighted word and more susceptible till the lure of gold than might be. Howsomever, methinks that betimes you Persians carry truthfulness to ane unco extreme."

"Besides," said Pyrron, "there was never a more perfidious treacher than the Persian Tissaphernes."

"Who?" said Vardanas.

"You know, the satrap of Karia under the second Artaxerxes."

"Oh, Tshishapharnas. He had been too much under Hellenic influence. Therefore he does not count."

"A true sophist, though he wear the Median trouser!" said Pyrron. "But continue your catalogue of our delinquencies."

"Next, Hellenes have the world's worst manners. They have no courtesy; they have no sense of fitness; they have no respect for authority. Lastly, for all your vaunted cleverness, you cannot make a decent suit of clothes, but wrap yourselves in blankets like savages."

Pyrron whistled. "My word! I'm doomed to the depths of Tartaros, O Minos."

"When comes my turn?" said Thyestes.

"I have finished," said Vardanas. "Now, Hellene, say what is horrible about Persians."

"Well, first come their pompous manners," said Thyestes, crossing his hands on his bosom and mocking the deep bows of the Persians. "Then there's their effeminate luxury."

At this, Vardanas held up the coat he was mending, staring at the tears and patches with eyebrows raised in so comical an expression that all burst into laughter.

Thyestes continued: "Then there's this eldrich custom of men's marrying their own daughters and sisters."

"What is wrong with that?" said Vardanas. "My own father, who is a good man if hard to live with, speaks of wedding my sister Nirouphar."

"The mere thought of sic incest gars the gods to shudder!"

"Your gods, perhaps; not mine. At least a man knows what to expect. This he does not when he weds a woman outside the family. And you Hellenes wed your half sisters."

"'Tis no the same. Although as a soldier I've had my share of robbery, rape, and manslaying, that's one sin nought could tempt me to commit. Forbye, there's the Persians' slavish obedience to their kings."

At this the twain began to shout: "How else can one run an orderly, civilized state?" "...the self-respect of free Hellenes..." "...who use their freedom to rob and murder one another..."

Pyrron, laughing, called: "Desist, you two! We've not yet heard from our Indian. Come, Kanadas, tell us what you consider repulsive about the usages of Hellenes and Persians."

"You no be angry?" said Kanadas, who had been silent as usual. Reassured, he began in his halting mixture of Persian and Greek:

"Persians are little wicked, but not so wicked as Hellenes, because Persians are more like us. Persians do one wicked thing. That is, cut off male parts from captives to make them—what is word?"

"Eunuchs?" said Pyrron.

"Yes, eunuchs. That is great sin. Brachman give those parts to men to keep race going. To maim them is insult to gods."

"But," said Vardanas, "how else can we keep order in our harems?"

"Try keeping to one wife apiece," said Pyrron. "What else, Kanadas?"

"As for Hellenes," said Kanadas, "I have not been in Hellas and so not know how Hellenes live at home. In Sindou they are very wicked."

"How so?" said Thyestes.

"They make love to other men. Is terrible sin among us, but you do it all the time."

Vardanas put in: "We have a saying, too: Beware the Hellene! First he flatters you; then he kisses you; then he sticks it up your arse; then he runs off with your wallet."

"Now, lads," I said, "that's not entirely true."

"Indeed?" said Vardanas.

"Nay, 'tis not. The southern Hellenes, Athenians and Spartans and such, make a habit of it, but in the North we deem it lewd and shameful. True, we make no such matter of it as does Kanadas, but our better sort of men approve it not. Nor do our neighbors, the Macedonians. The King Philip was slain by a Macedonian youth who had been buggered at a drunken revel and blamed the king for not punishing the fellow whose fault it was."

"It does happen among you, though," said Vardanas. "The story itself bears witness."

"So too does it happen among Persians," I said. "We all know about your painted boy-eunuchs."

"Alas! Some of my countrymen have caught the habit from Ionian Hellenes and other conquered peoples."

Pyrron cleared his throat. "There's a tradition," he said, "that the forebears of the southern Hellenes encouraged homosexual love as a military measure. It was thought that an army of men who satisfied each other's lusts would not need to drag a cumbrous train of women after them in the field. Others say the practice came from Crete."

"Where does this leave you, O Pyrron?" said Vardanas. "Do you prefer men or women?"

Pyrron smiled. "I differ from all of you. I love mankind in the abstract but have no passion for any individual, male or female. Now continue, Kanadas."

"Next wicked thing is way Hellenes make war. They break rules of warfare. In Sindou it is law that when sun sets, every army camps where it is. No Indian would surprise enemy by march at night, as Alexander did to Poros. Unfair."

"Somebody should have told Alexander," said Thyestes.

"He would not have heeded," said Kanadas seriously. "Next thing is killing people not warriors. In Sindou, warrior caste does all fighting, but fights other warriors only. Fights not priests, farmers, traders, workers. Hellenes kill everybody, no matter what caste. Wicked."

"You have a point there, old boy," said Pyrron.

"Then, men they kill not, they make slaves. Persians do too. No slaves in Sindou. Slavery cruel. How you like to be slave?"

"At no rate," I said. "But slavery's not so bad as that. Else what should we do with prisoners of war? We could not turn them loose lest they take vengeance upon us anon. We could not keep them and feed them in idleness for aye. The only other thing would be to slay them, and surely that's less humane than making slaves of them."

"In Sindou prisoners join army of winning king. No kill, no make slaves. Simple."

Vardanas said: "Without slavery there could be no civilization. The Greek thinkers say that if everybody had to toil for his own bread, nobody would have time to learn new truths, or teach his fellow man how to act, or make beautiful things like poems and statues."

"I must disagree," said Pyrron. "Here's one Greek thinker, at any rate, who disapproves of slavery. However, I don't like the Indian caste system any better."

"Why not?" said Kanadas. "Caste is perfect system. Every man has place in life, work to do, customs to follow. No need to worry or question. Everything—how you say?—organized."

"That's the trouble. In free, democratic Hellas there's no limit to the height an able man can rise, at least if he be freeborn. What if an Indian be born into a low caste with the spirit of a great leader or the intellect of a profound philosopher? What could he do with his ability? Nothing."

"Could not rise in this life, but could in next. Gods put every man in caste he earns by actions in former lives. If you be good now, you are promoted in next life. Perfect divine justice."

"Just like the fornicating army," said Thyestes.

"But if bad, you spend next life as insect," said Kanadas.

"That's like the Pythagorean doctrine," said Pyrron. "However, I shall believe in a future life when I see it."

"Have you no religion, then?" said Vardanas, sounding a little shocked.

Pyrron yawned. "I can only quote Protagoras: 'I have no way of knowing whether the gods exist or not, for the obstacles to knowledge are many.'"

I said: "Well, if ever we get home safely despite the perils of land and sea, I shall feel obliged to thank some divine power or other. Shall I thank Zeus, or the Persian Auramasdas, or the Gandarian Imras? Or are they all the same?"

Pyrron yawned again. "That were a subject for another evening."

"What of definite worth have we gained from this one?" I asked.

"There's my practical Leon, always wanting to know the precise value of everything! Let's say: To think of virtues and vices as matters of custom, not dogmatically true. And thus, I hope, to look upon strangers like these wretched Arachotians with a tolerant eye."

Vardanas said: "My feeling now is that all men are hopelessly bad, though in different ways."

"Perhaps," said Pyrron, "we can someday review our national virtues as we have our national vices. Could we combine the wit and intelligence and daring of the Hellenes, the courtesy and generosity and veracity of the Persians, and the sobriety and moral earnestness of the Indians, we should have a race worthy of ruling heaven as well as earth. And now to bed, my dear chaps."

"*Ea!*" said Thyestes. "But we've no told our blue-bearded comrade what we think of the Indians' burning widows, and their other cruel customs."

"I am sleepy, too," said Kanadas. "Some other time, perhaps. All I say now is Hellenes do one more wicked thing. They make poor Kanadas of Paurava go on this horrible journey, through wild countries, among fierce evil peoples, sleeping on hard ground and eating vile, unholy food. I think gods make your king into spider in next life because of that."

After another guide deserted, it dawned upon me that these folk never went more than a few leagues from their homes and could be made to do so only by force. Thereafter, I hired a man at each village to guide us to the next and then engaged another.

Ere it reaches Kandacha, the post road leaves the Arachotos and trends west over broken country. Here we suffered not only from heat but also from the wind. Boreas howled and shrieked all day. He stung our faces with sand and filled our gear and garments with dust until our eyes were like red-rimmed grapes looking out of brown masks of dirt.

The wind blew off Pyrron's hat. The first time, he rode after it while it rolled ahead of him like a runaway chariot wheel. He passed it several times but failed to retrieve it until Skounchas the Daha galloped by and snatched it up.

The second time, Pyrron tried to pick up the runaway hat from the ground as the Daha had done. Instead, he fell off his horse into a thornbush. He came back limping and bleeding from a score of scratches, while Skounchas rode behind him grinning and flourishing the hat.

"Philosophical detachment is sometimes difficult of attainment in the face of material annoyances," he said. "But, as Aischylos says, time teaches many lessons. I shall forgo my hat till we reach a more suitable clime." He began to tie a scarf over his head. "Oh, *damn* this abandoned wind!" he cried, as it whipped the scarf out of his hand and carried it far out over the waste.

"This is nothing," said Vardanas. "Around Lake Areios it blows like this for half a year on end. Be thankful; were it not for the wind, the midges would devour us."

"You can scoff at the wind," I said, "for you're the only fellow clad for it. Could I get one of those head bags in Kandacha?"

"I see no obstacle," he said.

Besides his Median coat and trousers, which kept the sand from stinging his skin, Vardanas had put on the headdress that Persians wear in such lands. This is a kind of bag pulled over the head. It has a hole that leaves the visage bare, but in these gales the bag is tucked up under the felt hat until all the face is covered save the eyes. This headgear not only guarded his face but also kept the wind from blowing his long hair into a tangle.

* * *

We reached a high plain flanked by hills. At its western edge, this plain breaks up into gorges, which level out into the valley of the west branch of the Arachotos River. The city stands on the edge of the tableland. A citadel rises from a nearby peak. Alexander found the Arachotian village of Kandacha here, renamed it Alexandropolis, and made it a major garrison town. Now, less than four years later, the village had been swallowed up by new construction.

At the sight of this bustling place, we looked forward to getting indoors out of the wind. This, alas, was not to be. I sought out the viceroy of Arachotia, a graying Hellene with a look of harassment, named Menon, son of Kerdimmas.

"Rejoice, Troop Leader Leon," he said. "It's good to see you. Did you say you wished quarters in the town? Dear me; more decisions! I fear it's impossible."

"Why, O Viceroy?"

"Because our own folk are moving into the city faster than new houses are built. We burst at the seams now. You I can put up in my own hut, but not your men."

I was tempted to ask him to pitch a few of these thieving Arachotians out to make room for us, but forbore. He might refuse, and the king had warned me against such overbearing.

"Thank you, but I must decline," I said. "My father taught me—and King Alexander showed me by example—that one must share the discomforts of one's men to keep them true. Now, how about the road to Phrada? Can I get my force thither without a guide?"

"Oh no, Hipparch. You must have a guide."

"Why? Our experience with guides has not been happy."

"During the windy season, the shifting sand often wipes out the road. Unless you know the lie of the land, you'll get lost in the sand dunes and salt marshes around Lake Areios."

"Then can you get me a trusty one? I'm weary of their desertions."

"Surely, surely. I know such a man—I can't think of his name—What is it? What is it?" Menon struck his palm against his forehead. "This responsibility is driving me mad. By the! Never let the king make you governor, Leon. It's the shortest road to your grave. Because I had some small success in Chalkidikean politics, the king set me over a province larger than all Hellas. It sounded wonderful until

96

I found myself in this howling wilderness, among all-depraved savages, with nobody I can trust, seeing the same few Greek faces month after month…"

Menon collected himself and said: "Forgive me, blessed one, but the cursed loneliness makes my mind wander. As Pindaros says, to fools belongs a love for far-off things. I'll ask my secretary for the name of that guide. Whence go you from Phrada?"

"Across the Waterless Plain to Karmana. We shall need camels to carry water. Can I hire camels at Phrada?"

"Given time; the caravan routes from the north run together there. Let me write to Stasanor—"

"Who's he?"

"Viceroy of Zarangiana; my opposite in Phrada. I'll tell him to spread the word you'll hire camels. The letter will reach him by royal post days before you do."

"Thank you."

"It's nothing, nothing. But do think again about staying the night with me." Menon placed a hand on my shoulder and toyed with my tangled hair. "It's seldom I get a handsome gentleman like you through here. I think we could be very close friends indeed."

So that was it. I affirmed my refusal and went back to my tattered tent outside the city. The wind drummed on the cloth and threatened to blow the whole structure into the distant Arachotos.

We spent two days there. We had our hair cut and beards trimmed by a Greek barber. We washed the dirt off in the west branch of the Arachotos. I replaced a few worn-out horses and mules with fresh stock. And, of course, we sweated and swinked to feed the elephant.

We set out again at the beginning of Boedromion, traveling mostly at night because of the frightful heat. Some Thessalians laughed at my Persian head bag and hat, but I said: "Laugh away, buckies; we shall see who laughs last."

Sure enough, within two days, tormented by the wind, they were tying scarves about their faces and cursing themselves for not having bought such headgear. Then Elisas brought out a dozen hats and head bags he had bought in Kandacha and offered them at outrageous prices. The men cursed him for a swindler, but he only shrugged and said:

"Everything is dear in a growing town. If you like them not, I will find others who do."

In the end, they bought all the head bags. Those who failed to get any cursed and struck Elisas for not having enough to go round. I rescued him from a serious beating. He, however, said with another shrug:

"A trader learns to take the rough with the smooth."

Menon's guide was a fat Arachotian named Dastiger, who rode a mule because he feared horses. I thought I might do better with him, being not exactly slim myself. True, he did not demand more money at every step.

Howsomever, Dastiger's vice was laziness. He took in ill part every moment on the road and tried by every sleight to cut it short. He was ever the last man ready at the starts and the first to urge stopping.

We forded the Arachotos and wound through the foothills of the Indian Caucasus. The next town of any size, Garis, was six hundred furlongs from Kandacha. I hoped to reach it in four or five days.

The morning of the third day we were halted for hours while a woman gave birth. When mother and child were seen to be doing well, I urged a greater speed to make up for lost time.

"You never cross desert thus," grumbled Dastiger in Persian. "You and your animals will all fall dead. Should go slowly, with many rests."

"Resting is what you are best fitted for," I said. "Beat more speed into that mule. Get up!"

"Always hurry, hurry, hurry. Outlanders crazy."

Toward evening I saw a walled village ahead on the banks of a wee river. "What is that?" I asked.

"Garis by name," said Dastiger.

I stared. "That does not look like Garis as I remember it, and I am sure the Haitoumans is bigger. Nor have we come any twenty-five leagues from Kandacha."

"You forget: Everything seems smaller second time, and journey goes quicker."

I called to Vardanas: "Will you ride on and see if this fellow be right?"

Vardanas and the Dahas galloped off, the wind whipping their dust plumes away. When they came back, the Persian said: "I cannot make out their dialect."

As we neared the town, Dastiger urged his mule ahead and got there first. When I came up, he was surrounded by laughing villagers, who seemed to know him.

I picked out one of the wiser-looking and said slowly in Persian: "Is this Garis?"

"Yes, yes, Garis by name," he said.

"Is that the Haitoumans yonder?"

"Yes, yes, yes."

"You see," said Dastiger. "You go so fast you get there before you think. Now we take long rest before marching again "

"Perhaps you have a woman friend here, eh?" I said.

Dastiger gave a shrill laugh and held his hands before his face. Then he dashed off to keep his tryst with more alacrity than he had shown since joining us.

I made arrangements for feeding Aias, then sat down to dinner, watching the sun go down behind the spurs. I was biting into a pomegranate and spitting the seeds when the beat of hooves and a hail in Persian made me look around.

A postman rode in from the west and pulled up at our camp. I got up and traded greetings with the lean, weather-beaten rider.

"*Auramasda thouvam daushta bia.*" he said, which means "May God befriend you." Then he said: "Outanas son of Pakouras by name am I. I ought not to stop, but never before have I seen an elephant. The temptation was too great."

I replied: "Your motto may not suffer you to stop for snow, rain, heat, or darkness, but it says nought about elephants. Get down and share a bite with us."

"One must eat, even on the king's business." He sprang down from his horse, laid his mailbags on the ground, and sat cross-legged beside them. I yelled to the cook and rejoined the circle. Outanas plied us with questions.

"Gossip is our stock in trade," he said. "If we get lost in a blizzard, any peasant will take us in for the news we bring of great events. Now tell me, pray, whither you are bound with this great beast, and why?"

I answered him as frankly as I thought prudent.

"Then," said Outanas, "there is nought to this tale that has been going the rounds in the West, that Alexander has perished in the monster-haunted jungles of India?"

"He was much alive when we left Nikaia two months ago," I said. "I have spoken to many postmen and officials along the way, and none of those had any such tale to tell."

Vardanas said: "Unlike certain other nations, we Persians know how to keep our mouths shut when so commanded."

"Even so," I said, "something would surely have reached us. Nay, I think you must needs put this story down as a baseless rumor."

"I know how they arise," said Outanas. "Somebody hears someone else say: 'Alexander must be dead, else Harpalos dare not do the things he does.' Then the one who overhears goes to his friend and says: I have it straight from the market place that Alexander is dead.'"

I heard Outanas with but half an ear, for I became aware that Dastiger the guide stood just behind me. That gave me a thought.

"Tell me," I said, "is this Garis?"

"Garis!" cried the postman. "Mithras preserve me, no! This is Parin by name. Garis is a good ten leagues further."

I rose and faced Dastiger. "So, vagabond—"

The guide sprang nimbly forward and snatched up my sword, sheath, and baldric, which I had laid on the ground while eating, and ran. I ran after him. Behind me the camp burst into commotion. Dastiger ran past the village and up the valley, parallel to the stream bed. As the sound of hooves came to my ears, he swerved away from the stream, across a field of standing crops, toward the nearest spur of hills. I pounded after.

The sound of hooves drew nearer. A Sakan arrow whistled past Dastiger's head. The guide looked back, ran a few steps up the slope, and vanished.

Confounded, I stopped. Madouas, the Daha who had shot the shaft, cantered past me to where our quarry had disappeared. I hastened up, puffing. Several others arrived from the camp.

Madouas pointed to a hole in the ground with a rim of stones around the top. It looked as though Dastiger had jumped down a well.

"An outlandish thing to do," I said, peering into the depths. "I see him not."

A Thessalian thrust a javelin down as far as he could reach. He said: "'Tis but four or five cubits deep, Troop Leader. I'm feeling bottom."

"Then whither has the thieving waf gone?" I cried. "Unless he be a witch and has turned himself into a crayfish!"

"Nay, he is no Hyrkanian wizard," said Vardanas. "He went through the tunnel. Look there!"

Though it was too dark to see clearly, I made out two openings on opposite sides of the well at the bottom.

"This is a *karis*," he continued. "It brings water from the hills to the plain without losing it to the air on the way. We sink a line of wells, like this. We dig a tunnel joining them at their bottoms. This tunnel comes to the surface at the head of a set of irrigation ditches, like those yonder. So Dastiger can slip through the tunnel, climb another well shaft, and make his escape."

"Lend me a sword," I said. "I'm going after him."

"It will get you nothing," said Vardanas.

I borrowed a sword nevertheless, lowered myself over the edge of the well, and dropped. I landed in shin-deep water with a hard sandy bottom. By stooping, I could walk along the tunnel. Thinking Dastiger would have chosen the uphill direction, I plodded up the gentle slope. The darkness was almost complete except for the dim light down the well I had just quitted. When that light grew small behind me, that of another well appeared in front.

I felt my way along, now and then stopping to listen. There was no sound but the faintest gurgle of gently flowing water. Fishes nibbled at my legs.

When I had passed three wells without finding Dastiger, meseemed Vardanas was right. Behind me a mass of earth fell from the roof of the tunnel with a loud splash. Visions of being entombed dampened my fire. When I reached the next well without success, I beat a retreat.

Back at the camp, I took a sword out of our store of spare weapons. Though the best we had, it was a crude, cheap blade, so notched as to be almost like a saw. As I began to grind a proper edge on it, Vardanas, observing my look of disgust, said:

"I grieve for your loss, best one. The worst is that you will have to charge yourself for the new blade."

"What?"

"Said you not at the beginning that every soldier who lost a weapon, otherwise than in battle, should have the cost of replacing it taken out of his pay?"

I glared at Vardanas, but Thyestes and some of the troopers had heard and burst into laughter. So I had to debit myself on the troop's payroll account. This, I thought, was carrying honesty to a foolish extreme. As I sat honing the blade, another thought struck me.

"Where's that postman, Outanas?" I asked.

Elisas said: "Gone, Troop Leader. When you went off after the guide, the postman leapt up as if to join the chase, but remembered his precious mailbags and forbore. He told me to thank you for the victuals and rode off."

"A pox!" I said. "I was fain to ask about the things Harpalos dare not do unless Alexander be dead."

Next morning the headman came to demand a fantastic sum that Dastiger had promised them for joining in his hoax. I chased the mayor back to the village, spanking his bottom with the flat of my wretched new sword.

From Parin the road descended as it westered. The foothills of the Indian Caucasus still rose on our right, with the mountains towering behind them, tier upon tier. On our left, the land opened out into vast level plains, dry, barren, windswept, and gravel-covered, with little sign of life save an occasional troop of gazelles or wild asses. The wild ass of these parts is a mulelike beast almost as large as a horse, which the Persians call a *gaur*.

Two days from Parin we came at last to the genuine Haitoumans, the Etymandros of the Hellenes. Here the river cuts through a yawning trough in the desert. The ford is deep and dangerous, unusable in spring.

Our column wound down the high side of the gorge. My people looked mistrustfully at the broad brown flood and then at me. At such times a leader's right to his post is put to the test. I forced

Golden into the water, step by step, the stones rolling and grinding under her hooves.

Soon the water was waist-deep for a man afoot. Some Persian king had caused a line of stakes to be driven into the bottom below the ford and linked by ropes, to stop people from being swept away. But half the stakes were gone.

Behind me the men came in one at a time. Their horses snorted and needed a touch of the spur. Elisas rearranged the contents of the carts to put things liable to damage from the water on top.

Golden, shivering, plodded on. Most military men do not deem a ford usable if it be more than twelve palms deep, and the Haitoumans was at least sixteen palms at its deepest.

At last the water shoaled. From the far bank the road slanted up the side of the gorge. I walked Golden up this road a few paces and looked back.

The carts floundered through the flood, the water curling round their wheels. On the far bank, Kanadas and Siladites talked to Aias. The elephant lumbered into the stream, playfully splashing water about with blows of his trunk.

As they neared the west bank, my people more and more swerved to the right to make a short cut to the road up the bank. I sat at the first turn and waved them past. "Haill on, lads!" I called.

Aias, too, swerved upstream. Where the water was but a few palms deep, his stride slowed to a halt. He swung his head from side to side. He started to pluck first one foot and then another, out of the mud, but seemed unable to advance despite earnest efforts. He raised his trunk and squealed.

I called: "What is the matter?"

"He stuck!" came back Kanadas' deep voice. "Soft bottom here. Go quickly; get help!"

Already one could see that Aias was lower in the water. I hastened up the road. Before me lay Garis: a mud-walled fortress, a walled caravan shelter, and a score of houses huddled round a small market place.

"Vardanas!" I cried. "Aias is mired. We must get all the draft oxen we can, with harness and ropes."

We dashed into the town, scattering people and dogs. Vardanas demanded: "Where is the chief?"

The people either did not understand or pretended not to. At last we found an old man who, though a little deaf, admitted he understood Vardanas when the latter shouted.

Vardanas said: "He says a Persian governor is the highest man here, but he has gone *gaur* hunting."

"Have they no elected headman? You know, a mayor?"

More shouting. Then: "The mayor has gone hunting with the governor."

"How about the postmaster?"

"He has gone hunting too."

"Are there no Hellenes?"

"None. Just the governor to collect taxes and keep up the caravan shelter, the mayor to enforce the laws, and the postmaster to keep the postal service running."

Thyestes pushed his way through the thickening crowd, saying: "O Leon, the great beastie's up to his knees in mud the now. Gin you dinna get him out sune, hell be freely buried."

Striving to keep calm, I said to Vardanas: "Then who does rule this dung heap?"

"Nobody, now. The hunters are expected back any day."

"Then tell him to order his people to fetch their oxen and tackle."

"He says he cannot."

"Why not?"

"They have no oxen, he says."

"Nonsense! I saw several in the fields."

"I know." Vardanas spoke in a threatening tone to the oldster. "Now he says they could not do it without orders from the governor."

Some young Garians had gathered round the elder and uttered approving sounds at each response he made. Then Kanadas arrived. The townsfolk gave him a wide berth, for with his height and blue beard and huge sword he was an imposing sight.

"Woe, woe!" he cried, weeping. "Hurry, Lord Leon! My beautiful Mahankal is up to his belly in mud! If he die, I go mad, kill everybody!"

In the distance, Aias trumpeted calls for help.

"Translate that," I said, and to Thyestes: "Blow the alert and line the lads up. Belike we maun butcher these knaves to make them help us."

Vardanas reported: "Now he admits they have oxen, but not enough harness for the task. Anyway, how do they know the elephant will not trample the town flat?"

A blast on our trumpet sent the Garians running for shelter, while the Thessalians lined up with javelins poised.

"Elisas!" I said. "Give me a small loaf of bread."

"Are you daft, man?" said Thyestes.

"Na, you shall see." I took the loaf and said to Vardanas: "Tell him I shall now begin to eat this loaf. If, when I have finished, they've not rounded up all the oxen within five furlongs, with harness, and all the rope in town, I'll order my men to slay them all and burn the town to the ground. If, on the other hand, they help us, they shall be fairly paid."

I began eating while Vardanas translated. A furious haver broke out betwixt the old man and those around him. I kept on munching.

When a third of the loaf was gone, the younger Garians scattered to their dwellings. The townsfolk reappeared, running out to the fields. When the loaf was nearly gone, Vardanas said:

"They say these are all the oxen they have, and if we do not believe them we should search for ourselves."

"It pleases," I said, finishing the loaf. "Let's forth to the stream."

Poor Aias was indeed in sorry plight, with his belly drooping into the water. His trunk was curled up over his forehead, and he sent out peal after peal of trumpeting. The villagers drew back from the awesome sight, and some of the bullocks tried to flee back up the road from the ford.

"Give me rope!" cried Kanadas.

Taking the end of the heaviest rope, of braided leather, he plunged into the water and waded out to his pet. He and Siladites passed the rope around the elephant's rump, shouting at each other in Indian.

Finding all the others looking at me, I realized that they expected me to direct the rigging of an elephant tackle. I had never done any such task; but, as we say in Thessalia, one never knows what one can do till one tries.

I grouped the oxen, small black beasts with humps on their backs like those of India, in six teams. One team was to pull each limb of the elephant, one on the main rope around his rear, and one on a loop around his neck.

One effect of this activity was that Aias, knowing it was for his good, stopped struggling and thus did not sink further into the mire.

Hours passed. We all became covered from head to foot with the mud of the Haitoumans. At the first attempt to pull, one of the ropes broke. We halted everything to strengthen that line.

Again I gave the command to go. Whips cracked, oxen heaved, and ropes tautened. Kanadas and Siladites screamed, "*Malmal!*"

With sucking and bubbling sounds, Aias drew one foot after another out of the mud and advanced it. The combined pull of the oxen staggered him, as they were pulling at an angle to the direction he faced. Then over he went on his side, with a snapping of ropes, a tremendous splash, and a scream as of twenty trumpets fouled with spittle.

"Whoa!" I shouted.

Aias rolled back on his belly, got to his feet, and started for shore, with every sign of wrath. The oxen fled up the road, while some of the Garians scrambled straight up the side of the gorge in their terror.

Siladites splashed after Aias, caught the end of his trunk, and tugged on it, shouting "*Thero!*" Aias let himself be halted short of the brink, uttering smothered gurgles and squeals as if cursing under his breath. The Garians straggled back. We unhitched and untangled the ropes. The townsfolk capered, grinned, and kissed each other as if the entire plan had been theirs.

We no sooner gained the top of the gorge, however, than the Garians began shouting. Vardanas explained: "They want their pay."

"Two and a half oboloi for each bullock," I said. "Find who the owners are."

That, however, was easier said than done. Every man screamed that he had furnished two, three, or more oxen, which was absurd. Not knowing the folk or the tongue, I could not settle matters. I sought out the deaf elder.

"Tell him," I said to Vardanas, "that I shall hand him money equal to two and a half oboloi per ox; or five drachmai, two and a half oboloi altogether. In the want of authorities, he shall pay each owner his share. If these people wish to fight over this money, that's up to them."

Although the old man looked frightened, I brooked no denial. I handed him a cloth holding the money and thrust him into the midst of his folk. Then I went back to camp, ignoring the uproar that broke out behind me.

"Get to sleep early, lads," I said. "We're off for Phrada the morn."

BOOK FOUR

Ariana

ON THE FIFTH DAY from Garis, we reached a small river, the Chasis. Here stood a ruined caravan shelter and a postal station.

"There was a village," the postmaster explained, pointing to broken ground where outlines of ruined house walls could still be seen. "Raiders destroyed it. Tell King Alexander that if he will build a fort and fix up the *sarai*, we could lure settlers hither. I for one should like some neighbors friendlier than the jackals."

We crossed the river and pitched our camp. On the far side, Vardanas pointed to a marker of stone.

"The bourne of Ariana!" he cried. "I, Vardanas son of Thraitaunas, welcome you to Ariana! Know you Vindapharnas?" He burst into rolling Persian verse. As nearly as I can translate it, it went:

Behold the Arian land, the hero-land!
The realm of sun and roses, where the hand
Of mighty Auramasdas governs all;
From where, round great Xaiarshas' golden hall,
The silver streams of Parsa rise and fall
Through spacious plain, past towering mountain wall,
Far down unto the Persian Sea's bright strand,

To where the wine-red dunes of singing sand
Before the Baktrian blast like serpents crawl...

"Methought this was Zarangiana," said Thyestes.

"It is," said Vardanas. "Zarangiana is but one province of Ariana. Ariana is the entire land wherein Arian speech is spoken."

"Mean you Persian?" said Thyestes.

"Persian and Median are the two main tongues that make up Arian. There are also Parthian and Hyrkanian and Baktrian and Sogdian and Karmanian and Sakan, as well as all the petty dialects of these. But welcome to my glorious homeland." Vardanas drew a deep breath, as if the air had become sweeter. For all I could see, though, the west side of the Chasis showed nought but the same vast, dusty desert as the side we had quitted.

"Hero-land or no, I'm for a bath," said Thyestes. "And tell your reeky Dahas to bathe, too, afore we fling them in willy-nilly. 'Tis becoming so we can sense them upwind at ten furlongs."

"Nor would one do you any harm either, laddie," I added.

The Persian looked unhappy. "Fain would I not offend my dear comrades by my stench, Leon. But you know our laws anent rivers."

"This is no river. The postmaster tells me it vanishes into the sand a few leagues from here, and there are no towns below us."

"But where can we bathe with decent modesty?"

"Below yonder patch of reeds. None shall go thither to shame you."

I posted a watch and plunged in. Out near the middle was a chain of pools extensive enough to swim a few strokes in. The Hellenes played boisterously, splashing and ducking one another. We scoured off the dirt with sand, and, at a signal from Siladites, the elephant filled his trunk with water and squirted us.

I was floating on my back when there came a great splashing and shouts of alarm from behind the reeds. I waded downstream to where Vardanas and the Dahas bathed.

The four Sakas danced on the edge of a pool, shouting and pointing. In the pool, Vardanas thrashed as though some sea monster had seized him.

I plunged in and pulled Vardanas out. When he could speak, he said: "I owe you my life, Leon. I was washing in the shallows when a frog leaped out of the reeds and alighted in front of me. In my terror, I fell into the pool. As I cannot swim, I was in peril of drowning when you saved me."

"You had been in no peril had you used your wits," I said. "Yon pool's no deeper than your breast, so you had only to put your feet down. And why should you fear a poor little frog?"

"All Persians fear frogs."

"In Hera's name, why?"

"We are brought up to think them evil spirits. Now that I have traveled and mingled with foreigners, I am not so sure about the spirits. But I cannot overcome the fear put into my soul in childhood."

"If you cannot swim, 'tis time you learned. Come hither and let me show you how to float."

"No, really, I do not feel well enough—"

"Come here! That's a command. I'll hold you..."

An hour's struggle taught Vardanas to float on his back, though betimes he nearly drowned his teacher when panic seized him and he caught me round the neck. As we were drying ourselves, I said:

"What said that Persian poem about wine-red singing sands?"

"Oh, that. You will see them shortly."

"What?"

"Yes. I believe they lie beyond Phrada, in the Desert of Despair. Our route to Nia lies thither."

"By King Zeus, you Persians have cheerful names for places! 'Twas bad enow knowing we had to cross the Waterless Plain, but the Desert of Despair is worse."

The Hellenes cruelly chaffed Vardanas over his frog panic, calling him "Froggy Vardanas." He took no umbrage, having a ready wit and returning as good as he got.

"I wouldn't make so much of Vardanas' irrational fear of frogs," said Pyrron at our evening's talk. "We all have, I daresay, something we fear beyond reason, did we but admit it. Elisas fears violence of any sort. I fear caves and similar enclosures. What do you fear, Leon?"

"High places," I said. "How about you, Thyestes?"

110

"Snakes," said he with a shudder.

"Yet snakes are kept as pets in Macedonia," said Pyrron.

"Forbye," I said, "they're kept in Thyestes' native Thessalia, too. We have a fine old mouser named Typhon, six feet long."

Vardanas gave a grunt that implied he cared no more for snakes than for frogs.

"Mauger that, I fears them," said Thyestes. "And how about our Indian Titan? What fear you, mighty Kanadas?"

"Nought," said Kanadas, scowling. "Least of all, you."

"O-ho!" said Vardanas. "I know better. True, Kanadas fears no mortal foe; none is braver in battle. But he fears foreign lands. He fears breaking his complex rules of religious purity. Most of all, he fears the spirit world. Ghosts and demons and fairies and other bogies terrify him."

Kanadas did not deny it. "That is only—how you say?—reasonable. A man I can hew down with my sword; but what can I do against spirits, which kill not only body but also soul?"

"If they exist," said Pyrron.

Thyestes said: "Now dinna tell me you believe no even in spirits, O Pyrron! Is there no limit till your skepticism?"

"All I know is that I've never seen a spirit. When I have examined one thoroughly, I shall believe. Even then I might be mistaken."

Vardanas said: "Having no religion, do you not even believe in a future life?"

Pyrron smiled. "I quote the divine Aischylos:

I think the slain
Care little if they rise or sleep again."

"Allbody knows there's spirits," said Thyestes. "My uncle Antagoras saw one back in the hundred and tenth Olympiad."

"Does everybody?" said Pyrron. "I'm somebody, yet I know nothing of the sort."

"By 'allbody' I didna mean philosophers, who, it is well known, believe aught save plain truths. They even think the world is round, when anybody with eyes can see 'tis flat."

"Well then, let's define all non-philosophers as 'everybody,' and see how far that gets us. Are you a witch?"

"Eh? A witch? What are you talking about, man? Of course I'm no witch!"

"Then would you say that most of your fellow Thessalians are witches?"

"What a daft notion!"

"Yet if you inquire of the majority of Hellenes which part of Hellas is populated almost entirely by witches, they'll name Thessalia."

"Is that true? All I can say is, the other Hellenes are sillier nor I thought."

Pyrron spread his hands. "So much for the confidence one can repose in what everybody knows."

"Belike I kens not my own powers," said Thyestes, casting a sinister smile toward Kanadas. "Had I thought I was sic a deadly night bird, I'd have raised some fearful cacodaemon to deal with those who fash me.

Phrada, on the Phrada River, is a dismal little town of low mud-brick houses with curiously domed roofs. When it came into sight, looking like some vast bakery or smeltery with many ovens, Vardanas said:

"Let me ride on, Leon, to warn the viceroy of your coming."

"Why?"

"To let him ride forth to meet you. It is the Arian way of honoring visitors."

"As Stasanor's a Hellene, he probably knows it not," I said, "and in any case he may not wish to honor us. But go ahead."

Vardanas raced off with the Dahas. In half an hour they were back with four more horsemen: a Hellene, and three Ariaspians. The latter are a half-nomadic folk of the region. Stasanor had several as auxiliaries in Phrada, besides a score of Greek mercenaries.

The Ariaspians wore the usual Arian trousers. One bore a lance, one a bow, and the third a device I had not seen before. The man wore a wide belt around his goatskin coat. This belt had a hook, and hanging from the hook was a long coil of rope made of braided leather.

People have asked me if the Ariaspians are the same as the Arimaspians, the Sakan tribe supposed to have a single eye in the middle of the forehead. All I can say is that Ariaspians, whose name means "noble horsemen," have two eyes like everybody else. As for the one-eyed Arimaspians, I have heard many traveler's tales, including no doubt many lies, but I have never found a man who claimed to have seen these one-eyed folk himself. So many tales of the wonders of the East have I found to be untrue that I doubt if the Arimaspians exist.

The Hellene said: "Rejoice, Troop Leader Leon. I'm Hippokoön, secretary to Stasanor."

"Rejoice!" I said, a little downcast that the viceroy had not bolstered my dignity before my men by coming to meet me himself. "Is the Stasanor in Phrada?"

"No. He's downstream at Alexandreia, seeing to the building." Alexander had founded another Alexandreia in Zarangiana, near Lake Areios, which was to become the provincial capital when the main buildings were finished.

"When look you for his return?"

"It is uncertain. Perhaps in a ten-day."

"Have you received a letter from Menon, foretelling my arrival and asking him to arrange the hire of camels for me?"

"I recall no such letter, but I'll look."

As we neared Phrada, we passed a pair of fire-altars with a Magos pottering around them. Then I knew we were in Persia proper, or Ariana as Vardanas would say. When I had chosen a camp site, I went with Hippokoön to the viceroy's house. The streets of Phrada were ankle-deep in dust, so that even at a walk our horses' hooves raised a cloud.

"Be glad it's not winter," said Hippokoön. "Then it's knee-deep in mud, which is even beastlier."

In the viceroy's house, the secretary got out a chest full of letters and went through the recent ones. Some, I saw, were in a foreign writing of many little loops and hooks.

"Syrian," said Hippokoön. "Most of the business of Dareios' empire was conducted in it. Learning Persian is bad enough, but Syrian, my dear, is simply appalling!"

There was no letter from Menon. As Stasanor had departed from Phrada on the same day we left Kandacha, he could not have carried it off with him. Either the letter had been lost on the way; or, more likely, Menon had neglected to write it. Were I Zeus, I would appoint a special fiend to harass those who do not write the letters they have promised.

I talked this matter over with my officers after Hippokoön had supped with us that evening. The secretary said:

"You'll find few camels here for hire, because this is the height of the caravan season and they're all in use. However, if you go a thousand furlongs northwest into Areia, you will come to one of the greatest camel-grazing grounds in Persia. There thousands are reared every year, and I'm sure you'll find some you can use."

"How far is that in leagues?" said Vardanas. After doing sums in the dust with our fingers we made it about thirty-five.

"Let me go," said Vardanas. "I can be there in three days and back in seven."

I was tempted to go on this jaunt myself. It would be a relief to shed my responsibilities and gallop off over the horizon without always craning my neck to be sure I did not get out of sight of my hipparchia.

But second thoughts prevailed. Nobody could beat a Persian at covering huge distances quickly without getting lost. With my weight I should only slow him down. Besides, there were many repairs to be made and precautions to be taken for crossing the Desert of Despair. I did not think any but myself could be trusted to oversee all the petty details.

Vardanas therefore went off with two of our Dahas and two of Stasanor's Ariaspians, while the rest of us sweltered in Phrada, breathing and eating dust. Every cart wheel was taken off, inspected, and greased. Every sword was honed to the sharpness of a razor, and every spear to that of a needle. Harness was repaired and replaced. The women sewed us extra waterskins and water buckets of leather. I bought an ox to drive along with us for a few days and then slaughter for meat.

* * *

Vardanas did not return at the end of seven days. This surprised me not, as I was a seasoned enough traveler to know that every journey takes longer than planned.

When the ninth day did not bring him, howsomever, I began to worry. Although Vardanas could usually take care of himself, no man can avoid his fate if the gods have really ordained it. Furthermore, we were falling behind our itinerary, which had been so drawn up as to enable us to voyage from Phoenicia to Hellas before the winter storms. With much more delay, we should be hitched fast in Asia through the winter.

The heat, dust, and flies annoyed the men. Having rested and done everything to ready our gear for the next leg of the journey, they became bored and got into mischief.

Two Thessalians fought over the woman of one of them. One received a knife cut and both got a flogging. A groom who had been ailing for some time died. A child was stung by a scorpion and almost died. My two remaining Dahas got together with another Saka, a Sakarauka living in Phrada, for a hemp party. Sakas drug themselves by breathing the smoke of burning hemp under a blanket, and my pair were useless for days afterwards.

To keep the demons of boredom from stirring up more trouble, I organized athletic contests: running, javelin throwing, and the like. I won the wrestling tournament myself; if the gods denied me beauty, they at least bestowed upon me a set of tolerably stout wrestling thews. The one man who might have dompted me, Kanadas of Paurava, refused to compete. When Thyestes taunted him with cowardice, he said:

"It is not that at all. I am good wrestler. It is that such close contact with men not of my own caste would defile me."

Thyestes chose this time to play a joke on his foe Kanadas. Recalling Kanadas' fear of spirits, Thyestes one night powdered himself all over with flour and put mud in his hair so it could be twisted up to make horns. Then, creeping to Kanadas' tent, he peered in and cried in a hollow voice, in his atrocious Persian:

"Me ghost of King Dareios! Because you insults gods of Persia, they sends me to destroy you!"

He screamed a wild laugh and thrust out his whitened arms. Kanadas gave a yell that must have awakened half of Phrada. He leapt up and tried to plunge through the wall of the tent he shared with Siladites. Instead, his head burst through a rotten spot of the tent wall, and he dashed off with the tent flapping about him like a cloak.

First Kanadas ran into the river, fell down, and came out covered with mud. Then he ran to the east gate of Phrada. The gate was closed, of course. But Kanadas was a mighty man, and terror lent him wings. He gave a great leap, caught the top of the gate, and swung himself over, screaming "Ghost! Ghost!"

The sentry on the wall saw a naked, mud-covered giant, with something flapping behind him like bats' wings, rush up to the east gate. There the specter seemingly spread his wings and flew to the top of the wall. The sentry uttered an even louder scream, leapt down inside, and ran to the market place shouting "Ghost!" too.

The caravaneers in the market place, awakened by the sentry, sprang up as Kanadas appeared. The moon, though past full, shed all too clear a light on the apparition. In a trice, all these men were fleeing out the west gate. Kanadas, wishing human help against his spectral pursuer, ran after them; but the faster he pursued, the faster they fled.

I got up to find Thyestes, still ghastly in his floured disguise, rolling on the ground with mirth. He told me the tale between spasms of laughter.

"Zeus rot your teeth, you fool!" I cried, and sent men to hunt for Kanadas. They found him standing bewildered in the desert, the muddy remains of the tent still draped about him.

When Kanadas found out what had happened, he said: "Lord Leon, I must kill this baseborn villain. He has always hated me and jeered at me, and my honor demands battle to death."

"I forbid it," I said. "I love you both and will not have either slain, at least until our task be accomplished."

"I do not care. Send me back to India or kill me, but I will fight him as soon as I get my sword. This journey is horrible enough without his persecuting me and making my life miserable."

"But look how much bigger you are! It would not be honorable."

"I dinna fear the great scut," said Thyestes. "I'm going for my weapons, too."

"Come back, both!" I shouted. "Skounchas! Spargapithas! Cover them with your bows!" When the Dahas had nocked their arrows, I went on: "Any fighting shall be according to my rules. Pyrron, blindfold them."

I cut two stems from the nearest tamarisk and trimmed them to sticks, each three feet long and as thick as a thumb. Pyrron put a Persian head bag backwards on each of the duelists.

"This will prevent them from seeing down past their noses," he said.

We led the warriors to a clear space, gave each a stick, and spun them round several times.

"Go to it!" I said. "Fight until one yields or until I tell you to stop."

The sight of two men, naked but for bags over their heads, stalking each other blindly in the moonlight, was one of the weirdest I have seen in a long and eventful life. Alas for heroism! We had turned them loose facing opposite ways, so no matter how they slunk, leapt, and slashed the air, they never came within ten paces of each other. The noise of the onlookers kept them from finding each other by sound.

Betimes a spectator shouted: "Beware! He's right ahint you!" Then both would whirl, making the empty air hum beneath their strokes. When Kanadas walked into a tamarisk, the touch of a feathery branch caused him to hew madly at the tree until he realized he was striking no human foe.

Our party was helpless with mirth when Thyestes called in a muffled voice: "Kanadas!"

"Yes?"

"Are you weary of having these shameless ones make fools of us?"

"Yes. Are you?"

"Aye. I'm also fair frozen."

"I, too." The Indian's teeth chattered.

"I says, fornicate this foolishness."

"Good! I say so, too."

They cast aside their sticks and pulled off their blindfolds. Thyestes said: "Kanadas, you're the only body in this dung heap who understands honor. Don your garments and come to my tent for a drop of hot wine to warm us, and a plague on all these—"

He called us names that were new even to a man of my warlike past. Thenceforth, he and Kanadas were the best of friends, as far as Kanadas ever became friendly with anybody.

Next morning, a plume of dust appeared in the distance. Two hours later Vardanas rode in with one of the Ariaspians, who hallooed to his friends and whirled a loop of his rope about his head.

"The rest follow," said Vardanas. "I have galloped all over Areia to find seven mangy camels."

"Where are the thousands Hippokoön promised us?"

"Driven off. After a band of Derbikan raiders seized some, the herders drove the rest out of harm's way. Luckily, I found an old camel herder who had not heard of the raid. He sent these under his son Dadarshes. But he sent them only on condition that we guard them until we sighted Phrada."

"You've earned a deep draft at any rate," I said. Anon, when he had told me the whole story over a cup of wine, I asked: "What does that Ariaspian with the rope he flourishes so grandly?"

"Know you not? We call that a *kamynda*. Let me show you. Where is that polluted ox?"

Vardanas got up unsteadily, for he had drunk deep. He borrowed the rope, mounted, and called to me to turn the bullock loose.

I unhitched the beast from its stake and struck it with a strap. It ran out into the desert. Vardanas cantered up beside it, whirling the loop of rope. He tossed the rope so the loop spread out and settled over the ox's head. The noose tightened as Vardanas pulled it. Soon he brought the animal to a halt, though it plunged and shook its head in trying to free itself until the rest of us ran up and caught it.

I had drunk deeply too, for I said: "Persians are not the only ones who know how to catch cattle. Wait till I fetch Golden, and I'll show you how we do it in Thessalia."

Again the ox was loosed. This time it ran for the river. I galloped up, caught its horns, and slid off my horse, using my weight to twist the animal's head and finally throw it. The act would have been more impressive if the ox had not carried me to the edge of the Phrada, so that we both arose covered with mud. Still and all, my Asiatic comrades marveled at the feat and looked upon me with new respect.

"'Tis nought," I said. "Every true Thessalian knight learns to do it afore he can walk."

The camels plodded in during the afternoon. Though I was no judge of camel-flesh, even I could see that they were poor creatures of their kind. One wobbled as it walked as though it would collapse if even a twig were placed upon its back. I asked Vardanas:

"How much did you promise for these things?"

"A drachma a day."

"Oh, you ninny! Even I know the going rate for camel hire is not above four oboloi a day in these parts."

"We had to have them; there were no others; you would not have liked me to spend a fortnight chaffering the old fellow down," said Vardanas in a hurt tone. "Besides, a gentleman does not like to bargain."

"One Persian gentleman has no sense about money, you mean. Next time I'll send Elisas to handle the commercial end of things."

I should have thought that, after riding thousands of furlongs, the Dahas and Ariaspians would have been glad to rest. But no, they must needs have a game of stick-and-ball ere we parted. We marked off a playing field in the desert and set a pair of large stones at either end for a goal. The game is played on horseback with a wooden ball and a stick that is flattened and curved at the end like a long-handled spoon. Each team tries to knock the ball through its own goal.

They played four on a side, Vardanas and three Dahas against four Ariaspians. Spargapithas was knocked senseless and had to be replaced. Two players became angry and belabored each other with their sticks until we parted them. Otherwise, it was a splendid game. The Phradan garrison, being in better practice, beat us 21-15.

From Phrada we took horse over a flat, boundless, yellow plain, bare but for a few tamarisks. The last foothills of the Indian Caucasus sank below the horizon behind us. The camels slowed us, because they went no faster than a man can walk.

The first morning after leaving Phrada, we were striking tents when a man said: "Somebody follows us, Troop Leader."

On the plain behind us, black against the rising sun, appeared two small figures. We delayed our departure until they came up, two weary Greek hoplites.

"I'm Oinopion of Orchomenos, Hipparch," said the elder in the old-fashioned Arkadian dialect. "This is my friend, Kteatos of Gortys. We're fain to join you."

"Oh?" said I. "What says your commandant of this?"

"He knoweth not," said Oinopion with a broken-toothed grin. "We dropped over the wall and marched all night to overtake you."

"What's your reason?"

The younger, Kteatos, spoke: "We can no longer endure this polluted desert, Hipparch! We yearn to see a tree or a brook; not this endless waste of sand and rock."

Perhaps I ought to have chased them back. But we had lost four men, wherefore I was not unwilling to strengthen my force at the expense of the Phradan garrison.

"Is the commandant likely to ride out after you?"

"Not he! He'll not even report our disappearance. He'll carry us on the rolls, instead, and pocket our pay himself. Perchance the Stasanor will not find out for years."

"Very well, provided you know what you're getting into. When there's work to be done, we all pitch in and do it. There's no swaggering about saying that this or that task is fit only for servants. Do you understand?"

"Aye," said Oinopion.

"Can you ride?"

The Arkadians traded glances. "We've not ridden of late," said Oinopion. "We thought thou wouldst suffer us to ride the wains."

"Nay! We're cavalrymen, and if you know not that trade, you'd best begin learning. First, take off those bronze cuirasses and greaves; the weight would kill your horses."

I mounted them on two of our gentler spare horses. They clung fearfully to the animals' manes, looking at the ground. "Marry! 'Tis a far fall, forsooth," said Oinopion.

The second day brought us to the Areios River, which flows into Lake Areios when it flows at all. Now it was but a shallow, sandy trough in the desert. At the crossing were a *sarai*, a postal station, and a well, but no town. Here we slaughtered the ox and cut its meat into strips to dry.

Then, following the caravan tracks and the advice of the postmen, we bore more to the south. We found ourselves crossing a belt of dunes of curious rosy sand, which gave forth a musical sound when trodden on.

"The singing sands," said Vardanas.

After we had struggled through the sand, a belt of low hills rose in front of us. We threaded our way through these and arrived at Nia with water to spare. By careful harnessing up, we had beaten the Desert of Despair.

Nia stands on a rocky hill in a flat plain. This hill is shaped like a wedge lying on its side, a gentle slope surrounded by steep cliffs on three sides. Hundreds of stone huts stand on the slope, and about the hill lie tilled fields watered by karises from the more distant hills. Several caravan routes meet at Nia.

From Nia we bore southwest. Two days brought us to an oasis where thousands of date palms stood. The sight inspired Vardanas to entertain us with a Persian song that lists three hundred and sixty uses of the palm tree. The tribe that owns the oasis lives by selling the dates. Like most of the folk of this region, they ride asses, even to war. Horses are scarce for lack of decent grazing. We loaded up with dates and filled our waterskins. Kanadas worried about the elephant.

"Not much good hay and straw left, Leon," he said. "He like not palm branches. He is not well. This no country for Indian elephants, or Indian men either."

Aias had in fact a drooping and shrunken look. He needed wooded country where he could stroll along tearing boughs from trees and eating the leaves by the talent. We did the best we could for him by chopping up palm fronds.

We set out across the Waterless Plain. The heat, which had abated as autumn wore on, rose as we proceeded farther south. Day after day we plodded through a wearisome sameness of landscape: flat expanses of rock and sand and gravel, now and then broken by a bit of a mound or an outcrop. Mirages shimmered on the horizon. By day there was little sign of life save occasional troops of *gaur* and gazelles. By night, wolves howled and hyenas laughed.

One day, the whole horizon in front of us became yellow. A huge yellow cloud rolled toward us.

"Sandstorm!" said Vardanas. "Cover your faces!"

"Close up!" I commanded. "Keep together!"

The storm crept slowly upon us, the air about us remaining calm. It took the storm a quarter hour to reach us. Then sky and landscape were blotted out by yellow-brown murk. The wind whipped our headcloths. It was like swimming under water in a muddy river.

I tried to lead my detachment but soon found I was not sure of the way. We huddled and waited.

After an hour the wind fell. Patches of sky and land appeared. We shook the dust out of our garments. I was about to order us to march when the wind started again. Down came the brown pall.

Pyrron sat on his horse beside me, muffled up to the eyes like the rest. I shouted through my wrappings: "O philosopher, how explain you the fact that, though the Arachotian wind blows harder than this, it raises at no rate so much dust?"

"The Arachotian winds have already blown away all the dust in Arachotia," he shouted back.

At sunset the sandstorm stopped for good. To my amazement, we seemed to be in an entirely different place. The post road had vanished, and none of the features was familiar. I consulted with my officers. Vardanas said:

"Let us stop for the night, Leon. In the morn the Dahas and I will make a sweep to see if we can pick up our road."

This seemed like a good plan. Next morning they went off. To keep them from getting lost, I rigged a tent pole atop Aias' back and tied a piece of cloth to it. This could be seen for many furlongs. I climbed up on the elephant myself to follow their movements.

The scouts came back at noon. "We have found no sign of the road," said Vardanas. "That cursed storm must have wiped out all tracks."

"Saw you no sign of other travelers?"

"None. We might have been whisked by magic to another province."

"We're traveling southwest, so if we go on in that direction we cannot go too far astray."

Thyestes said: "We maun wait until later, to tell which way the sun is setting."

This we did. However, we no sooner thought we had found our true course and marched a few furlongs than another sandstorm came down upon us. We halted again.

At eventide the dust blew away. We made a few furlongs during the night, guiding ourselves by the stars. The next day, sandstorms again held us up for hours. So it went for days.

Although we had plenty of food, fodder and water were getting scant. I lowered the daily dole of water, and we carried pebbles in our mouths to keep the spittle flowing. Every shrub along the way was torn up and fed to our beasts.

One morning Protos, a Thessalian, said: "Troop Leader, yesternight my father appeared to me in a dream. Turn back, lad," he cried, "afore the jackals pick the flesh from your bones!'"

"Fine advice!" I scoffed. "Now that we're over halfway to our goal, your goodsire's ghost would have us turn about and lose oursels allenarly."

"'Tis no the distance only, Troop Leader," said another. "Yesterday I saw three hawks flying from the left. You ken what that means."

"We maun pray more to the gods," said another.

"Go ahead," I said. "I've been praying for days the now."

"Prayer's no good enough," said Antimachos, another Thessalian. "Sacrifice is needed."

"What shall we sacrifice?" said Protos. "Outen the beasts we canna move."

"Say rather, whom?" said Antimachos.

This proposal aroused a storm of dispute: "Dinna look at me, body, or I'll knock the head from your shoulders!" "Some of these bairns would no be missed..." "'Tis fine for you who have none to say so, but any man who'd lay hand on mine maun deal with me first!" "We should draw lots!" "Why no the camel master? He's nought but a foreigner..."

"Hold your tongues!" I shouted. "The next man who proposes human sacrifice shall be the first victim. Do I hear any volunteers? No? I'm ashamed of you, acting like witless savages. 'Tis an old and true saying that the gods help them that help themselves. So let's push on, and let there be no more nonsense."

That night Oinopion, one of our new Arkadians, was caught trying to steal water. I flogged him and warned him that the next attempt would be punished by death.

But some never learn. The next night, Oinopion's comrade, Kteatos, was caught in the same way. As the men dragged him before me and accused him, I questioned him in the light of an oil lamp. He spat at me and snarled:

"Wouldst not do the like for thy lover?"

"Cut off his head," I commanded Kanadas. The Arkadian, however, would not kneel to give his executioner a clear swing. He struggled and cursed until Kanadas, losing patience, brought the huge sword straight down, splitting his head to the teeth.

Somebody shouted: "Leon! Look out!"

I dropped to the ground as a javelin whizzed over me. Oinopion, who had thrown it, ran off. In the darkness he tripped and fell before he had gone fifty paces. By the time he got up, the Thessalians were all around him, spearing him. He was dead when I reached the scene.

Next day we buried the dead and set out again. We met more sandstorms. The elephant grumbled; the camels moaned; the horses and mules hung their heads. When we could move, we walked to spare the animals.

The wobbly camel abruptly lay down and died. We shifted its load to others and butchered it while the camel master Dadarshes, a stupid and timorous youth, wept and wailed. We gave the camel's blood to the children to drink. We took over two hundred pounds of its meat with us, though it was too tough to eat raw and we could not cook it for want of fuel. We ran out of bread and could not make more for the same reason. Even as we left the spot, a swarm of jackals and hyenas appeared to quarrel over the carcass. Vultures dropped out of the sky.

The next day the country changed. It was still flat, but with patches of white caking. The soil became damp, though still no plants grew. Joyfully we dug a hole, into which water seeped. When we had a spoonful I tasted it. It was salt.

The white patches, too, were salt. They waxed larger, and the footing became treacherous. It was slippery mud under a thin crust of salt. A camel slipped and fell, thrashed about, and died. Dadarshes, weeping, explained that it had broken its back. This time we cut only a few steaks from it, because we were overloaded with food, while shy of fodder and water. Vardanas said:

"We must bear west, Leon. I have heard of this salt marsh. In spring it becomes a great shallow lake; it stretches many leagues to the south."

We bore right and at last passed out of the salt beds. A horse fell and could not be gotten up again. The elephant was a gaunt, shuffling wreck. Siladites had to goad him ever and anon to keep him moving.

There were more reports of portentous dreams and sinister omens. The cook told how, as he had walked away from the camp in hope of finding a place where water could be dug for, a viper crossed his path, reared its head, and said: "Go no further, man! The gods of Persia have doomed you!"

To keep the men's spirits from falling so low as to render them useless, I was driven to concocting false but favorable omens of my own. When I told how a white gazelle had walked three times around the camp at night and then galloped off westward, they became noticeably cheered. This experience made me even more doubtful than before of omens.

In midafternoon we were packing our gear for our evening's march when one of the Dahas began talking excitedly to Vardanas and pointing.

"Horsemen," said Vardanas. "Probably Asagartians."

The Asagartian nomads live northwest of the Waterless Plain, in southern Parthia. As these riders were several days' march from their usual haunts, I guessed they were raiders.

I put our trumpet to my lips, but my mouth was so dry I could not blow a note. I therefore told the men in a croaking voice to make ready for battle.

The horsemen grew from specks to clearly visible figures. There were forty or fifty of them, riding toward us without haste.

When they were a few plethra from us, the riders halted. Three cantered forward, raising their hands. I said:

"They wish a parley. Vardanas, you and I and Skounchas shall meet them: you to interpret their dialect and Skounchas to keep his bow handy."

We rode out to meet them. They were a ragged, sun-blackened lot, in gaudily colored shirts and long stockings. Most of them bore no weapons other than a knife and a kamynda coiled at their waists. One, who seemed to be the leader, carried a spiked club like that of Vardanas.

The leader began a harangue, which Vardanas answered now and then with a few words. After this had gone on for a while I said: "*Ē!* How about some translation, laddie?"

"Patience, Leon. He is telling me his pedigree to prove how honorable and important he is."

The Asagartian spoke again. There came a sound of hooves. I looked around to see one of the other nomads galloping up to Vardanas from behind, whirling his kamynda. The man had quietly walked his horse around behind us while the leader held our attention with his oration.

"Beware!" I shouted, but too late. The noose settled over Vardanas' body, pinning his arms. He was jerked off Rakous' back to roll in the sand. The nomad started to drag Vardanas away despite his roars and thrashings.

I spurred Golden after the nomad, passed Vardanas, and cut the rope with a slash of my sword. The Daha's bowstring twanged, and the Asagartian's horse tumbled head over heels, throwing his rider ahead of him.

"*Eleleleu!*" cried Thyestes behind us. The Thessalians charged. The Asagartians wheeled and raced off into the desert, scattering.

I circled round and drew up where the nomad had fallen. The man was getting to hands and knees. I dismounted, flung him on his back, and took his knife from him. Then I had to fend off the furious Vardanas, who tried to assail the man with his sword.

"Stop, fool!" I told him. "Would you slay our new guide?"

We bound the man's hands with his own rope. "What in the name of the Dog did they hope to accomplish by dragging you off?" I asked.

Vardanas replied: "They took me for the leader. I suppose they hoped to make you ransom me; you are too well armed for an open battle. Raiders look not for hard fights; they seek feeble victims and easy loot."

We mounted the Asagartian on a spare horse with his hands still bound, placed his own noose about his neck, and gave the end to a Daha to hold. Vardanas told him that if he guided us safely to the Karmana road he should live; but, if we perished in the desert, he should die with us.

The nomad surveyed the barren landscape, jerked his head south-westerly, and started off. We lost one more horse, but next day mountains began to rise over the horizon. The Asagartian indicated one tall peak. Vardanas said:

"He calls that Saka's-Hat Mountain. If we aim just to right of it, we shall find the post road."

After a moment, Thyestes said: "'Tis still abune a day's journey to yonder peak, and our water is nigh hand gone. Now that we ken the way, what for no slaying the savage to save his water?"

Vardanas and Kanadas protested that such an act were cruel and perfidious after we had promised the nomad life.

"He's had life," said Thyestes with a grin. "A whole day more than he'd be having otherwise."

I said: "How would it be to turn him loose afoot? We should save his weight and water without breaking our pledge. Belike his own folk would find him."

"No," said Vardanas. "The raiders are tens of leagues hence by now. They would take it for granted that we should kill him. He would die of thirst. It were less cruel to slay him."

Kanadas added: "I give him my own water and go without, sooner than let you kill him save water. If you Hellenes are cruel and treacherous, Indians are not."

"There's greatness of soul!" said Pyrron. "Can we let foreigners outdo Hellenes in generosity?"

"I could," growled Thyestes. "You're a ruckle of softhearted fools, but have it your own way."

The next day, with swollen tongues and croaking voices, we reached the foothills and found a hamlet with a karis. Refreshed, we pressed on and picked up the Karmana road at the foot of Saka's-Hat Mountain. I said to Vardanas:

"We'll loose the Asagartian the now. He can find shelter in the villages. If they learn he's a raider and cut his throat, that's his lookout."

When this was explained, the nomad burst into voluble speech. Vardanas said: "He is fain to join us as a soldier."

"What think you? We could use some more good men."

"I should refuse. All he wants is a horse. The instant he gets aboard one without his bonds, he will be off for Asagartia like a shaft from the bow."

"Let him steal somebody's horse else, then."

We left the nomad sitting sadly on a stone by the roadside and went on, winding up into the Karmanian mountains. The villages were no longer the stout-walled, self-ruling towns of Gandaria and Arachotia, but little open serf-hamlets. The serfs belonged to Persian lords who lived in castles on the hilltops. The villagers did not suffer from lack of defenses, for they were so wretchedly poor that not even nomadic raiders bothered to rob them. Usually, at the sight of the elephant, they all ran away and had to be coaxed back.

We stopped at one of the larger villages to rest. Aias began to recover, with plenty of food, water, and shade. The local baron, Mardounias, rode down from his castle with a falcon on his wrist to see what we were up to. When I had explained for the hundredth time what I was doing with an elephant so far from its native haunts, he fed us dinner at his stronghold, and we dined him in return. Without letting our guest know, for fear of loss of dignity, I took over the cooking and so managed to turn out a decent repast.

Mardounias, howsomever, was a dull fellow who talked of nought but boar hunting. I like hunting as well as the next man, but to devote an entire evening to the death of one wretched pig is carrying one's enthusiasm too far.

Soon, trouble arose betwixt my men and the villagers over a wee bag of rings and other gewgaws which one of the Thessalians said a villager had stolen from him. I misdoubt my man had stolen these trinkets from civilians in the first place, but what soldier was ever swayed by such an argument? I had to break camp and move on to forestall a battle. Thus, in the last quarter of Pyanepsion, we came over the mountains to Karmana.

Like Nia, Karmana is a spot in the middle of a barren plain where several roads happen to cross. Nearby, a rocky ridge breaks the plain. A castle on the last peak of this ridge dominates the town. Afar off, rugged ranges rise from the edges of the plain on all sides. Vardanas told us a tale of how Karmana was once ruled by a dragon, until the hero Artaxashas slew it by pouring molten copper down its gullet. Meseems it were an effective method.

In Karmana we paid off Dadarshes. The camel master demanded outrageous compensation for the two dead camels and had to be dealt with firmly. We bathed and had our hair cut and our clothes washed. I bought a new sword, for Karmana has skilled smiths who work the iron and copper mined in the province of Karmania. The town hums with the sounds of handicraft.

The rest, who had amassed goodly sums of pay during the march through the desert, did with them according to their natures. Thyestes headed for the brothel. Pyrron dribbled his money away in gifts to beggars and small loans to the men, most of which he never even tried to recover. Kanadas clung to every copper of his pay with the clutch of a drowning man. Said he:

"Sinful to spend good silver on strange women. Better to rule one's lusts. But I wish I had one of my wives, for I have desires like other men."

Vardanas spent most of his money on two fine new suits of clothes. For a somewhat vain man, he had long gone in rags without complaint; but his new splendor, I thought, was hardly called for. When he paraded the new raiment in front of me, I said:

"Congratulations, buckie! Why did you no tell me?"

129

"Tell you what, Leon?"

"Why, surely Alexander has appointed you viceroy of this province, has he not?"

Vardanas never kept money. On the other hand, he never borrowed, having a horror of debt. When his purse was empty he cheerfully went without until the next payday.

What was left of his silver Vardanas spent on a feast for the whole hipparchia on his birthday anniversary, according to the Persian custom. It is also the custom for those who attend to bring gifts to the giver of the feast. Vardanas said nought of this, and we should not have known but for a chance remark by Pyrron. So we rushed about the market place of Karmana, buying belated gifts. Some, like a bird in a cage, given by the Dahas, were hardly suitable for a man on a journey like ours.

It was a fine feast, considering what an out-of-the-way place Karmana is. We had mutton and pork broiled on skewers, and heaps of dates and melons. Whatever their faults, the Persians know how to cook, being surpassed in this regard only by the Babylonians.

Vardanas hired the town band to play for us after they had finished their nightly salute to the setting sun. They came in with ten drums of all sizes and a score of trumpets, some so long that the trumpeter had to rest the big end of his horn on another man's shoulder. At the bandmaster's signal, they banged and blew with all their might. As far as I could tell, each man played his own tune without heed to the others, making a dreadful din. Vardanas, however, assured me that this was a stirring battle hymn by one of Persia's most celebrated composers.

The Thessalians danced a country dance, the akrolax. I stamped and kicked with the rest, though my figure is hardly that of a born dancer. Later Vardanas got tipsy and began to declaim Persian poetry. He would have gone on all night had we not turned him upside down and plunged his head in a bowl of water.

We had trouble in Karmana with an accusation of rape brought by a woman of the town against Polygonos of Iolkos. The story of this case would make a book by itself, but I do not wish to fill my history with such petty and sordid details. My decision was that the woman had yielded willingly to Polygonos' lusts, but that he had then sought to cheat her of her fee. I made him pay her the going rate and fined him an equal amount.

We set out from Karmana with a wan-looking Thyestes, who was subjected to merciless chaffing about riding a horse for a change. We marched by winding roads, amid towering mountains and barren plains, westward toward Persepolis. The worst of the heat was now over. In fact, we became uncomfortably cold at night, especially the Indians, who began to shiver at any heat less than that of a furnace. The stony roads retarded us, as they had in Gandaria, so that we fell further and further behind our schedule.

There were few happenings worth telling. The Dahas slew a bear with arrows. I had never eaten bear and was surprised to find it the tastiest meat I had ever devoured.

For several days our progress was slowed by a curious dry fog, which blotted out the landscape as utterly as did the sandstorms of the Waterless Plain. For several more days we were stalked by a band of hillmen, who trotted along the ridges and peered at us from behind rocks out of arrow range.

"They would like to rob us but fear our weapons and the elephant," said Vardanas. "Keep strong watches. Wander not off at night. If you do, you will be found without your heads in the morning. Some of these tribes do not let a man marry until he has brought in a stranger's head."

The farther west we got, the more plant life we saw. While the land was still a desert by Greek standards, at least we could collect enough greenery to appease the monstrous appetite of Aias, who began to fill out a little. We saw real trees, mostly walnuts and willows. Flocks of wild sheep and goats bounded over the hills.

One morning, as we were arising, a great whinnying and braying and trumpeting arose from our beasts. Not fifty paces off, a lion was creeping toward us. We shouted and clashed our weapons, which checked the lion's advance. Then Kanadas guided the elephant toward the lion, who slunk off with a few roars to show us he really feared us not.

We crossed the border from Karmania into Persis in the first ten-day of Maimakterion. We were now, Vardanas explained, in the real

Persia. A few days later we reached Persepolis. As the Persians call both town and province "Parsa," I shall use the Greek names to keep them distinct.

Persepolis, standing in a corner of a plain beneath a small but rugged mountain, can be seen from afar in the clear air, so that it looks like a toy town. Only when one comes close does one realize the size of the palaces that generations of Persian kings raised here, magnificent even in ruins.

We came first to the city of Persepolis, a typical Persian mud-brick town, of modest size for the capital of a great empire. In fact, the Persian kings deemed Persepolis a resort and a ceremonial capital only. They came here for the great yearly festivals and rituals, especially those of *Naurous*, the Persian New Year, which takes place at the vernal equinox. The real business of ruling the empire was mostly done from Sousa and Babylon.

Then we passed through the groves and gardens about the palaces. The palaces stand on a great stone platform. The four main buildings on the platform—the palace and audience hall of the first Dareios, and the palace and audience hall of the first Xerxes—were burnt by Alexander. Their roofs had fallen in, their statues had been smashed, and their ornaments had been looted. But still the vast human-headed bulls of stone guarded the broken portals, and behind them lofty columns topped by animal heads rose like a forest over crumbling walls of bright-colored brick.

Several smaller buildings still stood intact upon the platform. Before the largest of these, the palace of Artaxerxes Vaukas or Ochos of bloody memory, stood a brace of armored Persian guards. Thither I bent my steps, rightly thinking it the viceroy's quarters and meaning to draw on the local supplies of fodder.

The guards stared sourly as I approached. One said: "Who are you and what do you want?"

I gave my name and added: "Is the viceroy in?"

"What business is that of yours?"

I stepped forward and roared in their faces: "Because I am an officer of the king on official business! If the viceroy be in, take me to him. If not, tell me where he is, or you shall rue your insolence!"

That took some of the haughtiness out of them. One guard jerked his head toward the door. The other went inside. Soon he came out again. Both bowed low as a stout Persian, beard curled in ringlets and perfume pervading the air, appeared in the doorway.

"Well?" he said, looking down his nose. "I am Phrashavartes by name. What is it?"

I started explaining my mission, but the viceroy cut me off. "My good man," quoth he from his high horse, "I do not concern myself with such matters. See my secretary Gimillos in the morning."

I began to protest, but Phrashavartes vanished into the palace. The guards, grinning, gripped their spears in case I should try to force an entrance.

Raging, I went back to our camp, beside one of the groves near the palaces. Vardanas said: "You should have taken me, Leon; I know how to treat these wantons. Then, too, you look like a vagabond. Appearance matters; you must dress your best."

"In what? I have but two dirty old shirts."

Then borrow one, or wear one of my suits. Polish your helm and other gear. My slave will help you."

Though it irked me to spend time on such foppery, I let myself be guided by my friend's advice. After dinner an argument arose among the officers over the size of the platform on which the palaces stood.

"There's but one way to settle it," I said. "Come, lads, let's pace it off. 'Twill clear the wine fumes from our heads."

We did and found the platform about six hundred paces long and three hundred fifty paces broad. The naked columns were an eerie sight in the moonlight.

I said: "When the king commanded the palaces burnt I whooped and danced about the blaze like all the rest. But I regret it the now. They were a gorgeous sight."

"No doubt," said Pyrron, "though a trifle too massive and gaudy for Hellenic taste. The Persians have no indigenous building style; hence these things are a disorderly hodgepodge of Hellenic, Egyptian, and Babylonian elements. But, as you say, it was folly to destroy them."

Vardanas had not gone around the perimeter with us. Instead, he sat on the wide processional stairway, weeping.

"What ails you?" I said.

"Alas!" he said. "I weep for great Xaiarshas' golden hall. I weep for all the other beautiful buildings which your people burnt. I weep for the sacred writings of Zarathoushtras, written in golden ink on twelve thousand sheets of cowhide. When will such glories come again?"

"I'm sorry," I said, "but that was lawful revenge for Xerxes' burning of Athens."

"Oh? But that too was revenge, for the Athenians' part in the burning of Sardeis."

"I never heard of that."

"It's true," said Pyrron. "Could we trace back all our feuds, we should probably find they originated in a controversy among the first men Prometheus made. Assuming, that is, that Prometheus did in fact create the first men."

"What's your idea of the origin of man, O skeptic?" I asked.

"Since nothing has been proven, I haven't yet formulated a definite belief on that score. However, I'm intrigued by Anaximandros' hypothesis that men are descended from fishes. The unintelligent manner in which they often behave" (he waved a hand toward the ruins) "lends support to the theory."

"Our myths have a first man, too," said Vardanas. "Gaiamarthen, begetter of the Arian people. But I do not fret over which myth, if any, be the true account."

Thyestes said: "If your Gai-something begat the Arians, whence came the rest of us?"

"That is simple. Some Arians had intercourse with demons."

"*Papai!* Mean you that I'm half demon?"

"Of course. I am sure, however, that your demonic forebear was of the highest quality. He must have been a king of the fairies at least."

"*Phy!*" said Thyestes. "Fairies, forsooth!"

We made our second assault on Artaxerxes' palace in royal Eastern style, riding upon the elephant. A canvass of the detachment had procured me a decent shirt and kilt, and I wore the bronze cuirass of one of the dead Arkadians. Vardanas, however, far outshone me. Aias knelt in front of the portal to let us clamber down. This time there was no insolence as Vardanas, with haughtiness that matched that of the viceroy, strolled up to the guards and said:

"Fetch Gimillos, fellow."

Gimillos was a tall, thin Babylonian in a long brown robe. He rubbed his hands together and said: "Welcome, gentlemen, seven times welcome. And what can I do for you? How can I serve you?"

"You can do something better than let the Eyes and Ears of the King stand out here bandying words with these louts," said Vardanas.

"I am sorry; I am sorry. Do step inside." Gimillos led us through a maze of rooms to a chamber piled with records. "Sit down, my good sirs, sit down." When I had told him my mission, he said: "I suppose then you have come and will pay your taxes?"

I thought he was joking, but he was not. "Pay what taxes?" I cried. "Is everybody mad?"

"No, sir, seven times no. To guard the welfare of the people of Persis and to build the public works they demand takes money. There is the head tax and the road tax and the traffic tax and the horse tax and the property tax and the precious-metal surtax and the—well, to find all the taxes that apply in your case, I shall have to go over the schedule. Shall I visit your camp this afternoon and appraise your worth?"

"Do not be ridiculous. My property, so-called, belongs to King Alexander. For a governor to tax his king's property were absurd."

"I am sorry; I am sorry. Inflexible are the viceroy's orders. All must pay, the tall and the short, and the sober and the drunken."

"There will be changes when the king returns," I said.

The Babylonian raised his hands. "Ah, my dear sir, who knows what the gods have in store? And how do we know the king yet lives? All sorts of tales—"

"He lives, fear not."

"But he is not in Persis, and we are. No, no, sir, it is better to resign oneself to the inevitable. And who can evade the stars? They predict that Alexander will perish in the demon-haunted Eastern jungles, and we must needs make ready against that day. Perhaps you had better stay here in Persis; we shall have use for stalwart arms and deadly spears."

Vardanas yawned. "We waste time. We have not forced our way over a thousand leagues of mountain and desert, past ravenous beasts and hostile tribes, to be robbed by some petty clerk. Others have sought to stop us; the jackals have picked their bones." He suddenly seized Gimillos' long black beard in one hand, whipped out his dagger with the other, and touched the point to the Babylonian's throat. "I had no qualms about killing you now, did I suspect you of meaning us ill."

Gimillos leaned as far back as he could, his eyes popping. He tried uneasily to smile.

"Pray, gently, dear sir, gently! If this be a jest, it is not in good taste, and if this be a joke, ill-taken it is."

"No jest," said Vardanas. "Tell your governor that if he wishes to gather taxes from us, he must fight for them. It were not the first time we cut our way through greater numbers."

"Alas! As you say, I am but a poor clerk; crushed between the upper and nether millstones am I. If you be not here to pay taxes, then why do you come?"

"To collect, not to pay," I said. "We wish fodder from the public store. Arrange it."

"You can pay the going rate, of course?" said Gimillos.

"Whether or not we can, we will not." I flapped Eumenes' authorization in Gimillos' face. "Read this."

Gimillos stared at the papyrus, moving his lips in a painful effort to puzzle out the Greek. He said: "Fiends take it! Although I cannot understand half of it, I will assume this document is as you state. But what then? I assure you that Phrashavartes will not honor it, for all your threats and bluster. And if you try to seize the stuff by force, seven times seven soldiers will spring to arms to thwart you. So let us be reasonable, dear sirs."

"What is your notion of reasonableness?" said Vardanas.

The Babylonian, who evidently liked to ride on two anchors, went on: "Let us look at it this way. As a man of peace, I abhor violence; and, moreover, urgent letters to finish have I. Verily, they will use up the rest of the morning. This afternoon to your camp I shall come and appraise your worth. You will still be there, will you not?" Gimillos winked broadly.

136

Vardanas hesitated to tell even so small a lie, so I spoke in his stead: "Surely, surely. Come, Vardanas. We must prepare a suitable welcome for our friend Gimillos."

Back at camp, I called the officers together and said: "Strike the camp quickly and quietly. We must be off within the hour."

Soon we were clattering along the Kyros River on the road to Sousa. When I told what had happened, Pyrron said:

"These viceroys are all so sure Alexander will never return that each is preparing to make himself an independent king."

Vardanas said: "The jackal fell into a dye pot and thought himself a peacock."

I said: "The Babylonian said something about Alexander's death's being written in the stars. What make you of this star science of theirs?" Pyrron smiled. "I, too, am a prophet, without any stars to guide me."

"How mean you?"

"Why, I prophesy that you will die, and you, and you, and so shall I. I prophesy that the sun will rise tomorrow and that there'll be rain and cold weather in Athens next winter."

"But these predictions from the stars are more particular than that!"

"It's all the identical type of phenomenon. The astrologer scrutinizes the heavenly bodies and says: Ares conjoins Kronos, wherefore a king shall die. But how many kings are there? Scores that we know of, and perhaps hundreds in unexplored lands. Some are dying all the time, so how can the astrologer help being right?"

The fifth day after we left Persepolis, we caught up with a caravan going our way. When we came to a flat stretch where we could pass, we rode by, waving and trading jests with the caravaneers.

At the head of the line, a man guided a camel out before us and held up a hand. "Who commands this host?" he called.

"I do," I said, and gave my name.

"It is good," he said. "I am Thouchras by name, leader of this caravan. There is danger ahead."

"What danger?" I asked.

"We enter the mountains that border the land of the Houzans, where wild hill tribes live. The tale is that they have thrown off your Greek king's rule and begun waylaying and plundering again."

"Indeed?"

"I have been at my wits' end to get my folk through safely. If you will join me, we shall have a better chance than traveling separately."

"I fear you will delay us too much."

"It will only be for two or three days. Then we shall reach the plains of Houza."

"Very well," I said, and passed the word.

"*Vaush, vaush*," said the caravan leader, which means "good." "True, I am as brave as a lion, and my people are mighty fighters. But there is nothing like a troop of trained soldiers in such a strait."

Our road joined the upper reaches of the Eulaios River, which wound snakelike through the ragged mountains that sunder Persis from Sousiana. We crept through narrow gorges and under frowning cliffs. Castles loomed over us. Little could be heard over the murmur and rush of the river. The sky darkened, and the first rain we had seen since India pelted down upon us.

Thouchras, the caravan leader, sought me out to boast of his bravery. On the second day after we joined the caravan, he said:

"You should have seen me in the land of the Iautians when my caravan was attacked, Hipparch. By Mithras, I built a rampart of the bodies of those I slew! There is nought I love better than a good, rousing fight. I shall almost be sorry if the hillmen assail us not." He brandished his sword toward the frowning, rocky hills, shouting: "Come, villains, try conclusions with Thouchras the Dauntless!"

As if in answer to Thouchras' boasts, a troop of horsemen trotted over the nearest ridge on our right. More and more came into view until at least a hundred were to be seen.

Shouts and screams came from the caravan. Seeing men pointing in the other direction, I looked and discerned a band of foot archers pouring over the crest on our left. Thyestes blew the alarm on our trumpet. My hipparchia, with the speed of long practice, drew itself into a compact formation with the wains on the inside and the elephant in the rear, ready to charge out.

"Stand by for orders, lads!" I cried. "*Iai* for Thessalia!"

I turned to Thouchras. "Draw your men up!" I said. "If you will take the first shock, we will launch a countercharge on their flank..."

But Thouchras was in no mood to talk of battle plans. Pale under his native swarthiness, he turned his camel about and went bouncing back along the road, crying: "All is lost! Auramasdas save us! Every man for himself!"

Similar cries of despair arose from the other Persians. In a trice, the whole mass of camels, horses, mules, and carts had turned about and was fleeing without order back toward Persis. Vardanas screamed at them not to be fools, that they were going to their deaths. A few collected their wits and attached themselves to us, but the rest fled on.

We poised our javelins and nocked our shafts. The men looked to me for the next command.

The strange horsemen broke into a gallop down the slope. They aimed, not at us, but at the fleeing caravan. In fact, they swerved to keep out of range of our bows. On the other side, the footmen ran toward the same quarry.

The sun twinkled on weapons at the far end of the valley. We could not clearly see what happened because of the distance and the dust of the pursuit. Howsomever, thin despairing screams told us the hill-men had caught the fugitives ere they reached the end of the valley. I think a few men on good horses got away, but the rest were all taken.

It would have been folly for us to attack so large a force. Hence I ordered my people and the Persians who had joined us to take up our march again with all possible speed. Even so, the barbarians could have closed with us had they wished. Before we issued from the valley, they galloped past us along the hillcrest, waving plunder, herding captured beasts, driving the women, and carrying the heads of caravaneers on their lance points. None, however, came close to us. Though they outnumbered us ten to one in fighting strength, our resolute bearing and the fearsome sight of Aias kept them off.

Vardanas was much cast down by this tragedy. "I am ashamed of my countrymen," he muttered. "By the favor of Auramasdas, Leon, I will show you how a proper Persian acts. Verethragnas aid me!"

Rakous bounded uphill toward the disappearing raiders. Vardanas whirled the kamynda he had taken from the Asagartian. I divined that he meant to ride up to the foe, snare one of them with his rope, and drag him back to us. That would bring the whole pack down upon us in a trice. I spurred after him.

"Come back, fool!" I cried. "That's an order!"

He paid no heed but galloped ahead. A trick of the ground enabled me to cut in between him and the tribesmen, I caught Rakous' bridle and hauled the big horse around.

"Let me go, Leon!" cried Vardanas.

I led him back, protesting bitterly, to the troop. As he was not mad enough to set out after the hillmen afoot, that ended the matter, except that I had to bear the berating of my friend until his anger cooled.

"You practical Hellenes!" he fumed. "Cold and calculating, like a lot of grasping Phoenicians! No manly spirit, no honor! May you be kinless, for cheating me of my exploit!"

When he had finished, I said quietly: "Each to that at which he excels, as we say in Thessalia. If you're so eager to show your manly spirit, get behind our Persians and harry them. They lag."

He did so, albeit grudgingly. For days thereafter, Vardanas was sunk in such bottomless gloom that I feared he might even slay himself. When I asked him what ailed him, he said:

"I am baser than the veriest slave, Leon, for speaking to my best friend so churlishly."

"'Tis nought, buckie! I gave it no thought, so why should you? Cheer up!"

Still he continued to brood, nor could I say aught to lift his spirit, until one day he suddenly became his old gay self. As I came to know him, I found that these fits of gloom were a part of his nature that nought could relieve. Being a rather even-tempered man myself, I found such extremes of emotion hard to understand. As Sophokles said, man is the most wonderful of all natural wonders.

BOOK FIVE

Sousiana

FOLLOWING THE EULAIOS, we came down out of the Persian mountains into the Sousian plain. This is a land of many names. Some call it Sousiana from Sousa, the principal city. To the Hellenes it is Kissia, from the Kossian tribe. To the Persians it is Houza, from the Houzans or Ouxians. To the people of Sousiana itself, however, it is Elymais or Elamis, a name which goes back to the days when it was a powerful kingdom, in an age of which all definite knowledge has perished.

The road came close to the river at intervals only, where the Eulaios made sharp bends in its winding course. Elsewhere, swamps and thickets fringed the river, spreading far out over the plain where tributaries joined it. Wild cattle and swine abounded in these wooded parts. Had I not hurried my men along, they would have lingered forever and aye for the hunting.

We had killed a buffalo cow and were cutting it up when there came a scream from the river. I thought I heard Thyestes call my name and looked up. He was really shouting:

"Lion![2] Took one of the women!"

Irtastouna, the concubine of Charinos of Krannon, had been seized while going for water. We had heard much roaring since we

---

2   Leōn.

reached the plain, as well as the snarl of leopards. But, since such beasts as a rule avoid a company as large as ours, we had grown careless of them.

We seized upon weapons and ran toward the river. There was a shout of, "There it goes!" though when I arrived I saw no lion. However, blood and spoor in the soft soil led us into the thickets. The men spread out, beating the bushes and havering excitedly.

"Silence!" I shouted, trying to listen.

By bellowing and cursing I quieted them. Then came another chorus of shouts: "I hear it!" "Over yonder!" "Come on!"

They dashed off, crashing through shrubs and pushing through the branches of willows and poplars. Hearing a growl, I ran after.

I came to the edge of a small open space as several men threw javelins at the lion—or lioness, as it turned out to be. The animal had dropped Irtastouna's body and was trotting off into denser growth when the volley of spears fell about her. One struck her. She sprang out of sight with a snarl.

I shouted: "Keep together! Dinna go off by yoursels!" Though I have never hunted lion, I had heard enough to convince me that a dense thicket is no place to go poking after a wounded lion by oneself.

But, in their excitement, the men paid me little heed. Several dashed after the lioness, and I ran after them.

I overtook this group as Charinos, burning with grief, plunged to the front. With a roar, the lioness bounded into sight again and sprang.

Charinos brought up his spear and braced himself. The javelin caught the lioness' hide somewhere, and Charinos was bowled over. The lioness landed on top of and a little beyond him. As he started to wriggle out from under her hindlegs, she whirled and opened her mouth to seize him.

Thyestes, coming up, thrust his javelin into her open mouth. The point came out through her lower jaw. Roaring, she reared up and, with a stroke of her paw, knocked the shaft whirling away.

Now Kanadas came up on the other side. He swung his great sword in both hands and smote the lioness across the back. Her hindlegs gave way. As she fell, a score of spears, including mine, were buried in her vitals.

We buried Irtastouna, bound up Charinos' scratches, and consoled him as best we could. We skinned the lioness, albeit the skin had too many holes to be of much worth.

Along the way, several other changes had betided among the women and children. Two of the concubines had run away, and three new women had been added to our train. One more child had been born, and one had died. So, one might say, we were just about holding our own in point of numbers.

Now the Eulaios joined another river, the Pasitigris. A couple of leagues below this confluence, a town called Soustara stands atop a cliff and watches the river sweep through a gorge below it. Here the survivors from the Persian caravan left us, as we were now in more or less law-abiding lands.

We shopped in Soustara. I found that most of the people spoke not Persian but Syrian, then the common tongue of travelers and traders all over the western half of the former Persian Empire. As I knew nought of that tongue, I had to trust Elisas for the chaffering.

During a round of the market place, Elisas and I found some freshly butchered sheep, hanging in the stall of a flesher. I said:

"Let's buy one of these for the lads' dinner. If we get a live sheep, that ninny of a cook will haggle it all up in butchering it."

Elisas then had a long bargaining session with the flesher. At last he said to me: "The best price I can get is eighteen and three quarter drachmai."

"That's outrageous!" I said. "Ere I left home, a good sheep brought no more nor twelve. And this a sheep-raising land, too!"

There seemed to be no help for it, however. We had remarked before on the rise of all prices. I paid. But, as I turned away, the flesher spoke to his helper in Persian:

"Set five drachmai aside for the sutler, as I promised."

The flesher, seeing an obvious Hellene before him, took it for granted that I could not understand Persian. On the other hand, Elisas, hearing the flesher speak Syrian, had assumed that the tradesman did not speak Persian either. I sprang forward, caught Elisas by the arm, whirled him around, and dealt him a buffet that sent him sprawling and the sheep rolling in the dirt. Then I leapt upon the flesher and gripped the front of his tunic.

"Auramasdas smite you, offspring of a frog and a viper!" I roared in Persian. "Give me those five drachmai, dog-face, or I will wreck your shop!"

Trembling, the flesher handed over the money. I looked around for Elisas, but he had disappeared. This was wise of him, for in my rage I might have knocked all his teeth down his throat. I suffered him to collect a commission of one part in ten on our purchases, but here the abandoned wretch had tried, by taking advantage of my ignorance of languages, to get more than one part in four!

I carried the sheep back to camp myself. We ate without Elisas. I never expected to see the little rascal again and was casting about for means of filling his place. I could not do all the buying, because I had other duties and because it would not be dignified for the hipparch to spend all his time thus. Vardanas was a fool about money; Thyestes was testy with foreigners and, moreover, spoke little besides Thessalian Greek...

I was gnawing a mutton chop and thinking when Skounchas the Daha came in with a piece of old leather on which Elisas had scrawled a note in execrable Greek:

ELISAS OF CHALYBON GREET
NOBLE TROOP LEADER LEION

I sorry you catching me taking big commission. Was too much temptation. My head still buzz from blow. If you wanting me work for you, I promises not do again. You forget commission, I forget buffet. Do that please?

"Where is he?" I asked Skounchas, but the Daha had an attack of inability to understand me, doubtless from fear for Elisas' skin. At last I wrote on the other side of the sheet:

Come back. Your sin is forgiven if not forgotten. Next time you plan to cheat me, let me know beforehand what you wish done with your body.

* * *

When Elisas returned, I commanded him to teach me Syrian. I found it, however, far more difficult than Persian, unless indeed Elisas made it hard for me on purpose, as he was in one of his sullen moods for days thereafter.

Persian, you see, has inflections much like those of Greek, and many of the words are even alike. Thus "father" and "mother"[3] are *pitar* and *matar*. But Syrian I found entirely different from Greek, in grammar and words alike. Forbye, where Greek gets along with four guttural sounds, the *gamma, kappa, chi,* and rough breathing, Syrian has twice as many: a battery of gasping, coughing, retching, and gargling noises. One day I was practicing them when Thyestes rode up and began to pound my back, thinking that I was choking.

We rode through the fertile fields of Sousiana, where bountiful crops were breaking the soil. On some of the farms, enormous horses stood in paddocks. Vardanas said:

"Mithras smite me if those be not from the royal Median herds! What do they here, so far from the plain of Nisaia?"

I said: "I should guess that as soon as the Persian government fell, every horse thief within a hundred leagues of Nisaia hastened thither to seize as many horses as he could, ere Alexander could stop him."

"Alas! What wickedness have I lived to see!"

"I would not say so," I said. "While 'tis fine for the king to have thousands of giant horses, other folk as well can put the breed to good use. Could I fetch a herd of yon beasties to Hellas, my fortune were made."

Vardanas laughed. "You should have been a trader, Leon. I see the mercenary gleam in your eye whenever you see a chance to squeeze an obolos out of a deal."

"What's wrong with trading?"

"I thought your philosophers viewed it as ungentlemanly, as do men of my own class among the Persians."

Pyrron, who had been whispering to himself, cleared his throat. "Some do, Vardanas. But I, though a philosopher, regard such attitudes as mere prejudices, effected by time and place and circumstance.

---

3   *patēr kai matēr.*

I sneer at no honest occupation. My sister's a midwife, and I have no shame about assisting her with chores. Those whose property supports them in idleness are wont to aggrandize themselves by contemning the labors of all those less fortunate than they. But why heed them?"

"A sound point of view for a philosopher," said Vardanas, "but I can fancy the outburst if I told my father I was going into business. He likes to call himself a Persian of the old school, who knows nothing but how to ride, to shoot, and to tell the truth."

"Men of my class feel the same," I said, "though they except horse trading. As for me, I agree with Pyrron. And speaking of your father, you'll soon be home. What's your home like?"

"We have two, like most of the landowners hereabouts. One is a house in Sousa; the other, where we spend our summers, is in yonder hills." He pointed toward one of the ranges that broke the horizon. "You are lucky to see the Houzan plain in winter. In summer it is so hot that barley grains pop on the sidewalk, and a lizard that tries to cross the street in daytime is stricken dead."

"If it's hotter than the Arachotian desert, I'm glad to miss the Sousian summer. How much family have you?"

"There is my father, Thraitaunas son of Tachmaspas; my mother Rhautagouna; my father's other wife Houtausa; then my brothers Kambouzias and Ariakas; and my sisters Nirouphar and Mousa and Gambia. My sister Artaunta is married and dwells in Hagmatana. I had another brother, Tachmaspas, who fell at Issos, and a brother who died in infancy."

"I come of a big family, too," I said.

"Ours is not really large. The Persian king was wont to give prizes to the largest Persian families, on the ground that only thus could he get enough faithful Persians to help him rule the lesser peoples of the empire. Now I suppose Alexander will do the same for all these Hellenes whom he is sowing hither and yon in Asia."

"I'd better harness up, then," I said with a smile.

"What will you do for a Greek girl? There are few indeed in Persia."

"The king seems to like his men to wed Asiatic lasses. He'd better, seeing that he himself married one. Belike your father would give me one of your sisters."

146

I meant it as a jest, but Vardanas looked grave. "Oh, my dear Leon, pray do not speak of such a thing to him!"

"And why not? My family is as respectable as his, as you shall see if you come to Thessalia. We belong to the knightly class and to the clan of the Aleuadai, the noblest family of Thessalia."

"It is not that," said Vardanas, looking miserable. "I would not offend my dear companion; but Father is fearfully proud of being *Ariatshisha*—of pure Arian lineage. Although most Persian families in Houza are more or less mixed with the Houzans, we are pure Persian. He would never consider a non-Arian son-in-law."

"*Phy!*" I said, a little put out despite Vardanas' apologies. Although I had never seen the Persian's sisters and had no idea if I should even like them, it was irksome to be deemed inferior merely because one was a stranger. I found it hard to cleave to the spirit of international tolerance on which Pyrron had been lecturing us. But I bethought me that if the case were reversed, my family would be just as shocked by the thought of giving one of my sisters to Vardanas; nor would they easily accept my bringing home a foreign bride.

Early on the second day after we left Soustara, Sousa rose out of the plain ahead of us. We could see it from afar, as it is built on a clump of mounds or low hills. Ere we reached it, we forded a river which the Hellenes call the Koprates from its dung color, but which those who live along it call the Dida. The city itself stands beside another river, the Chavaspes—not connected with the Chavaspes of Gandaria, though they both bear the same name.

As we came closer, I could see the mounds upon which Sousa is built. Each mound is walled and fortified, while another wall encloses all the mounds and the bulk of the houses of the city. The three largest mounds are crowned with temples, palaces, and barracks; the houses of lesser folk spread over the smaller mounds and the low places between them.

This was the biggest city that any of us had seen in years, larger by far than Taxasila, though not in a class with Babylon. Howsomever, like most cities in Persia and Mesopotamia, Sousa had a shabby look because half the mud-brick houses had been abandoned and were crumbling into ruin.

147

There was a glitter of arms and a clank of marching soldiery on the plain to the east of the city. Here, on a spacious drill field, several thousand youths marched to and fro. They wore the Macedonian foot soldier's helmet and cuirass; they carried the eight-cubit pike, and the Macedonian star-and-crescent pattern adorned their bucklers, but Median trousers flapped about their legs. They had dark, big-nosed Persian faces.

Near the road stood a group of officers conducting the drill. Two commanded of the rest: a pock-marked Macedonian in full general's regalia, and another man whose garb combined trousers with a Greek officer's helmet. The Hellene spoke to the other man: "Advance!"

"Advance!" shouted the Persian in his own language.

The soldiers started forward raggedly.

"Persian countermarch!" said the Macedonian.

"Persian countermarch!" bawled his companion.

Now, "Persian countermarch" is a simple maneuver. The leading man in each file turns and walks back to the rear between the forward-moving files, and the man behind him follows, and so on. However, a man bearing a long Macedonian pike must hold it straight up during the maneuver, lest it foul the pikes of his neighbors. And woe; woe! The recruits' pikes leant in all directions. Hence there arose a clatter of pikes colliding with pikes, and cries of anger. In a twinkling the men became a milling mob.

The Macedonian officer dashed his helm to the ground and cursed. Now that I could better see his face, I recognized Archelaos son of Theodoros, whom I had known in the old days before Issos. I rode up and called his name.

"Leon!" he cried. "Hermes attend us! I thought you had been eaten by some gryphon or dragon beyond the sunrise. Be it true the East is full of warrior women, pygmies who live on the smell of flowers, and other marvels?"

"Not so full as the tales make out, though there's much of interest. What do you here?"

"Did you not know? I am a general." He indicated the Persian. "This is Brigadier Masdaros. He and I are trying to make phalangites out of Persians. Beside us, Sisyphos had it easy. But what are you doing with this enormous elephant?"

I told him of my mission. "Whom seek we for governmental fodder?"

Archelaos jerked his thumb northward. "Go to Aboulites' offices on North Hill, in the palace of Dareios the Great. Perchance you can stable the elephant with the others."

"Other elephants?"

"Yes, we still have eleven that belonged to Dareios the Little. Another one died. All they do is eat their heads off. I claim their keep should come from the civil budget, while old Aboulites insists it must come from the military, as if these polluted beasts were of any use to me! So far he has had the better of it in our daily squabbles before Kallikrates, the fiscal officer."

"Have you barrack room for us? It's years since we have slept in real beds, not counting brothels."

Archelaos silently counted my hipparchia and whispered to Masdaros. Then he turned to me, shaking his head and smiling.

"Yes," he said. "A company of replacements marched off to join the king a few days ago, so we have room. Vivanas!" He spoke to a young Persian aide. "Lead this party to barracks and see that they are made easy."

We left the officers shouting at the recruits and headed for the city. Vardanas, easily cast down by anything that showed his countrymen in poor light, stared gloomily ahead.

"Who are those?" I asked Vivanas.

"Well-born Persian youths whom the king ordered trained in Macedonian tactics, Hipparch," he said.

"How long has this been going on?" said Vardanas.

"About two years," said Vivanas. "The orders were issued long before that, but it took much time to assemble the men and gear."

Vardanas rolled his eyes heavenwards. "Auramasdas befriend me!"

"Alexander thought we were overthrown for want of steady infantry," said Vivanas with an embarrassed air. "In a few more years…"

"In a few more years!" said Vardanas. "Alexander may be right, but I fear that trying to make phalangites of noble Persians is like carving a tombstone with a razor."

"How mean you?" I said.

149

"They are so imbued with the idea that the only gentlemanly way of fighting is on horseback that they have no heart for footwork. I fear not even years of practice will remedy that."

"That, as Pyrron would say, is but a foolish prejudice. The object of war is to win, be it mounted, afoot, or swimming."

"That may be," said Vardanas, "but such feelings cannot be changed by a mere command, come it from never so mighty a king."

We passed into the city, through the winding streets, and up the ramp that led to the top of the principal mound. This mound was fortified by a parapet round the edge. The top was crowded with barrack buildings, among which stood the ancient temples of the Sousian deities Sousinax and Nana. Worshipers crowded past soldiers, and the sound of hymns mingled with the clatter of the armorers. The temples were crumbling. Workmen crept about on them like flies, bricking and patching, but the onlooker felt that they would never catch up with the natural process of decay.

Vardanas said: "Let me leave you here, Leon, to go home. I shall soon be back."

Vivanas made us comfortable. As we were settling in, an uproar from another part of the barracks brought me in haste to find the cause.

It was not a quarrel but a celebration. Kanadas and Siladites had come upon a group of fellow Indians who cared for the eleven elephants that dwelt in Sousa. In their joy at finding countrymen, both my Indians were shouting in their native tongue. As all the other Indians shouted too, it sounded like a riot. They laughed and wept and embraced one another, and ended by dancing round a circle, clapping hands and snapping fingers.

Having combed the burrs out of my beard and borrowed a clean shirt, I climbed the stair that led up the side of North Hill. The retaining wall was decked with low reliefs in enameled brick of life-size animals, in red, white, and gold, such as a goat-horned lion with eagle's wings and hindlegs.

At the top of the stair, a gallows reached out over the steps. From this gallows hung three men in Sousian dress of good quality. I had to duck lest I brush against their feet. They had begun to stink.

After this cheerful introduction to the civil government of Sousiana, I went on and asked for Aboulites. After waiting in anterooms
until hunger gnawed my vitals, I was told the viceroy could not be
seen, but that his son Vaxathras would tend to my needs.

Vaxathras was a plump little man in a gorgeous robe of silk. As
many in Hellas have never seen silk, let me say that it is a marvelous
lustrous fabric that comes over the caravan routes from the Sakan
country. Howsomever, nobody knows where it grows, or indeed if it
be the fleece of a beast or the fiber of a plant. Vaxathras also wore a
fillet of silver thread about his hair. His beard was curled in ringlets;
the ends of his mustache were waxed so they stuck out like spikes;
and his face was powdered and painted, with a red spot on either
cheek. He was so cordial he bounced.

"Come, my dear Hipparch, welcome!" he cried in Persian with a
strange accent. "What can we do for you? Fodder? Nought easier!
Let me countersign your order. There, present it to Ashinas. Where
are you staying?"

"In the barracks on the hill," I said.

"Oh, my dear fellow, that will never do! You must move up here
to the palace, with the rest of us civils. There is room for you and two
or three of your officers. You have some chests of specimens, have you
not?" (I wondered how he knew.) "Have your men fetch them here,
too, along with any other things of value. We live in disturbed times.
When can we expect you? This afternoon before dinner time? What
else can I do for you?"

After Phrashavartes' haughtiness, such eagerness to please took
my breath away. I mumbled assents without stopping to think and
left Dareios' palace in a daze. Only when I ducked under the feet of
the hanged men did I begin to berate myself for agreeing to Vaxathras'
proposals without scrutinizing them more closely.

As I entered the barracks, I heard the sound of sobbing. When
the crowd opened out for me, I saw that it was Vardanas, sitting with
his face in his hands and weeping bitterly, while Thyestes and Pyrron
and Kanadas sought to comfort him.

"What is it?" I asked.

Vardanas tried to tell me, but each time he opened his mouth he
was overwhelmed by a flood of tears. At last Pyrron said:

"His mother's dead."

"When did she die?"

"Two months ago, but he only now learned of it."

Vardanas' lamentations went on and on. Our efforts to comfort him only seemed to bring on more sobs, until I thought he would weep the day and night away. Never had I seen so unbridled a spate of emotion.

I told Thyestes of the plan to move the officers to the palace. "Of course," I said, "somebody maun stay with the troop."

Thyestes spoke a rude word. "Aye, I kens. You'll go up there and wallow in Persian luxury the now, leaving poor Thyestes to scratch fleabites here in barrack. It never fails."

"Na, na, buckie," I said. "I thought we'd take turns."

"What is this?" said Vardanas suddenly, his lamentations stopped as though cut off with a knife. I told him about Vaxathras.

"You must not go there!" he said. "Especially you must not take the chests there!"

"Why not?"

"I came to warn you. Aboulites and Vaxathras are plundering the Sousians worse than any of Alexander's other governors. Once they get the chests in their power, they will make away with you and keep the stuff for themselves. Trust them not!"

"What shall we do, then?"

"I bid you to my father's house; fetch the chests with you. They are not fully safe even there, but I do not think Aboulites will molest a man of my father's rank. At least, he will not until he has tried all kinds of guile."

I had an instant of wonder whether, if Vaxathras and his father were such ready-for-aughts, I was safe in the hands of Vardanas and his father either. However, having been on the road with Vardanas for five months and found him a man of the nicest scruples, I thought I could trust him if I could trust any man.

"Vaxathras expects us today," I said. "Should I send one of the men with my apologies?"

"Do not send even one of our men; he might be seized as a hostage. Find some aide of Archelaos or Masdaros to take the message." He spoke to the troop at large. "I would bid you all to stay with us, had we room. But my father has other guests, so Leon and Pyrron are the only ones we can bed. The rest shall, however, be bidden to dine with us in turn."

On the way to Vardanas' house, the Persian said: "I trust that my friends will comply with our code of manners to the extent of bowing to my father."

Thyestes muttered something about "silly servile ceremonial."

I said: "Flank Guard Thyestes, either you shall show good manners—Persian manners, that is—or you shall go back to barracks. I willna have our dear friend shamed."

"I meant nought," he said. "If he say we maun stand on our heads, I'll do it."

"Also," said Vardanas, "you will see that when my stepmother enters, I stand up until she gives me leave to sit. It were a delicate compliment to your host if you did likewise."

Thyestes said: "Ha! I thought the Persians treated their womenfolk like slaves, but it seems they defer till them, as do the Egyptians."

"Not quite," said Vardanas. "If any folk make slaves of its women, it is the Hellenes, who shut them up in the back of the house and do not present them to guests or let them eat with the men."

"That has its advantages," said Thyestes. "We thus see to it that the men get a chance to put a word in edgewise."

"And like most human institutions, its disadvantages as well," said Pyrron, clearing his throat. "As a philosopher, I hold all manners relative and matters of convention. But, as I believe in adapting myself to circumstance, you shan't find me backwards with my Persian bows."

Vardanas' house stood in spacious grounds against the western wall of the city, where the wall overlooked the Chavaspes. At Vardanas' knock, a peephole opened in the door in the blank brick wall that faced the street. The door opened. There came a barking of dogs and sounds of bustle within, as though people rushed about with last-minute preparations.

We trooped past the porter, doffing our hats and helmets. The dignity of our entrance was marred by Pyrron's tripping over the doorsill and almost falling.

The man who greeted us was tall but bent, with a long gray beard and an arched nose like that of Vardanas. He wore a long robe of plain materials.

"Welcome!" he said. "I am Thraitaunas son of Tachmaspas by name. May Auramasdas befriend you! Enter, friends of my son, and use my house as your own."

From Thraitaunas' gravity no one would think he had been scurrying about like a frightened mouse to ready his place for guests. It struck me that he was as uneasy about us as we were about him. I gave him my best Persian bow and broadcast compliments and blessings as if he were a king instead of a minor landowner.

As my eyes grew used to the gloom of the anteroom, I saw that a number of other people were lined up behind Thraitaunas. First my host presented a lean dark-skinned man of his own age, with shaven face and head, as Beliddinos, the high priest of Mardoukos in Babylon. Then he introduced his family: his surviving wife Houtausa, a thin pale woman with downcast eyes; his son Kambouzias, whose beard was just beginning to sprout; his son Ariakas, about eight; his daughter Nirouphar, almost my height; his younger daughters Mousa and Gambia.

Under Vardanas' direction, the camp men brought in the chests and stowed them in a locked storeroom. Kambouzias showed me to a long narrow bedroom and said: "When you have washed and decked yourself, lord, my father is fain to show you his garden."

Like all Persian gardens, that of Thraitaunas was of oblong shape with a cross-shaped water channel running the length and the breadth of it, a summerhouse at the farther end, and trees around the edge against the walls. Everything—paths, pools, benches, and plants—was arranged with rigid symmetry. Thraitaunas handed me a cup of water.

"Water of the Chavaspes," he said, "which our kings used to send the length and breadth of the empire so they could always drink it."

To me it tasted like any other water, though I knew that Persians distinguish among fine shades of taste in water as most nations do in wine. I uttered fulsome compliments.

"You speak Persian well," he said. Then he showed me round the garden. "This is a rarity, the yellow double rose of Isatis. Alas, Troop Leader—what is your name again? Ah, Rheon." (Like many Persians, Thraitaunas could not make an *l* sound.) "Alas that you will not be here two months hence, when they will all be in bloom! For four months this garden is a blaze of color, where now you see but thorny stumps and snags. What says Gautarzas?

"In spring, their tryst with us who live to keep,
The spirits of the dead, long buried deep,
In form of roses fair, with courtly bows
Do gaily greet us, then go back to sleep."

Nirouphar, the eldest daughter, came into the garden with Pyrron and began showing off the plants. There was little understanding betwixt them, as she spoke almost no Greek and he had but few words of Persian. Nevertheless, "showing the garden" is a Persian ritual to which all guests must submit, whether or no they are fond of flowers.

Nirouphar wore red trousers and, over them, a kind of long embroidered saffron coat. She was a handsome filly, tall and well made. Her strong back and graceful croup promised some man many long delightful gallops. She had the same high-bridged nose, dark complexion, and curly raven mane as her brother Vardanas.

Now Vardanas appeared, looking far different from when I had seen him last. His long robe glimmered with gold and silver thread. The waxen ends of his mustache swept out like the horns of a wild bull, and a large red spot was painted on either cheek. This custom illustrates Pyrron's theory of the relativity of manners. Among us, face paint is deemed effeminate in a man; but Persians use it on formal occasions even when the man is as manly as one could wish.

"Tell us your adventures, Rheon," said Thraitaunas. "My son has given me but a few words."

We sat on benches in the garden and sipped wine while Vardanas and I told our tale. When one of us got dry, the other took up the account. Thraitaunas was stirred by the parts about fighting and hunting, muttering, "*Vaush, vaush!*" and plying me for further details.

The Babylonian priest, Beliddinos, clad in a long embroidered robe, gazed keenly upon us and shot out searching questions regarding war and statecraft. Meanwhile the servants busied themselves with the hearth in the courtyard, around the corner from where we sat. The delicious smells of Persian cookery wafted into the garden and seduced my thoughts from our narrative. I foresaw another defeat in my lifelong battle against my waistline, a conflict wherein the final skirmish has not yet been fought.

Pyrron made heavy going of this conversation in a tongue of which he was largely ignorant. And, methinks, he was a little put out, as he was used to being the man to deliver any lectures that were to be uttered. He rose and began to wander about the garden, whispering to himself.

Presently Nirouphar, as dutiful hostess, joined him. They sat by themselves and spoke softly, heeding us not. By bending an ear, I made out that she was giving him a lesson in Persian. Pyrron, always obliging, entered into the spirit of it but mangled the words until the lass could not help laughing, drawing a frown from her father. I felt a twinge of annoyance—not that I knew or cared aught about the wench, but it irked me to see this gangling booby garner the most nubile maiden present without a visible effort, while poor plain Leon, with his snub nose and his thick wrestler's form, sat solemnly answering the queries of a pair of ancients.

"...and here we are," said Vardanas, winding up his tale.

"Good!" growled Thraitaunas. "Were I young, I too would travel afar; I too would serve strange kings; I too would see unearthly sights. But woe! My aches and ills! My knee bothers me; last month an aching tooth drove me all but mad. Now, my son, I trust you have had your fill of travel. I need your help with the stock. I am too old for much riding. And we have some special new stock to care for."

"Do you mean we got possession of some of the royal herd of—" began Vardanas, but his father cut him off with a gesture.

"Later, later," he said. "Are you home for ever and aye?"

"Not yet. I must needs go to Athens with Leon first."

Thraitaunas scowled. "I said I needed you! Must I then give a direct command? Or has travel sapped your respect for your father's will?"

"I gave my word to the king," said Vardanas. "After we deliver the elephant I shall be free."

"Fie! But a promise is a promise, I suppose. We shall speak of this anon."

The talk then turned upon lighter matters until Houtausa heralded dinner. We went into Thraitaunas' living room, where small eating tables had been set up.

Like all the other rooms, this one was long and narrow. That is the way with Sousian houses, and the reason is this. To make the houses livable in the heat of summer, the builders pile two or three feet of earth on the level roofs. This means that the rooms must needs be narrow, because the only timber that can be had for holding up this great weight is palm trunks. Since palm trunks are not very strong, the roof beams made from them must needs be short.

Thraitaunas' house slaves served a sumptuous feast. I will not delay the tale with an account of the menu, though I can remember every course to this day. It ended with a spiced and sweetened fruitcake which the Persians call "dessert." I asked Thraitaunas:

"What is this I hear about the sins of Aboulites and Vaxathras?"

"No more than one must expect when your king appoints a sly Houzan as governor instead of an honest Persian. It is the old story: taxation in advance, extortion, tomb robbery, plundering temples. Saw you three hanged men in the city? They were taxpayers who resisted Abourites' demands."

I said: "One man's wickedness becomes all men's curse, as we say in Thessalia. I swear by Zeus—or Auramasdas, if you prefer—that no more will I trust one of these governors ere I ask among his subjects what kind of man he be."

"Do that," said Thraitaunas. "It may keep your throat uncut till you reach your home. An uncut throat is always a useful thing to have, ha! Beriddinos stays here for the same reason you do."

Beliddinos shot a hard glance at his host as if to warn him not to talk of his affairs. But the old Persian was the kind who would speak his mind about whatever he pleased. Besides, we were all a trace tipsy. Indeed, any Persian gathering is apt to involve what seems to a Hellene like heavy drinking.

"Beriddinos has gathered funds for rebuilding his tumbledown temple," said Thraitaunas, "since your government has not given him the money Arexander promised. Ho, ho! Would not Abourites like to get his talons into your cargo, my friend?"

Beliddinos said: "Do not let our host give you false ideas, Hipparch. But a pittance have I collected; barely enough have I gathered to begin one wall of the new house of God, from pious Babylonians in Sousiana. Whither go you hence?"

"That depends. I must find Menes, viceroy of Syria, and I may wish to see the treasurer Harpalos. Do either of you gentlemen know where they are?"

Neither knew, but Thraitaunas said: "I will inquire. Though I am old and racked with pain, though I must bow the knee to a dirty Houzan, still I have connections."

Beliddinos said: "In any case, to make Babylon your next goal you will wish. There will Harpalos be if he be not in Tarsos, and there news of Menes can you surely obtain."

"Have you something in mind?" I said.

Beliddinos smiled thinly. "I mean that to Babylon I, too, must journey, and thought we might join forces. Never could the treasury of Mardoukos sustain the hire of so many stalwart guards as your troop comprises."

Vardanas cried: "Splendid!"

I said: "It sounds good, sir; but let me think about it, lest some forgotten obstacle rear itself in our path after we have made our arrangements."

"Surely, surely," said Beliddinos. "For one so young, caution you have learned; for a bluff soldier, worldly wisdom has come to you fast."

"You need not fear," said Vardanas to me. "I have known Beliddinos all my life."

"Thank you, my son," said Beliddinos to Vardanas, and then to me he said: "The first thing to think about is time. How soon will you leave? The sooner the better, ere Aboulites' ruffians come knocking for us."

"I thought three or four days would suffice for rest and refit."

"Excellent. Think on my proposal and speak to me about it; ponder it and let me know your mind."

Thyestes and Pyrron had made hard going of the conversation in Persian. Nirouphar spoke: "Father, it is a sin that you never let Dorymachos give me more lessons in Greek when he was teaching my brothers. Then we could all speak in that tongue; our Greek guests would not be put out of countenance."

Thraitaunas snorted. "My Greek is as bad as Pyrron's Persian, and I do not think Beriddinos knows any Greek at all. Anyway, it is ridiculous to talk of educating women. There is already too much education of men. Learning has caused most of the world's woes, ever since Tachmarthen forced the demons to teach him the secret of letters. Had Dorymachos not filled Vardanas' head with Greek nonsense, he would not have gone gadding off to the ends of the earth. He would not have left his poor, sick old father to struggle alone with the property. His Greek education was another of your mother's silly ideas."

"My mother had more sense than you!" said Nirouphar.

"Silence, wench!" roared Thraitaunas.

"I will not be silent!" cried his daughter. "That is what you say whenever somebody catches you in the wrong. I am sick of it!"

"Go to your room!" he thundered.

"I would not stay!" she cried, sweeping from the room.

Vardanas, glaring at his father, struck both fists against the table. I thought he also was going to rise and burst into heated speech, but he mastered himself and said: "Pray forgive us, friends. You know how families are."

"Indeed I do," said Beliddinos with a chuckle. "One of my own have I, and betimes the domestic disputes bid fair the roof to bring down."

Poor, timid Houtausa had spoken never a word. Thraitaunas drank and said: "A lively minx, my daughter. Being my wife will tame her."

Thyestes shuddered. Beliddinos said: "Do you still mean to go through with that, Thrai?"

"I said so, did I not? I thought we would marry in the spring, when the roses are out. Come to the wedding if you be in these parts."

"What if she does not wish it?"

"What do you mean? She is a good girl; she will do as I tell her."

"Like unto an itch that cannot be scratched is a contentious woman in the house. Why has she not wed one of the youths of the city? Fair she is, and over sixteen she must be. In Babylon, seven times seven suitors would she have."

"She is nineteen, but she is unwed for two reasons. First, there are no pure *Ariatshisha* youths around here; all have vile Houzan blood. One did come dangling after her last year, but I soon sent him packing, I can tell you. Second, I am an infirm old man; I need the care of more than one wife. Houtausa is not strong enough."

"It were a pity not to mate her to one young enough to get her with child. As we say in Babylon, friendship lasts for a day, but posterity goes on forever."

"What mean you, one young enough? I can still do my duty as a husband! You shall see. But enough of airing our private affairs before guests. Have more wine. Tell us more of your deeds of dought, young men; pray do."

After I had gone to bed, I was kept from slumber by the sounds of a terrific quarrel. Though I could not make out the words, I knew the voices of Thraitaunas, Vardanas, and Nirouphar all speaking in loud angry tones. It struck me that the three looked much alike, allowing for differences of age and sex, and probably had the same impulsive, headstrong natures. Hence no house was big enough for all at once.

I thought Thraitaunas' plan dreadful. Besides my Hellenic horror of incest, it seemed plain that his old age and her youth would be made wretched by this monstrous marriage. She ought, methought, to wed a good sound man of suitable age; a Persian equivalent, say, of Leon of Atrax. I had no thought at all of courting her myself. For one thing, she was a foreigner; for another, she was a whit more saucy and forward than I thought suitable for a wife.

Next morning, as I set out for the city to tend the hipparchia, I fell in with Beliddinos, also going to town in a tall hat and a plain brown tunic and carrying a walking stick with the top carven in the likeness of a dragon. His two slaves came with him, one bearing a pick and one a shovel.

"Whither bound?" I said. "You look as if you were setting forth on a treasure hunt."

"Not far wrong are you, my son. But the treasure I seek is the kind most men would cast away as rubbish."

"What is it, then?"

"Come and see, if you will," he said.

"You will see, forsooth," said Thraitaunas. "Were Beriddinos not one of my oldest friends, I would have him chained up as a dangerous madman."

"Hear the ignorant scoff! Well, my son, are you with me?"

Burning with curiosity, I walked with the Babylonian to one of the more ruinous parts of the city. We went into a lot encumbered with piles of broken brick that had once been a spacious temple. Beliddinos gave directions. The slaves began to dig in the places he pointed out with his stick.

Now and then they brought up a piece of brick, which they handed to Beliddinos. He studied it at arm's length (for age had made him farsighted) and cast it aside. Meseemed that, if Thraitaunas believed his friend a little mad, belike the Persian was not far wrong.

A few townsfolk gathered to watch, but with less interest than I should have expected. I said:

"O Beliddinos, were I to start digging in a vacant lot in Atrax, all the folk would think I dug for treasure and would come running with spades to forestall me. Why do the Sousians not do likewise?"

"They know me," he said. "Folk act as you describe in a town where for the first time I dig, but the Sousians have long since given me up as queer."

A slave handed Beliddinos a brick, which he stared at, turning it so that the light struck it slantwise and exclaiming softly in Syrian, the tongue spoken by most Babylonians.

"What is it?" I said.

"Look here." He held the brick so that I saw that the surface was covered with little marks. It was as if a flock of wee birdies had run

161

back and forth across it while the clay was yet soft, until the face was wholly covered by their tracks.

"That is writing," said he. "Back to Babylon I must take it to be sure, but I think this is a foundation brick stamped with the inscription of King Tammaritos, who ruled Elamis before the coming of the Persians."

"A strange kind of writing," I said.

"Not at all. For thousands of years we used it in Babylonia. But alas! Yearly the number of those who can read this clay writing grows less. The day may come when the archives of our collected wisdom will lie mute for want of any who can decipher them."

"Then why collect more written bricks?" I said. "Are there men who will pay for them?"

"Nay, no such vulgar motive have I. The thoughts of past ages I seek, to keep the noble deeds of the men of yore from utterly perishing. When we get to Babylon, you must see my collection. Inscriptions of Sargon the Conqueror and Chammyrabis the Lawgiver have I."

I felt an awe of a man so deeply learned, but my own duties called. When the slaves had dug a while longer without finding anything worthy of note, I excused myself and went to the citadel.

The rest of the day I spent in caring for my hipparchia: checking and renewing equipment, touring the market place with Elisas to buy provisions, doctoring the sick, comforting the downcast, and calming the quarrelsome. The elephant was well tended in the royal pens along with the others, though the keepers complained that Aias ate as much as any two other elephants together.

Meanwhile, Vardanas swaggered about the town, calling upon his many friends. Once he passed me in the street, driving a two-horse chariot and waving gaily. I envied his looks and charm but consoled myself with the thought that Fate gives it to some to cut a dash and to others to do the world's serious work. As the fable says, no man can be first in everything.

As I walked about Sousa, I avoided dark corners and cast furtive glances over my shoulder, lest Aboulites' minions come upon me unawares. In the late afternoon I finished my tasks and hastened back to Thraitaunas' house, bringing Kanadas. My heart beat faster at the thought of conversing with a fair and well-bred lady, though I told myself I was being foolish. I had to speak sharply to myself to keep from breaking into an undignified run.

I found Thraitaunas in his garden, dictating in Persian to a slave who wrote the message in Syrian—something about selling a foal. It is curious that most Persians are unlettered in their own tongue, although some can write Greek or Syrian, and although there are systems of writing Persian.

I presented Kanadas and asked where everybody was, for the house seemed quieter than was its wont. Only Ariakas and another lad of eight were to be seen, building a kind of fort in one of the trees.

"The philosopher has taken Nirouphar to walk the dogs on the city wall," said Thraitaunas. "Kambouzias has gone with them to chaperon and interpret."

"Oh," said I, with so dour a visage that the old man gave me a look informed with suspicion.

"Know you whether they went north or south?" I asked.

"No, but I daresay you can find them."

"With your leave, I will. I have a matter on which to speak to Pyrron."

"Indeed?" said Thraitaunas.

I left him talking with Kanadas and went out to the wall. Walking on the wall at sunset is a simple pleasure enjoyed, I suppose, by city dwellers of high and low degree the whole world over. Thence I could see across the low parts of the city, though the mounds cut off the view in other directions.

The sun was setting in purple and gold behind the mountains that part Sousiana from Babylonia. The sky was blotched and barred with clouds. A cool wind flapped my cloak. In the city, families were out weeding their roofs, for many Sousians raise flowers or vegetables on the earthen dressing atop their houses. Others pushed stone rollers over their roofs to flatten the earth.

Not knowing which way to turn, I went north, walking swiftly and looking sharply into the faces of strollers. When I had almost reached the northwest angle of the wall, I saw three crested Hellenic helmets. Two sat on the heads of Archelaos and Masdaros, the military commanders. I returned Archelaos' wave and Masdaros' bow.

The former presented the third man, Zenophilos, who commanded the citadel.

The three officers were taking the air with their wives, who were veiled against the gaze of the curious. Archelaos cried: "Rejoice, O Leon! Are you being well treated?"

"Aye, General; none better."

He lowered his voice. "Have you had any trouble with Aboulites?"

"Not yet," I said, and told of Vaxathras' reception.

"You were wise not to move into the palace where those shameless ones could get their clutches on you. I should have warned you yesterday but did not think of it quickly enough. When I bethought me, I sent word to Aboulites that if he molested you I would hang him from his own gallows." He turned to the other two officers. "Leon and some of his Thessalians saved my life in a skirmish in Phrygia in the old days, and I am not one to forget it."

"'Twas nought," I said.

"Still," he continued, "I would not advise you to stay here too long, lest you rouse Aboulites' greed. Despite my boastful threat, he wields great power."

"I'm off as soon as I can be," I said.

"Oh!" cried one of the ladies. "A storm is upon us!"

A great rain cloud had crept up from the southeast. The officers bade me good night and hurried away. I walked quickly back along the wall. Ere I reached the place where I had gained the top of the wall, the storm overtook me. First came a rattle of hail against the brick. A hailstone the size of a fist struck my head and dizzied me. Then rain drove down. By the time I reached the next watchtower, where a crowd of strollers huddled, I was soaked.

The rain being over, I took up my search again. A little south of the stair leading down to the street near Thraitaunas' house, I met Nirouphar, Pyrron, and Kambouzias. They were dry, having taken shelter in a tower before the rain began. The dogs climbed all over me, for they had taken a liking to my smell. Nirouphar said:

"O Rheon, how glad we are to see you! Pyrron has been telling me about philosophy, and my poor brother is having a difficult time translating."

I sympathized with Kambouzias. The abandoned wench, to flatter Pyrron, had urged him to tell her all about his theories. Kambouzias' Greek was adequate for such simple sentences as: "I have placed the lamp on the table," or "Please pass the salt," but in philosophy he was quite at sea. Nor could the lass have learned much about such an advanced subject from his fumbling translation.

Pyrron, happily unaware of this, said: "I'll go ahead, old boy, pausing for you to interpret. Now, the third mode of inconsistency in our percepts arises from the differences between the sense channels in the different cases. For example, an apple gives the impression of being *yellow* to the sight, *sweet* in taste, and *fragrant* in smell, but these sense impressions have no necessary connection, one with the other. Thus it follows that what appears is no more a certain, determinate thing than something else..."

"Excuse me," I said, "but if I know not whereof you speak, how do you expect the maiden to know either?"

Pyrron shrugged. "That's what she asked for."

"Oh, pray do not stop him, Rheon!" said Nirouphar. "I love to hear him lecture. It sounds so profound, even when I understand it not."

I sighed and took up my translating, pausing now and then for a hearty sneeze. I suppose any passer-by could have seen that I had eyes only for Nirouphar, while she had eyes only for Pyrron, who had eyes for nought but his fine-spun webs of reasoning. Betimes we had to halt the lecture to untangle Pyrron from the dogs' leashes, for he would absently let them run in circles round him until he was helplessly enmeshed.

We returned to Thraitaunas' house to find a gilded litter in front of the door, with two bearers and two armed guards. A eunuch came out, leading the boy who had been playing with Ariakas. Thraitaunas' son exchanged farewells with the boy and his keeper. The boy got in, and off they went, the eunuch walking beside the litter.

We went in and found Thraitaunas deep in converse with Kanadas, with whom he got on quite well. In fact, I think Kanadas was the only one of us whom Thraitaunas liked, despite the Indian's odd ways, such as his insistence on cooking his own dinner and eating it by himself in a corner. Just now Kanadas was talking on his two favorite subjects, to wit: his dislike of the journey and the foreign lands it took him through, and the moral superiority of Indians over all other men. In spite of Kanadas' lack of tact—or perhaps because of it—his sobriety, piety, and imposing person impressed the old Persian. Thraitaunas was polite to the rest of us because we were the guests of his son; but, as he scorned all non-Arians, I do not think he really approved of us.

Indians, forbye, also call themselves Arians. Hence, although Kanadas was nigh as black as an Ethiop, a Persian gentleman had liefer have him in the family than a Hellene like me.

Thraitaunas looked up. "Well, did you get caught in the rain?"

"We found shelter, Father," said Nirouphar, "all but poor Rheon—"

I interrupted with a terrific sneeze. "Sir, who was the boy playing with your son? I saw him depart in great state, as if he were a young prince."

"He is, or was," said Thraitaunas. "That was Prince Vaukas, the son of the unlucky Daraiavaus." For so the Persians pronounce "Dareios."

"Oh," said I, regretting I had not passed the time of day with this sprig of former Persian royalty, if only to have something to tell about afterwards to make myself more interesting and impressive to others.

I sneezed through dinner and did but peck at the excellent food. Next morning I had a violent cold and fever. When I appeared at Thraitaunas' board, the family united in demanding that I go back to bed and let them nurse me.

I let them persuade me, looking forward to Nirouphar's tender care. She did devote me some time in the morning, but her ministrations proved more brisk and practical than tender.

"Keep covered and drink all of this water you can hold," she said. "No; no wine for you until you are on the mend!"

Then her father commanded Nirouphar forth to entertain Pyrron, while the graybeard sat on my bed by the hour and told me about his own ailments. If half the things he said were wrong with him were true, he had been dead six times over. Lucky for me that my sickness was no grave one, else I had wasted away from the mere contemplation of all the ills to which mortal flesh is heir!

The best thing that betided that day was when a Persian postman came in and gave me a letter, saying: "I have searched the city for you, Troop Leader. This is from the great king."

"Many thanks," I said, and tipped him two oboloi. The letter read:

EUMENES OF KARDIA GREETS
LEON ARISTOU OF ATRAX

King Alexander commands me to tell you that he follows your letters with the utmost interest. Already, mindful of your warnings about the Chaibara Pass, he has changed his plans for sending elephants westward by that route. He asks that you continue as you have been doing and write him forthwith should you find yourself in need or in danger. In addition to the praise of the king, pray accept my good wishes as well. We are now sailing down the Hydaspes, conquering as we go.

I learnt anon that when the king commanded Krateros to march to westward with a herd of elephants, they went, as a result of my advice, by Chaarena in the south instead of by Gandaria in the north.

That night I was kept awake by another familial quarrel, which led me to wonder if this were a nightly ritual. Although I was still unwell the next day, the thought of another session with Thraitaunas' symptoms drove me to rise despite all protests.

"I thak you, sir," I said, "but duty cobes before adythig else. I bust prepare our departure."

Between my cold and an uneasy feeling that I was growing fonder of the sight of Nirouphar than was good for me, I went about my business with such a gloomy mien that one Thessalian asked me if the omens were bad.

That was a good question, as I had not had any omens read in Sousa regarding the next stage of our journey. I had meant to, but between fear of Aboulites and interest in Vardanas' family I had forgotten. That night at dinner I spoke thus to Beliddinos:

"O wise one, till now I have bought omens at each stage of the journey, though I have grown increasingly doubtful of their value. This time I have not yet done so. But I know the fame of Babylonians at reading the scroll of Fate. What think you? Should I go to an oracle monger as before, or can you read our future in the stars?"

"Far different from what vulgar fortunetellers assert is the pure Babylonian star doctrine," he said. "We hold that the gods, who live in the stars, by their radiations affect events on earth. But in a general sense only, they affect them. Thus when in the ascendant is Nerigal, likely is war; but that tells not if Leon of Atrax will be slain in battle. I think we can, by long study and observation, the effects of the gods' influences on kings and nations dimly see. But as for casting horoscopes for common men like you and me, as to whether we should lend or borrow, or ride or walk—faugh! Mere quackery is it, my son; foolish deceit it is."

Then how about the run of omen casters: the liver inspectors, bird watchers, and the like?"

"Believe as you list, and ill it becomes me to contemn my colleagues. In confidence, however, the more I study such matters the less faith in them have I. Somewhere in the sphere of the gods, I doubt not, is a perfect scheme of correspondence between omens and future events. The flight of birds, the form of the liver of a sacrifice, the mysteries of name and number, and the aspects of the heavens are all conjoined in one vast, mystic web of causality. But how much do we know about this? Not so much as we pretend, I warrant."

"Then think you I could as well save the king's money and not buy omens?"

"I think you could. Of course, you will still have to tell your men the omens are good, for less worldly in such matters than we are they "

I spent a day counting our money and casting accounts. The results of my reckonings filled me with forebodings.

Despite his boasted connections, Thraitaunas had learnt nought of the whereabouts of Menes and Harpalos. Therefore I bade Thraitaunas and his family a decorous farewell at dawn on the morn of the twenty-third of Poseidon. To feast my eyes on Nirouphar once more, I stretched out my leave-taking until even old Thraitaunas, for all his love of ceremony, became uneasy. That something was amiss in the family I could divine from the formal way they addressed one another.

At last Vardanas said: "Be off, Leon; I have another leave to take and will ride after. Rakous will catch up with you in no time."

He winked. Thinking that this farewell was with a sweetheart, I demurred not. I clasped hands in the Persian manner with Thraitaunas. Then, followed by Beliddinos and his servants on mules, I rode to the west gate to meet the hipparchia. We all trotted out through the gate, over the bridge of stone that spans the Chavaspes, and across the plain toward Babylon.

It was a misty morning. As I rode, I pondered on the mysterious ways of Fate, which forestalls the union of couples, otherwise attracted to one another, by causing them to be born of different nations. The pathos of it all made a tear run down into my beard. Thyestes said:

"What ails you, body?"

"'Tis but the tailend of my cold," I said, which was not altogether false.

Then I squared my shoulders and put all that behind me. What little I knew of Nirouphar implied that she would be at best ill-suited to me, even supposing the many obstacles to a closer relationship could have been overthrown. Although my years of living with Hyovis had made me think well of Persian women, I desired no foreigner for a legal wife, let abee one who took such a vigorous part in familial disputes.

Fate had been kind after all. I was lucky to have escaped entanglement. Not even a god, they say, could be at once wise and in love. What I really needed, I told myself, was a good long canter in a whorehouse in Babylon.

The sound of hooves at a run brought me round. Three figures loomed out of the mist. One, I saw, was Vardanas, another his Kolchian slave, who had been with him since erst I knew him. The third was a Persian woman. So, I thought, has he brought his sweetling along? And did it mean we should have a vengeful husband or outraged father on our trail?

"Who's this?" I said.

"You know her," said Vardanas. The woman pushed back her hood and behold! It was Nirouphar. "She could not bear the old man any longer, let alone wed him. He is a terrible tyrant in his family, you know. So she has run away to see the world, trusting to my protection."

BOOK SIX

Babylonia

"BY THE GODS AND GODDESSES!" I exclaimed. After a moment of stunned silence, I nodded to Nirouphar and said: "Greetings, lady!" Then I turned upon Vardanas and said in Greek: "Herakles! Man, are you out of your mind?"

"What mean you, Leon?" said he, bristling. "If your men can drag a train of concubines all over Asia, why cannot I travel with my own sister, a virtuous and respectable maiden?"

"Gods! Dinna you see that sic a plan will fair ruin our expedition? We have no facilities for highborn ladies, and this running away from home will cause us untold trouble. It may bring disaster dire upon us. Take the lass back to Sousa; I'll not have her hung around our necks like an anchor stone."

"It is you who are mad, Leon. She will cause us no trouble—"

"Take her back, I say!" I shouted. "That's a command!"

"I will not."

"And who commands this hipparchia, my fine callant?"

"You do. You can dismiss me from your service. In that case, I will seek what employment I can find. But under no conditions will I return my sister to Sousa."

"What for no?"

170

"In our last quarrel we broke all filial ties. My father struck Nirouphar and would have beaten her had I not held him off by force. She swore she would never look upon him again, and I promised her I would not compel her to do so."

I almost burst out, consigning him and his pestilential sister to Arimanes and telling them to get out of my sight. Howsomever, caution held my tongue in check while I pondered the matter. Not only was Vardanas dear to me as a friend, but I had found him of priceless help in translating dialects, charming officials, scouting to find the best route, commanding the Dahas, and plying his mighty bow and deadly mace against our ill-wishers. Without him, our expedition had come to grief ten times over.

As bullying would plainly do no good, I resorted to reason. "Hearken, my dear friend. I have nought against the lass, who'd be a splendid ornament to any household. But suppose your father write the king or one of his governors, saying we've kidnaped his affianced bride and demanding punishment? Our mission were placed in peril, for I gather he's a man of influence."

"Fear not; he does not carry so much weight as he likes to pretend. And as officers of the king we are not without influence ourselves. I will say it is a private family quarrel, in which no outsider may meddle. Nought will come of Father's protests, if he make them."

"But even if you be right on that score, where shall she sleep? We have no lordly pavilions to assure her due comfort and privacy."

"That is simple. I will give her my tent and move in with you."

"Auramasdas save me from Persian generosity! I'd be blither of it if you did it the other way round; if—ah—"

He laughed. "You mean if I kept my tent and commanded her to occupy yours, you slavering satyr!"

He translated the jest into Persian, whereat Nirouphar laughed heartily, too. Persians, men and women alike, while far more modest than we about their persons, and no more incontinent, are extremely free with their speech. I have heard well-bred Persian ladies tell jokes that would shame a Corinthian bawd.

I made one more effort to regain the reins of our affairs. "But what shall she do for service? You brought no lady's maid with you, unless you can buy one in Babylon."

"I fear I shall never have enough money for that. Kerketas the Kolchian can do her heavier personal work, and mayhap I can hire one of the soldier's women to wash and tend her garments."

With a sigh of dismay and foreboding, I said: "So be it, then. But I take no responsibility for the dame or for any disaster that befall us on her account."

"I understand," he said.

Around the campfire that evening, I broached the subject to Vardanas again. Not that I had much hope of turning this headstrong chariot team from their course, once they had taken the bits in their teeth. Howsomever, every furlong's added distance from Sousa would make the maiden's return less likely. Therefore, this was my last chance.

"Vardanas," I said, "have you thought deeply on the upshot of this adventure of your sister, as regards your own future?"

"What mean you?"

"Will not your wrathful sire disinherit you, or whatever they do in Persia to offspring who flout them?"

"I suppose he might. I had not considered."

"A good family property," I went on, "is not lightly to be cast aside. With it one always has a place to go if all else fail. If you're moneyless, the family can send silver to fetch you home. If you're taken prisoner or seized by pirates or slavers, they'll redeem you. Many a good body has ended up chained to a galley bench or sweating in a mine for want of property to ward him."

"Mithras! I never thought of that." Vardanas sighed. "Perhaps I shall make it up someday with my father, who really loves us in his crabbed way. But I see not how or when this will come to pass."

"And what will you do with your sister meanwhile? She should have long since been safely wed."

"I do not know that, either. Mayhap I shall have to marry her myself, for want of well-born Arian men to give her to."

"*Pheu!* Another of your horrid Persian ideas. What will you do after we reach Athens? Your term of service ends there, unless you make arrangements to re-enlist."

Vardanas stared at the embers. "Auramasdas preserve me! Never have I planned so far ahead."

"Begin now, or you'll find yourself in Hellas ere you reach the next turn in the road."

"I suppose my bonus will support us for a while. Then perhaps I could enlist with some king or viceroy as a mercenary."

"If we get to Athens with our bonuses intact. I cast our accounts yesterday, and the results overjoyed me not."

"How so? Has somebody been stealing from the money chest?"

"I think not; the seal was intact. But we're running further and further behind schedule, so the whole cost of the journey is proving more than we thought. Also, everything I buy for the hipparchia seems to cost more than expected. Elisas says he does not understand these rising prices either."

"Are you sure the Syrian is not causing the sellers to charge extra and return part of the difference to him on the sly?"

"Again, I think not. We've been through that and understand each other. He may have a reasonable commission on purchases, but I keep a close watch upon him."

Vardanas shrugged. "I have never understood money. Ask Beliddinos. Babylonians know more about money than any other folk."

I put my problem to Beliddinos, who was quizzing the Dahas as to whether it was true that in their land the sun never shone. Quoth he:

"Simple it is when you understand it, my son; clear it becomes with explanation. Ever since the great Kyros set up the Persian Empire, to wring all gold and silver from their subjects has been the policy of the Persian kings. And what became of this wealth? Was it spent on public works to ease the lot of their subjects? Nay; it was piled up in bags of coin and bars of metal in Sousa and Hagmatana and Parsa, or made into statues. So, as precious metal became scarcer in the empire, business ran slower, for every man clutched what coins he had, not knowing when he would get his fingers on more."

I said: "That Gandarian guide, Kavis, said somewhat the same, though I did not expect an unlettered barbarian to understand these matters."

"Now," continued Beliddinos, "this vast treasure your Alexander seizes, and in an orgy of profusion spends it: leading armies to India, and paying his soldiers lavish bonuses, and ordering vast public works. Like the Tigris in spring, the stream of money in the empire rises. Now every man spends his money quickly, lest its value shrink while it lie in his wallet. So business thrives, and prices rise, and traders bless the name of Alexander."

"What will happen when he has spent all the Persian treasure?" I asked.

"By the four teats of Ishtar, that am I also curious to see! No doubt he will have to do as other kings: from his subjects' purses to rape more money to run his government and pay his soldiers. Then, perhaps, less deafening will sound the chorus of blessings!"

"You do not seem to think well of the way the Persians ran the empire," said Vardanas with an edge in his voice.

"They were men; therefore full of sin and folly were they. Before the Persians, ruled the Medes, and before the Medes, ruled the Babylonians and Assyrians, but I do not say they did any better. After the Persians have come the Hellenes, and we shall see how they fare. Through its cycle of empire runs each race, as ordain the stars. Who knows? Perhaps, after the Hellenes, some folk yet unheard-of may to the rule of the world arise."

We descended by gentle slopes through gaps in the low hills betwixt Sousiana and Babylonia. At our camping places Beliddinos performed a mighty exorcism to keep at bay the demons which, he said, lurked in the waste.

"It may be," he said, "that they be neither so common nor so fell as the reports of the vulgar make them out, but well it is on the safe side to be."

At first Vardanas sought to compel his sister to ride in the carts with the soldiers' women. But Nirouphar had other ideas. She preferred to ride horseback with the officers, and ride she did. For one thing, she was an excellent rider; for another, her trousered Persian woman's garb (which differs but little from that of the men) was well suited to equitation.

When Nirouphar dismounted for the midday meal, Vardanas forbade the grooms to give her a leg up when she went to mount. That halted her not; she simply vaulted upon her beast man-fashion and soon was jogging among us again.

"Shameless hussy!" exclaimed Vardanas. "How shall I preserve your innocence and purity if you persist in mixing with this crowd of strange, rough men? I am half minded to spank you."

"Try it, brother dear," she said.

He swung Rakous about as if to seize her bridle, but Nirouphar wheeled her mare and slipped to Pyrron's other side. Twice more Vardanas made as if to catch her, but she dodged out of his reach like a skillful player of stick-and-ball. The rest of us roared with laughter, giving poor Vardanas no support. Pyrron believed in greater freedom for women; Beliddinos had the prudence to keep out of others' disputes; while I, still deeming myself wronged by the Persian, took a grim satisfaction in his difficulties.

"Vardanas!" she said. "As you say, I am an ignorant girl who has led a sheltered life. But if I am to face the wide world, I must know about it for the safety of my honor. And how better to learn than from such traveled men of the world as you and your friends?"

"Oh, I give up! Ride the elephant if you like, but do not shame me before all."

"Now, that is an interesting thought!" She called up to Kanadas: "O mighty Indian, may I ride your beautiful beast?"

Presently she was swaying in the booth atop the elephant, like an Indian princess. Howsomever, when the novelty wore off, she clambered down and resumed her seat on horseback where she could more easily talk with the rest of us. For a while she quizzed Pyrron on the grammar of the Greek language, which she was making earnest efforts to master. When she wearied of this, she ranged her horse beside mine.

"O Rheon," she said, "tell me why you look so solemn and downcast! In Sousa you were gay and happy. What is your trouble?"

"You may well ask, madam, being my chief trouble yourself."

"I? Why, what do you mean?"

"Your brother consulted me not ere bringing you along. It was not only a surprise but also a most unwelcome one."

"Mithras! What have I done that is so dreadful?"

"It is not what you have done but what your father is likely to do, such as stirring up the king's officials against us. Troubles! I thought we had undergone every kind an ingenious and hostile Fate could devise, but when I saw you I knew that Fate's quiver was not yet empty. Moreover, a swiftly moving hipparchia like ours, on urgent business, is no place for a delicately reared lady. You will tire from our pounding pace, or sicken from our coarse food, or become bored and commit some womanish folly that will bring disaster upon us. Or the mere sight of your beauty will tempt some lewd lord or officer to attack us to gain you as a prize."

During my tirade, she had stiffened her lips to keep back the tears. Now she drew herself up and said: "My good Troop Leader, it were well if you came to know me before accusing me of weakness and folly."

"My dear Lady Nirouphar, as I explained to your brother, I have nought against you personally. But a hundred years' acquaintance with you would not alter the fact that you are a woman, and moreover a lady, which makes matters worse."

"You confuse me with one of your sheltered Greek milch cows who never see the outsides of their fathers' houses ere they wed. As you have seen, I can ride with the best, and at need I can fend for myself in other ways, too. However, I will keep out of your way and cause you as little bother as I can."

She betook herself to Beliddinos and thereafter used me with the same cold courtesy that had obtained between Vardanas and me at the start of our journey in India.

The road wound snakelike across the Babylonian plain, for the surface of this plain is cut up by coiling streams and pocked with lakes and marshes. Swarms of wildfowl flew overhead. In the distance, besides herds of antelope and wild asses, we sometimes saw ostriches. The Dahas went off in chase of them until I forbade it. While it cannot fly, the ostrich outruns a burdened horse with ease, and my lads never got within bowshot. Lions and leopards abounded

176

in the thickets, but we had had our lesson and suffered no more losses from these beasts of prey.

As the plain grew flatter and the watercourses larger, fields of sprouting grain became thicker. Here the Babylonians, mostly small dark folk, till their fabulously fertile soil.

A little group of horsemen with lances appeared in the distance, keeping us in sight but never coming close. They followed us all day. When they appeared the next day, I pointed them out to Beliddinos.

"Be wary," he said. "Perhaps a band of Kossian robbers are they." Then he returned to the theological argument in which he was engrossed. "If you like, I will concede that, as our various religions on one supreme deity agree, you could say that Auramasdas and Brachman and Zeus are but other names for Mardoukos. But it does not follow that the rituals are so effective, or the beliefs so true, or the morals so pure, of those who worship this god as Auramasdas, and so forth, as they are of those who revere him as Mardoukos."

"But all priesthoods say their doctrines are the truest," said Vardanas. "Thus our Magians say their doctrines come straight from the prophet Zarathoushtras, inspired by the good God."

"Come now," said Beliddinos. "Zarathoushtras may have been a good man, but he lived only a few centuries ago, whereas the holy traditions of Babylonia go back thousands of years. As our doctrines are the oldest, they must be the purest, because they have lasted the longest."

"I do not see how that follows. Rather they are more likely to have become corrupted in all that time."

"But everyone knows that the men of ancient times were closer to the gods and hence wiser than we!"

"I am not even sure of that," said Vardanas. "Time was when men made weapons of bronze, not knowing how to smelt iron. You cannot say knowledge had not advanced in that respect."

"The knowledge of how to slay each other more swiftly is no true advance in civilization."

"Well then, aside from the contradictory assertions of competing priesthoods, how shall we choose among the doctrines of the various religions? If they have things in common, they also disagree on many things. The myths of the Hellenes, for instance, say nothing about the evil spirit Arimanes, rival to Auramasdas for the rule of the universe."

"Maybe truth different to different men," said Kanadas. "Men see different parts of it, like story of blind men feeling elephant."

"That is like some of Pyrron's theories," said Vardanas. "It is a shame he cannot speak Persian, for he loves a disputation."

"What is his belief?" said Beliddinos.

"Why, he is actually an atheist! And such a good man in most ways, too."

"Like the Judaeans?"

"What are Judaeans?" I asked.

Beliddinos said: "A warlike, godless Syrian tribe whom for rebellion King Naboukodreusor deported. Many were settled in Babylonia, where still they dwell."

"Have they no gods at all?" I asked.

"Not quite. They have a bloodthirsty little tribal god called Iaves. But all other gods they impiously deny and contemn. They deem it sinful to make statues of gods, even of their own fierce Iaves."

"It does seem absurd," said Vardanas. "I am told the Judaeans' religion makes them haughty and forbidding, so they will not eat or treat with other men."

Kanadas clucked over the iniquities of the Judaeans, whereupon Vardanas burst into coarse laughter. "Behold him who speaks!" he cried. The Indian had the grace to look shamefaced.

"Not so hostile are all Judaeans," said Beliddinos. "Many are men of sense and virtue, and some have even come over to Mardoukos. But hard to deal with are their priesthood. I fear their intolerant doctrines are subversive of good order and morality. For, while we may argue points of doctrine among ourselves in an intellectual way, the sinful mass of men need impressive religions, with many gods, exciting myths, and beautiful images and ceremonies, to make them act virtuously. But the priesthoods must respect one another and not strive to undermine one another's creeds or divert one another's revenues. This insolent Judaean claim to a monopoly of all religion has in it the seeds of bloody upheavals and persecutions."

* * *

178

The plain was now broken only by occasional low mounds. Sometimes we saw none for leagues at a time, and again several were in sight at once. I gave them no thought until one morning Beliddinos was missing at marching time. I found him and his servants scratching at the surface of a nearby mound. When I taxed him with the delay, he smiled a vague, otherworldly smile and held up a slab of brick covered with bird-track writings.

"What is that?" I said.

"An ancient letter. It is of no value; the writer wants to know when the addressee will pay him for the five sheep as he promised. But it shows that here, too, stood a town in ancient times."

"Mean you this knoll was once a town?"

"So are they all." Beliddinos gestured round the horizon. "Folk build a town, and their houses crumble in the rains, and they cast them down and build new ones on the rubbish. Higher and higher rises the town, its own hill building, like the hills of Sousa." Beliddinos dropped the tablet, dusted his hands, and came back with me to the camp. "Were not my priestly duties so heavy, fain would I spend my life digging up the history of my people. In the mounds of Babylon is more history than in all the other books and inscriptions in the world."

"I envy your wisdom," I said, "but, while ancient history is a fine study, I find the modern world all I can keep up with." I cast a glance of perplexity toward Nirouphar, who, using her poor brother as interpreter, was trying to talk of cultural matters with Pyrron.

It became a nuisance, though, when Beliddinos began to run off from the hipparchia at every stop, to grub in a mound. Once he came back waving a brick and crying: "Soumerian!"

"What is that?" I asked.

"The kings of Soumer ruled this land just after the Flood. A few can still read their writing, though we know almost nothing about them."

Pyrron, when this was explained, quoted:

"The day shall come, the great avenging day,
Which Troy's proud towers in the dust shall lay!"

* * *

Beliddinos tenderly wrapped the tablet in a cloth and stowed it in a saddlebag. Meseemed he had two souls in one body. One was that of a shrewd, farsighted, self-possessed temple official, who took his sacred revenues seriously but not his theology. The other was that of an unworldly seeker after pure knowledge, whose true deity was not Mardoukos but Kleito, the muse of history.

That afternoon, the concubine of Trooper Machaon went into labor. We camped at once to await the birth. The pains went on for hours. The woman was still groaning and screaming after the stars had come out. The women clustered about, whispering big-eyed among themselves, muttering charms and fetching amulets. Word got around that this would be a hard birth if it came off at all.

Then Nirouphar and Pyrron went into Machaon's tent. The shrieks continued for another hour, then died out. Then came the thin first cry of an infant. The men broke into cheers and clapped Machaon on the back.

Later still, Nirouphar and Pyrron came out. I went up to them as they were washing their hands.

"I think all's well, old boy," said Pyrron. "It was a difficult birth, as we anticipated. When Nirouphar's strength proved insufficient, I was compelled to lend my own clumsy hands. And incidentally, our Persian beauty can make a living any time as a midwife. I, of course, have had experience from assisting my sister, but Nirouphar knows her way around the birth canal, too."

"It was nought," said Nirouphar. "Many a time and oft have I helped the women of our serfs with their deliveries. These troopers' women are as big boobies as our peasantry. To hear them, one would think that birth was wholly a matter of magical spells and not a natural event at all."

"Good, good for both of you," I said. "I've cooked your dinners myself, mistrusting our cook to do you justice. You must be starved."

Nirouphar gave me a sharp look. "So you do think of others' feelings sometimes, Troop Leader?"

I answered her sally not. But later, after she had eaten, I took her aside.

"Lady Nirouphar," I said, "I owe you an apology for thinking you a useless burden. You have earned your passage by today's work, for a successful delivery cheers the men while a death casts them down and leads them to find evil omens in every shadow. Pray accept the thanks of one who has not always used you with due courtesy."

"Very well. Let there be a truce between us at least. But I would have done the same in any case."

I saw that she had not really forgiven me, so I tried another approach. "Forbye, I need your help."

"So?"

"To keep the men well in hand, a hipparch needs to know what they are saying when he is not about. Thyestes and I thought Klonios would serve this purpose when we made him a double-pay man. Klonios is a fine old fellow, but he has been a common trooper too long to think like an officer."

"Well?"

"I see that you gossip a deal with the women. That is natural, but you can make your gossip serve the king's purposes. Most of the men tell everything to their women, and the women pass it around. Now, if you would—"

"So, you would have me tattle on your men because you cannot govern them yourself?"

"Madam, without such a source of news, no officer knows when his men are planning mutiny or desertion. They do not send a delegation to warn him; witness the plots against the divine Alexander himself."

"I would not blame the men for resenting your strictness."

"Forsooth, I am strict, but I try to be just. And we owe our lives to that strictness. Had I not pounded their battle drill into them, we had been lost when the Asagartians or the Houzans attacked us. Remember, these are not gentlemen, but ignorant, superstitious, lustful loons, good soldiers though they be. Remember also that your and your brother's safety are bound up with the hipparchia's discipline."

"I will keep my ears open. But look not for me to come running to you with every petty complaint I hear them utter."

Next morn I was brought out of my tent before dawn by a yell from the sentry: "Horse thieves!"

A group of Kossians had crept up and were cutting out two of our horses. They got their halters loose, mounted their own animals, and were starting to lead our beasts away when my lads ran out after them, naked or nearly so and waving swords and javelins. It looked bad, because the rest of our horses were not bridled. By the time they were, the thieves would be out of sight.

I was shouting commands and watching one of the Dahas string his bow when more yells made me turn. The horse theft had been but a feint. A dozen more Kossians rushed out from behind some nearby date palms while we were all watching the pursuit. They darted into the camp and began to snatch up whatever they could find and run back toward the palms, where their fellows held horses ready.

Those not already chasing the horse thieves rushed upon these new invaders. Kossian arrows whistled about our ears. I went after one robber making off with a saddlebag. The bag was so heavy that, even though the thief was better built for running than I, I gained upon him. As I came up he dropped the bag, but too late. Turning to see how close I was, he stumbled. Before he could recover, I sworded him well. Then I dragged the bag back to camp.

A single arrow from Madouas, the Daha who had been so prompt with his bow, had picked off the man leading our horses. Thereupon the other thieves fled, leaving two of their number dead.

A Thessalian was struck in the arm by a Kossian arrow, but the wound soon mended. Vardanas' Kolchian slave, however, had unwittingly gotten in the way of a Kossian, who stabbed him in the belly. The hurt did not seem grave, and we did what we could for the man.

In their haste, the thieves had seized all sorts of things like blankets and loaves of bread, but much of the loot they dropped in their flight. The only costly articles they got were a good helmet and an iron cooking pot.

The loot I recovered turned out to be the bag holding Beliddinos' written bricks. When he saw what was in it, Thyestes burst into a guffaw.

"You should have let the limmer get away, Leon!" he said. "'Twere a waur doom nor death itself, after dragging yon monstrous burden far over the plain, to open it and find nought but bricks within!"

182

Beliddinos looked sharply at my officer. Although the priest denied knowledge of Greek, I suspected him of knowing more than he pretended. He said:

"Mardoukos bless you, Hipparch. Though these tablets seem worthless to some, I would not sell them for seven talents of silver. Should you need help in these parts, do hot hesitate to call upon the Temple of Mardoukos."

We made good our damages as best we could and went on. Vardanas' slave, however, soon worsened and three days later died of a wasting fever. When we had buried him, Vardanas complained:

"This is terrible, Leon! Without my slave, I must care for my own gear like any baseborn pauper! And I shall never save enough from my pay to buy another."

I answered: "Cheer up, buckie! We have a saying in Thessalia:

"When the gentleman's faithful slave be dead,
The gentleman maun slave in his stead."

Seven days out of Sousa, we came to the Tigris River. For three days we followed its northern bank. Then we crossed by a bridge of boats. Aias, however, had to wade, for the villagers who kept up the bridge assured us that the elephant's weight would sink it. The brown water rose swirling to Aias' belly, but he made the passage without ill hap. The road continued west, parting from the Tigris. I like not the Babylonian plain, despite its fabulous fertility. The air is too hazy to see the horizon, and the land is cut up by canal banks, standing like earthen walls running in all directions and shutting off the view. The watercourses are also planted with endless rows of date palms. All this, after the immense clear views of Persia, gave me a closed-in feeling. Betimes I rode the elephant instead of my horse to see farther.

Nirouphar kept trying to pump all Pyrron's knowledge out of the poor man, despite the barrier of language. Although she could now speak a few simple sentences of Greek, her knowledge was quite inadequate for philosophical discourse. She essayed to enlist me as an interpreter, but after a morning's struggle I said:

"You are a charming young woman, Lady Nirouphar, but I cannot control my horse, command the hipparchia, round up stragglers, watch out for foes, compute our expenses, replenish the elephant's store of food, and translate Pyrron's philosophy into Persian all at once, especially as much of it I cannot understand myself. You must needs find another victim."

The only other man who was competent to interpret was Vardanas. Howsomever, when Nirouphar besought her brother to do so, he discovered that he had to take the Dahas on lengthy scouting rides to ward us from robbers and keep us from going astray in the maze of canals.

So Nirouphar's converse with Pyrron was reduced to simple language lessons. When her mind became weary with these, she ofttimes clambered up to sit with me in the booth on Aias' back, to ply me with questions about our adventures in the East and life in my homeland. The formal and distant manner in which she had been treating me inevitably mellowed. Had she been Greek, I might have been shocked by her unladylike forwardness, but in a foreigner it only added to her exotic charm.

"O Hipparch," she said, "my great ambition is to read and write Greek proficiently. When I was little I picked up a smattering of Greek from Dorymachos while he tutored my brothers. But I forgot nearly all of it, save the alpha-beta, for lack of practice until you came. Have I ever shown you my library?"

"Your library, Nirouphar?"

"You will not laugh?"

"By Zeus the king, I swear I will not!"

"Here it is." From her wallet she brought out a small roll of papyrus, a fragment torn from a larger book. With the greatest labor she began to read in Greek, syllable by syllable:

"The har-dy war-ri-ors whom Boi-o-tia bred,
Pen-e-le-os, Lei-tos, Pro-tho-e-nor led:
With these Ar-ke-si-la-os and Klo-ni-os stand,
E-qual in arms, and e-qual in com-mand ..."

* * *

184

Only the memory of my promise kept me from laughing at her pronunciation. I knew the text to be the closing part of Book Two of the *Iliad*, which some call the "Catalogue of Ships." It was the dullest and most difficult section of the epic she could have chosen. Still, she was vastly proud of such reading skill as she had.

"If Fate allow," I said, "someday you shall have a complete *Iliad*. I will read it over with you and explain the hard parts."

Thereafter we were friends, if not intimate ones. She reported the women's gossip to me without reserve. Soon I felt for her something more than friendship, admiration, and the simple animal lust which the sight of a comely lass arouses in any healthy youth, Athenians excepted.

I was, I feared, falling in love. In view of Vardanas' attitude toward non-Arian suitors, I knew not what to do about my passion. Vardanas would not entertain a suit for honorable marriage, and to ask Nirouphar to become my concubine would affront both Persians. It might even jeopardize our mission. So, for the time being, I kept a tense and uneasy silence.

As everybody knows, falling in love is something which a sensible man avoids. The man of sense relieves his lusts with light women, weds a girl of good family and ample dowry chosen by his parents, and goes through life without succumbing to the pleasant madness of love. At least, so our parents teach us. But, despite these wholesome moral precepts, most men seem to fall in love sooner or later and become prey to the follies which that state entails. Perhaps the precepts need revision to make them fit the nature of men more closely.

I was not the only one to feel thus. A warm affection sprang up between Nirouphar and the elephant. The lass was always fussing over him and bringing him dainties, until he paid more heed to her than to any of the men.

"O fickle monster!" said Vardanas. "We wear the soles from our shoes and the seats from our trews, fetching this creature from India. We save it from a hundred deaths by starvation, thirst, and the weapons of evildoers. And then the ungrateful animal jilts us for a flutter-witted jade!"

* * *

Beliddinos, as I have stated, had two sides to his character: that of a zealous seeker after historical knowledge, and that of a shrewd and worldly temple official. As we neared Babylon, however, he displayed another aspect: his official character as head of the chief cult of the world's greatest city. Day by day he became more solemnly unctuous and dignified. He addressed us all as "my son," called upon Mardoukos and his other grim Babylonian gods to witness every statement, and scattered blessings, exorcisms, and other sacred formulae like rain.

Only rarely, now, could one catch the flicker of amusement that used to pass over his lean, ascetic face during a solemn pronouncement of divine intent or cosmic doom. By the time we reached Babylon, those who had not known him in his holiday mood would never have thought him other than as the holiest, loftiest, purest pontiff in the world, devoted to the glory of his dour divinities.

And so, at the beginning of Gamelion, we came to Babylon. First the villages clustered more thickly, and we passed fair estates and villas.

"Most of these were built by noble Babylonians," said Beliddinos. "But, because of their sins, great Mardoukos allowed the Persian kings from their owners to take them and to their Persian supporters to give them."

Then we reached the outer or suburban wall of the city. This is a low brick wall three hundred furlongs around. It is merely to keep Arab raiders and other robbers out of the suburbs, not to provide a strong defense.

We passed through this wall and marched league upon league through an ever-thickening pattern of villages and wheat fields. Some people ran at the sight of the elephant. When it was seen that we meant no harm, hundreds of naked brown children swarmed after us, yelling, chasing one another, and begging.

Then the main walls loomed over the lines of date palms like a chain of mountains. Pyrron, with Vardanas acting as translator, was arguing the shape of the earth with Beliddinos. He said that it was round, the Babylonian that it was flat. Pyrron dropped his learned reasoning to whistle at the sight of the walls.

"Zeus on Olympos!" he said.

If he, who had seen Babylon before, was so struck by the sight, you can imagine the effect of this colossal if worn and shabby old city on me who had never seen it. I had missed it on my way east because my troop was sent straight from Opis to Hagmatana.

The main wall of Babylon is about thirty cubits high and so wide that two four-horse chariots can pass one another between the towers. These towers bestride the wall every hundred cubits and are nearly twice as high as the wall itself. I was told that the wall is eighty furlongs in circumference (with gaps where the Euphrates flows through the city) so a prudent man does not set out for a stroll around the city on the wall after dinner, as he may in most cities. Yet diligent scrutiny showed that the brickwork was crumbling in many places. Brickers moved about the wall, repairing it, but it would take an army of them to keep ahead of the decay.

The guards waved us through the east gate. As far as my eye could see stretched rows of houses. Here and there the ground rose to a low hill crowned with palaces or temples. It was as if some god had picked up all the cities in the world and set them down together in a clump.

"How finds a man his way about so vast a place?" I asked Beliddinos.

"Not difficult is it when streets are straight," he said. The main streets are indeed nearly straight and cross at right angles, as in Peiraieus.

"If you like," the priest continued, "I will show you the way to my temple. Perhaps we can quarter you on the sacred precincts."

"Many thanks," I said. "That were a princely kindness!"

As we rode, the traffic waxed denser. Never have I seen such a throng of moving people, save when refugees flee an invasion.

"Is aught amiss in the city, that such masses swarm the streets?" I said.

"No. This is the hour when men go home from work. Like this every morn and even it is."

We came to the inner city wall, smaller than the main wall but still a decent defense. Inside the inner wall we passed a huge open space piled with broken brick.

"What is that?" I said.

"Those are the remains of the great Tower of Babylon, or as we called it the *zikoras* of Mardoukos. It stood yonder." Beliddinos pointed ahead of us. "Three hundred cubits it rose above the plain. From its top one could see from Sippara in the north to Nippor in the south; from its lofty peak the will of the gods as revealed in the stars we studied."

"What happened to it?"

"In the years following our trouble with the first Xerxes, the tower was neglected. Unfilled were cracks; stolen from the casing were bricks. By the time Alexander came, into a vast heap of rubble it had crumbled. Orders to rebuild it he gave. So his men have hauled the bricks of the old tower over here and dumped them, but they have not yet begun work on the new."

As we went on along the Street of Mardoukos, as this avenue is called, traffic got thicker and thicker. At the crossing of two broad avenues, a packed mass of travelers halted us. Slowly we edged up to the crossing. I was about to lead the hipparchia across when a Babylonian civic watchman, with a bronzen helm on his head and a stone-headed club suspended from his belt, stepped into the center of the crossing. He blew a blast on the ram's horn. Then he flung out his arms with palms turned outwards, as if to halt us and those coming toward us from the opposite direction.

"What is this?" I said, starting to guide Golden across.

"Stop!" cried Beliddinos, catching my mantle. "He is a—how would you say it—a commander of traffic. Everybody below the rank of king, general, or governor must obey his commands."

I halted. Amazingly, all traffic east and west through the crossing halted too, obedient to the guard's gestures. Now he turned so as to face east and made beckoning motions with both arms. At once the traffic between north and south began to flow. I sat impatiently while horses, mules, asses, camels, oxcarts, wains, chariots, litters, a flock of goats, and hundreds of folk afoot, bearded men and veiled women, poured past in front of me.

"How long does this take?" I asked. "Must we stand here till nightfall?"

"Nay; the traffic man will soon beckon us. In a city of such size we cannot let traffic manage itself, lest the streets be hopelessly blocked and confusion reign."

The watchman stepped out again, halted the flow between north and south, and beckoned us onward. Seeing that I commanded the hipparchia, he gave me a salute with his club as I passed. I waved to him and rode on.

After a jog to the left, we reached the Street of Adados, a broad avenue leading westward to the Euphrates River. Before it reached the river it passed between two sacred places. On the left stood the temple of Mardoukos, which the Babylonians call Esagila, or the Lofty-headed Temple. On the right was a great temple compound where aforetime rose the Tower of Babylon, which was called Etemenanki, the Cornerstone of the Universe.

Beliddinos guided us to the left, into the grounds of the temple. Amidst the groves stood a small temple, very old-looking. Dragons in enameled relief paraded around its worn brick walls; gilded ornaments on its cornices gleamed in the setting sun. To one side were signs of construction, where a space had been cleared and the raising of walls begun. The new building, as planned, was larger than the old, and together they made a shape like a thick letter *gamma*.

"There," said Beliddinos, "the new temple of Mardoukos stood ere Xerxes razed it and raped away the great golden statue of the god. Since then we have used the old temple, but with your king's help and the favor of the gods we hope to restore the new. You understand, by 'new' I mean a mere two hundred and fifty years old."

Priests and temple servants came running to greet their master. Those of higher degree kissed his hands, while the lowlier ones bowed to the ground. There was much formal blessing and invocation of the gods, for the Babylonians are a ceremonious folk. A group whom I took to be Beliddinos' family swarmed out of a walled enclosure to greet him also, albeit less formally. At last Beliddinos said: "Come, Hipparch."

He led us across the avenue to the grounds of the tower. The site where once the tower rose is a broad bare dusty place, like a parade ground, surrounded by low buildings arranged in a hollow square. In these buildings the lesser priests and attendants dwell, and pilgrims from other parts of the country stay. Here room was found for us and our beasts. Scented soap fit for kings and high priests was given us to wash with.

Evening—which, as says the Poetess, brings together all that the light-giving dawn has scattered—fell softly. Priests and pilgrims clustered about us, showering us with questions about the elephant. What did he eat? Was it true that elephants lived a thousand years? Had he any joints in his legs?

Weary though we were, it was late at night when the sweet sound of hymns, wafting from Esagila, lulled us to sleep.

Thenceforth we saw little of Beliddinos, who was swallowed up by his duties, as a hero of Babylonian myth, named Ionas, was swallowed up by a whale. Though still cordial when he saw us, he was no longer intimate, but brisk, suave, and dignified, as one must be to put great designs into effect without revealing one's inner self. The morning after we arrived, Beliddinos presented to me a man whose name, he said, was Peithagoras of Amphipolis, a student of divinatory science at the temple of Mardoukos.

"He will show you about and guide you to the offices of the government," he said.

"Rejoice, Hipparch," said Peithagoras, a Hellene who had taken to Babylonian ways. He curled his beard, used perfume, wore a long robe with sleeves, and carried a walking stick with the top carven in the shape of an eagle. At the same time he affected the most extreme Attic dialect, as to remind his hearer that Amphipolis was an Athenian colony.

"My dear old thing," he said, "there's no use going to the offices today. All the chaps are at some beastly conference. Let me send my slave to make you an appointment with my brother's secretary."

"Your brother?"

"General Apollodoros. Perhaps the general himself could give you a moment, though he's frightfully busy, you know. Meanwhile let's look about the temple. Their divinatory methods are centuries ahead of ours. I'm a student of these things, you know. Who's that simply divine young Persian with you?"

"Vardanas of Sousa."

"Fetch him along; fetch him along. And any others who want to come."

I called out my officers and Nirouphar and Pyrron and made them known to Peithagoras, who led us about the temple compounds with his tongue wagging like a poplar leaf in the breeze.

"Now here, darlings," he said, "is the hepatoscopy room. They call that chap fiddling with the sheep's guts a *machos*." He spoke in hesitant Syrian to the blood-smeared diviner, who answered.

"The liver-gate is long on the right side and short on the left," said Peithagoras. "That means our arms will be successful. Now in here is the astrological library. All those stacks of bricks are reports on the aspects of the heavenly bodies. The astrologers claim their records go back to the Flood, thirty-four thousand years ago. Let's see—ah—here's one. Reign of—ah—Naboupalesar. I can't really read these ghastly little scratches yet, though I'm learning. Isn't it wonderful, darlings, that by taking a few sights on the planets and a little calculating, you can tell your state of health and wealth and welfare a month or a year or a decade from now? It never fails, if you remember to take every aspect into account."

He rattled on like that for hours. I recalled that Beliddinos, who ought to know about such matters if anyone did, was much more skeptical about the prophetic powers of astrology, but I forbore to contend the matter.

Peithagoras showed us other sights, like the golden statue of Mardoukos, glowing softly in the dim light of the old temple. This statue was not the one that Xerxes stole, but the one he left behind. It showed the god, long-bearded and stern, seated upon a golden throne. Coiled about his feet, also worked in glowing gold, was a lizardlike dragon, called a *sirous* by the Babylonians. This beast was also depicted on the outer walls of the temple and on the knob of Beliddinos' walking stick. The air was heavy-laden with incense, and somewhere out of sight a chorus was practicing a hymn with a wailing up-and-down tune. Peithagoras said:

"These blighters say the statue weighs eight hundred talents of solid gold, but I think if we bored into it we should find a wooden core with a thin golden covering. Don't try it, though; my priestly friends wouldn't like it. Now let's go outside, O best ones. This incense gives me a perfectly foul headache."

He took us out on the river wall, so we could look up and down the Euphrates as far as the hazy air permitted. North of this spot, the river makes a sharp bend, passing around the citadel. Thence it flows slowly southward past the sacred enclosures.

Below us, long lines of wharves and quays spread out to north and south along this bustling waterway. There were great sluggish barges piled with produce and moved by poling. There were sharp-nosed little sailing vessels with overhanging bows and sloping masts. There were timber rafts, heaped with brushwood for fuel, drifting down from the Assyrian mountains.

Strangest were bowl-shaped vessels of stitched hides, perfectly round, floating downstream piled with melons and other cargo, each with a hobbled ass reposing on its side atop the load. The boatman keeps this curious vessel in midstream by an occasional stroke with a square-bladed paddle until he reaches his proper wharf. Then, with much splashing and spinning, he forces the bowl-boat to shore. When he has unloaded, the boatman sells the wooden framework of the boat along with his cargo, rolls up the leathern covering, ties it upon the ass, and sets out upstream again.

While others took in the view, I cast a glance over my people. It cost me a pang to see Nirouphar shamelessly clutching Pyrron's arm. Peithagoras sidled up to Vardanas and spoke low in his ear. The Persian turned a dark face upon him and spoke a curt "No!"

"Don't be nasty about it, darling," said Peithagoras. "I can get prettier boys than you any time. Not every blighter gets a chance to befriend one so well connected as I."

He left Vardanas and went to work on Kanadas. Presently I heard the Indian growl something in his native tongue and spit into the river.

"By the twelve postures of Kyrene!" said Peithagoras. "What crowd of barbarians have I fallen into? But come, old things, it's time for lunch. Perhaps a drop of wine will soften your hearts."

The afternoon I spent on the business of the hipparchia: writing the king, counting our money, and conferring with Thyestes and Elisas. According to our figures, if we were very thrifty and traveled swiftly, we could reach the Syrian coast with the soldiers' discharge bonuses intact but hardly anything to spare. It would be hard to last out the sea voyage from Syria to Athens without spending any money, as the voyage would be long and slow with many stops.

"There's no doubt," said I, "that we must present our money order to Harpalos for more funds."

"Aye, buckie," said Thyestes. "If the king's own treasurer willna honor it, who will?"

"Think you I should call the men together to explain our plight?"

"Na, you mauna. 'Tis only the thought of those lovely bonuses that keeps the lads under rein. By Zeus, let them think the silver's not likely to last, and they'll plunder the cotters or desert. As it is, 'twill be a prodigy gin we lose not one or two in this fornicating great city, by desertion, murder, or some sic way."

"Tell them to go in pairs on leave and wear their swords at all times," I said, "and gif I find they've started any trouble with the Babylonians, I'll make them wish they'd never left Thessalia."

A pity it is that I did not take my own advice.

Two days later I rode forth on Aias, with Peithagoras, to attend General Apollodoros' secretary. First we crossed a great bridge with boat-shaped stone piers that carries the Street of Adados across the Euphrates. Then, at Peithagoras' direction, I turned north and followed a winding course up the right bank.

Peithagoras, as excited as a child over his elephant ride, babbled unceasingly. He pointed out the canals and overflow basins with which the Babylonians try to tame their mighty river. The wharves swarmed with merchants, shouting and waving their hands as they chaffered. The Babylonians gathered in gabbling crowds to see the elephant as he lumbered past, but we proudly pretended not to notice them.

We followed the bend of the Euphrates where it flows around three sides of the citadel. At the southeast corner of the citadel we turned north on a wide avenue paved with great slabs of stone. On each side rose a brick wall. Along the base of these walls strode long lines of life-sized lions, depicted in low relief in bright enameled brick, some white with yellow manes and some yellow with red manes.

There were also a number of brick posts several feet high along both sides of the street, separating the walkers along the sides from the beasts of burden in the middle. I have never seen such shrewd and splendid street construction in a Hellenic city.

"This is Enemy Street," said Peithagoras. "It has a long Babylonian name meaning 'The Street Whereon May No Enemy Ever Tread,' but it's called 'Enemy Street' for short. They carry Mardoukos along this way when he visits Ishtar in the spring festival. You should be here in Elephabolion; the Babylonians put on a perfect whiz of a parade."

Enemy Street was a furlong in length. At the far end rose the largest gate in the world. Two colossal brick towers loomed over it, and round them stood smaller fortifications.

"The celebrated Ishtar Gate," said Peithagoras. "And there are the equally famous Hanging Gardens." He pointed to a mass of greenery looming over the wall of the citadel, to the left of the Ishtar Gate. "I say, have the driver stop this creature. Here's where we go in."

We clambered down and marched in through a double door in the wall of the citadel. This door, dwarfed by the Ishtar Gate though large by most standards, was set in a doorframe that was painted bright red to scare away the demons.

Inside was a pair of anterooms. In one, Greek guards lounged; in the other, taxpayers stood in line to give their money to clerks, who entered the payments in ledgers and wrote out receipts. Then we came to a big open court swarming with people, and round about it the entrances to more offices. The air was full of Greek, Persian, Syrian, and other tongues.

I will not tell how I was passed from clerk to clerk and from secretary to secretary until I was dizzy; the details are now hazy. Harpalos, I learnt, was still in Tarsos and had not yet sent word that he was making his winter trip to Babylon. Menes I should find at Alexandreia-by-Issos, where he was building a new city for Alexander.

Half the folk I saw seemed to be idling or gossiping, while the other half worked frantically to clear their tables of mountains of documents. At length I was passed up to General Apollodoros himself, Peithagoras' brother, a man of much my own size and shape but older. Peithagoras told him of my mission.

"Good for you!" bellowed Apollodoros, and clapped me on the back. "India to Athens on an elephant, eh? By the God! You could write a book about it. Now what's all this about fodder and stuff?"

He gave the necessary orders. As I was bidding him farewell, another Hellene passed the door of the chamber. Apollodoros shouted:

"*Ē! Agathon!*"

The man, a native of Pydna in Methone, turned out to be the commandant of the citadel. He questioned me about India until I protested: "I could talk all day about my journey, gentlemen, but I must get back to my hipparchia. The elephant will be getting hungry."

Peithagoras said: "Why not invite the hipparch to tomorrow's feast, brother dear? Then you could question him to your heart's content."

"It pleases," said Apollodoros. "Tomorrow at sundown in the Hanging Gardens. How about the other officers of your troop? Who are they?"

I listed them. He invited Thyestes, Vardanas, Pyrron, and Kanadas.

"Shall I get boys or girls for any of these people?" said Apollodoros. "How about you, for instance?"

I did not want to go into tedious explanations to the effect that, albeit I preferred girls, there was now only one lass I wanted. Vardanas, too, would prefer a girl, and so would Thyestes. Pyrron and Kanadas would be just as happy without companions.

"Have two good, bouncing wenches for Troop Closer Vardanas and Flank Guard Thyestes," I said. "That's all."

When we came out on Enemy Street again, we found Siladites in a dispute with a Babylonian watchman. The argument lost no vim from the fact that neither could understand the other.

Peithagoras spoke Syrian to the guard, who waved his club and jabbered. Peithagoras said to me: "Oh, dash it all! It seems we've broken some of their beastly traffic laws."

"How now?" said I. "We've not driven Aias in a drunken or reckless manner."

"No, but it's forbidden to stand a beast or vehicle on Enemy Street. The sign says so."

"What sign?"

"This." Peithagoras pointed with his stick to the nearest of the brick posts. I saw, now that I looked closely, that the column was inscribed with writings in the Syrian and Babylonian languages.

"How am I supposed to read that stuff?" I said. "What says it?"

Peithagoras peered at the post and conferred with the guardsman. "Let's see—ah, that's it. It says: ROYAL ROAD. LET NO MAN LESSEN IT, ON PENALTY OF LAW. BY COMMAND OF BOUPARES, GOVERNOR, FOR DAREIOS, KING OF KINGS. This blighter also claims that crowds gathered to see the elephant and blocked traffic."

"What should I do now? Slay myself?"

"I'll manage it, darling." Peithagoras spoke low to the guard and passed him a coin. The guard smiled, saluted, and went his way.

I was trying on the new shirt that Vardanas persuaded me to buy when he came to me and said: "Leon, I am in a strait."

"What?" I said.

"You say General Apollodoros will have a woman for me at the feast. But now Nirouphar insists that I escort her thither."

"I suppose you refused; no Hellene would take his sister to such an affair."

"No, I did not refuse. We are not so bigoted in Persia. Besides, you know not my sister. She has a mind of her own and a burning curiosity."

"Well, what then is the problem?"

"Kanadas and Pyrron have declined the general's invitation, and I really do not think I can manage two women at once."

"And you a polygamous Persian? Shame on you!"

"It is not so much a matter of numbers as the fact that Nirouphar and I have quarreled. We are on strained terms."

"What about?"

"I gave her twenty-five drachmai to buy us some things we needed, and, do you know, the abandoned wench spent every drachma on a Babylonian gown? It is not only a foreign fashion, but an indecent one, being so thin that she might as well be naked. She has no more sense about money than a rabbit."

"Hearken to the god of thrift and prudence! But I see the solution to your problem. I will escort your sister fair, leaving you free to cope with your Babylonian wench."

"Splendid! I knew I could count on you," he said.

With my gear newly polished, I awaited with pounding heart for the sight of Nirouphar in her transparent Babylonian gown. Alas! She appeared in her regular Persian coat and trousers, for Vardanas had given the gown to Elisas with orders to sell it for what he could get.

We rode Aias to the citadel. Warned by my experience of the day before, we sent the beast back with Siladites, with orders to return for us in three hours. We entered the courtyard that I had seen the previous day, passed through doors into another court, and turned right into an alley between two rows of houses. Others streamed into this alley with us, men and women in the varied garb of many nations. After fifty paces, the corridor opened out. There stood one of the world's great wonders, the fabulous Hanging Gardens of Babylon.

These gardens, so-called, are really an enormous building at the northeast corner of the citadel, so constructed that it looks more like a hillock covered with greenery than a work of mortal man. The ground floor of this building is open on three sides and surrounded by a wide border of trees and shrubs. Stout stone pillars and arched vaults of brickwork support a massive roof, bedight around its edge with gilded dragons, lions, and other creatures.

Atop the roof, in a thick layer of soil, stands a grove of trees and shrubs, many of them rare and exotic. I learned that Harpalos the treasurer, when he resided in Babylon, brought such plants at vast expense from distant lands and planted them here, being an enthusiastic gardener like Artaxerxes the Resolute. Harpalos also refurbished the Hanging Gardens building, which had fallen into disrepair.

Spacious stairways lead to the roof. In summer the rulers of Babylon hold feasts by moonlight in the delightful roof garden, looking out over Babylon as the gods were once thought to look out over the works of man from their seat on Olympos. Now, however, because the air was cool with the threat of rain, the tables were laid on the lower level. Still, strange it was to eat in a great gilded hall and look outwards, not at walls, but at masses of greenery.

A machine of chains and leather buckets hoists water from a well in the vaults below the building right up through the ground floor to the roof, where the water runs through channels in the gardens and pours in little artificial waterfalls over the edge of the roof to wet the gardens on the lower level. This apparatus is kept groaning and squealing night and day by slaves who endlessly turn windlasses in the bowels of the building.

Apollodoros, a wreath on his hair, met us at the entrance. The women he had procured for us were a pair of bay fillies named Nin-Zerbanis and Nin-Nika, behung with shawls and veils and ribbons and gewgaws. Zerbanis, who was short and plump, he presented to Thyestes, while Vardanas received Nika, a large and solidly built dame.

"Hoots, what a bonny deemie!" cried Thyestes in broad Thessalian. "General Apollodoros, my lord, you ken what makes a soldier happy!"

Apollodoros smiled and led us to couches which we shared with our companions. So long had it been since I had reclined at a meal that I scarcely remembered how to behave. Most of our companions were Greek officers of the forces at Babylon, but sprinkled among them were Babylonians, Persians, and other foreigners. Most of the diners, also, were accompanied by women—of no high degree, if I could judge—or by painted pleasure boys. A handsome middle-aged Persian was presented to me as Stamenes, viceroy of Babylonia.

As soon as we were settled, the Hellenes began throwing questions about my journey. As I was feeling gay and friendly, I so let my tongue wag that only by catching the words in my teeth did I avoid blurting out something about the money we bore.

In a corner, an orchestra of harps, lutes, flutes, cymbals, and drums played wailing music, and a music girl sang in Syrian a naughty song that began: "In the street I saw two harlots."

With an effort I kept myself from staring at Nirouphar, who looked so beautiful in her Babylonian coiffure and cosmetics that my heart ached. We talked in Persian between bites, on what subjects I recall not.

I like the Babylonian ways of cooking meat, albeit I do not care much for roast grasshoppers, and their vegetables (lentils, endives, and lettuce) are tender and delicious. I boggled a bit at the salted bats, which in Babylonia grow to the size of pigeons. In the end I found my bat edible, but there was hardly enough meat on the creature to repay the trouble.

The fruit—peaches, apricots, plums, and figs—was being served when I first caught a glimpse of Stamenes, the viceroy, and Agathon, the commandant, talking low and staring at me. Stamenes leant back in a carven chair while the Hellene bent over his shoulder and spoke in his ear. As soon as I looked at them, they turned their gaze away. I did not quite like the look of things; but, since I was full of good food and inflamed with love of Nirouphar, my suspicions were hard to arouse.

The wine was proffered, along with beer and palm wine, though I have never cared for these latter when real wine could be had. A trumpet blast signaled the libation. I noticed that most of the Hellenes had adopted the foreign habit of drinking their wine straight, even as I had. Apollodoros stood up, made a speech, and presented me to the company.

"Get up and tell them what you have told me about your journey, Troop Leader Leon," he said.

I had liefer fallen through the floor, but I rose on quaking legs and looked out over a meadow of gleaming cuirasses, shimmering silks, rings and other baubles winking in the lamplight, and wine-flushed faces.

"Though no orator," I began, "I'll try to give you a truthful tale, unadorned by tricks of rhetoric…"

I launched into my account. For the first half hour all went well. Then the audience began to fidget, cough, whisper, and make love to their companions. I raised my strong voice and kept on. I had got the hipparchia as far as Karmana when I felt a tug on my shirt tail.

It was Vardanas. "Cut it short," he hissed. "You are boring them."

"So from Karmana we came to Babylon, and here we are. Oh, there were a few small adventures like being attacked by nomads and lions, but nought to speak of. Thank you for your attention." I sat down.

The audience cheered, no doubt in relief that I was not going on all night, and began to talk among themselves. Soon the music could hardly be heard above the roar of voices.

Apollodoros stood up and belched. "Now hear this!" he shouted. "It's time our fair guests showed us some of the dances for which

Babylon is famous. Get up, girls, and go to it. What's that abandoned tune you dance to?"

Somebody spoke to the orchestra, which burst into a wild tune. About twenty women, including Zerbanis and Nika, let themselves be pushed out to the middle of the floor, whence tables and couches were drawn back.

The oldest of the women lined the others up in pairs, facing each other, gave them directions, snapped her fingers, and led the first figure—a lively affair with much spinning, arm waving, stamping, and finger snapping. Bright-colored skirts and robes billowed and whirled.

Anon, at a signal from the leader, the women doffed their shawls and veils and threw them in a heap in the center of the floor.

Now the orchestra changed to a slow dreamy tune. The women moved with slinking, serpentine motions. At another signal, they shed their outer robes and tossed them on the heap.

The orchestra played a martial tune; the women marched about in warlike poses. After a while the men began to shout: "Take it off! Take it off!" Off came their jackets to join the heap on the floor.

I felt a nudge and heard Vardanas' voice: "Nirouphar and I must go, Leon. I do not mind the show, but this is no place for a Persian girl of good family."

"But—" I began as he took Nirouphar's arm and forcibly drew her away from me. She protested and hung back, but he was the stronger.

"Nin-Nika will keep you company," he called back.

I wanted Nin-Nika not, nor did I want to start a dispute in public. Angry and unhappy, I turned my eyes back to the dance.

Now the orchestra caterwauled as if in deepest grief, and the women went through motions of mourning.

"Take it off!" yelled the men. Thyestes was among the loudest shouters. He pounded his table and screamed at his Zerbanis.

Off came the skirts, leaving the lassies in thin shirts and gay petticoats. A yearning tune brought off the shirts; and a furiously passionate melody, the petticoats. The women danced naked but for jingling ornaments.

In a frenzy of lust, Thyestes vaulted over his table, picked up Zerbanis (who must have weighed nigh as much as he) and bore her out of the hall. I had a glimpse of him as he carried her up a stair lead-ing to the roof garden. Other men did likewise with their wenches. Drinking vessels fell to the floor; men tripped over couches and fell. Fights broke out. The noise was deafening.

All of a sudden the breath was knocked out of me by a heavy weight that landed in my lap. I found my arms full of Nika, clutch-ing my neck, pressing her big brown breasts against me, smothering me with kisses, and muttering in broken Greek: "I love! You come! I make happy!"

Now, I am ordinarily cautious almost to the point of timidity, but under the circumstances I do not think I can be blamed for yielding to overwhelming forces. Besides, I was always so grateful to any woman who was not repelled by my plainness that I could deny her nought. I got up unsteadily, saying: "Hold it, lass; wait till I get this fixed."

For, what with the wine, the scenes I had witnessed, and this pas-sionate assault upon me, I found when I stood up that the hang of my kilt left something to be desired in soldierly smartness.

"You come! I show!" she panted.

She led me almost at a run out of the hall. Instead of taking one of the stairs to the roof garden, howsomever, she led me into one of the corridors between the rows of governmental buildings surround-ing the Hanging Gardens. Save for an occasional wall lamp, the place was almost entirely dark. I should have fallen on my face but that my guide knew the way.

Then suspicion began to edge passion out of the saddle. I braced my feet and slowed the woman's rush.

"Whoa!" I said. "Not so fast, kimmer. Whither away?"

She paused for breath, and a noise made me turn. But it was too late. Strong arms caught my wrists and twisted them behind me. I tore one arm loose and threw off the man who clutched it, but, ere I could do more, something smote me on the pate, and I swooned away in a shower of stars.

I awoke in a dark prison cell, shackled to the wall, with a lump on my head like the egg of a goose. When I had drunk a bowl of water left within my reach, I felt life return despite a headache. My indignant shouts brought a jailer. Instead of answering my questions, he shuffled off.

Presently there came the sound of many feet and the light of lanterns in the gloom. A cockscomb helmet shadowed the face of Agathon, the commandant. The other well-clad visitor was Stamenes, the viceroy. A pair of armed men of great girth and thew walked behind them.

"Awake, I see," said Agathon, grinning. "People who visit our fair city should pay more heed to our ordinances. With so much street traffic we must needs be strict, lest chaos ensue."

"What mean you?"

"Come, come, Thessalian, you know well enough. You left your elephant standing in a forbidden zone; you blocked traffic by causing a crowd to gather; and lastly you tried to bribe an officer of the law in the performance of his duty."

"I bribed nobody!" I shouted. "It was that Peithagoras who paid the guard."

"My, such a beastly temper! We know otherwise. Now we come to the penalty. We've been punishing such offenses lightly, but too many evildoers flout our just laws. It's time we made an example. So we've dug back into the archives."

"Long way back," said the Persian. "Babylonians wonderful. Keep records back to creation of world."

"And we've found just what we need!" said Agathon. "My dear fellow, you'll die when you hear. Back when the Assyrians ruled the land, some old king named Sennakrops—"

"Sennacheribos," said Stamenes.

"—decreed that any man who left beast or vehicle standing in a forbidden zone should be slain, and his body impaled on a stake before his house as a warning. Now, as you don't dwell here, we can't impale you in front of your house—"

"But can kill, oh yes!" said Stamenes, drawing a finger across his throat.

"However," said Agathon, "as you're one of the king's valued servants, we don't really wish to do anything so horrid. We'd rather let you off with a fine. Now, we know you're taking chests of treasure to Hellas. If you'll tell us where they are, the fine will be adjusted accordingly."

I thought. By "adjusting the fine" the Methonean meant setting the forfeiture at whatever sum we had with us. Any excuse will serve a tyrant, as it says in the fable.

While they probably would not kill me ere they got possession of the chests, for fear they might not be able to find them without my directions, it was likely that, as soon as they seized the treasure, they would slay me, regardless of promises, lest I report their crimes to the king. Therefore, my game was to keep them from finding the chests as long as I could. I said:

"When we entered the city, we buried the chests in one of those piles of broken brick from the Tower of Babylon."

The two officials traded glances. Agathon said: "That tells us little, my friend. There are millions of bricks in that dump. To search it through would take a lifetime."

"Look beneath the piles nearest the inner city wall," I said. "The chests are under the second heap in from the Street of Mardoukos."

They went away, leaving me in darkness. Time passed with heavy-footed tread. I was fed and watered enough to keep me alive. I thought sadly of Nirouphar, whom I might never see again. I listened to the rustle of mice, scratched the bites of countless vermin, and cursed my folly in letting down for a moment the bars of my suspicion.

I thought that surely my hair must be turning gray with age when Agathon and Stamenes came back. I knew that days had passed since they had been there last, though how many days I could not tell, for no daylight came into the crypt.

This time they brought with them a man who bore a kit of tools which I soon recognized as those of a professional torturer. Agathon said:

"So, little old Leon plays jokes on us, eh? But important officials like us don't care for jokes. This gentleman" (he pointed to the torturer) "will entertain you for a while. Then we shall ask where the money is, and if you don't give us the truth, well..."

I set my teeth. The executioner heated his tools in a brazier.

"You shall rue this outrage," I said, repeating my words in Persian for Stamenes' benefit. "The king will impale you. My orders are to write him every few days. If the letters stop, he'll know that ill hap has befallen me."

"We don't fear the polluted king," said Agathon. "He'll never return. Grab the blighter, boys."

The two muscular guards seized me and stretched me out despite my struggles. Unchained and well fed, I could surely have handled one at least. As it was, howsomever, I could do little but curse and threaten.

At the first touch of the hot iron I gave a fearful yell. "I'll tell!" I said.

It was not very heroic, but I was sure they would sooner or later find and seize the chests and then slay me. Therefore, to prolong the torture, merely to prove I could bear it, would not be a practical form of heroism.

I told them where the chests had been stowed in the precinct of the tower. Stamenes said: "You play more games, yes? We look there first thing, while you were still asleep from bump on head."

"We went over those grounds with the utmost care," said Agathon. "Give him some more, Kousouros."

The executioner applied his iron again. I yelled until I thought I should bring down the ceiling.

"I oversaw the stowing of those chests myself!" I shouted when the torturer paused in his ministrations. "An they be not there, they've been moved. With so many cells and storerooms on the tower grounds, you could easily have overlooked this one."

Agathon, fingering his beard, looked at Stamenes. "It might be worth trying. We can always set Kousouros to work on him again."

"All right," said Stamenes. "But give very good directions."

I told them exactly how to find the storeroom in question, and they and their ruffians went away. I was left alone in the dark again, wishing that I could swoon to ease the anguish of the burns.

Time passed. The burns pained me until I chewed my clothing to keep from crying out. Monstrous blisters formed.

Then came a sudden trampling; and the sound of voices. A group of masked men rushed into the block of cells. One held a torch while two others, with a chisel and a sledge hammer, cut my chains with a few heavy strokes.

"The bracelets you'll have to manage for yourself," growled the leader. "Now, up and run for it!"

We ran down the corridor. I staggered and stumbled, limping from the pain in my burnt leg. Upstairs we clattered, through a labyrinth of chambers and corridors, across courts, and out a great door which I recognized as the main entrance to the citadel. It was night, and a sodden drizzle blotted out everything beyond the range of my rescuers' torches. Outside the citadel, something huge and black loomed over me. It was Aias.

"You're in no shape to sit a horse, eh?" said my chief rescuer, whose voice, muffled by a scarf about the lower part of his face, I could almost recognize. "Were you tortured?"

"Aye." I pointed to my leg.

"Zeus! You were at that. Here's some salve for your wounds. When you've applied this, you'll forget about complaining to the king. Now up this ladder with you, and take care that in passing through Harpalos' demesne you don't flee the ashes only to fall into the coals."

He slapped my back. I struggled up the rope ladder, panting. Kanadas' strong arms hauled me headfirst into the booth on the elephant's back. The man who had spoken to me handed up a heavy bag that clinked.

Forward, Vardanas called softly: "Advance!"

With the familiar jingle of bits, clatter of hooves, creak of axles, and commands of "Get up! Get up!" the hipparchia moved north on Enemy Street. The masked men put out their torches and ran off into the darkness.

We rode through the Ishtar Gate. Who guided us I could not tell. We shuffled through dark and dank, passed the inner city wall, passed the main city wall, and came to the suburban wall. A Greek voice said: "Fare you well!" A man at the head of the column swung his horse about and galloped back toward the city.

"Aside from this cursed burn," I said, "there's nought amiss with me that a good repast and a bath won't cure. But I must needs ride the elephant till my leg heals. Hand me up some victuals, Elisas. And tell me what befell, somebody. How came I to be rescued?"

"'Twas our friend Beliddinos," said Thyestes, riding beside the elephant. "When I'd taken my pleasure with the wench, I looked down the stair to see four soldiers at the foot. These commanded me to give mysel up. No being minded to put my head in the lion's mouth, I made a running jump and came down with my heels on the breast of the foremost. It tumbled him on his back with muckle clatter.

"Then I ran for it afore the others could spit me. I dinna ken how I got out; but somegate I did, and lost my pursuers in the alleys. Then I was lost mysel and didna win back to the temple till dawn. When I learnt you hadna yet returned, Vardanas and I roused the priest from his slumbers and told him.

"The poor wight was hard to awaken, for he'd been up late hearing confessions. But, once he kenned what was afoot, he got up quickly enough. It would, he said, be like those all-depraved rogues in the citadel to frank you up in prison on a trumped-up charge in order to seize our silver. So he had his slaves drag the chests out of the store-room on the tower grounds and hide them in the temple."

My leg hurt fiercely. I bethought me of the bag the masked man had given me. He called it salve, but it clinked like money. Sure enough, it was full of shiny didrachmons, tetradrachmons, and even some massy dekadrachmons. I could not count them on the rocking back of the elephant, but my hand told me there were several pounds of silver here.

This might be salve for the soul, but it did my burn no good. Again I appealed to Elisas, who, thanks to Athena the Foresighted, had provided himself with a pot of ointment made of bear grease, bitumen, and the gods know what else. It eased the pain a little. The Syrian even passed me a file with which to work on my fetters. One might have thought him endowed by Apollon with prophetic gifts, so shrewdly did he foresee all contingencies.

Thyestes went on: "Day broke and you hadna come back. Instead, the sun brought a company of soldiers, who searched the tower and temple grounds. They wouldna say what they sought, but we could guess; and there were over many to fight. But nought did they find."

I asked: "Where had the chests been hidden?"

"Those rascally priests! By Zeus, 'tis the end of my faith in religion!"

"Where was it, man?"

"Ahint the statue of Mardoukos there's a hollow space ben the wall, with a grille of little holes in the brick. The entrance to the chamber is by a secret door in another room. When some great rich worshiper comes to question the god, a priest with a deep voice hides hissel in the hollow and speaks through the grille, and the poor gowk thinks it's the god. Well, our friends hid the chests in this wee chamber."

"But how was I rescued?"

"When the second day came without sign of you, Beliddinos went to work. None of us durst go near the citadel for fear they'd clap us up, too, but he sent a priest to inquire. The folk at the citadel said they kenned nought.

"Then Beliddinos summoned that Greek diviner, Peithagoras, and told him they'd made some new horoscopes which showed that Alexander would sune return from India. Beliddinos then brought Peithagoras to a session with the temple's seer. The seer went into a trance and said he saw a long line of crucified men, the wicked governors and generals whom Alexander would punish when he got back. There was also some stuff about a Thessalian officer chained in a dungeon— nought but guesswork on Beliddinos' part.

"As Beliddinos expected, Peithagoras went till his brother and told him of these prophecies. He taxed Apollodoros with kidnaping you. Apollodoros denied this but admitted he kenned that Agathoun and Stamenes had some sic plan in mind.

"In terror, Peithagoras besought Apollodoros to get you out, lest the king on his return blame both Amphipolitan brothers for the crime along with those who really did it. So Apollodoros and some trusted men of his bodyguard snatched you from the cell when Agathoun and Stamenes were no looking. That was Apollodoros who spoke to you afore we departed."

"Beliddinos surely proved a friend to his friends," said Vardanas, riding on the other side of Aias.

I called down to Pyrron: "You cannot now say prophecy never serves a useful purpose."

Pyrron laughed. "If I may quote the divine Euripides:

"*The best diviner I maintain to be*
The man who guesses or conjectures best.

* * *

"But I see your point. Neither should we say that ancient history is useless, for Beliddinos might not have gone to so much trouble on our behalf had we not rescued his bag of old bricks from the robbers."

"Whither are we bound?" I asked.

Thyestes said: "This is the road till Kounaxa and Opis, on the Tigris."

"But, man, we want the western road, to Sippara and Thilabos, up the Euphrates!"

"Na, that's what we planned, buckie. But Apollodoros sent us forth ane's errand on the Tigris road, mauger it be longer. Gin Agathoun and Stamenes send scouts after us, they'll think we're taking the short way to the Syrian coast and scour the Euphrates road, while we're safe on the Tigris road."

"The man has his wits about him," I said, "but the orra distance will cost us a pretty copper."

"Trust Leon to think of that!" said Pyrron. "My dear fellow, are you sure you're not of Phoenician extraction?"

"Nay," I said shortly. "And neither am I related to Aisopos' grasshopper, who trusts to the morrow to take care of itself."

So base is human nature that, mingled with my thankfulness at my escape, was resentment that the hipparchia should have gotten along so well without me and, moreover, that they should have saved me from the fruits of my own folly. It was then that I resolved no more to kill myself overseeing every detail of their equipment and conduct. Those who had not by now learned how to behave never would. I would, I swore, give more responsibility to the other officers and the double-pay trooper, and judge by results.

The road led us north through the fertile plain of Sittakia, where the Tigris and Euphrates rivers approach to a hundred and fifty furlongs of one another and then flow apart again. Heavy rains in the Assyrian hills had caused the Tigris to overflow, so that great stretches of land on our right were flooded. Millions of waterfowl sported in the lakes and marshes and rose whirring at our passage.

On our left, Vardanas pointed out the site of the battle of Kounaxa, where Kyros the usurper beat the army of Artaxerxes the Resolute but was himself slain. One of Vardanas' grandsires had fought on one side and one on the other. The place was of interest to me because it was thence that Xenophon's ten thousand began their retreat.

"After that bloody treacher lured their generals to a parley and murdered them," growled Thyestes.

"They should have known better," said Vardanas. "Anyway, Artaxashas" (for so the Persians pronounce Artaxerxes) "was not himself such a villain. He was a weak, easygoing man, and why he was called 'Resolute' I cannot imagine. He let himself be ruled by his blood-thirsty mother and equally savage wife."

"As no Hellene would let his women do," said Thyestes, who liked the last word.

At Sittakia we found a bridge of boats across the Tigris, though again Aias had to ford despite the swiftness of the broad brown flood. Going up the left bank of the Tigris, the fertile plain of Sittakia gave way to barren land in which a few prickly shrubs, of interest only to camels, broke in broad flats of clay. Snow-capped Persian mountains lined the horizon on our right.

As my burn was still too sore for riding, I stayed atop the elephant. For days I craned my neck to the rear, but none pursued us. Although riding Aias made me feel like an Indian king, my friends, riding before me, tended to ignore me rather than crane their necks to call up to me.

The first few days after we left Babylon, Nirouphar rode with me betimes in the booth atop the elephant and was tenderly solicitous about my burn. As the wound healed, howsomever, she returned more and more to her horse and to conversation with Pyrron in the mixture of Greek and Persian with which they now communicated. From my perch I watched them with pangs of jealousy. Vardanas, too, regarded this sight with visible unease.

At the beginning of Anthesterion we came to Doura. Here the land rises to cliffs overlooking the river, and the stronghold of Doura is perched upon these cliffs. The garrison gave me fodder without making difficulties. From here on, Kanadas grumbled because he could no longer buy rice but had to adapt himself to our barbarous diet.

Beyond Doura I rode Golden again. The burn on my leg left a large, unsightly scar, which still aches in damp weather. The Baktrian mare had grown spoilt while I rode the elephant. She tried to bite when I approached her and bucked me off when I first mounted. I mounted again, got a grip on her mane, and quieted her with a few good cuts of the whip. I have had horses I could treat as pets, but not this cross-grained beast.

North of Doura, I paid some gingerly court to Nirouphar, seeking quietly to show her my good points and, at the same time, to wean her from excessive admiration for Pyrron. Since she had been solicitous of me when my burn was bad, I was equally so toward her. Was her tent comfortable? Had it any leaks that should be mended? Was her pallet soft enough to give her good nights of sleep? Did the gait of her horse tire her? If so, would she like to try another mount? Was there aught in the way of special food I should try to obtain for her?

To my astonishment, she took my well-meant queries amiss. "Troop Leader Rheon!" she said sharply. "As I have told you many a time and oft, I am no piece of fragile Egyptian glass that shatters if you look crossly at it. I am comfortable and in fine health and spirits. When I have aught to complain of, I will let you know."

Then for some days she devoted more time than ever to Pyrron, leaving me crushed and glowering.

When I wrote to the king, I said I had been in trouble with the traffic laws in Babylon and hinted that Stamenes and Agathon might not be all they should as governors. However, I did not go into details of my imprisonment and torture, in consideration of the bag of silver Apollodoros had given me.

Perhaps I was wrong to let myself be bought off, when a strict sense of honor would have demanded vengeance at all costs on my tormentors. For years the question bothered my conscience. But at the time it seemed to me that I had enough to do to carry out my mission, without attempting to reform the whole Alexandrine empire.

One day, when I rode ahead of the column, Vardanas rode with me. I could see he was troubled. After he had fumbled for a while, I said:

"Out with it, man. Is it about your sister?"

"How did you guess? It plagues me that she should be so assotted with the philosopher. Yet I know not what to do about it. Were he a

Persian of good family I could betroth them. But as it is…Not that Pyrron is not a fine fellow in his way. He has never taken advantage of Nirouphar's folly. Still, either one is born an Arian or one is not."

"Have you taken her to task about it?"

"Yes, and it only caused a quarrel. She is unfair to me. She expects my protection but will not obey my commands."

"What would you have me do?"

"Speak to him. Perhaps persuade him to keep his distance until this spell passes."

"Why speak you not yourself?" I asked.

"As a civilian, Pyrron is not under my rule. But you as hipparch command us all. Besides, he is so learned that I should feel shame to chide him."

"*Papai!* That's a fine task to give me. Especially…"

"Especially what?"

"Oh, fie! Dinna you ken I'm in love with the lass myself?"

Vardanas' eyes rounded. "Why, no, I did not know. Oh, my dear friend, how dreadful!"

"Meaning that, as I, too, am but a loathsome non-Arian, my suit were hopeless?"

"I would not so put it, but you grasp the gist."

"I had thought it plain to all," I said. "For the last ten-day I've been sighing and staring. I've hardly eaten or slept."

"Really? I ask your pardon, but I have seen no lessening of your good healthy appetite. Since you ever present a stern and serious front, I saw no change in your mien."

"So much for sympathy. If I complain of the burn on my leg, you'll tell me to chop the limb off."

"Alas, with what fortitude do we bear others' misfortunes! But that still leaves Pyrron. As you and he are in a sense rivals, you should be glad of a chance to break up this unnatural infatuation."

"Unnatural! As if a Hellene were some sort of slimy monster! If it be hopeless for both of us, why should I interfere? And if it be not, I'd not use my rank against him."

"You mean it were dishonorable? A noble sentiment!"

"Belike, but that's not quite what I had in mind. The men obey me, not only because I can outwrestle them all, but also because I'm fair with them. Let it be thought I was ranking a man out his woman and trouble would soon raise its head."

"Oh dear!" said Vardanas. "Why could not my father have sent the wanton to some good Arian city like Parsagarda and wedded her to some respectable youth, as he did with my sister Artaunta? How shall we untie this tangle?"

"Let's both speak to Pyrron, stating the case and asking what he means to do. Thus I shan't appear as one meddling in his affairs from selfish motives, but as the just leader demanding that you and he compose your differences."

A day passed before we got Pyrron away from Nirouphar. Then the lass joined a group of our women who, having the Asiatic feeling about exposing the person, were going around a bend in the river out of sight of our camp to bathe. I said to Pyrron:

"O philosopher, 'tis time we gave our Persian frog another swimming lesson. Help me to teach him."

Vardanas did not look happy at the form of my stratagem. Though he had gotten over some of his horror of nudity, water more than knee-deep still frightened him. But the noble fellow did not quail.

It turned out that, although Pyrron was himself a poor swimmer, he was an excellent teacher of swimming. He had read everything ever written in Greek on the subject, and he had infinite patience and good humor. This time we got Vardanas to swim three strokes by himself before he shipped a mouthful of muddy Tigris water and put his feet down to cough it out again.

While we dried ourselves, I said: "Pyrron, Vardanas has a matter to speak to you about."

"Go right ahead, old boy," said Pyrron.

Though usually glib, Vardanas stammered and stumbled. At last he got it out. "...it simply will not do for a respectable Persian girl to hang about one man all the time. Her reputation, already worn thin from leaving home, will now be in utter shreds. I blame myself that I let her talk me into bringing her. But you, my man, what do you intend?"

Pyrron waved his hands helplessly. "Gods on Olympos! I've done nothing but attempt to elucidate the mysteries of philosophy to one who seemed interested. I had no conception that your sister contemplated me with mundane desires."

"Your wisdom is not of this earthly plane," said Vardanas. "Anybody with eyes could see she is assotted with you."

Pyrron's voice rose to a squeak. "But I'm not out to marry her or seduce her or anything else! As I've asserted before, I desire no mortal lovers of any age, sex, or race. Athena is my only passion."

"Well," said Vardanas, "we cannot go on like this. You will break her heart even if you cause no scandal."

"What would you have me do? Insult her?"

"You could at least dissuade her from sticking to you like a burr to a dog."

"On what pretext? So long as anybody shows an earnest desire for enlightenment, I consider it my duty as a philosopher to satisfy—"

"Oh, rubbish!" I said. "'Tis plain to the silliest wight she hangs upon your words for love of your sweet self and not for your philosophy. No woman could possibly understand your reasoning anyway. Why, I can scarce understand it myself."

Pyrron cleared his throat. "Now you come to a point on which I have a strong opinion. With the divine Platon, I hold that we Hellenes commit a national injustice and deprive ourselves of a valuable resource by relegating our women to the status of slaves—"

"For Hera's sake, dinna lecture! We wish you to dissuade Nirouphar; not necessarily by rudeness, but, say, by seeking other company. Talk to Vardanas and me, or discuss Indian theology with Kanadas."

"That's not a bad idea," said Pyrron. "To tell you the honest truth, I'm becoming a little tired of being plied with questions about man and the universe to which I don't know the answers and to which I think nobody else has the answer either. Let Leon woo her while Vardanas and I discuss philosophy. Perhaps she'll become enamored of Leon, and Vardanas can make a match between them."

"Out upon you!" I cried. "If that's a joke, 'tis a poor one. Know you not that I should like nought better, did Fate allow?"

"Why? Oh, you mean that you, too—my word, how blind I must be to the human drama about me! Well then, if you love her, what's amiss with my suggestion?"

"'Tis Vardanas' cursed Arian-race nonsense," I said. "Tell him, Vardanas."

Vardanas explained the Persian doctrine of racial purity.

"All right," said Pyrron. "You and Leon are good friends, aren't you?"

"Surely," said Vardanas. "None better."

"If Leon were demonstrated to be an Arian after all, would you find him acceptable as a brother-in-law?"

"Why certainly—well, perhaps. But it must needs be a better proof than some of your Greek tricks of logic. You know, proving Achilles could never catch a tortoise when we all know he could. What are you coming to?"

"Thanks to the coaching of your attractive and quite intelligent sister, I've acquired a fair smattering of the Persian language. Now, I've observed that many of the words of Persian sound recognizably like their Greek synonyms." Pyrron gave as examples the words for door, man, foot, and ship.

"It's therefore my hypothesis," he went on, "that the Hellenes and the Persians are ultimately of common ancestry. For, if you compare these same words in Syrian, you find no resemblance whatever. As far as I know, this is a point which none of my colleagues has ever raised, as none of them considers any foreign language worthy of study. Someday I shall compose a treatise on the subject. There should be lists of words having the same signification in the various languages, in parallel columns—"

"Excuse me," I said, "but aren't you straying off the subject of Nirouphar's future?"

"Oh yes, to be sure. My point is that, if Hellenes and Persians are of common lineage, then, if Persians are Arians, Hellenes must be Arians also. Thus are Vardanas' racial objections refuted."

My hopes rose, but Vardanas frowned in thought. "It were not so easy," he said. "However our forebears wandered and interbred in legendary times, we Arians certainly do not mean 'Greek' when we say 'Arian.'"

I said: "Prince Vaxouvartas of Baktria must have deemed the Hellenes Arian, since he married his daughter to Alexander. And aren't the Baktrians the purest Arians of all?"

"No purer than we Persians," said Vardanas. "And a conqueror takes what women he pleases. But, even if the racial obstacle be overcome, there remains the barrier of religion."

"Must I then become a worshiper of Auramasdas?"

"That were a necessary though not a sufficient condition. It were but the first of the labors of Samas. But I cannot decide the matter now. While my father live unreconciled, and my sister's wayward heart be turned elsewhither than toward him who desires her, there is no prospect of a wedding feast in any case."

We dressed and went back to camp. Nirouphar also returned. She bent a suspicious look upon us and said: "What plot have you three been hatching?"

"Pyrron has striven to make a philosopher of Leon and a swimmer of me," said Vardanas. "I fear with but little success in either case."

BOOK SEVEN

Syria

WE RODE UP THE LEFT BANK of the Tigris, passing through a gap in a low range of hills that lies athwart the river's path. We forded the Lesser Zabatos and marched through sparsely settled country, a desert save close upon the river. We sighted bands of marauding Arabs. Warned of their thievish ways, we kept close watches and were not molested.

The land waxed hillier, the air became cooler, and mountains appeared in the distance. We were in Assyria, the Arthoura of the Persians. The folk in the villages were larger and stouter than the Babylonians, with powerful frames, big noses curved like plowshares, and thick black beards.

I questioned Vardanas on the religion of Zarathoushtras, without committing myself. After all, I thought, when all other obstacles to my union with Nirouphar be overcome, it were time enough to proclaim my conversion.

At first, what Vardanas told me pleased me. Magianism seemed to have a more sensible answer to the problem of evil than other religions. Most start with a crew of all-too-human gods, as full of lust and folly as any mortals. Then people like Platon assure us this cannot be true; the gods are all-wise, all-good abstractions. When one asks whence comes evil, they throw out a cloud of words, like the ink an octopus squirts when one corners it in a seaside pool. It is all very confusing.

The Magians, however, frankly suppose two rival gods, of good and of evil, equally matched, who strive for the mastery of the universe. Every man must choose which of the twain he will side with. But my zeal for Magianism waned when I learned of the rites I should have to undergo to join it, such as that of washing my face in cow's urine.

We crossed the Great Zabatos, another tributary of the Tigris, and passed the site of the battle of Gaugamela. The battle had taken place five and a half years before, on a broad plain reaching almost to the horizon, on which rose a rank of low hills. The scene awoke strong memories in those of us who had fought in this great conflict.

We camped in sight of the battlefield on a chilly night and spoke in hushed tones of our memories. Knowing that Vardanas had served in Masdais' heavy horse on the Persian side in that vast struggle, I asked:

"Why in Hera's name did Masdais lead his division back to our camp after he had broken through our center? Had he assailed our foot from behind, when the Sakas made their fierce attack on our right, we had been in an evil plight indeed."

"Dareios had commanded Masdais at all costs to rescue his mother and his children."

"For this he threw away the battle?" said Thyestes. "What a silly carle!"

"Do Hellenes then count it a vice to love one's family?" said Vardanas.

"Na, na; but, like the dog with the bone in the fable, Dareios lost his battle outen getting his family back, through trying to grasp overmany things at once. What sort of body was he?"

"Not without virtues. Kind and courteous to his subjects, as far as the rules of courtly manners let him be. He labored hard to make them prosper after the oppressions of Artaxashas Vaukas. But his efforts had not borne fruit when the Macedonians fell upon him. True, he was no warrior, but timid and hesitant. When he did the right thing at last, like training his soldiers in the Greek methods of fighting, it was always too late. And he did twice flee from a battle, leaving his men to die for him. That is why I came over to Alexander with Nabarzanes; honor commands not to follow such a craven forever and aye. In peaceful times, though, he had made a good enough king."

"'The first in banquets, but the last in battle,'" quoted Pyrron. "Still and all, he suffered from the king's disease."

"What is that?"

"Self-conceit, which, as the proverb says, leads to self-destruction."

"I do not think him self-conceited. In his last days, when Bessos was hustling him through Media and Baktria, he became pitifully humble."

"Better beans and bacon in security than cakes and ale in fear," quoth Pyrron. "Nonetheless, he killed that Hellene who tried to give him sound advice."

"That adventurer, Charidemos of Oleus? My cousin Bagabouxas saw the whole thing. Charidemos besought Dareios to give him command of the entire army. When Dareios refused, Charidemos burst into rage. Before the whole court he shouted that all Persians, the king included, were womanish weaklings. One Macedonian, he said, could dompt ten of them. No king could be expected to bear such insults. As for self-conceit, I have heard naught for a year but complaints from you Hellenes about the same vice in Alexander. At least poor Daraiavaus never claimed to be a god."

"Of course you've heard complaints against the king," said Pyrron. "That's why most of the Greek states abolished kings and instituted democracies."

"Democracy is a fine ideal," said Vardanas, "but anyone can see it is doomed."

"Why so?"

"Because, as your own philosophers have pointed out, no state can be democratically ruled if its citizens exceed a few thousand. Suppose Alexander made his empire a democracy? The citizens could never come together from so vast an area to vote. If they did, such a huge disorderly throng, speaking a score of tongues, could not transact any business."

"What's wrong with a small state?" demanded Pyrron.

"Nothing save its size. Soon or late, a larger state swallows it, as a large fish swallows a small. There is strength only in union, as your own Aisopos said. Union can only be brought about by conquest, as the quarreling states of Hellas have often proved."

"The small states of Hellas did passably well against the great Dareios and the great Xerxes."

Vardanas shrugged. "Those Persian defeats were such accidents as happen in the life of any great empire. Forget not that when you won Marathon and Salamis, the Persians had already conquered hundreds of nations, from Kyrene to India. Then for years the Greek democracies attacked us. But even when Greek methods of warfare drew ahead of ours, we could always break up the invasion by playing off one Greek state against another, or bribing a general to desert and lead his men home. When Persia fell at last, it was to a powerful kingdom like itself."

"You're well informed in such matters," said Pyrron. "I doubt if many young Persian gentlemen could match you."

Vardanas grinned. "I had a good Greek teacher, Dorymachos of Acharnai, who studied under the godlike Platon and taught me the rules of rhetoric and the tricks of debate. To return, why does Alexander appoint so many Persian governors? Because Hellenes are unused to doing things on an imperial scale. Either they are overwhelmed by the task, or they cannot resist stealing from the treasuries they are set to guard."

"From what we've seen, Hellenes are not the only pilferers in positions of responsibility," said Pyrron. "But touching on the destiny of democracy: If you be right, which I don't admit, something precious will have gone from the world. To try to expound the delight of living in a democracy to one who has never experienced it is like explaining color to a blind man."

"I know that not," said Vardanas. "From what I hear, the Greek democracies spend all their time cutting each other's throats, as if they were wild Gandarian tribesmen. Peaceful and orderly civilized life, however, needs the rule of an all-powerful king, above the passions of feud and the hatreds of faction."

Pyrron said: "I must pit you against some of the more extreme democratic orators in Athens. The bout were worth the ticket."

Vardanas was not finished. "Moreover, war can be ended only by making the whole world into a single peaceful empire. Such an empire can be ruled only as a kingdom, for the reasons we have seen."

"I wouldn't call the Persian Empire peaceful," said Pyrron. "The viceroys were always revolting, and whenever a king died, his sons waged a civil war for the throne, like that which ended at Kounaxa."

Thyestes growled: "By Zeus, who wants to stop war? In a warless world the manly virtues would wither. Besides, soldiers like me would be out of work!"

During the night, a yell from the sentry brought us out of our tents. "Ghosts!" he screamed. "The ghosts of them that fell in the battle!"

I looked in the direction the sentry's trembling finger pointed, and fear squeezed my heart and stopped my throat, too. The light of the setting moon shone on a mist that moved toward us from the river. It was not a solid mist, but broken into columns and streamers about the size of a man. This broken mist advanced upon us with an eldrich effect. Around me rose a murmur of prayers and exorcisms. Kanadas' teeth chattered with terror. My own hair stood up; had I been alone I might have run, but a hipparch must set an example.

"Stand fast, lads!" I croaked. "If Thessalians dinna flee from living coofs, why should we fear their wraiths?"

Then came Pyrron's clear lecture-platform voice: "An interesting natural phenomenon!" He stepped forward and passed his hand through the first ghost. Then he turned and cleared his throat. "None of my colleagues has yet precisely defined the relationships prevailing among air, mist, and water. Air and water are commonly deemed distinct elements, yet in the case of mist we have an apparent intermediate form. We know that mist and cloud are made of water, but where does the water in mist go when it disappears? Perhaps the answer is to be found in the atomism of the great Demokritos—"

He had begun to pace about as he spoke, and now he stubbed his toe and measured his gangling length upon the ground. He got up, uttering mild curses, which were lost in the laughter of the hipparchia.

The following night we camped beside a village in the midst of a wide stretch of ruins. This is all that remains of the city of Ninos, the capital of the Assyrian Empire until the Medes and Babylonians destroyed it about the time of Solon and Periandros. Many tall tales are told of King Ninos, who built the city, and his queen, Semiramis, who reigned after him. But, as Beliddinos warned me that most of these stories are false, I will not repeat them.

The villagers called the ruins "Nineva." But when, with Elisas' help, I sought to question them in Syrian concerning the history of the city, it turned out that they knew less about it than we did.

From Ninos the course of the river trended westward. For a time we had the use of the Persian royal highway, stretching along the left bank of the Tigris between Ninos and Amida. This great road, which runs over five hundred leagues from Ephesos to Sousa, formed the backbone of the old Persian postal system. The surface was still in good condition, albeit not kept in such fine repair as under the Persians. Because of the time of year, the traffic was light, though single riders and men afoot were not uncommon.

We planned not, howsomever, to follow this splendid road all the way westward because it leads through Armenia and Kappadokia, which were out of our way. Forbye, these provinces of the Persian Empire had declared their independence when Dareios fell. Alexander's generals were unable to subdue them, for both lands were under the rule of powerful native kings who had served the Persians as governors and were well tempered in the arts of war and statecraft.

Swiftly we marched northwest for five hundred furlongs, through groves of date palms and orchards of cherry trees, to Bezabde. This is a fortified town in a crook of the Tigris, just short of the Armenian border. Here the road forks. The royal highway continues northward into Armenia, while the caravan road to the Syrian coast crosses the Tigris and trends west.

In Bezabde were many Armenians—stocky, hook-nosed men like the Assyrians. They trim their thick black beards to a point and wear the Armenian national hat. This is a cap bound about with long ribbons, which sits low over the nape in back and is gathered into three knobs forming a kind of crest over the forehead. There were also Kordians, big fierce-looking hillmen who dwell in southern Armenia, and their handsome women clad in bright clothes and speaking with loud, commanding voices.

On our first day in Bezabde, I saw one of these Kordians walking about the streets with a pair of curious objects on his back. These were flat structures of wood and leather, like unto the lids of oval boxes or baskets. I stopped the man, a tall, stout, red-faced fellow smelling of garlic, with blue eyes and great brown mustaches that swept out like buffalo's horns. I asked him what the things on his back were, but he could not understand me. However, Vardanas could follow the man's speech half the time, as the Kordians speak an Arian tongue.

"He calls them snowshoes," Vardanas explained. "On them he walked down hither from his village in the hills." The Persian pointed toward the snow-covered Armenian mountains to the north. "It is even colder there than here."

I shivered, for winter was now at its depth. Many a time and oft we had our tents blown down and our garments soaked by heavy storms. Most of us, tired of freezing our arms and legs, had bought native coats and trousers. Thessalians, used to a rugged climate, do not have the prejudice of southern Hellenes against warm raiment that fits the body. Forbye, it was hard to buy olive oil to anoint our bodies with in this land.

Aias, unused to icy blasts and lacking fur to keep him cozy, caught cold and grumbled unhappily. That night, Kanadas, bundled up to the eyes, came to me and said:

"Troop Leader, he die if we do not keep him warmer. We must get great blanket to cover him, or else stop and stable him till spring."

I summoned Elisas to help with the reckoning. It soon transpired that the delay would be more costly than the covering, could we but obtain a large enough sheet of crude cloth at a just price. Elisas said:

"There is a fair grade of woolen tent cloth for sale here, not too dear."

"All right, buy enough for a blanket for Aias."

"Not so fast, Troop Leader! It may take all the tent cloth in town to clothe the elephant. If we try to buy it all at once, the price will fly up like sparks from a fire. Let each of us go in turn and buy a piece, not as if we really needed it."

"How much need we?"

Elisas spread his hands. "Have never measured an elephant for a suit of clothes."

222

"Then do so."

"Oh, noble Hipparch! I fear the monster and cannot approach him!"

So, in the gathering dusk, the early stars looked down upon Kanadas, Siladites, and me, pottering about Aias with a rope to measure his vast dimensions. I decided that stuff for four two-man tents would suffice.

The next day Elisas, Vardanas, Thyestes, and I each strolled into the market place, fingered the tent cloth, sneered at its quality, and bought a bolt after a long haggle. All, that is, but Vardanas. As he hated chaffering, he closed his deal before he should have and paid nearly twice as much as the rest of us.

While the women sewed the bolts into a blanket, I visited the Greek garrison, which looked nervously northward toward the Armenian mountains. The commandant, Myson of Corinth, told me:

"With the world so unsettled, we never know what day will see us at war. I'm told the king of Armenia has sent a polite letter and a gift to Alexander, but one never knows if Alexander will deem that submission enough."

"What sort of soldiers are the Armenians?" I asked.

"Fell fighters when well led. By the! They have some heavy cavalry I shouldn't care to stand in the path of. Come and see for yourself, Hipparch."

"Whither?"

"I'm about to ride up the road a few furlongs to meet the Armenian commandant. We shall be back in an hour or two."

So it befell that I rode Golden at a walk beside Myson, while eight hoplites from the garrison, their bronzen helms and cuirasses brightly polished, clanked along behind us.

As Myson said, the border lay hardly out of sight of Bezabde. A pair of stone markers, one on either side of the royal highway, showed where it was. Myson said: "Shoulder—arms!"

The shields that had been slung over backs were brought around; the pikes that had been trailing in the gravel came smartly up to the right shoulders. Ahead of us a little knot of figures sprang apart. Four Greek border guards and an equal number of Armenians had been playing at knucklebones. Now they stood solemnly at attention, leaving their dice and stakes where they lay.

Along the road from the other direction, winding down from the hills, came a group of Armenians, mounted on big horses of the Median kind and wearing coats of iron scale mail with heavy cloaks over them.

The fat Armenian officer clasped Myson's hand and called down blessings upon him in his own tongue. They dismounted. Myson presented the Armenian to me as Bagrates. The latter had brought along a secretary who spoke a little bad Greek; but, when we found that both Bagrates and I were fluent in Persian, I took the interpreter's place.

The commandants exchanged a medimnos of flowery compliments and drank a cup of wine to the eternal friendship of Alexander's empire and the kingdom of Armenia. Then they got down to business.

"My king, the high and mighty Arkloathos son of Arouandas," said Bagrates, "demands to know why you are diverting caravans to the southern road, instead of letting them follow the Persian royal highway through his dominions as heretofore."

When this had been translated, Myson said: "Tell him we're not diverting anybody. Because of the rumors of war and unrest, the merchants prefer to take the southern road rather than be caught in Armenia in time of trouble."

"Ah, but who spreads these rumors of war and unrest, and what are his motives?"

"Tell him I don't know any more than he does. Rumors, like weeds, grow without cultivation."

"Surely the able and intelligent Company Leader Myson does not expect me to believe that he knows not what goes on in his own district?"

The session became strained. Bagrates was no longer a jolly fat man, full of flowery compliments, but a man out to wring every advantage from an opponent. Myson became frosty too.

"Tell him," he said, "I don't know whence the rumors come. If that makes me stupid in his eyes, I must bear his disesteem as best I can." When I had translated, Myson continued:

"Now I have a complaint. Three nights ago, a party of raiders crossed the border from Armenia and attacked the farm of Louxos son of Hananas. Louxos lost three sheep and was wounded in the leg as he strove to drive off the marauders. From their garb and speech, he thinks they came from around Zachos. We demand that the sheep be returned and Louxos be compensated for his wound, which will cripple him for a month if not for life."

"How do you know these people came from Armenia? Did anybody see them crossing the border?"

"No, but they came thence and fled thither..."

This wrangle went on for half an hour, until at last Bagrates told his secretary to note the matter and promised to look into it. Then he came back with a complaint about a party of hunters who, chasing a wild pig, crossed the border into Armenia and damaged the vineyard of one Sardoures.

Myson retorted with a complaint about a lion that made its lair on the Armenian side but crossed into Alexandrine territory to carry off the livestock of Myson's people.

"Mighty though he be," said Bagrates, "we cannot ask my king to command the wild beasts to respect man-made boundaries!"

At last they agreed upon a joint Helleno-Armenian lion hunt. Each commandant would pick some deserving men from his garrison to take part.

Now Bagrates brought up another matter. Had the noble Myson done aught about forcing the wife of Tigranes son of Marouas, who had run off with a cobbler of Bezabde, to return to her husband? He, poor man, was going mad trying to till his farm and care for his seven children at the same time. Why had she not come back?

The conference took three hours. Then the two commandants, who had been barking complaints and accusations, smiled, drank another toast, clapped each other on the back, mounted, and rode off.

"He's not a bad fellow," said Myson, "but for all his fat, sleepy look, he's sharp as a razor. You dare not yield a finger lest he take instant advantage."

While these words about Bagrates seemed just, I could not help thinking that Myson had not done badly at taking instant advantage himself.

* * *

We were packing to leave Bezabde when a Kordian swaggered into our camp and demanded to see me. He was the one whom I had questioned about the snowshoes on our first day in the city. Vardanas explained:

"He says he is an expert muleteer, camp man, groom, and guide, and can fight like a demon in a pinch. Will we hire him?"

The man looked strong, and I thought our force could use another pair of hands after its losses. "How far is he willing to go with us?"

"The farther the better, he says."

"All the way to Athens?"

"To the edge of the world, if we will take him, so it be far from Kordavana."

"What's the matter? Has he done murder? We're not a traveling sanctuary for fugitives."

The Kordian, whose name was Inaudos, whispered to Vardanas. The latter said: "He fears his wife."

And so Inaudos was with us when we set out. He had just finished hitching up one of the mule teams when a bright-clad Kordian woman appeared at the camp. With a screech she rushed upon Inaudos, waving a cudgel.

The Kordian cast a terrified glance around. The nearest refuge was the back of Aias, who stood awaiting a prod from Siladites to set him in motion. For all his bulk, Inaudos climbed up the elephant's harness and blanket like a monkey and tumbled into the booth.

The woman danced with rage about the elephant but did not dare come close. Inaudos put his thumbs in his ears, twiddled his fingers, and stuck out his tongue in a Gorgonian grimace.

Then Thyestes blew the trumpet, and off we went. The woman trotted after us, screaming curses, until our fording of the Tigris left her behind.

As a result of heavy rains in the Kordian mountains, a sudden rise in the Tigris had washed out the bridge at Bezabde. It was a nasty fording, like that of the Haitoumans in Arachotia. Although the water at the ford was no more than thigh-deep, it was abominably cold and dismayingly swift. We dismounted and led our beasts, the men holding each other's hands to steady themselves.

We had nearly crossed when I heard a shriek. Elisas had slipped and was instantly swept into deeper water. Knowing him to be no more of a swimmer than Vardanas, I plunged in after him and soon caught up with his thrashing form.

However, when I started to haul him out, he caught me round the neck in a death grip. Every time I got my face out of water for a quick breath, he dragged me under again. I struck at him, trying to stun him, and tore at his hands to break his grip, but Pan gave the little man the strength of a bear.

It would have gone ill indeed with me had I not felt a grip on my belt and found myself pulled into shallow water. Inaudos the Kordian stood over us, talking a spate in his own tongue and, I suppose, chiding us for our folly. When Elisas recovered, he was so voluble in his thanks to Inaudos and to me that fain would I have stunned the fellow again to quiet him.

Now the road bore westward, betwixt the snowy Masios Mountains on our right and the sweeping plains of Mygdonia on our left. This fertile land had turned from brown to green with the winter's rains. Alas! The rains had also made the road into a river of mud in which we splashed, slithered, and stuck. Once, when the way went down a rather steep hill, Aias balked and would descend the slope only by sitting and sliding on his colossal backside.

Now it was the elephant's turn to earn his passage. When a cart stuck fast, at the Indians' commands he placed his head against the back of the stalled wain. At the cry of "*Zouk!*" he pushed until the vehicle came free.

We had thus impelled the carts through a slough one day and were riding along again covered with mud, when I found myself at the head of the column beside Nirouphar. For several days I had had but little speech with her. I had been busy with heaving our vehicles through Syrian quagmires, while she had been making much of her friend the elephant, who was slowly getting over his cold.

While no orator, I have seldom been at a loss for words to suit the occasion—not polished Athenian rhetoric, perhaps, but plain, blunt words. With the Persian damsel, howsomever, my tongue seemed to swell up and fill my mouth.

After I had uttered some foolishness about the weather, she cast a glance toward Pyrron. The philosopher was striving, with his smattering of Persian, to learn from Inaudos about the customs of the Kordians, such as their habit of burying food beneath the floors of their houses, and keeping cheeses in pots for years. Nirouphar said:

"Troop Leader Rheon, I am utterly vexed! Would you could help me!"

I braced myself. "If there is aught I can do, dear lady, do you but name it."

"For days the wise Pyrron has avoided me. He talks but to you and my brother and the other men. Pray, find out what I have done to offend him!"

"You have done nought. It is only that Pyrron cares but little for the beauty of women."

"Do you mean he has the Greek vice?"

"Nay. I meant that the passions of the body mean little to him. His mind is always in a philosophical cloud. To him, you and I are but moving shadows; the real world is that of the intellect."

"But who spoke of the passions of the body? No such thought entered into our converse. I was learning Greek culture and had even come to understand a syllogism when he abruptly broke off our discourse. Please ask him what I must do to be deemed worthy of his wisdom again."

I said with a grin: "Let's say the rest of us became jealous of him for taking all the time of the fairest lady among us, and warned him to give us our share."

"Oh, rubbish! You know my brother is off scouting most of the time, while Kanadas merely grunts when I try to talk to him. I would not company with Thyestes, for he is a lustful man and ignorant, who regards a woman as nought but a sheath for his yard. As for you, you have been immersed in the hipparchia's affairs, and you gave me to know at the outset that you did not wish me underfoot."

"I thought that wretched quarrel was long since over and done with?"

"It is; but still you are not the sort of man with whom a prudent person takes liberties."

"Everybody seems to regard me as an ogre. But I am really a shy, timid wight beneath the bluster."

She looked astonished, then burst into laughter. "If a lion come to me and say, 'I am really a lamb beneath the mane and claws,' I shall believe him. If you are indeed a hare at heart, you hid the fact most masterfully."

"So it would seem. And that is not all I have been hiding."

"What mean you?"

"Is it not plain, woman? Love for you drives me to distraction. I burn in Tartaros with the thought of you."

She recoiled in her seat and looked at me as one would look at a scorpion in one's porridge, or so at least it seemed to me in my excited state.

"I know I am no thing of beauty," I muttered, "but I do have a good heart."

"It is not that, dear Rheon," she said gently. "In sooth, I should call you rather handsome in a rugged manly way. It is that you are not an Arian. Therefore, you should not even speak of love."

"I meant no offense, but that is the way of things. I am after all of a good landowning family, of the knightly class. For that matter, neither is Pyrron an Arian."

"Oh—but—but he is a philosopher. Philosophers belong to no nation but to the world. He says so."

"That is not how your brother looks upon the matter. Philosophers are born of human parents and beget human children like other men."

"Pyrron has never made lewd advances to me!"

"Who said he had? But you and he have been close enough on this journey to give rise to all kinds of surmises."

"And why should I not get as much education as opportunity allows? You Hellenes are worse than the men of my own nation. You cannot believe that a woman might wish to better herself. When you see one trying to learn, you are sure it is but an excuse, and that she really suffers from an itch beneath her trousers and seeks a hard horn to scratch it with!"

"My dear, I never said—"

"Nay, but you thought. And why should I not speak with Pyrron? You and the Indian go for hours without saying a word, but I am not like that. And Pyrron at least has never called me a useless burden."

"Oh, do stop twitting me on that!" I exclaimed. "I know I am a base boor, an unmannerly lout from the backwoods of Thessalia. I am unfit to give you a leg up in mounting. What can I do to gain your forgiveness?"

"You have it, good Rheon. I will not mention the matter again. And look not so sad. There are many girls of your own nation who would be glad to belong to so fine a hero as yourself."

"I want none of them the now. But what is fine about me? I am but a poor fumbling rustic, grappling with a task beyond his abilities."

"Say not so! You have most of the virtues I lack. I am flighty and easily turned from my path; you drive for your goal as straight as a migrating duck. I am often foolish and impractical in my judgments, while you shrewdly keep the final effects of every act in mind. I am carried away by the whim of the moment, but you keep your feelings under tight rein. When the cart wheel came off yesterday, few officers but would have flown into a rage and beaten the nearest servant or soldier within range of their fists. What said you? 'Come, lads; less chatter and more work. Let's get it back together,' as if such mishaps were to be expected."

"They are, so why waste effort in railing at them? But much though I esteem your praise, you do make me sound like a man with all the duller virtues."

"I find you not dull at all, once I get you opened up. After the constant turmoil of my family of passionate excitables, your solid good sense is a comfort. Betimes I could almost wish the gods had indeed made you an Arian!"

She shed a small tear. I did, too, partly to see her in sorrow and partly in self-pity. She said:

"Dry your tears, dear Rheon. Here comes my brother. If he see us thus, he will be sure you have dealt me a deadly thrust behind the nearest tussock. Now that I think, mayhap it was he, his mind full of brotherly forebodings, who commanded Pyrron to leave me forlorn. What know you of this?"

I looked surprised. "I know nought of any such thing!"

"'Put no faith in any Hellene!' But my brother's solicitude is wasted, for I no more regard Pyrron as a possible mate than I would a statue. In answer to my questions, the philosopher told me he had tried the pleasures of love, found them overrated, and forsworn them. No such drooping ascetic for me, thank you! And no lewd remarks from you, either, my good Hipparch!"

Our sorrows were blown away by a gust of hearty laughter. Vardanas, coming back with his Dahas from a scouting ride, cast sharp looks upon us but said nought.

We reached Nisibis, a large, well-fortified town that bestrides the Mygdonios River where the latter passes through a ravine from the northern hills to the southern plains. Broad fields of wheat and barley and rich orchards surround Nisibis, and there are many rose gardens of the Persian type. Thence we set out for Rhesaina and Karrai. It was just after we left Nisibis that we had trouble with witchcraft.

Charinos of Krannon, whose woman had been killed by the lion in Sousiana, had a new concubine named Alogouna whom he had picked up in Babylon and who was paid by Vardanas to do washing and other light work for Nirouphar. Simon, another Thessalian, had a Persian concubine named Mandana, by whom he had two children. Mandana had been ailing—some wasting internal disease for which medicine can do nought. In Mygdonia, however, she picked upon Alogouna as the source of her trouble. Methinks she did so merely because the Babylonian had a sharp tongue and was, forbye, younger and better favored than most of the soldiers' women.

The first I knew of this was when Thyestes brought Simon to me. "Troop Leader," said the soldier, twisting his feet and scowling, "you maun do something about that witch."

"What witch?" I said.

"Charinos' hussy. She has bewitched my Mandana so that she's sick to death. None of us is safe while the witch live."

I will not repeat all the long discussion. Charinos could cite no real evidence of witchcraft; he had only his concubine's sick conviction and his own vague suspicion. This suspicion, however, he had communicated to several of his comrades. They, too, came to demand drastic action against Alogouna. I, for my part, fetched in Pyrron to argue that their fears were based on nought but groundless superstition.

Argument, howsomever, got us nowhere. Charinos denied that his quean had been working goetic magic; the others remained as stubbornly sure she had been. I closed our last meeting with these words:

"There's no proof that any lass has done aught to any other, by natural or uncanny means. Are we savages, to convict folk on vague suspicion or womanish jealousies? Go back to your tents, buckies, and pray to Apollon to cause any evil spell to recoil upon the sender. There shall be no violence or persecution, d'you ken?"

They went sullenly. For a few days nought betided. Then, at Rhesaina on the Chaboras, Alogouna disappeared. All, including Charinos, protested utter ignorance of what had befallen her. For several days I knew not if she had been murdered, or had hidden in Rhesaina, or had flown away on the back of a demon conjured up by her sorcery. Then Nirouphar told me:

"She fled and hid in the town, Rheon. I so advised her. The men were all ready to strangle her and bury her quietly that night. You would never have known."

"Thank the gods you saved us from that! At this rate you'll prove as necessary to me as your brother."

"Oh, fie! I will wager you say that to all the women."

We reached the upper Euphrates at Europos, which the Syrians call Karchemis. Here we saw again the frantic commercial bustle of a Syrian town. Everywhere people made things: jewelry and glassware and weapons and embroidered garments. Everybody who was not molding glass or hammering gold or stitching cloth was lying in wait to sell his wares.

When we had camped outside the walls, I entered the town with Elisas to buy provisions. Pyrron went along, too, because, he said, he could not bear to miss any new sights.

As soon as we put foot upon the narrow, muddy street that wound between the jutting angles of mud-brick houses, hawkers swarmed about us. Their voices rose to a roar.

"Lovely beads for your lady!" "This dagger is forged from the magical ore of Damascus! Feel the point!" "This flask of perfume will melt a heart of stone!" "Look at this fine tunic! Just feel these goods!" "Naughty pictures, to give your comrades a laugh!" "How about a beautiful rug for your tent?" "Come, O Hellene, and meet my sister! Nice clean girl, very passionate!"

I was about to buy a string of beads for Nirouphar when Elisas said in Greek: "Stay away from them, Troop Leader. Let me handle purchases. I know my own folk. Bastards."

I should have taken the sutler's advice without comment, but Pyrron had to pry further into matters. "That's a peculiar thing to say, Elisas. Why are you so severe with your own nation?"

Elisas shrugged. "Because I am one. Born in Chalybon. I know their good and bad points. Skillful workers, shrewd merchants. Very religious; castrate selves for love of goddess Atargatis. But not philosophers. Not soldiers any more either."

"How did this come about?" said Pyrron. "Do you mean you were fighters once?"

"Oh yes, mighty warriors, like great king Keretos. But all separate; each city with its own little king. We could not get together to fight foreigners, so they always conquered us: Egyptians, Judaeans, Assyrians, Babylonians, Persians, and now Macedonians."

Pyrron smiled. "That sounds like Hellas."

"It is. And it will be the same with you Hellenes, divided into many little quarreling states. You will see. But from being conquered so often we have lost our—how would you say—self-respect." Elisas sighed. "Sometimes I wish I could be a fine warrior and gentleman like you. But Baalos did not make me one, and it is too late to change." He wept.

This confession made me feel friendlier toward the little man than ever before. I gave him a gentle clap on the back, which all but felled him, and said: "Cheer up, laddie! If you're no swordsman, at least you foresee what supplies we shall need. That's no mean virtue."

During our stay in Europos, Elisas went around with the mien of one sunk in deepest gloom, though he brushed aside my questions as to what ailed him. When we were packing to leave, he came to me with a moneybag and said:

"Troop Leader Leon, I am a worthless vagabond. Even after you beat me in Soustara, I still took more than my just tenth from the tradesmen, though I became more careful. You, however, not only forgave my earlier sin, but also saved my life in the Tigris. Since then my sins have weighed me down. In Karchemis I have prayed to Baalos in the temple and have confessed to the priest. To him I bared all my sins. He told me I should suffer the lash of the seven demons of guilt until I told you my fault and repaired my wrong. So here is all the money I have taken from the merchants, over my allowed tenth, after deducting my offering to the temple. Does it please my lord?"

"Zeus!" I said. "As that playwriting fellow said, wonders are many, but none is more wonderful than man." I counted out the money. "Let's say no more about it. If you can keep yourself as honest as this for the rest of the journey, I'll try to reward you at the final reckoning."

"I thank you, noble Hipparch," he said, and turned away.

"One moment," I said. "To keep the demons of guilt at bay, hadn't you best give me back those two didrachmons you just now picked up from the pile?"

"You are my father and mother," he said, and handed me back the two coins. "Good for my morals that you have such sharp eyes. I thought you would not notice."

The road bore southwest and wound through a pass, called the Syrian Gate, in the forest-clad Amanos Mountains. When we came out of the pass and sighted the sea before us, I raised a shout of "the Sea!" as Xenophon's men had done many years before. The Thessalians echoed it.

On a strip of land betwixt the Amanos and the sea, I found the half-built city of Alexandreia-by-Issos. The workmen were laboring on the town in leisurely fashion. The sight of the elephant brought the work to a halt as everybody downed tools and rushed to see the sight.

"Who commands here?" I said, first in Greek, then in Persian, and lastly in my foul Syrian.

A Syrian said: "I am the master mason Pabilos, contractor for stone work. Can I sell you some fine building stone? If the noble hipparch mean to settle here, he will want a good stone house, not a mud hut that melts in the rain—"

"Save your breath, friend," I said. "I seek the viceroy Menes."

"He is at Myriandros; he comes here but twice or thrice a month to see how the work progresses. Would you not like a good building lot if I can get one for you at half the regular price?"

"Nay! Whither lies Myriandros?"

"Half a day's journey along the coast." Pabilos pointed southwest. "If the noble hipparch want a house in the Greek style, I can—"

"No house, thank you," I said, and led the hipparchia off on the coastal road.

Myriandros was no half-day's journey for the hipparchia; so hardened were we to travel that we reached it in two hours. A soldier directed us to the house of Achatos, the mayor. There were a pair of ruffianly guards lounging in front of the door, who reminded me unpleasantly of those at Persepolis.

The first man they fetched was Mayor Achatos, a tubby Syrian with a worried look. "Good Troop Leader," he said, "cannot your business be put off? Will it not wait till the morrow?"

"Why?"

"Our noble viceroy—may Baalos bless him—is sick. Indisposed is he."

"What ails him?"

"A toothache."

"Then my business will not wait. I am here on the express orders of King Alexander."

Achatos sighed and disappeared. Presently he came back with another Syrian, Menes' secretary, Chiramos. I had to go through the same argument again. At last Chiramos went away, promising to do what he could.

Achatos gave me a sharp look. "Are you intimate with the king? Are you close to him?"

"I am in constant touch with him by post," I said. "What about it?"

"Then can I make a plea to you in confidence? May I submit a private petition?"

"Surely."

Achatos jerked his thumb. "Can you do aught toward getting *him* out of here?"

"Menes?"

"Yes. In confidence, mind you. My life is in the hollow of your hand. But I am beset; I am desperate; I am frantic."

"What is the matter with him?"

"Oh, no doubt he is no worse than other officials. But, as he likes Myriandros, he settles here for months at a time. The town has to pay for his keep and that of his folk. He takes my best rooms and then complains about the quarters. His bodyguards pinch my daughters' buttocks and make lewd proposals to them. It is but a matter of time before they are raped or seduced, if indeed it have not already befallen unbeknownst to me. Could you persuade Alexander to order him to Damascus or some such place big enough for him? You would not find the town of Myriandros ungrateful."

Pressed for money as we were, I should probably have wrung as big a bribe as I could from the man, had not a roar from within interrupted us. A muffled voice exclaimed in Persian:

"I care not if it be Alexander's pet monkey, sent from India to plague me. I said I would hear no more petitions today! Get rid of him!"

There was a murmur of speech, and at last the same voice said: "Oh, Mithras smite the fellow! I will see him, but only for a moment."

The man who strode out was a tall stout Persian with a graying beard and a cloth tied around his swollen jaw. He mumbled in bad Greek:

"I am Menes. What is your business?"

In Persian I told him of my mission. "So I need a ship, arranged to carry an elephant. Here is my letter of authorization from Eumenes."

He glanced at the letter, then groaned and clutched his jaw. "No, no, it is not the letter, but my cursed tooth. I have tried medicine, magic, and prayer; but nothing does any good."

"In Thessalia we knock the aching tooth out with a hammer and a nail when it gets unbearable."

"I thought of that." Menes lowered his voice. "But, do you know, Hipparch, I have a deathly fear of such surgery? I, a big strong man who has fought in great battles? Now, let us see this letter." He moved his lips as he read it slowly, then pursed them. "I doubt if I can help you. Where is this elephant?"

"Outside in the street."

Menes and I walked out. The viceroy looked a little taken aback by the hipparchia, drawn up around our carts as if we expected a battle. Our experience with governors had made us wary. At the sight of Aias, however, Menes turned to me with a smile on his stern face.

"The pain of my tooth went away as soon as I laid eyes on the beast," he said. "It must be a good omen."

But then he frowned as he sauntered round the elephant, looking him up and down. "What does it weigh?"

I asked Kanadas, but he knew no more than I. "Nobody knows," I said. "After all, there is no scale in the world for weighing such a mass. I should guess several hundred talents."

"Hmm," said Menes. "That looks bad. It is not so much the weight as the fact that it will all be gathered into one place, if you understand me. Also, as the elephant moves about, the ship will tip. Let me think. It would take one of the largest rates..." he continued, half to himself. "We have a pair of eighters, the *Terrible* and *Horrible*, at Tyre. Then we have the four fivers of the *Victory* class, the *Victory* and *Triumph* at Arados and the *Fame* and *Glory* at Sidon. But these are all laid up out of commission, and it would take months to refit one and make it into an elephant barge. There are also some big ships in reserve at Alexandreia-in-Egypt, but those would do no more good than these I have mentioned."

"Why are there no suitable ships in readiness?" I asked.

"At the close of King Dareios' naval effort in the Western Sea, King Alexander sent word to lay up most of his larger ships, because they were too costly to run and were no longer needed for battles. The three-bankers, he said, would suffice to keep down pirates."

"Will you swear by Auramasdas that you have no ships that could carry Aias?"

"May you be kinless, Hellene, for doubting the word of a Persian gentleman!" he burst out. Then he added in normal tones: "If you wished to wait till summer, however, and I could find enough tax money, we might convert a ship now in reserve."

"We cannot wait so long."

Menes shrugged. "The king should have written me about this sooner. Even if we had a ship, it would do you little more good than these hulks I have spoken of. Nobody in his right mind would set out on a voyage to Hellas in the depth of winter. A gale would sink you ere you rounded Cape Anemourion."

"Well, then, tell me what to do. I must get this beast to Athens, and it is too far to swim."

Menes thought. "Your best chance is to go overland to Ephesos."

"Ephesos! But that is hundreds of leagues!"

"True, but there Philoxenos has some larger ships still in commission, to watch the truculent Greek states."

"Who is Philoxenos?"

"Admiral of the Aegean."

"This is terrible news! Our resources will not take us thither."

Menes shrugged again. "I do but think of your good. At best a sea voyage with the elephant will be dangerous, and I would cut it as short as I could."

I beat my head with my knuckles. Any such lengthening of our land journey would eat not only into our bonus funds but into Xenokrates' gift also. Of course I could present my draft to Harpalos in Tarsos, but, from what I had seen of Alexander's officials, I was doubtful of his honoring it.

"What is the route?" I asked. "The itinerary that Alexander's surveyors gave me went only to the Syrian coast."

"Let me think. The main road from Kilikia runs northwest to Tyana in Katpatouka." (This is the Persian name for Kappadokia.) "Then it takes a winding course westward and joins the Persian royal highway at Ipsos in Phrygia. After that, follow your nose to Ephesos. Of course, we are at war with Arivarates of Katpatouka, but hitherto Antigonos has kept the post road from Kilikia to the west open. So you should have no trouble."

"Why could I not follow the southern coast, where the climate is milder and the threat of war less imminent?"

"There is no continuous road along the southern coast; broken it is by many capes and bays. There are tracks and footpaths from one village to the next, but often one must march far inland. This time of year, even the tracks will be washed out."

Now it was my turn to groan. Further argument failed to move Menes, whose tooth now began to hurt him again. In a rage he shouted:

"I cannot do the impossible! I have no suitable ship and cannot get one before midsummer. Take your monster to Egypt or to Arimanes for all I care. It is not my fault that you thought not of such matters beforehand."

Much as I should have liked to yell back at him, I saw that this would only antagonize him the more, and there was yet something he could do for me if he would. I said:

"I fear you are right about my stupidity, Menes, but it is too late to begin the journey over. Will you do me one favor?"

"What?"

"Write me a letter to Philoxenos, explaining why you could not give me a ship and asking him to do so instead."

Menes grumbled: "I am not his master. If he refuse, I can do nought. But I will write your wretched letter, if only to get rid of you."

He stamped back into the house, holding his jaw and roaring: "Chiramos! Where is that polluted Syrian? You cannot trust these Syrians for an instant; turn your back and they sneak off—ah, there you are! Come along, come along, do not keep me waiting. I have an urgent letter to get out."

As he dictated, the pain in his tooth abated. Or, at least, he felt he had been too severe with me, for he mixed his dictation with advice and apology: *"Menes, viceroy of Syria, greets Admiral Philoxenos.* Excuse my outburst, Hipparch. *This letter goes by the hand of Troop Leader Leon of Atrax.* I am not myself, with my toothache and all. *The king, our master, has commanded Leon to take an elephant from India to Athens.* The cold on the Anatolian plateau may be too severe for your beast, though. Perhaps you should wait in Kilikia for spring. *To carry this creature across the sea, the king commanded me to prepare a ship.* But watch out for Harpalos. In confidence, he is a tricky scoundrel. *However, such a cargo would need a ship of the largest size.* But if you get through to Antigonos you should be all right. He is loyal at least—"

Chiramos threw down his tablet and burst into tears. "Noble Viceroy!" he wailed. "How can I take dictation when you speak partly to me and partly to your visitor? Pray, pray address one or the other until you have finished!"

Menes' tooth gave him a twinge, for he shut his eyes and groaned. Then he opened them and howled: "You sniveling Syrian blockhead! I will—"

He chased Chiramos out of the room, leaving me to think about the advice he had given.

From Alexandreia-by-Issos, the road northward goes through a pass near the sea. The Syrians call this the Kilikian Gate, while the Kilikians, on the other side, call it the Syrian Gate. Beyond this Syrio-Kilikian Gate we passed Issos and splashed through the ford at the Pinaros. Recalling that Vardanas had fought on the Persian side not only at the Granikos and Gaugamela but also at Issos, I said:

"Was it you whom I smote so hard on the head at Issos that I broke my sword and had to pick one up on the field? It was that sickle-curved Thracian blade I bore ere that thieving guide stole it."

Any Hellene would have said yes to make a good story of it. But Vardanas, after thought, said: "No, Leon, none struck me on the head at Issos. But several tried."

North of Issos the land opened out into the Kilikian plain. This is a fertile country of deep, soft soil. The air was cool, mild, damp, and hazy. The rains had turned the roads into strips of mud even deeper than those of Syria. We crossed the Pyramos at Mopsou-hestia, supposedly the home of Mopsos the diviner in Trojan times, and the Saros at Adana without mishap.

Pyrron continued to keep his distance from Nirouphar, who found herself thrown into my company for want of other persons with whom to converse. She said:

"Come, O Rheon, tell me of your home and family. Who are your folk?"

"We are knights of Thessalia, a branch of the Aleuadai, with much the position in our land that your family has in yours. If none has been born, wedded, or died in the last year, they're as follows: There is my father Aristos, a short stout fellow, as mild as milk. Then there is my mother, Rhoda. She is taller than my father and rides him with a tight rein."

"Indeed? I thought all Greek men ruled their women with rods of iron!"

"So they boast, but it is not the whole truth. When last I heard from them, my mother's mother was still alive and hearty, albeit well past sixty. There is my elder brother Demonax, who is really the best man of the lot of us, and his wife Zobia and their two infants, and my younger brother Aristos, and my sister Phila, and a couple of widowed aunts and an orphaned cousin who live with us. I also have two married sisters who live elsewhere, and a brother who died."

"Do not tell me the names of all those others yet! I shall find it hard enough to remember those you have already named. It sounds like a big, bustling family, like ours in Sousa."

"Oh, it is all of that! I will warrant that during our quarrels we out-shout any other family in Thessalia."

Thus were things made intimate between us. Nirouphar had one of the most attractive qualities a woman can have, that of drawing a man out and making him feel important. Betimes, when I became too pompous, her brother would gaily puncture my dignity with some needle-pointed Persian witticism; but she never did. No wonder I loved her!

At Adana I called a council and said: "Lads, we now near the lair of Harpalos. Several of those we have met have dropped hints of warning against this man. It seems likely, therefore, that he will not only refuse the money the king has empowered us to draw from the treasury, but will also try to seize what little we have left. That's the pass we face; how shall we put the horses to it?"

Vardanas said: "We had better keep the women out of his sight, if the tales of his lechery be true."

"That reminds me," I said, "that his brother Philippos in India advised me to give him something in the female line to get on his good side. What think you of such a proposal?"

"'Tis over-late to think on that," said Thyestes. "For a slave girl of the sort that would excite the old satyr, we maun go back to Babylon and spend ten or twenty pounds of silver."

"Besides," said Vardanas, "when was the tiger's appetite sated by a lamb chop? If he mean to rob us, he will hardly be deflected from his aim by such a gift."

Thyestes said: "I misdoubt he'll try to lure us into soft quarters in his palace, there to seize us in our sleep. So let's refuse all sic offers and camp in a place where we can either fight or flee."

Vardanas said: "And let us keep not only more sentries on duty, but one or two mounted pickets to watch the roads. My Dahas are good at that."

Kanadas said: "Keep half of horses saddled, half of mules hitched, and elephant ready to move."

Pyrron said: "While I'm not a military man and so unaccustomed to guarding my life and liberty against dastardly plots, it would seem advisable not to let more than one of us into the treasurer's grasp at any one time."

"Good," I said. "And we'll do more than that. We'll keep half our men under arms at all times."

Thyestes frowned. "I'm no sure about that, Leon."

"Why?"

"The men are getting clean worn down with pushing ahead, day after day. They're beginning to grumble that we shall never reach Hellas and they'll never have a chance to rest again. They'll no like continuous duty."

I agreed to a four-man watch, which was one quarter of our remaining Thessalians. I also bought some extra lengths of chain with which I bound the chests, and doubled the guard over them.

I also wrote the king daily, telling of my suspicions and of the precautions taken. Of course, Harpalos might still crush us by overwhelming force; but I could think of no more ways to guard against attacks by stealth and treachery.

And thus, in the first third of Elaphebolion, we came to Tarsos. The Kydnos flows through the town and then opens out into an estuary that forms a fine harbor. The town itself is of mixed Hellenic and Syrian culture. In the market place we saw sophists disputing, Phoenician traders chaffering, and Greek mercenaries swaggering. All business stopped at the sight of the elephant. People ran alongside, heedless of their dignity, to shout questions in a Greek dialect that I could hardly understand. The liveliness and curiosity of the folk made me well nigh feel as if I were once more home in Hellas.

Despite the pleas of the populace, I would not stop in the market place. We went on out the north gate on the road to Kappadokia. I looked for a defensible knoll to camp on; but the plain is flat in all directions around Tarsos, though we could see the Taurus Mountains against the sky line to the north.

We therefore chose a grove of trees several furlongs north of the city. When I had made sure that the camp was guarded against sudden surprisal, and that sharp eyes were watching in all directions, I returned to the city. To command respect, as Vardanas had taught me, I rode upon the elephant, clad in my finest raiment. Elisas, who came with me, could have ridden Aias also, as there was room for four in the booth. But, still dreading the beast, he preferred his mule.

Harpalos had taken over the palace of the Persian viceroys. This structure stood in a park surrounded by a high brick wall with spikes along the top. At the gate stood a pair of hoplites in gilded helms and cuirasses. I gave my message, and soon a young Hellene came to escort us to Alexander's treasurer.

Inside the wall was an elegant park where flourished trees and shrubs from many distant lands; for, after money and women, exotic plants were Harpalos' next most pressing passion.

The palace was a spacious structure of tawny brick with a fine stone portico upheld by marble columns in half-Hellenized style. Large though the palace was already, Harpalos was adding a wing. Masons chipped, carpenters hammered, and plasterers scraped.

As the usher led us toward the portico, he said: "If we chance to meet the treasurer's second—ah—wife, Glykera, we must prostrate ourselves and cry: 'Rejoice, O Queen!'"

"Queen?" said I, with a gravid glance at Elisas. "Mean you I must flop down on my belly to some unknown strumpet—"

"Not so loud, good sir, please! If you wish aught from the treasurer, you must, like the octopus, take on the color of your surroundings."

The front doors of the palace stood open, with guards erect beside them. Inside, we passed through a shadowy audience hall whose roof was upheld by a forest of pillars, like unto the audience halls at Persepolis but on a smaller scale. From the remoter rooms of the palace came the clink of the coiners' hammers. After a wait in an anteroom, we were ushered into the treasurer's private office.

Harpalos son of Machatas was a stout man who looked much like his brother Philippos. He was oiled and scented and clean-shaven and clad in a shimmering silken robe like that which I had seen on Vaxathras in Sousa. One could have mistaken him for a gelding. From the pomp of his surroundings I expected him to be as haughty as a Persian king. Instead, he rose and greeted us warmly, embracing me and patting Elisas' cheek. The only odd thing about him was that his bulging green eyes stared in a way that reminded me of a fish.

"Rejoice, blessed ones!" he cried in a good if Macedonian-accented Greek. His fat made him wheeze as he spoke. "I have heard of your coming and of your exploits; my brother has written me from distant India. Ah—surely the spirit of my deified first wife Pythonike has watched over you, to bring you through so many perils safely! Have a drop of this; it is real Chian. When did you see the divine Alexander last?"

"Last summer," I said, sipping the marvelous wine.

"Have you heard about his wounding?"

"Nay. What's this?"

"Ah—he climbed the wall of the city of the Mallians at the head of his men, leapt down inside, and fought the Indians almost alone before his men could reach him. An arrow pierced his lung, and his life is despaired of, if indeed he have not already perished."

"How terrible! What a calamity!" I said. "Pray the gods will speed his recovery. Is there aught more to tell?"

"No; this is the latest news to arrive, though it was sent from India nearly a month ago."

I was not merely being polite in my concern for the king's health. Alexander had no heirs. If he died now, his generals and officials would scramble for power, and a mere troop leader with a chest full of treasure would be swallowed at a gulp by the first one to lay hand upon him. To enjoy any kind of protection, we—the hipparchia— should have to shop for a new master.

Howsomever, I did not need to believe that Harpalos was telling the truth, or that Alexander had died forsooth. The king, for all his small size, was a man of great strength and endurance who had recovered from the gravest of wounds ere this.

We got down to business. I handed over Eumenes' letter authorizing me to draw upon the treasury, explained Menes' refusal to give us a ship, and brought out a statement of our expenses.

"Explain it, Elisas," I said.

When Elisas had done so, Harpalos said: "Let me praise the order in which you have kept your accounts, O Hipparch. You should see some of the statements I receive! Nothing but wild guesses as to whither the money has gone. Now, ah—as to this, the king's word is of course law. Leave this letter to me, and all shall be taken care of."

"When, O Harpalos?"

"Do not worry, best one. A transaction like this takes at least a few days. You will have to confer with my man Pygmalion, to reckon the cost of your remaining journey. And he, alas, is not here."

"Where then is he?"

"Ah—he went home to Byblos for a visit. I expect him back soon. Meanwhile, make yourselves comfortable. I hear you are camped in the mud on the Kappadokian road. Surely we can find space for you in the city?"

The man seemed so friendly and charming that it was hard to refuse. Even Elisas, who took no sunny view of human nature, cast me a longing glance. I found myself weakening.

But, as says Hippokrates, appearances are deceptive. Just then the lamplight caught a huge ruby in a ring on Harpalos' thumb. This was the kind of gem one would look for in the headcloth of an Indian king. Harpalos had not, I thought, bought that jewel in the open market on his salary. I said:

"I thank you, my lord treasurer. But I think we'll stay where we are."

"My dear old chap, why make life so hard for yourself?"

I smiled. "I've found it best to keep the lads roughing it. Then they mind it not. But, if once I bed them down on soft cushions, they hate to move on. When they do strike the road again, I get nought but sulks and grumbles over lack of comfort. Nay, you'd best let us be, for we yet have a long hard road before us."

245

He seemed a little hurt, but accepted my refusal on condition that I would take dinner with him. He wanted all the officers at once. Remembering Babylon, I refused again, allowing him only one at a time.

"A man of grim and austere principles you must be," he said. "Would I had more such men to serve me! Perhaps someday we can do something about that." He winked one bulging green eye.

That night I dined with Harpalos and some of his officials. Although I expected an oriental orgy like that in Babylon, nothing of the sort occurred. Nor did "Queen" Glykera appear.

Yet I was struck by the sumptuousness of this dinner. Off golden plates we ate delicacies from as far away as Babylonia and Persia. Though the rigors of the journey had rendered me almost slim, a month of Harpalos' dinners, I thought, would make me too fat to mount a horse.

My couch mate was a man named Sabiktas, clad as a Hellene but speaking with a strong accent that led me to class him as some sort of Thracian or Bithynian. He was, he explained half jestingly, Alexander's viceroy of Kappadokia.

"I was legally and officially appointed," he said, "and I can prove it. But what good does that do me, when that whipworthy rogue Arivarates holds sway in my province? If Antigonos, whose duty it is, would rouse himself to drive out the dog-faced usurper, I could rise to my just position in the world. Every year we hear of some stunning victory Antigonos has won over the Kappadokians. But then it turns out that the boundaries remain where they were, and the usurper is as firm on his throne as ever."

After the meal, some of the officials got a puckle drunk and rallied Harpalos on his success with women. To hear them talk, one would think him a satyr and a Herakles rolled into one. He lolled on his couch, soaking up the praise with a bland smile, until he fixed his fishlike stare on me.

"Leon!" he said. "I am told there is a handsome girl in your hipparchia; the sister of that Persian officer."

"Well?" I said.

"Fetch her here some evening; we will have a mixed dinner. Some really lively entertainment. Ah—I will find a good bouncing wench for you."

This was only one of several remarks which showed that Harpalos knew more about our expedition than he had any right to know. He must, I thought, have spies everywhere. If he wanted me to fetch Nirouphar and then provide me with another woman, one needed not the wisdom of Solon to see that he had lewd intentions toward the Persian maid. As we say at home, wine is wont to reveal the mind of man.

Back at the camp next morn, I called my friends together. "Bring your sister," I told Vardanas.

"Now," I said, "our great sausage of a treasurer is fain to entertain our Nirouphar at dinner the night—"

"Oh, good!" cried the lass. "I have not seen a party since Vardanas so cruelly dragged me forth from that one in Babylon."

"I'm sorry, Nirouphar dear, but I fear you cannot go to this one, either."

"You are a beast, Rheon of Atrax! Why can I not?"

"Because Harpalos, though no athlete, needs no mounting block to vault upon his chosen steed." I reminded them of Harpalos' repute as a judge of many-gaited women, and told them of his proposal to me.

"Oh," said Nirouphar.

Vardanas said: "I have heard rumors of this man's lechery. His fellow officials did not unduly puff up his prowess. We must hide my sister."

"But where?" said I. "In the bottom of a cart?"

After we had talked the matter over without agreement, I called in Elisas and put the problem to him.

The Syrian smiled. "No need to hide her in a cart, noble Hipparch. Let me fix her up, and you shall see."

"What do you mean?" said Vardanas.

"No harm, Lord Vardanas. I will not hurt her honor."

Two hours later, Elisas led in a shuffling beldame with straggly gray hair hanging down before her face.

"Arimanes!" cried Vardanas. "What has he done to you, Nirouphar?"

"A little flour in the hair," said Elisas. "Some of the shabbier clothes from the soldiers' women, a touch of cosmetics, a little practice in acting like a crone, and behold!"

I suppose Elisas had once been involved in some sort of slaving or kidnaping, so well did he know the art of hiding a woman while she walks about in plain view. We were none too soon with our disguise. Ere noon, our Dahan picket galloped in to warn us of a party approaching from Tarsos.

Then a group of Harpalos' mercenaries arrived with a wagonload of wineskins and the treasurer's compliments. The wine was Rhodian, fine stuff albeit not Chian. I put it under guard, for swifter than the flight of a falcon can a generous supply of liquor ruin a military unit.

I accompanied the mercenaries back to the palace to send my thanks in to the treasurer and ask about Pygmalion. No, he had not returned. When I got back to camp, Vardanas said:

"A fellow was around here with a bid from Harpalos to dinner. All the officers are to come; also Pyrron and Nirouphar."

"What said you?"

"That we could do nought without you. He asked after my sister, too, saying he wanted a look at her. We showed him Nirouphar in her haggish guise, and he went away frowning."

"Go you to this dinner and represent the rest. Pick up what news you can."

"That's no all, Leon," said Thyestes. "I just had a whin of a talk with the Persian lass, and she has something to tell you."

"Fetch her, then," I said.

When Nirouphar came in, she said: "Do you remember the man in charge of the gift of wine this morning?"

"Aye."

"Well, while the men were unloading the skins, this fellow got Kronios and a few other troopers aside and quizzed them about camping here in the mud. He said: did they not think it uncommonly cruel of the hipparch to keep them out in the rain when nice soft berths awaited them in Tarsos? Kronios told me about it, for he has been aiming a stiff spear at me ever since his woman ran away."

"I will show the baseborn lout!" said Vardanas, but the rest of us shushed him. Nirouphar continued:

"I also heard Porygonos say: if you, Rheon, love sleeping out, nobody is stopping you, but they like a little comfort ere they die."

I said: "That's serious. What think you I should do, Thyestes?"

"Call the ruckle together and make a speech, telling them as much about our true plight as you dare."

I groaned, being no willing orator; but it had to be done. I talked softly and finished: "What I'm trying to say is: 'Twill be time to thank the benevolence of this gentleman when he's given us our silver and let us out of his grip, without trying to steal it back."

The men were quieted for the nonce. But, weary of the road and of my everlasting prodding and pushing, they remained sullen.

The next day Pygmalion was still absent. I insisted on another word with Harpalos, who was all smiles and promises.

"I know how eager you are to get on, dear Leon," he said. "But in another day or two he will surely be back. If not, I will write him.... No, there is nobody else whom I would trust with such a reckoning. Pygmalion is a skilled computer who has studied arithmetic under the wise Babylonians."

That evening, Thyestes went to the palace to be entertained. Harpalos sent a wagonload of his exotic dainties to our camp. This was a clever man. Rather than stiffen our resistance by openly attacking us, he would dissolve it away in the juices of kindness and generosity.

The next day there was still no Pygmalion, and another load of good things to eat and drink arrived at camp. Harpalos also sent some soldiers of the garrison and a troop of harlots, all wreathed and garlanded for revelry. While Pyrron was feasted at the palace, I strove to keep my men sober and orderly. Despite my efforts, howsomever, an orgy was soon under way. When words ceased to avail, my officers and I resorted to blows.

The next thing I knew, four Thessalians laid hold of me and bore me, cursing and struggling, to the banks of the Kydnos, into which they tossed me. The waters of the little river, though but a few palms deep, were like ice. Thyestes followed me with a splash.

When we had dragged ourselves out, I said: "Buckie, saw you who's back of this? An I knew who he was, I'd kill the dastard."

"'Twas none of our lads at all," replied he between chattering teeth. "'Twas those all-abandoned men and women the treasurer sent to corrupt them."

When we got back to camp, the disturbance had somewhat abated because some of the people had fallen into drunken slumber. As nobody was on watch, we had no trouble getting to our tents and arming ourselves. Nearby, Vardanas held his four Dahas in a ring around Nirouphar's tent. Kanadas and Siladites guarded Aias.

"Oh, there you are!" cried Vardanas. "What befell you?"

"I'll tell you later," I said. "Get your bow. To massacre the whole hipparchia were a remedy too strong for the disease, but we can at least drive out the polluted Tarsians."

We made our plans. Thyestes blew the trumpet. When silence had fallen, I roared in my best battle voice:

"I will count three, and then every man or woman who belongs not to the hipparchia shall be slain with arrows or trampled by the elephant. One—two—three! Go to it, lads!"

The elephant gave a frightful squeal and lumbered into the camp. From his back Vardanas' bow twanged. One of Harpalos' soldiers yelled as the arrow skewered his leg. The Dahas walked into the firelight alongside the elephant, bows drawn.

In a trice the visitors scrambled up and fled. I saw at least two men rise up unsated from women in order to run. And so ended the mutiny.

The next day the men were contrite as I held court and doled out fines and beatings. One, however, had disappeared. I ought to have searched Tarsos for him, but I had too much else on my mind. He was only Polygonos of Iolkos, the least worthy of the Thessalians, and no great loss.

There was still no Pygmalion at the palace. Struck by a thought, I asked the young usher about the missing mathematician.

"That old Phoenician?" said the usher. "He died a month ago. The treasurer sent his body back to his folk in Byblos."

As soon as I got back to camp, I gave orders to strike our tents. Off we went again. Meseemed that Harpalos was keeping me dangling until he learned whether Alexander lived. If the king died, Harpalos would feel he could seize us with impunity.

We could not reach the Kilikian Gate, the pass from the Kilikian plain to the highlands of Kappadokia, by nightfall. We did, however, camp in the shadow of the Taurus. Just to make sure, I took another look at our treasure chests. No sooner had I laid hands on them than I cried:

"Immortal Zeus!"

"What is it?" said Thyestes and Vardanas, running up to the tent at the sound of my voice.

I whispered: "Those are not our chests!"

Thyestes' mouth fell open, and Vardanas sat down. The latter said: "Mithras grant that you be wrong!"

"Not so loud!" I said, tearing at the chains. "I know our chests well. I've been in and out of them often enough. Ours had three bronze clasps each, while this one has but two and that one is closed by a sliding bolt. They're the same size and shape as ours, but anybody from Karia to Carthage can see the difference. Oh, why did I no look at them more closely this morning!"

At last I got one of the chests open. It held nought but bricks. I opened the other, though I knew it would prove to contain bricks too, as indeed it did. Thyestes said:

"It maun be that one of the parties the treasurer sent out to provision us looked our chests over. Then last night during the party, his men traded for ours a pair as nearly like them as could be found in Tarsos. The men we had guarding them had wine as a chain about their wits, too."

I beat my head with my knuckles. "Woe, woe! What in Hera's name shall we do the now, bodies? We're fair ruined. How shall we ever face Alexander?"

"'Tis a sad outcome to our labors," said Thyestes. "Could we no steal our chests back from Harpalos?"

"Nay; he'll have stowed the treasure in his vaults and be on watch for us."

"Well then, what for no seize one of these villages and gar the folk to disgorge their hordes? I kens some tricks with fire that'll wring silver from the most beggarly looking loons." Thyestes smiled a sinister smile and made motions of brushing hot metal against flesh.

"None of that!" I said. "We have troubles enow without inviting more."

"It need no be a town on the main road, that could easily send a waul till the government. And sin time began, that's how commanders of troops have refilled their coffers."

"I said nay! The king forbade it ane's errand."

"You're either addle-witted or fainthearted, Leon Aristou, to let that stop you in time of need."

"Hold your tongue, an you can think of nought better! I'll carry out my orders to the letter or die trying."

"Then what shall we do indeed?" said Vardanas, tears running down his face. "Slay ourselves? Turn pirate or highwayman?"

For a while we sat in deepest gloom. At last Thyestes said: "We maun ask the philosopher. Though a fool in the feck of practical matters, he does have a store of his own kind of wisdom."

When appealed to, Pyrron said: "My word, this is a shocking surprise! But I don't think we're reduced to such drastic measures as suicide yet. We still have the elephant, so it's our duty to carry on and get the animal to Athens. 'Before virtue have the deathless gods set the sweat of man's brow.'"

"But how?" I said. "We cannot get Aias to Ephesos without men to ward him and gather fodder for him, and we cannot hold the men without money to pay them. Let them hear we're moneyless, and most will look for another master."

Pyrron said: "If Siladites has taught Aias a few tricks, we might pass a helmet for gifts in the villages."

"We might thus collect a whole drachma a day," I said. "Man, you have no idea of how much this creature eats! And the Anatolian villagers are thrifty carles."

For half an hour we talked of ways to beg, borrow, earn, or steal enough money or food to get us to Ephesos, but without finding a solution. Then one of the treasure guards put his head into the tent and said:

"Troop Leader, the sutler is lief to speak with you."

Elisas came in, glanced at the brick-filled chests, and said: "Lord Leon, if you come with me, I will show you something you will like."

Inaudos the Kordian was with him. The twain conducted us to the carts. Inaudos, grinning, thrust his arms into a cart full of food. Under the sacks of flour, on the floor of the cart, lay our money.

Inaudos went to another cart full of hay. Underneath were piled the animal skins and other specimens from India.

"Did you do this?" I said.

"Yes," said Elisas. "Inaudos helped me. We thought chaining up the chests and posting guards all around them would only draw the treasurer's eye to them. Did, too. So we moved all the treasure to these carts and put earth and firewood in the chests. Then when Harpalos' men took our chests and left chests full of bricks, they only traded bricks for sand and wood."

"Why didna you tell me? We've nigh hand died of grief and shock!"

"I was not sure you would like the plan. You are a godlike man, terrible in your wrath. We thought that if nothing befell our chests, we would put the treasure back into them after leaving Tarsos."

"Oh, bless you both!" I cried, hugging and kissing them. "Little friends have surely proved great friends." I went to the cart with the money and counted out fifty drachmai for each. "Here, billies, do as you like with it. Though we're short of funds, I'll take this out of my own pay if I must."

"Too much," said Elisas. "You saved my life, so this is a small thing to do for you in return."

"Take it, and dispute me not, lest my normal thrift make itself felt again. Off with you!"

Some of the men overheard our talk and gathered to learn what was afoot. When they understood the stratagem of the sutler and the Kordian, they cheered them, too.

"It were fitting if you rewarded their quickness of wit out of your own purses," I told the Thessalians sternly. "Were it no for them, yesternight's folly had left us destitute."

Shamefaced, the Thessalians dug into their purses to add to the reward I had given. Some cursed Harpalos with all the vigor of old soldiers and uttered grandiose threats of vengeance against him.

Pyrron said: "Be thankful you've taken your head safely out of the wolf's mouth, as the wolf said to the crane in the fable. And now, an interesting question for speculation has just occurred to me. What will Harpalos do when he discovers that his men have brought him two chests full of earth?"

253

"By the Dog!" I cried. "I know not what he'll do, but I know what we'd better do, and smartly! Strike the tents! Tonight we shall march till we drop!"

Dusk closed down upon us as the road wound up through the foothills toward the defile called the Kilikian Gate. There was a clatter of hooves behind us and a hail. I rode back to see what was up. A rider was trying to reach the tail of our column, but his horse would not go near the elephant, and there was not enough room to pass around the beast. The man waved and shouted:

"In the name of Harpalos, treasurer of the empire, you are commanded on pain of death to return at once to Tarsos!"

I glanced back, caught Vardanas' eye, and made the motion of shooting. Vardanas' bowstring twanged. The man screeched and fell off his horse, which bolted.

"Hide this carrion," I said.

Inaudos and another camp man hauled the corpse to the mouth of a narrow ravine and tossed it behind a thicket.

"Now hasten!" I said. "We've gained a few hours by slaying that wight; let us see that we make good use of it! Get up!"

The ramparts of the Kilikian Gate closed in upon us. Crags of limestone loomed over us like the towers of some Kyklops' castle. There was scarce room for our carts and the elephant betwixt the cliff on one side and the swift cold stream that furrows the pass on the other. The roar of the river almost drowned the creaking of axles and the clatter of hooves. On our right rose the cliff face where an inscription tells of Alexander's passage through the gate on his way to Issos, but it was too dark to read the writing.

We made another sixty or seventy furlongs ere we halted again. We not only suffered great fatigue but also feared, in the darkness of the gorge, to stray off the road into the river.

The next day we pushed on, with no further sign of pursuit from Tarsos. The gorge broadened into a vale of tamarisks, on both sides of which rose the steep slopes of the Taurus, clad in somber forests of oak and fir. Although the footing became easier, it now began to rain.

We struggled on, but the rain turned to snow. Kanadas said: "Must stop, Troop Leader."

"Why?" I asked.

"Elephant get cold, die. Must make fire to warm him."

"We dare not start a fire here!" I said. "Between Harpalos' men behind and Arivarates' men before, we're in peril every moment on this road."

"No, no, must have fire! Otherwise elephant freeze feet, die! What is use of all this work and travel if my beautiful Mahankal die?" The Indian began to weep.

"A plague upon it!" I said. "Very well; let us begin to look for a sheltered spot."

I peered ahead into the grayness. As there was no wind, and the snow was damp, every feathery frond of the tamarisks was coated with white. Within another furlong we found a little vale where a brook came in from the side. A naked crag, leaning out over this dell, provided some shelter. Soon we had a small fire blazing, while melting snow made puddles all around us.

"I like it not," I said to Thyestes. "We sudna stop nor light a fire till we're past Tyana."

"I thinks 'tis safe," he said. "Seldom maun Arivarates' men come so far south. And 'twould take a gey forcible officer to gar his men go plowing athort the country on sic a day!"

As Thyestes usually insisted on more care against possible foemen than the rest of us thought needful, I cast off my forebodings and rode out with Vardanas and the Dahas to set up mounted pickets.

But, to the man in fear, everything rustles. My heart all but leapt from my mouth when there came a crashing of feet and a flurry of snow. A spotted deer, fleeing for its life, almost blundered into us, scrambled for its footing, recovered, and started off in a new direction. With the speed of lightning, Spargapithas whipped his Sakan bow from its case and let fly. The deer fell dead.

Just then a leopard, shaggy in its winter coat, bounded toward us. I suppose the snow had deadened our sound and scent so that the beast, intent on its quarry, was unaware of us. Our horses snorted and reared. Seeing us at last, the leopard slid to a stop, gave a spitting snarl, and scampered off. Spargapithas loosed a second shaft but missed. He cursed in Sakan as he searched for his arrow.

Vardanas said: "He fears we will take the deer back to camp and eat it before his watch be over."

"Tell him to worry not," I said. "We'll not touch tooth to it ere he come."

We took the deer back to camp, where the men received it with cheers, despite their dank condition, and helped to skin the beast. I told the cook:

"Stand back, fellow; this is one nice piece of flesh I'll not have spoilt."

I prepared to roast the deer myself, heedless of loss of dignity. The snow kept falling. The wind rose and the air grew colder. Aias squealed and grumbled unhappily. Kanadas, feeding his pet's insatiable maw with hay, said:

"Must rig tent, Troop Leader, to keep cold wind off him. Blanket not enough."

I told Thyestes to work on that. For hours the men cut poles, pinned tent cloths together, and wrestled with ropes. Twice they had the contraption nearly up when it fell down. Aias moaned and gurgled sadly. Meanwhile I cooked the deer.

It was late afternoon when the elephant tent was rigged at last. It formed a covering over Aias' back and one side, while the crag protected his other side. Alas! We no sooner got the tent up, the last rope tied, and the last peg driven, when Aias gave a playful tug with his trunk. Down came the tent in a heap.

Thyestes smote his thigh. "Furies take the great stirk!" he shouted. "Gin he want it back up, let him put it up hissel!"

The Indians scolded the elephant, who hung his head and drooped his eyelids in shame. Nirouphar talked to him, explaining the error of his ways and patting his rough leathery trunk, until he was cheered up again. Then it was not hard to put the tent back up a second time.

The light faded; the deer was done. The cook was making ready to serve it when a sentry said: "Troop Leader! Here comes our picket!"

Spargapithas rode in and dismounted. Vardanas said: "He says you forgot to relieve him."

It was true; between the elephant tent and the deer, I had left the Daha out longer than I meant to. On the other hand, he ought not to have left his post while he still could stand. I began a terrific scolding, with Vardanas translating.

"He smelt the deer," said Vardanas, "and feared you had broken your word not to eat it before he arrived."

I cut off a piece and gave it to Madouas, whose turn at picket duty it now was. "Eat this on your guard," I said.

The Daha was mounting his horse when a sentry yelled. Ere we could reach for our weapons, a swarm of armed men sprang out of the earth, it seemed, and rushed upon us.

They were Kappadokian hillmen, clad in loose trousers, high boots, and sheepskin coats, with felt hats or fur caps on their heads. They bore bows and spears; a few had shields or helmets. There were at least a hundred.

Never was a surprise attack more skillfully planned or more adroitly carried out. They had crept up from two directions, hiding behind knolls and crags, until a sudden rush brought them breast to breast with us in a few heartbeats.

A man who ran with the rest, but fell behind because he was weighed down by a coat of scale mail, called out: "Yield!"

Some of my men, who had grasped swords or javelins, cast them down. Thyestes, on the other hand, drew his sword, shouted, "*Eleleleu!*" and ran toward the leader. Perhaps he was being heroic. But, without wishing to cast any slight on his memory, I think he merely did the first thing that came to his mind, as men will when surprised.

Ere I could move, bows twanged and javelins flew. One arrow, shot at close range, drove through Thyestes' canvas corselet. Such was the force of the shaft that the cruel point pierced through his body and out the other side. Another arrow struck his neck and a javelin his leg, but the body wound was the one that did for him. He staggered and fell, his sword flying out of his hand. Behind me a slave cried out as another arrow, missing Thyestes, wounded him in the thigh.

Taken unawares and outnumbered five to one, the rest of my men cast down their arms. I followed their example, seeing no advantage in adding my death to Thyestes'.

"Who is the leader?" said the armored man in good if accented Attic.

"Leon of Atrax, troop leader for King Alexander and commander of this hipparchia. Pray, sir, who are you?"

"Arivarates son of King Arivarates of Katpatouka," said the Kappadokian. He was a young man, his beard a mere down. "What is your mission?"

"If you'll let us take down yonder tent, you will see."

"Stand still."

Arivarates the younger motioned to a couple of his men, who cut the ropes holding up the elephant tent. Down fell the tent. The men who had cut the ropes leapt back with yells of terror at the sight of Aias. The other Kappadokians wavered.

Now was the time, had we been ready, to have seized our arms and set upon these foreigners, while the Indians drove the elephant at them. I looked around, but none of the Thessalians met my eye. All sat or stood with hanging heads, in that dazed state of shame and wretchedness that seizes a man first captured; for everybody knows that in four cases out of five, capture means lifelong slavery.

Ere I could form a plan, Arivarates shouted in his own tongue. The Kappadokians rallied. Several bows were trained upon my midriff.

"Hold still, all," said Arivarates. He strolled forward and looked up at the elephant. "For the love of Ma! I have heard my father tell of seeing these beasts at Dareios' court, but this is the first one I have seen with my own eyes." He turned upon me and said in stern notes: "A mighty reinforcement for that all-daring knave Antigonos!"

"Nay," I said. "This is but a peaceful scientific expedition."

"How so?"

I told the Kappadokian prince the tale of our mission. When I had finished, he said: "A fetching tale, could one but credit it. However, it is my father's place to decide what shall be done with you. You must come to Mazaka."

"Where is that?"

"Forty leagues hence."

"Herakles! That's no afternoon's stroll."

"There is no help for it. Gather your gear and ready yourselves to march. You will have to walk."

"At least let us take care of our comrade," I said, pointing to Thyestes.

"Then be quick."

I hastened to Thyestes. As I thought, he was dead. We buried him on the spot, and Pyrron preached a short eulogy on the Poet's text:

The lot of man; to suffer and to die.

We all wept, though many of the Thessalians had not liked Thyestes because of his strictness and rough ways. Some had even held his base birth against him, resenting, as they put it, "being ordered about by one who is no better than we are."

As for me, I felt lost without him. He was a simple soldier, with neither Vardanas' charm nor Pyrron's wisdom. He had his faults, being lustful and sometimes cruel. But he was brave and trusty and hardy, with a good practical mind for military matters, virtues sorely needed in an enterprise like ours.

BOOK EIGHT

Anatolia

ARIVARATES TOLD OFF one of his men to walk with each of the Thessalians and Dahas and two with each of the officers and Pyrron. We stumbled through the mud while the women, children, and servants, weeping and wailing, rode the mules and carts. Others of Arivarates' men led the horses. Siladites was allowed to ride the elephant, as there was no other way to guide the beast; but Kanadas was forced to stamp through the slush behind me. Nirouphar rode in the booth on Aias' back.

After the first few hours, we suffered the torments of sinners in Tartaros. This was not from cruelty on Arivarates' part, for he was a kindly captor despite his gruff manner, but because our legs were unused to all-day walking and our shoes were not soled for icy mud.

Happily for us, not much was left of the first day of our captivity. When darkness came, Kanadas sat down wearily by me and said: "Now you learn what slavery is like, Leon. After while you do not think it good thing any more."

"Would I had as long a pair of shanks as yours, man," I said.

"What is this?" barked Arivarates. "Keep apart and do not talk to each other unless I am there to listen. I know what you are thinking of: plans of escape. You had better give up any such hopes."

"My dear prince," I said, "I can think of nought the now save the pain in my legs. If I ran, I couldn't go ten paces ere they folded under me.

"Oh!" said Arivarates. "Let me see. You need the muscles kneaded to limber them, like this."

He dug his fingers into my calf with such force that I yelled.

"That is how to do it," he said. "You and the Indian shall massage each other's legs, and I will make the other prisoners do the same."

The next day we tottered off on our road again. The Kappadokians strode easily beside us, watching us closely. We had no converse with them because of the differences of language, but they did not even talk much among themselves. Like the other folk of inner Anatolia—the Paphlagonians, Lykaonians, and Phrygians—they are stocky, hairy, and hook-nosed like the Armenians. In manner they are slow, stolid, and silent. But, if they lack the liveliness of Hellenes and Syrians, they are more honest and true than either.

The valley opened out on the Anatolian plain, a wide, brown, gently rolling expanse, cut here and there by steep-sided valleys through which small swift rivers flow. Patches of melting snow lay everywhere. There were few trees and little sign of life, except for fowl flying overhead, occasional flocks of sheep, and once a herd of wild asses in the distance.

We reached Tyana the second day after our capture. So crippled were we that we staggered along with our arms about the necks of our Kappadokian guards. One of our three remaining slaves escaped on a mule, so Arivarates made all the menservants of the hipparchia, too, dismount and walk.

Arivarates let us rest in Tyana; it was either that or carrying us. After a day and a half we went on. The wind rose and whipped at us, so that we had to reel along leaning against it.

Now and then one of King Arivarates' messengers would gallop past, spattering us with mud; or a troop of armored cavalry would clatter up, exchange some words with Prince Arivarates, and ride on. King Arivarates was evidently getting ready for a summer of hard fighting.

Between his duties, Prince Arivarates rode beside one or another of us and conversed in Greek or Persian, asking sharp questions. As

I had spoken but the truth when I pleaded that this was a scientific expedition, I saw no reason not to be frank.

On the second day from Tyana, we came into a wide flat land of frozen marshes. In the distance a tremendous mountain rose over the horizon, rearing a snow-covered cone above a ring of forested foothills. Arivarates said to me:

"That is the holy mountain of Ma, which the Hellenes call Mount Argaios. Legend says a fire-breathing dragon sleeps beneath it. When he stirs, the earth trembles, and someday he will come forth to burn up the entire land. *Ea!*" he cried to Pyrron in front of us. "Watch your step, man. If you stray off the road into these bogs, you will sink from sight in a trice."

He turned back to me. "That man has convinced me that he is a veritable philosopher. No ordinary man could be so awkward and absent-minded. But I will lay no wagers that he will so convince my father, who is not overwhelmed by love of Hellenes."

"From your speech," I said, "I had said you had some Greek education yourself."

"True. I have spent a year in Athens. We admire Hellenic culture, but we should esteem it even more if we could get rid of all the Hellenes." He grinned.

"You are making a good start," I said, indicating the column.

"Not bad. My father thought me mad to raid so far south with only a company of foot. But I told him my sturdy hillmen could take care of themselves. And behold! I have taken the cream of Alexander's men, with a monster and a chest full of money."

"Thank you for the flattery. But what will you do with the elephant? This land is too cold for these beasts, and he'll eat you out of house and home."

"That is for my father to decide. If all else fail, he should give us plenty of steaks."

Two days thereafter we reached Mazaka. This city clung to a low spur of Mount Argaios, surrounded by vineyards, orchards, and sheep-folds in the midst of an otherwise wild and barren land. The houses were made of timber from the forests of Mount Argaios and slabs of stone from a quarry on the banks of the Melas. The Mazakans looked at us curiously but did not run and point and shout as had most other folk.

We were herded into a stockade. They let us have our tents, though of course no weapons or edged tools. As soon as they left us, I called the men together and said:

"Lads, some may think all's over but the slave block. But that may no come to pass after all. We dinna ken whether this king will slay us, sell us, or turn us loose. So there shall be no letting down of discipline—"

"So say you!" said Geres of Lapathos. "As for me, I've had all the soldiering I want for the now. Any wight who wants me to obey maun make me!"

The only answer was to spin Geres around and deal him a buffet that stretched him in the dirt. Howsomever, Geres got up and came for me like a wild bull. He was as heavy as I and a puckle taller, so I had my hands full. We were slugging away, and I was bleeding at the lip and wondering if I had not taken on more than I could cope with, when, as I pressed my foe backwards with a rush, I saw a foot shoot out and trip Geres. Down he went. Nobody noticed that he had been tripped, for the yelling crowd pressed in upon us from all sides.

Ere he could rise, I sent him a good swing to the side of his jaw. This time he stayed down. Later Inaudos the Kordian caught my eye, winked, and wiggled his foot.

Thereafter there was no more argument about discipline. I made Klonios of Skotoussa, the double-pay trooper, flank guard in Thyestes' place, after warning him to cast no more lovelorn looks upon Nirouphar. Though too slow and easygoing to make a first-class officer, Klonios was well liked and altogether the best choice open to me.

King Arivarates lived in a palace of rough stone, like unto the other houses in Mazaka but larger. The royal standard, a gilded eagle with two heads, stood on a pole before the entrance. We were marched in under heavy guard, after having been taken to the bathhouse to make ourselves presentable.

The king, a massive graybeard, sat on a throne of carven black stone, from the back of which rose a golden two-headed eagle. On one side stood Prince Arivarates; on the other, a brawny soldier with Kanadas' two-handed sword.

I gave a Persian bow and said: "Rejoice, O King!" When I snapped my fingers and hissed at the others, they did likewise.

King Arivarates chewed his mustache. "So," he rumbled. "What shall I do with you, Hellene?" He spoke Greek with a much stronger accent than his son's.

"Send us on our way to Athens, King," I said.

"Ha! We shall see. My son tells me you claims to be a what-you-call scientific expedition, eh?"

"True, O King."

"With tame philosophers yet?"

"Aye. Behold the wise Pyrron of Elis!"

"Ha!" The king chewed the other end of his mustache. "I have read lots of Greek books. Wonderful thought you Hellenes have. Have beginnings of a good little royal libraries here. But"—and he fixed Pyrron with a glare—"no books by any Pyrron of Elis. What have you written, if you are so wise?"

Pyrron looked shamed. "Well—ah—King," he said, "the truth is that I've never written a real book. I have a multitude of treatises planned. I keep reading and taking notes. But there's always so much to observe, and so many interesting things to do and talk about, that somehow I never get around to serious composition. When I do sit down to write, I always discover I'm out of papyrus, or I've mislaid my notes, or I need a reference book that's in Athens."

"Ha." The king pulled his beard. "You know somethings? This is all a clever little scheme by Harpalos to get reinforcements to Antigonos. I suppose Harpalos will next try to send soldiers through my country dressed as dancing girls. Those branded rascals will not let me alone. I writes nice letter to King Alexander, saying I will be friends with him. What happen? Every year Antigonos invades my country and I have to drive him out again." The king smote the arm of his throne. "So you think you fool old King Arivarates, eh? I have a little surprises for you. Come forward, you so-called philosopher."

Pyrron stepped forward. A lackey brought a stool. The guard with Kanadas' sword also advanced and placed himself behind Pyrron.

"Put the behind on the seats," said King Arivarates. "Comfortably, eh? You better be. We will see who is a philosopher. Honorable calling, philosophy, and it make me angrily to see some how-you-say ignoramus pretending to be real philosopher.

"So. My son has prepared a list of questions. You answer them all right, I let you go, with all your specimens and property except your slaves and money. Those I need, for damages done to my kingdom by Antigonos. But if you do not, off goes your head, and all the rest will be sold into slavery. You understand, eh?"

"This is an unusual proposal," said Pyrron, "but I'm as ready as I shall ever be. 'It is not strength, but art, obtains the prize.' How many questions are there, O King?"

I felt an immense admiration for Pyrron, who seemed as cool as if he were merely facing a fellow sophist in the Athenian market place.

"Ten," said the king. "Take your time, for I should not like my beautiful palace dirtied with your blood. But do not think Gasys cannot swing that Indian sword. He has been practicing for hours, on cabbages. Go ahead, son. Numbers one, aim, shoot!"

Prince Arivarates stepped forward with a roll of papyrus. He said: "Thales of Miletos was asked: What is easy? and: What is hard? What answers did he give?"

Pyrron muttered to himself. The king said: "Come, speak up, man! I cannot hear."

"I'm sorry; that's a habit of mine. Thales said it is easy to give advice to others, but difficult to know oneself."

"That is right," said the prince.

"Good! Good!" cried the king. "Give him a cheer, everybody. Is maybe the last one he will ever hear."

"Second," said the prince, "what did the statesman Solon hold to be the first rule of life?"

"To hold the moderate course," said Pyrron.

"Right. Third, how did Anaxagoras of Klazomenai describe the sun?"

"As a mass of red-hot metal, larger than the Peloponnesos."

The king said: "Maybe you make them too easily, son."

"They wax harder," said the prince. "Fourth: what did Antisthenes say was the greatest boon?"

Pyrron hesitated and mumbled, then said: "To—to die happy."

"Give three maxims of Pythagoras."

"Does this count as one question or as three?"

"As one."

"That's not just!" said Pyrron.

"Ah, but who decides what is just, yet?" said the king. "Go ahead, or Gasys will earn his pay."

"Be it noted that I comply under protest. The three maxims are: Don't stir fire with a knife; don't sit on your quart; and don't eat your heart."

"What does that mean?" said the king.

"Is that a question?" said Pyrron.

"No, I mean yes, I mean no. I ask it, but it is not one of the ten."

"Then the answer will have to wait."

"I will wager you do not even know the answer," said the king.

"As it happens I do, but since this isn't one of the ten, it makes no difference. Next question, O Prince."

"Pray do not interrupt, Father," said the prince. "It puts me off my stride."

"No, I am really interesting," said the king. "We will count the answers to this as one of the ten. Explain those three maxims, Pyrron."

"By 'Don't stir the fire with a knife' he meant 'Don't stir the pride and passions of the great.' By 'Don't sit on your quart' he meant 'Don't use tomorrow's sustenance recklessly.' By 'Don't eat your heart' he meant 'Don't waste your life in unnecessary troubles.'"

"Good maxims!" said the king. "You all be carefully not to stir my passions, eh? And it seems to me that taking elephant to Athens is eating your heart. But go ahead, son."

"Sixth—I mean seventh—" said the prince, "how did Demokritos describe the universe?"

"One of my favorite philosophers. He said: The universe is made up of atoms and the void; all else is mere appearance."

"What a wicked atheist!" growled the king.

"Eighth: what said Protagoras about his belief in the gods?"

Pyrron rattled it off: "I know not whether the gods exist or not."

"Any fool knows they exist," said the king. "You better have some harder questions, son."

"You shall see, O sire. Number nine: what did Anacharsis say were the safest vessels?"

Pyrron stared at the ceiling and at the floor, moving his lips and muttering. The wait became embarrassing. The executioner shifted his grip on the great sword and shuffled his feet to assure his footing.

"Those that have been hauled out on shore," said Pyrron.

"Right," said the prince. "Tenth and last question: what did Aristippos say was the main advantage of being a philosopher?"

This time the wait was even longer. Gasys sighted on Pyrron's neck and made small passes with the sword.

The king sighed and looked sad.

Pyrron's mien became desperate. He licked his lips. Sweat beaded his brow.

There was a sharp hiss from the audience as Vardanas spoke in a loud whisper: "*If—all—laws—were—repealed!*"

"Oh," said Pyrron. "The advantage is that if all laws were repealed, one would go on living the same as before. I think such a conclusion is factually open to question, but that's what the chap asserted."

"You pass," said King Arivarates. "Even though there was a little cheating on the last question. But then, once I saw you was a really philosopher, I would not cut off your head for missing one little question. At least not indoors—catch him, somebody!"

Pyrron had swooned.

The king feasted us that night in celebration of Pyrron's feat. My soldiers ate with the king's guard while the officers and Pyrron dined with the king, and Nirouphar with the queen. King Arivarates was about to seat Pyrron on his right when Pyrron said:

"O King, as Troop Leader Leon is of higher rank than I, he ought to have the place of honor."

"But you won the games! The party is for you!"

"I know, and it's very kind of you. But, you see, Leon is a serious, dignified sort of chap who cares for such distinctions, whereas they mean virtually nothing to me."

"The vagabond tries to shame me, King," I said. "Seat him there if you have to call your guards to help. The left will suit me as well."

I will not describe the repast save to say that, next to the Spartans, the Kappadokians are the worst cooks of all the nations whose food I have eaten. The king plunged into a subject that was much in his mind.

"How would you like to live in Mazaka?" he said.

"Why—I should have to consider the matter carefully, King," said Pyrron. "What had you in mind?"

"I wants some learned Hellene to stay here to write history of Katpatouka."

"Has it a history?"

"Indeed yes, a long history! Nearly all gone now, except for a few old documents and traditions..."

I lost the thread of the king's talk because I became engrossed in speech with Prince Arivarates, who sat on my left. He was eager to hear about the Eastern lands. From an account of our adventures I passed naturally to the subject of money.

"Think us not ungrateful, O Prince," I said. "However, if you send us off without an obolos, 'twill go hard with us." I explained about the need for money to keep Aias fed, and the unexpectedly heavy costs of travel.

"That may be," said the prince, "but you cannot ask us to give up such a sum when Alexander's generals have ravaged our land and forced us to wage a costly war against them."

"If Alexander were here, no doubt your father and he could arrange things peacefully. But why should we be punished for Antigonos' deeds? Or why should Xenokrates, for whom the fifty talents are meant?"

The prince shrugged. "As Alexander is head of the Greek confederacy as well as king of Macedonia, all Hellenes share responsibility for his acts. Besides, is it not a Greek saying that necessity knows no law but to conquer? Well, we have the necessity of conquering Antigonos, and this money is useful for that purpose."

I pressed the prince further. "As the Kappadokians deem themselves a cultured folk, they should do all they can to forward an enterprise of benefit to all mankind. It is their duty to posterity."

The prince became nettled. "Do not presume too far on our generosity, Hipparch. You will only anger my father, and then it will be worse for you." He dropped his voice. "Let this business lapse for the nonce. You cannot leave for some time in any case."

"Wherefore not?"

"Weather. You know not how lucky you were to find Katpatouka so warm at this season."

"Warm!"

"Yes, warm. Any time in the next fortnight a blast of cold may freeze the streams and make the earth as hard as brick. It would slay your tropical monster as quickly as leaving a fish out of water. Now, since you will be our guests for a while, relax, make yourselves agreeable to my father, and perhaps a chance will arise to do something about your money. But do not press the matter further now."

"I thank you for the advice," I said, and turned my attention to the king. The elder Arivarates was telling Pyrron of the glories of Kappadokia. He said:

"First was a great empire of Chatti, with capital at Chattysas. Sixty leagues northwest; I can show you ruins. Phrygians destroyed it."

Pyrron asked: "Could the Chattians be the same as the Keteians mentioned by Homer?"

"Maybe; Chattian kingdom was about the times of that Trojan business. Then we had another kingdom with capital at Pteria; Lydians destroyed it."

"When was this?"

"Times of King Kroisos. And that story about how the Persian king started to burn Kroisos and then changed his mind is a big lie. The rascal burnt himself up, right to the last cinder. Since then, Lydians, Medes, and Persians rule this countries. But now the land of the two-headed eagle is free again and, by Ma, we will stay free! We are a great people with a great past and a great futures, but nobody knows about us. You Hellenes say: 'Kappadokia? Oh yes, that is where our strongest slaves come from!' Bah! So maybe you will stay and write history, yes?"

"I don't know, King Arivarates," said Pyrron. "I'm frightfully grateful for the offer, but duties call me back to Hellas."

"So? What duties?"

"When I set out, my city, Elis, fitted me out with new clothes and other gear, and money to enable me to join Alexander. In return, I promised to tell the citizens all I learned on my travels. Besides, my sister, with whom I live, will be fretting over my long absence."

"Write her a letters."

"I would, but I'm not authorized to use the royal post, and I've met nobody on his way to Elis for a year."

"I can change a mind about letting you go," said the king.

"No doubt, but a history under duress is likely to be a pretty poor piece of literature. You know how it is with creative intellects."

"So? We shall see, my friend of the godlike intellect..."

After it was over, I asked Pyrron: "Why not write this history the king wants?"

"My dear old chap, you have no idea of the size of the task of writing a book. Why, Herodotos spent fifteen years in travel and research, preparing to write his history!"

"Perhaps this would not be so big a book."

"It would still be a task of months, if it were done at all creditably."

Pyrron now dwelt in the palace, and the rest of us in the barracks of the royal guard. For the next two days I had little to do but see that the elephant was well cared for and listen to the grumbles of my men about Kappadokian cooking.

Then there came a day of stir and bustle in the town. No Kappadokian said aught to us, as most could speak no tongue we knew and all were taciturn by nature. But as I lunched with Pyrron, Vardanas, and Klonios, in came Prince Arivarates.

"I have been looking for you," he said. "The news we have been awaiting has come. Antigonos has passed through Ipsos to attack us. My father and I ride to meet him as soon as the levies come in."

"I hope you come through it sound," I said. I could not quite wish success to his arms, as Antigonos was after all another servant of my master King Alexander.

"Thank you, Hipparch. Now, before I go, there is this to be said. You people worry about your money, which my father wishes to keep."

"That's a soft way of putting it," I said.

"Then hearken. Next to beating the Hellenes, my father wants that history of Katpatouka more than anything. If you can write it while we are gone—well, I make no promises, but something might be done."

"I should be glad to," said Pyrron, "but how could I compose a work of that size in half a month?"

"There is not so much Katpatoukan history to record as you seem to think. Seek out Rhatotes, the high priest of Ma, who is also my father's librarian. He knows as much of our history as any man and has custody of the records."

"I fear nobody will be able to read my scrawl," said Pyrron.

"Then tell Zardokes—my father's second secretary—to copy your writing in a neat hand. This need not be an immortal monument of scholarship; I do but wish something to show my father on our return."

Pyrron sighed. "I'll do my best."

So we went to the temple of Ma. We had to wait hours to see Rhatotes, as he was busy with prayers and sacrifices to the Kappadokian war goddess.

When Rhatotes at last received us, we found him a forbidding-looking man: tall, gaunt, stooped, and hook-nosed, like a plucked vulture. Despite the chill, he was sweating and blood-spattered from beating animals' brains out with a club. When he knew our mission, however, he was helpful enough. He took us back to the palace and showed us the library.

A small chest held all the documents bearing on the history of Kappadokia: a few summaries of the land's history, traditions, and legends, some letters and treaties from the days of Persian rule, and a few inscribed clay tablets from ancient times. These last, however, were in tongues that had long been out of use. Not even Rhatotes could read them.

Pyrron turned the documents over. A gleam came into his eyes, like a horse that feels its oats.

"I'll do it!" he said. "Leon! Fetch Zardokes, please. Tell him to bring all his writing materials. And hasten!"

I was astonished, not only because Pyrron almost never asked favors, but also because his manner had utterly changed. When I came back with the scribe, Pyrron and Rhatotes were sorting the documents so that the oldest were on top. Then, under Pyrron's direction, Rhatotes began translating, slipping into Persian when he could not think of the Greek for something. Pyrron scribbled notes and sometimes dictated passages to Zardokes.

I marveled to watch him. Pyrron, hitherto self-effacing, good-natured, lazy, awkward, and vague, was transformed into a brisk, energetic, forceful fellow with a godlike ability to grapple with the mass of strange names and unfamiliar facts. To watch him aroused the same awe that one feels when watching a skilled sculptor shape a block or a skilled fencing master show the methods of fighting with and without armor.

He looked up at me. "Oblige me by running along, Leon," he said. "It distracts me to have somebody staring at me when I'm working."

Thereafter I minded my own business, namely the hipparchia. Two days later the levies from the district round Mazaka had all marched in for the weapontake. I watched King Arivarates and his son (who was really his nephew and adopted son) ride off at the head of their mailed lancers, with the gilded two-headed eagle bobbing on its pole before them. They were followed by hundreds of Kappadokian peasants with spears and axes on their shoulders.

The Kappadokian horse, I thought, could ride over anything Antigonos could bring against them. On the other hand, the foot, though made up of big sturdy-looking men, was neither armed nor drilled to the point where they could stand against the long Macedonian pikes.

That night Pyrron, whom we had not seen since he began his work, came to dinner with the rest of us. His eyes were red from staying up late and peering at old papyri by lamplight.

"How goes the history of Kappadokia?" said Vardanas.

"Coming, coming. The first section is nearly complete, down to the time of the Lydian conquest."

"Wonderful!" said I.

"Not so wonderful, considering that hardly anything has come down from distant times. I'm sure more historical materials once existed, but the demons of destruction—fire and water, strife and stupidity, mice and mold—have had their way with them. Luckily I was able to squeeze a few traditions out of the king before he rode away. Now I'm trying to locate the oldest men among the educated class around Mazaka, to see if they can tell me anything."

Vardanas said: "Tell us what you have learned so far. Give us a summary."

Pyrron said: "I'm sorry, old boy, but I can't."

"Diplomatic secrets?"

"No. If I told you the tale, I should never get it written. That's how it is with writing. I can be full of enthusiasm over some treatise I'm going to write and even get some of it on papyrus. But then some chap invites me to dinner and begs me to tell it to him. As I'm fond of talking and don't like to refuse a reasonable request, I do. Then I find that all my vital force has leaked away, like wine from a punctured skin, and the work is never completed." He sighed. "That's no doubt why I have never written a real book in my life, though I've collected material for a hundred."

"Then dinna even think of telling us," I said. "For a chance to get our lovely silver back, we can bridle our curiosity."

The next half month we spent in repairing our gear and resting up for the next leg of the journey. When rain roared on the roofs, when snow scudded through the streets, when the bitter wind howled around the corners, we were glad to be behind Mazaka's stout stone walls and not out on the bleak tableland.

Then the weather softened. I went to the commandant of the garrison, Tibios, and asked him to lend us back our weapons. I explained:

"The lads have been pressing on for so long that they're out of practice at formal maneuvers. I desire to exercise them."

At first, Tibios curtly refused. He was sure we were up to some desperate scheme. Our position was a little odd, as we were technically captured enemies.

At last I set Vardanas on Tibios. Soon the Persian's charm had softened the old Kappadokian's suspicions, like butter in the sun, and he agreed to joint exercises with his men. Thus, he frankly explained, there would always be a strong armed force to watch us. So we galloped and threw our darts in company with Tibios' gray-bearded veterans and fuzzy-cheeked striplings.

Otherwise Mazaka was a sleepy little capital, the more so when the king and most men of fighting age had left. A minister named Myattales ran the kingdom in the king's absence, but he let us alone and we had no dealings with him.

I saw almost nought of Nirouphar, who dwelt with the king's womenfolk and, Vardanas told me, thrilled them with her tales of feminine fashions in great cities like Sousa and Babylon.

Rumors swept the city: King Arivarates had repelled Antigonos; Antigonos had defeated and slain the king; the king had wiped out all the Macedonians and was advancing to the conquest of Phrygia...

At last a rider galloped in from the west and vanished into Myattales' study. The minister came out on the front steps of the palace. A trumpeter blew a flourish. When hundreds of Mazakans had gathered, Myattales made a short announcement, which was translated for me as follows:

"Our Lord the king has defeated the Hellenes. Those of the enemy who were not slain or captured have fled back to Phrygia. The king returns at the head of his army tomorrow or the next day. Give thanks to Ma for this victory."

The Mazakans nodded, grunted a few approving words, and went their ways. Not for them any bonfires or drunken revels in celebration!

Two days later the king rode in. First came his long column of heavy horse; then his peasant levies; then groaning wainloads of wounded; then several score of wretched-looking prisoners; and lastly a mounted rear guard.

There were speeches on the front steps of the palace, of which I understood not a word. The royal family came out to kiss the king and his son, the latter with his arm in a sling. Pyrron, red-eyed and swaying (for he had not slept in two nights), stepped up and handed a big roll of papyrus to the king.

"This is the history of the noble and ancient kingdom of Kappadokia," he said. "If it looks rather messy, O King, that's because it is a mere rough draft with corrections. Zardokes will soon have a smooth copy prepared for you."

The king opened the scroll, glanced it over, then folded Pyrron in a bearlike hug and gave him a loud smacking kiss.

"So? You are a good boys, even if you are a fornicating Hellene!" he roared. "Now you have to write another chapter, about how old Arivarates beat the skirt off Antigonos! I tell you about it at dinner."

At the feast of victory, the king related with gusto how he had caught the invaders in the marshes south of Lake Tatta. The turning point of the battle came when Antigonos sent a company of Macedonian foot across ground that turned out to be boggy.

"They got stuck," said the king. "My peasant boys do not like to face men in armor, because we are too poor for that kind of luxuries. But now they swarmed over these poor stuck Greeks, and those huge long spears did no good at close quarters. Everywhere was Hellenes in shiny breastplates shouting 'Quarter! Mercy!' Well, we chased them halfway to Ikonion. Antigonos rode off with his cavalry, and some of their foot got away into the hills this side of Ikonion. But I do not think Antigonos will try another invasion this years."

The weather now turned balmy. I went to Prince Arivarates and said: "Could we now set out for Ephesos?"

"I think so," said he, with his usual air of gravity beyond his years. "You will still get a lot of cold wind, but except in a bad year we seldom have snow so late."

"How about our money?"

A smile lit the prince's somber young face. "As I expected, my father is delighted with Pyrron's history. So you will find your money chest restored to you intact." He lowered his voice. "In fact, since you have been hard put to it to keep to your schedule of expenses, I have taken the liberty of adding twenty talents to it on my own responsibility."

"O Prince!" I cried. I knelt and kissed his hand.

"I feel we can afford it, because we captured Antigonos' pay cart containing hundreds of talents' worth of money. Antigonos either expected to campaign in Katpatouka all summer or hoped to bribe some of our barons to go over to him. But pray say nothing of this. My father admires Greek philosophy, but not that much."

"What's to become of our slaves?"

"Those my father is determined to keep. One, a good Katpatoukan, will be freed. The other my father will put to good use. If you must have more, you can buy them in Alexander's territory."

Thus we set out from Mazaka on the second of Mounychion. The king and the prince saw us off with great cordiality. The king slapped our backs, kissed us, and bellowed jokes, while the prince bowed gravely and shook our hands.

In later years, after Alexander's death, Eumenes invaded Kappadokia on the orders of Perdikkas the regent. Eumenes defeated and captured old King Arivarates, whom he crucified along with his chief men. Prince Arivarates escaped to Armenia. During the wars of the Successors, the prince retook Kappadokia with the aid of Arkloathos of Armenia. There he yet reigns, and very ably, too. So, belike, the elder Arivarates' boast about the freedom of Kappadokia may come true after all.

King Arivarates sent a small troop of light horse with us. He said it was to protect us, but I think it was to make sure we did no warlike acts against him.

Returning to Tyana, we stopped to witness the spring festival in honor of the local goddess of fertility. The priests built a bonfire, dug a trench, and filled it with glowing coals from the fire. While a band of musicians played a monotonous little tune on lyres and flutes and drums, six priestesses in paint and bangles girt up their skirts to the knee and walked the length of the trench barefoot on the hot embers.

Somebody belched behind me. It was Vardanas, who had filled himself with barley beer at the inn. "I can do that," he said.

"Each to that at which he excels," I said. "You'd best leave fire-walking to the fire-walkers, laddie."

"I will wager I can walk farther on those coals than you!"

"Out on you! I had all the burns I want in the dungeons of Babylon."

"Fie! You are no sportsman. I will show you!"

Vardanas sat down and pulled off his boots. Then he rolled up his trouser legs and walked to the end of the trench.

"For the honor of the Persian race!" he cried, and stepped out upon the coals.

He made his first step without flinching, but then something went wrong. With a yell, Vardanas hopped off the embers, sat down, and clutched one foot. Everybody—Thessalians, Kappadokians, priests, and priestesses—burst into laughter. Vardanas wept, not I am sure from pain but from shame.

"The mouse has tasted pitch!" I said. "Get your bear-grease ointment, Elisas. Here's a fire-walking priestess who could not quite
make it."

From Tyana the road took us to Kybistra and thence to Laranda
in Lykaonia. Our escort turned back at the Lykaonian border. Lykaonia is mostly high, cold, barren, windswept plain, broken here and
there by small conical mountains. We kept close watches, because
the Lykaonians have the name of lawless hillmen who rob travelers.
Nought befell us, however, except that once a pair of huge lionlike
sheep dogs attacked us and had to be slain.

Now that we were back in Alexandrine territory, I took up again
my series of reports to the king, explaining the interruption. I urged
Alexander to come to terms with the worthy Arivarates. On the other
hand, I warned him against Harpalos, who, I was sure, was looting
the treasury to an indecent degree.

There was a chance of these letters' falling into Harpalos' hands as
they passed through Tarsos, but I thought it unlikely that the treasurer would try to stop and censor all the royal mail. In any case, honor
demanded that I make a serious attempt to avenge myself on those
who had injured me or tried to. As the Persians say, kindness to the
lion is cruelty to the lamb.

In Laranda, soldiers of Antigonos' garrison stopped us, as we
had plainly ridden from hostile territory. Their commandant, a solemn Spartan named Nabis, walked up and down, looking gloomily
at us.

"You tell a fine tale," he said in Doric dialect, "but what proof have
you-all got?"

"Plenty," I said. "Hand me the documents, Klonios. Here is a letter from Eumenes, in which all loyal subjects are commanded in the
king's name to help us and further the expedition. Here's authority to
requisition governmental fodder. Here's a letter from Menes, viceroy
of Syria, to Philoxenos..."

Nabis made a show of studying the documents, pursing his shav-
en upper lip and frowning over the edge of the papyrus at us. As he
sometimes held them upside down, methinks any pieces of writing
would have done as well. At last he said:

"I reckon you-all can go on. In fact, the sooner you get that two-tailed monster out of town, the better I'll like it."

Off we went on the road from Laranda to Derbe. As spring came on, the trees along the watercourses put out new leaves and the tamarisks turned pink. The brown earth became green with new grass, and flowers carpeted the plains. Herds of wild asses grazed hock-deep in the growth and galloped off braying as we neared them.

Spring also filled the hipparchia with new energy. Though it seemed we had been on the road since our childhood, home at last began to look real instead of like some mythical place beyond the edge of the world. I no longer had to drive and harry my people to keep them moving. Smelling their oats, they often hurried me on faster than I intended to go.

The Thessalians began talking of their plans against the day of their discharge. One would open a shop, another buy a farm, and a third pay off his father's debts, while a fourth meant to spend all his bonus on wine and women and then go to Macedonia to seek service under Antipatros, the regent.

I made no more progress with Nirouphar, though the spring made my love burn brighter and more painfully. She was pleasant and gay and courteous, but then so she was to all. Pyrron's promise to hold aloof from her was gradually forgotten, until she was spending almost as much time with the philosopher as formerly. I once mentioned the fact to Vardanas, hoping to rouse him to renew his ban.

He grinned. "Not Auramasdas himself could keep my fair sister from conversing with somebody. On the whole I think she is safer with the philosopher than with you, highly though I esteem you. He is not a lustful man, whereas you..."

"I am as virtuous as the next!" I said.

"Ah, but do you remember that girl in Karmana, the one with a cast in her eye?"

"Let's not rake old ashes. For that matter, I recall some of your escapades, too."

"But I do not even pretend to be a safe escort for blooming young virgins!"

* * *

278

From Derbe the road led us to Ikonion. According to the Lyka-onians, Ikonion was the first place to emerge from the waters after the Flood. Here the gods, to repeople the earth, made men of mud and caused the winds to blow the breath of life into them. From Iko-nion we made a long march northwest to Ipsos, where we rejoined the Persian royal highway.

Now the going became easy. With the coming of spring, how-ever, the splendid road was thronged with traffic, which ofttimes slowed our progress until we could edge past. After a while, we took to putting the elephant at the head of our column instead of the tail. Then when Vardanas or Klonios rode ahead, shouting: "Way! Way for King Alexander's men!" the travelers took one look at Aias and leapt for the ditch. Sometimes they kept right on running across the nearest fields.

There were horses, mules, asses, camels, oxen, and men afoot. There were chariots, carts, and sleds. There were herds of sheep, goats, and cattle. Platoons of Greek or Macedonian soldiers strode eastwards in heavy Iphikratean marching boots, while gangs of slaves, mostly swart Gandarians and Indians captured in the last two years' battles, shuffled westwards on bare feet, with hanging heads.

Betimes a Persian postman galloped by, blowing a horn to clear the way. Whenever one flew past, we all sang out: "Neither snow, nor rain..." Again, a solitary Hellene, wrapped in a cloak and his face shaded by a traveling hat, plodded along with a walking stick or jogged on a mule, on his way eastwards to seek his fortune or just to see the world.

The road led us along a river between the massive Paroreian Mountains to Prymnessos, which sprawled on flat land with a castle on a crag above it. Thence we marched to Keramon-agora, where they make fine carpets. Then we entered gracious Lydia, with its vine-clad hillsides and fields of wheat and purple crocuses, from which the folk make saffron. We saw the long-robed Lydians at their wild rites in honor of Kybele.

And thus, on the last day of Mounychion, we came down the Hermos River to Sardeis, the jewel of western Anatolia, often de-stroyed but always rising again from its ruins. The city bustles with business and manufacture like a Syrian town. The streets near the market place are lined with racks on which dyed stuffs hang to dry; the spring breeze stirred their billows of crimson and yellow.

South of the city rises Mount Tmolos, crowned by a marble arcade built by the Persians as a lookout. From the city below, the arcade is a mere white fleck topping the dark forested slopes. The mountain thrusts out a spur toward Sardeis, and on this spur stands the citadel. Thither we took our way.

Antigonos son of Philippos, viceroy of Phrygia and Lydia, was a tall, lean man, even taller than Kanadas. He had one cold blue eye in a somber, scarred face with a close-cut graying beard. He limped and rested his weight on a stick.

"A scratch I got at Lake Tatta," he said. "It will soon be well. What is your mission?"

I told my tale, which I now knew so well that I could repeat it in my sleep. I ended: "How is the king? I heard in Kilikia that he was badly wounded. Have you had any later news, General?"

"Yes, I had a letter from Eumenes but the other day. Alexander has quite recovered and is now nearing the land of Patala, in the delta of the Indus River." Antigonos stared piercingly at me with his one eye. "Now that you have given me the official explanation of your journey, suppose you give me the real reason."

My jaw dropped with surprise. "This is the real reason, O Viceroy! What thought you?"

"Come, come, Hipparch, tell me not that the king let a score of good Thessalian cavalrymen go while they still could fight?"

"That he did. After all, I have been eight years from home, and some of the lads nine."

"That is your tale, is it?"

"Aye, good sir."

"What message did the king give you for Antipatros?"

"Alexander never mentioned the regent's name to me." I became angry. "If you doubt me, write the king yourself. You should have an answer ere we sail from Ephesos. By Herakles, I had my orders from the king himself, as my documents prove, and I know not what call there is to question me like a criminal!"

"Documents can be forged," said Antigonos. He fondled the sheets of papyrus I had handed him, then suddenly made a motion as if to tear them up.

"*Ea!*" shouted, laying hand to hilt.

Antigonos held out the documents to me with a small grim smile. "You see, my boy, you are not so free and independent as you seem to think. I could confiscate or destroy these documents, and then where would you be? Or I could have you crucified for threatening me." He paused, looking through me with that one terrible eye. "Come."

He led me to a room in the citadel where several other Macedonians sat over a wine jug, though the wine did not seem to have cheered them.

"My fellow commanders of western Anatolia," said Antigonos. "Kalas, viceroy of Mysia and Hellespontine Phrygia; Asandros, viceroy of Karia; Pausanias, commandant of the forces at Sardeis." To the others he said: "This fierce-looking young fellow is Leon of Atrax, of King Alexander's mercenary Greek horse. Or so he claims."

"Leon!" cried Kalas. "Are you not one of those who joined the Thessalians at Gordion?"

"Aye. Thank you for remembering me, O Kalas." When I first joined Alexander's army, Kalas commanded the Thessalian Division. I had not seen him for seven years.

"What is your rank now?" he asked.

"Troop leader, in command of a special hipparchia on detached duty."

"Not even a brigadier? Hermes attend us! You disappoint me. You were always bold in battle and crafty in council, as I remember."

"But then I'm no Macedonian, let alone an old companion of the king. So I'm lucky to have risen as far as I have."

Antigonos said: "Then you are he who you say you are, after all."

I passed over the remark and said: "What brings all you gentlemen together?"

Antigonos spoke with a smile that was half sneer. "This you might call a recrimination party. We had an admirable plan—oh, a masterly plan—for a three-pronged attack on the Anatolian foreigners. But the gods saw matters otherwise. I have been beaten by Ariarathes of Kappadokia." (He gave the king's name the Hellenized form.) "Kalas has been beaten by Bas of Bithynia, and Asandros has spent the month in a fruitless chase through the Pisidian hills after the wild mountaineers. Now each of us seeks a way to blame the others for his failure. I, for example, lay the whole collapse to their insistence on attacking when we lacked enough men to face the barbarian hordes. For pointing this out, my dear comrades here impugned my courage."

"I said we should never have enough men, and by Zeus I still say it!" cried Kalas. "How can we, when as soon as we get a company of dung-footed peasants whipped into shape, the king orders them to march off eastward to join him in some foolhardy scheme like raping the queen of the Amazons?"

Asandros said: "You people may carry on your quarrels, but I had rather find a remedy for our woes. For one thing, let us not talk of failures and collapses. Let us rather say the enemies' dispositions made it desirable for us to execute strategic withdrawals according to plan."

"Bugger that fancy talk!" said Pausanias. "Antigonos is right. You were trounced, and you know it."

Antigonos said to me: "Pausanias spent the time sitting here on his fat arse, so he is in a position to contemn all the rest of us."

"Furies take you, Antigonos!" cried Pausanias. "Those were my orders. If you spent more time on the army and less on trying to make a second Athens out of Smyrna—"

"Hold your tongue, you dog-faced sodomite!" roared Antigonos.

The generals all sprang to their feet, shouting and shaking fists. They even forgot their Greek and began cursing each other in Macedonian, which I could barely understand. Ere it came to blows, Antigonos held up his hands and bellowed for silence.

"What impression must we make on our young visitor?" he said. "He has the king's confidence—or so he claims—and will undoubtedly write our divine master an account of this meeting. That is, if no—ah—sad accident befall him first." He leered at me. "Lucky for you, stripling, that you arrived when we were all together. Thus none dares do you ill, lest the others know. Ah, a band of brothers, a band of brothers!"

Asandros said: "We should get on together better if you were not always kicking our rumps, Antigonos."

"Maybe, but some people's rumps cry out to be booted. And now to business. Leon has just come through Kappadokia, with Ariarathes' blessing. He can therefore tell us about that land. Question him, fellow bunglers."

They questioned me for two hours. I answered with fair candor. However, as I had a kindly feeling for the two Arivaratai, I puffed up the Kappadokian forces to twice or thrice their real strength, to discourage the Macedonians from another attack.

When they ran out of questions on Kappadokia, they sounded me out on a plan to send the elephant to Athens with the Indians and join their armies with my Thessalians for their next campaign. I politely refused, and presently they dismissed me with authority to draw fodder. As I left the chamber, their voices rose in anger behind me.

We spent a day in Sardeis resting and repairing. I went with Pyrron and Vardanas to look at the tomb of King Alyattes of Lydia, and at the gardens which Artaxerxes the Resolute planted with his own hands. It is said this Persian king had a passion for gardening that surpassed his interest in the duties of kingship.

I saw no more of Antigonos and am not sorry for it. He terrified me. He was a strange man. Toward Alexander he was loyal while the king lived, but after that he played his own game in the most ruthless and crafty manner. Those who served under him swore by his kindness and justice, but his rivals among the Successors found him a bitter and malignant foe. It took the combined forces of most of the other Successors to finish him off. Old One-eye fell at last at the battle of Ipsos a few years ago, being more than eighty years old.

We rode on to Ephesos. Here a broad and beautiful avenue leads down from the theater on a hillside, through the city to the quays, where the Kaystros makes a sharp turn and empties into the sea. Vardanas remarked:

"One can tell one is in a Greek city with eyes shut, from the way the people reek of onions and olive oil!"

I stopped in the market place to ask after Philoxenos, the admiral, and got a dozen contradictory directions. I finally found my man walking along the quays and looking at the shipping. He was a good-looking brown-bearded Macedonian, not much older than I. When

I told him of my mission and showed him my documents, his eyes lit up with interest.

"I will do it on two conditions, Hipparch," he said with a grin.

"And what are they, O Admiral?"

"One: that if ever you write a book about your journey, you will give me credit for helping you, thus making my name immortal."

"I, write a book? What a daft idea! But then, General Apollodoros made the same suggestion in Babylon. If I do, I'll surely tell of your help. And the other condition?"

"That you give me a ride on the monster."

"Nought easier."

I pushed through the crowd around the elephant and called up to Kanadas to help the admiral up. I turned the hipparchia over to Klonios, told him to find a camp site, and climbed up on the elephant, too. By now I had overcome some of my feeling that I had to manage every detail of the hipparchia's existence myself.

"Come with us, Vardanas," I called.

"The naval anchorage lies yonder," said Philoxenos, pointing.

Kanadas turned Aias' head. Presently we came to the sailors' village, with long rows of shacks and thousands of sailors and rowers and their slatternly women and swarming children, all of whom rushed up to see the elephant. Philoxenos asked me about Aias' weight, but I had to give him the same answer that I had Menes, to wit, that I knew it not.

There were scores of ships. Many of the smaller ones were hauled out on the beach, while the rest rode at anchor off shore. The great majority were common two—and three—bankers, but there were a few larger ships looming over the rest like tuna among herrings. Two great gilded fivers were rowing in from exercises.

Philoxenos pointed again. "I think that is our ship, the *Destroyer*. Ē! Thoas! Bring a boat! Kylon! Run and fetch Iason!"

Presently a boat appeared, rowed by a burly sailor. From the other direction a man came out of the store sheds at the end of the sailors' village and walked along the beach toward us.

This is Iason of Rhodes, my naval architect," said Philoxenos. These are Leon of Atrax and Vardanas of Sousa, on a special mission from the king. Tell Iason what you have told me."

I did so, though I had to repeat myself several times because Iason's attention kept wandering to the elephant. Philoxenos added: "We shall row out to the *Destroyer* to look her over with a view to converting her."

"Oh dear! What a wicked thing to do to such a pretty ship!" said Iason. "A mere floating pigpen—or elephantpen, I ought to say."

"The elephant will make her stink no worse than she does," said Philoxenos. "Let us go."

He and Iason hopped into the boat. I got in more cautiously, knowing that I was no experienced mariner. Vardanas said:

"Leon, had I not better stay here?"

"What for?"

"Well—ah—Kanadas might need help with the elephant."

"Rubbish! Get in."

Looking miserable, he did so, clutching the gunwales. The sailor rowed us out to the *Destroyer*. This was the biggest ship of all, an eighter. As landlubbers sometimes ask how a ship can have eight banks of oars, let me explain that no ship does, for it would be so high and its uppermost oars so long that rowers could not manage it. The *Destroyer* had eighty oars arranged in four banks of twenty each, two banks on each side. Five rowers pulled each oar of the upper banks, while three pulled each oar of the lower banks. As five and three make eight, the ship was called an eighter.

We climbed a ladder of rope, with wooden rungs, that hung down the side. Sailors helped us over the rail. As we stood on deck at last, Vardanas, looking greener than ever, whispered:

"My first time aboard a ship, Leon! Would it were my last!"

Philoxenos took us on a walk around the mighty ship. The *Destroyer* was a good sixty paces long, with a raised forecastle bearing two light catapults for throwing darts, and a raised quarter-deck including the officers' cabins and a pair of steering oars. Down the middle of the ship ran a raised grating of sections that could be taken up. Philoxenos stepped into an open section of the grating and led us down a ladder to the oar deck.

Here all was dark and cavernous, the only light being that which came through the oar ports and the grating overhead. The oar deck was empty of life, save for mice. Though the ship was in commission, the rowers came aboard only when it was about to put out. The place stank. The oars lay lengthwise in bundles.

Philoxenos looked about, fingering his beard. "What make you of it, Iason?"

The Rhodian said: "Maybe we could take out the middle third of the rowers' benches and make a pen in their place. How much space does your little old monster need, Hipparch?"

"He should have room to turn around in. He is about seven cubits high and ten cubits long."

"That would mean taking out at least seven or eight rowing spaces on each side—"

There was a loud thump, followed by curses in Persian. Vardanas, the tallest present, had struck his head on an overhead beam.

"That made me see stars all right," he said, rubbing his head. "If it be too low for me, how would you ever get an elephant in here?"

"A right smart point, blessed one," said Iason. "Can you make him lie down for the whole voyage?"

"I'm sure not," I said. "Certainly he could never crawl into a low space like a badger creeping into its hole."

"Then there's nothing for it but to take up a section of the main deck, letting the elephant's back show to the whole world."

"Do not take it up clear across the ship," said Philoxenos. "It would make it too hard to get from bow to stern."

"I can leave a catwalk two planks wide on each side." Iason hopped down to the lowest part of the oar deck, next to the side of the ship. He stamped on the floor boards. "Look here, you-all, these planks would never, never hold that weight. Your monster's feet would go through the bottom of the ship as if it was papyrus."

Philoxenos said: "There are those timbers we salvaged from the wreck of the *Arrogant*. Could we lay a course of them over the regular floor, at right angles to the planks?"

"I should think so, if we sawed them to size."

I said: "I see not how you plan to get Aias on and off the ship. There are no cranes or hoists in the world for lifting such a weight."

Iason said: "Tell you what: I'll build a ramp down from the main deck to the oar deck. How steep a slope can the elephant walk?"

"I know not, though I should think you could work it by running the ramp the length of the pen."

Iason clapped a hand to his forehead. "By the Dog! Here's the worst obstacle yet! I daren't put the elephant anywhere but right in the center of the ship, for fear he'll make it list or ride out of trim. But that's where the mast is."

"We can unship the mast for the voyage to Peiraieus," said Philoxenos. "This time of year the winds are too strong and gusty for safe sailing anyway. For that matter, you will have to take out some of these pillars."

"I can't take out too many, lest the hull be weakened."

Philoxenos touched an overhead beam. "But these deck girders will have to go, as they are right where the elephant's body will be. Without the girders your pillars will be mere posts, serving no purpose but for the elephant to scratch himself against."

"Herakles!" said Iason. "That's true. Let me think. Let's not get hasty, best ones, or we're liable to send both ship and creature to the bottom of the Aegean."

Vardanas paled at these words. At last Iason said: "I reckon I can run some heavy timbers along the stringer angles to strengthen the sides, in that way making up for the loss of the girders."

"We must block the oar ports in the waist, too," said Philoxenos.

"That's all very grand," I said, "but how shall Aias reach the deck?"

Philoxenos said: "We can build a mole out to deep water. I have enough idle rowers and sailors, eating their heads off at three or four oboloi a day, to do the job in a few days."

"Then how shall we get him off at Peiraieus?"

"They have some real fine piers there," said Iason.

"Aye, but how high from the water are the tops of these piers?"

"Oh, maybe three feet."

"That leaves the main deck of the ship several feet above the pier level, and Aias cannot jump nor yet climb down a rope ladder. You'd better build a big gangplank for him, lest we have to sail back to Ephesos with him for want of means of landing him."

Next day the naval camp stirred with activity. Iason and his helper went out to the ship with writing tablets and measuring cords. Sailors hauled timbers from the sheds to the beach at a point near the *Destroyer*, which was towed in toward shore until she almost touched bottom. From the ship rose a mighty banging as carpenters knocked out the pegs that kept the deck planks and other parts in place.

While waiting for the work to be accomplished, my friends and I began touring the neighborhood. First, we visited the site of the new temple of Artemis. For years the Ephesians had labored and taxed themselves to replace the one that Herostratos had burnt thirty years before to immortalize his name. The temple stands on the plain, eight furlongs from the center of the city. The base had been finished, and most of the columns were up. The half-built temple was shrouded in masses of scaffolding, and the atmosphere rang with the sound of hammers.

Pyrron went up to a tall, handsome, middle-aged man with his hands full of plans, who was directing the building. He said: "I am Pyrron son of Pleistarchos. Are you not Deinokrates? I think you used to know my old painting teacher…"

Pyrron presented Deinokrates to Vardanas, Nirouphar, and me, saying: "This is the man who laid out Alexandreia-in-Egypt."

I could never have done as Pyrron did, because I am overcome by shyness before men of godlike intellect. However, Deinokrates greeted Pyrron and the rest of us affably; so heartily, in fact, that nobody else had much chance to say a word. Not even Nirouphar, whose tongue was seldom still for long, could break into the spate of talk.

"Welcome! Rejoice!" he cried in a Macedonian accent. "Look at our new temple! Will it not be magnificent? Four times as large as the temple of Athena Polias in Athens! Where is your elephant? I saw it the day it arrived. Magnificent beast!"

"Aias is at the camp," I said.

"Could I ride on it? Splendid, splendid! I shall be there. Know you what I should like to do? I yearn to carve Mount Tmolos into a statue of Alexander riding an elephant! But alas, the king turned down my proposal to make Mount Athos into a statue of him, holding a city in one hand. He said nobody would live in the city because of lack of nearby farm land to feed them. *Ea*, Praxiteles!"

A white-bearded man came out of the temple's interior. The great sculptor was as shy and quiet as the architect was boisterous and forward. When he murmured "Rejoice!" Deinokrates boomed:

"You must give Praxiteles a ride on the elephant, too. Now let me show you what we plan. The columns will be forty cubits high. As you see, they will be the most massive columns in the world, to strengthen the structure against earthquakes. Round the base will run a sculptured parapet wall..."

When we got away, my head rang with architectural terms like "the small Ionic volutes of the capitals" and "the large dentils of the bed mold of the cornice"—most of which I did not understand.

I got back to camp to find that Kanadas, Siladites, and Elisas had worked out a money-making scheme with the elephant. Siladites guided the beast, Kanadas helped riders on and off, while Elisas chanted in his throaty Syrian Greek:

"Come hither all Ephesians! Come hither all Ephesians! Ride the mountainous monster from the deadly jungles of distant India! One little obolos, one sixth of a drachma, for the thrill of a lifetime! Ride the greatest beast the gods ever made...!"

They had already collected a handsome pile of small coins. Had this happened at the start of our journey, I should have demanded that the money be turned into our general funds. Thus I should have caused much bad feeling for the sake of a few oboloi. Now, however, I merely smiled, praised the mercenary trio for their enterprise, and insisted only that Deinokrates and Praxiteles be allowed to ride free because they were great men.

It was one of the prouder moments of my life when that pair came to camp the next day with a slim man of about my own age, who, I learned, was Praxiteles' son Kephisodotos. I rode them back to their temple on Aias' back. I had little to say to the older men, though. Deinokrates kept booming about his grandiose plans for the temple and for even larger structures. Praxiteles seldom spoke at all.

Kephisodotos Praxitelou, however, crowded close to me and spoke in low intimate tones in soft Attic. "This altar work pays well," he said, "but I really yearn to get back to portrait sculpture. I should simply love to do a bust of you, Hipparch."

"An ugly lump like me? You're daft, man!"

"Not at all, dear boy. Just look at those strong planes of your face! And these godlike arm muscles!" He kneaded my arm.

"Well, if you would fain make a statue of Sokrates, you could do worse than take me as a model. 'Tis said I'm spit of the old satyr."

"Do stay in Athens for a few months!" he urged, holding my hand. "As soon as this beastly altar's done, my father and I shall be back in Athens like bullets from a sling. Do stay! There's nothing like being sculptor and model for real intimacy. It'll be just too utterly divine!"

I was not unhappy to reach the temple and bid farewell to my importunate young suitor. I wondered if there was aught amiss with us Thessalians, that we should scorn this masculine love which southern Hellenes regard as the noblest of life's joys. However, along with my father's lumpish form, I had inherited my mother's stubbornness. Therefore, I cast aside my doubts and resolved to cleave to the morals of my family and nation, and let others jeer at them as rustic and barbarous if they would.

The work went swiftly forward on the *Destroyer*. All day the sound of hammer and saw drifted in from the anchorage. An endless train of men carrying baskets of earth and stones trudged to the beach and out the mole to dump their loads.

The first thing to be finished was the new gangplank. I looked at it and said: "How much weight will it carry?"

Iason said: "The gods know just how much, but it sure is made of thicker timbers than we use for horse gangplanks. I'm willing to bet it'll do."

"Still, I should like to see Aias tread upon it. My guardian spirit tells me it were not safe to trust it without a test."

Iason ordered a crew of rowers to pick up the gangplank and place thick keel timbers under each end, so that it made a kind of bridge a couple of palms above the sand of the beach. Somebody went to fetch Aias and the Indians; somebody else, Philoxenos.

Aias proved contrary when we tried to get him to step on the gangplank. First, when Kanadas headed him toward it, he walked around it. Kanadas said:

"He think it silly to climb over plank when it is easy to go around."

By coaxing and prodding, Aias was persuaded to put his weight on the plank. He had his forefeet solidly planted and had just placed one of his hind feet on the gangplank when it broke with a rending crash. At the loss of support, the elephant jumped off the gangplank with a squeal and started back for our camp at a swift shuffle, despite the yells of the Indians.

"You see?" I said to Iason.

"Immortal Zeus!" said the naval designer. "That thing of yours must outweigh Mount Pelion. We've got to make the gangplank of keel timbers, as if it was the drawbridge of a castle or siege tower."

Philoxenos said: "But think, man: such a gangplank will be so heavy that we could not handle it by simply picking it up and tossing it over the side. We need a mast to hoist it with, but we cannot have one because of the elephant's pen."

Vardanas said: "If all else fail, we could push Aias overboard and let him swim to shore."

"Buckie," I said, "any wight who thinks to push an elephant overboard has his work cut out for him. More like, he'd pick you up with his trunk and toss you into the wine-dark sea. Still, that brings another thought to mind. This clever elephant understands everything the Indians say to him. Now, here's my idea. We'll carry the mast on deck. He shall pick up the mast with his trunk and put it into its hole. Then we'll use the mast to hoist the gangplank into place."

Iason said: "You forget, to do so the elephant's got to stand on the main deck, which can't support such a weight."

"Could you not strengthen this deck as you propose to do with the oar deck?"

"No, because it would take such heavy planking that the ship would be top-heavy and unsafe. But I think I have it. We'll ship, not our regular mast, but a short jury mast with a pulley block at the top. This'll be light enough for the sailors to manhandle into its socket without a hoist, and we'll strengthen the deck only where the elephant has to step to get on and off the ship."

"What's a pulley block?" I asked.

"It's a wonderful new invention: a block of wood with a little old wheel in it, so a man can pull a rope through it more easily than through a simple hook. The king's having the whole fleet outfitted with them."

While we waited for the work to be done, Pyrron led us on a series of all-day picnic parties. We saw the sacred cypress grove of Ortygia, where Leto is said to have given birth to Apollon and Artemis, and where the Kouretes hid the divine children from the wrath of Hera. (I cannot help it if Delos also claims to be the birthplace of Apollon.)

To the south we rode to Priene, where the philosopher Bias was born. We went to busy Magnesia and to Panionion, where people from all Ionia gather in winter for the festival of Helikonian Poseidon.

To the north we visited Kolophon, where the philosopher Xenophanes was born and the seer Kalchas died. The Kolophonians claim that Homer was born there, but so do the people of other Ionian cities. We watched the famous cavalry at its exercises and visited the shrine of Apollon Klarios.

Another time we rode to Teos, where the Ionian Dionysia was in progress. We stayed there over three nights to see some of the plays, games, and religious services.

Here we had one incident. We had gone to a tavern after a play and were awaiting our wine when a gaunt, elderly Hellene sitting near us, who had already drunk deeply, suddenly cried: "That for you, Persian dog!" and spat in Vardanas' face.

At first, Vardanas was too surprised to move. Then, with a snarl like that of a leopard, he went for his dagger. He was bringing it down in a stab across the table when I caught his wrist. He was strong, but I was stronger; for an instant we remained locked in our effort.

"Let's no stab the body ere we know his reason," I said. "Put your knife away, man, and let me question him."

Vardanas relaxed. The Hellene had drawn himself back so that he nearly fell off the bench, his face ashen with terror. All the talk in the tavern had died as people turned to watch us.

"Now," I said to the Hellene, "talk, or you'll have not only my friend whom you insulted to deal with, but me as well."

The man sighed and mumbled: "I am Onetor of Lampsakos. Know that, over thirty years ago, Persian troops of the viceroy Ariobarzanes, serving under the tyrant Philiskos, seized my city. My father, mother, and brothers they slew before my eyes. My wife they raped before my eyes, many times, before they took her away as a slave. My sons they carried off to make into eunuchs. Ever since, I have hoped for a chance to requite those painted fiends, but it has never come. I was never strong enough for soldiering, and when Alexander invaded the Persian Empire I was too old to serve him. Now it's too late. I am a man without honor, lower than a slave. I have failed in my duty of vengeance."

The old man burst into tears. Vardanas, weeping also, went around the end of the table to sit beside Onetor, put his arm around him, and comfort him. He told the Hellene tales of friends and kinsmen of his who had been robbed or enslaved or slain by the invading Macedonians, until half the folk in the tavern were weeping, too. In the end Vardanas swore eternal friendship with old Onetor, and a sobered lot of revelers left the tavern.

I doubt, though, whether any of those there, if ever in later years he took part in the sack of a city, stayed his hand from the usual crimes of such an occasion because of this moment of sympathy for the victims of war in a tavern at Teos.

During our tours of the neighborhood of Ephesos, Pyrron kept up a steady stream of talk. Much of the talk was heavily philosophical, and I could make but little of it. On the other hand, when he guided us round the monuments and buildings and sacred places, telling the myths and histories connected with them, I found it fascinating. How he carried so much knowledge in one mind I know not, though I saw that he replenished his store when he could by questioning the priests and custodians.

But Pyrron was one of those enthusiasts who never know when to stop. From the time she met him in Sousa, his wide knowledge had fascinated Nirouphar. Starved for facts about the great world, she had striven to draw all she could from him. As lecturing was to him what bread and wine are to most folk, he had gladly complied.

Now, howsomever, she found herself stuffed with all the knowledge that one human mind can absorb in such a limited time, and longed to be let out of school for a while. But Pyrron kept relentlessly on, expounding the theories of Pythagoras and Demokritos and other sages about the nature of matter, the form of the cosmos, and the origin and destiny of mankind. So it came to pass that Nirouphar hung less and less eagerly on his words. As a well-bred Persian she was too polite and tactful to tell him to hold his tongue, but betimes I caught her in a yawn. More and more she reined her horse to walk abreast of mine.

While we were touring, Elisas disappeared on his mule into the interior of Anatolia. He came back four days later with a fat roll of carpets, which he had bought in Sardeis.

"Will sell these in Athens," he said. "Why do you not buy Lydian wares to sell, too? Not rugs, please, because if we sell against each other the price will go down. But there are dyes, gaming sets, and other Lydian products that should sell well in Hellas."

I was tempted to take the Syrian's advice, having a bit of the commercial spirit despite my knightly upbringing. But I forbore lest my dignity as an officer suffer from such huckstering. Several of the Thessalians, though, did buy Lydian goods for resale in Athens, and some made neat profits.

At last Philoxenos sent word that the *Destroyer* was ready, and that fifteen talents of hay and greens had been placed aboard for Aias in the space once occupied by the oars and benches.

On the nineteenth of Thargelion we marched down to the beach. Here we dismounted and turned our horses and mules over to the dealers who had bought them. Many of the men wept, and hugged and kissed their mounts. I tried to kiss Golden good-by, but had to jerk away quickly to keep her from biting off my nose. The wagons and most of the camp gear had been sold, too.

"Let's go," I said, and led the hipparchia out on the mole.

The *Destroyer* lay at the end of the mole, which sloped up so that its outer end was on a level with the main deck of the ship. Vardanas and I headed the column. Behind us, Kanadas and Siladites led the elephant, who had been acting fractious of late. Then came Pyrron, talking philosophy to Nirouphar, followed by Elisas, the Thessalians, and the women and children. Lastly came the cook, the camp men, and the grooms bearing the heavier burdens, such as some squealing young pigs which Elisas had bought to assure us fresh meat on the voyage.

I stepped on the deck. Behind me, Aias balked.

First he reached out his trunk and touched the deck and the railing. Then he extended a foot and tried the deck. Though the planking had been strengthened at this point, it still sagged and creaked beneath the elephant's weight. Aias drew his foot back, squealing.

The Indians jabbered at him, crying *"Malmal!"* Siladites pulled Aias' ear with his goad. Still the elephant would not move, but shook himself and squealed angrily, lashing the air with his trunk. Behind him, the rest of the hipparchia waited. The children became unruly.

"Elisas!" I said. "Have you any more melons?"

"Nay, Troop Leader. We have not seen a melon since we left Syria."

"What else have we to tempt him?"

The Syrian shrugged, looking at me past Aias' legs. "This is a poor country for fruit this time of year. I will try some dried figs."

Elisas made one of the camp men put down his load. The Syrian opened the bag and took out a small sack of figs. As he feared to squeeze past Aias' legs, he tossed the bag of figs to Kanadas.

The Indian fed a fig to Aias, who flipped it into his mouth with his trunk and reached out for another. Kanadas backed off, trying to lure the elephant forward. But Aias stood rooted to his spot, waving his trunk and grumbling. Several times Kanadas went through this performance, but the elephant refused to move for the sake of a fig. The crowd of Ephesians laughed and jeered. Kanadas said:

"If we could offer big fancy cake, he might move."

I said, "See if there's a big fancy cake in Ephesos. If not, get the best you can. The rest of you, come on forward. Fear not; Aias will no step on you if you're careful."

The hipparchia crowded past the elephant to the deck. Elisas disappeared shorewards.

The camp men and grooms put down their burdens and lined up for their final pay. The ship's captain, Polyphron of Miletos, lent me a table on which to spread out money and pay sheets. I paid them off without major disputes and bid them farewell. One said:

"Any time the king sends you to the land of the Hyperboreans, Hipparch, let me know and I'll join you."

"I too," said others. With many farewells, they filed back past the elephant and down the mole.

"Inaudos!" I said. "Go you not also?"

The Kordian fell to his knees. "Let me come with you, Hipparch! I be your personal servant! Only three oboloi a day, with food and one new suit a year! I save your life, maybe!"

"I hadn't planned on this. Why are you so eager to come? Surely your wife will never track you down in Ephesos, and you can find work here."

"I want to see Athens. Everybody talk about Athens. I feel like fool, to come so near Athens and then turn back."

"All right, we'll carry you on the payroll as far as Athens."

Captain Polyphron said: "I 'ope you'll not wait much longer, 'Ipparch. It's a long row to Samos harbor, and fain would I not reach it after dark."

I told him of the difficulty with Aias. The Indians still stood by the elephant's head, now coaxing and now scolding. At last Kanadas shouted a long sentence in his own language. Then he and Siladites turned their backs, stepped on the deck, and walked down the ramp to the pen.

Aias tried the deck with his forefoot again, then quietly stepped aboard and inched down the ramp after the Indians. The ship's structure groaned with the weight, but held.

Elisas arrived sweating with an enormous loaf of bread under his arm. He panted: "Where is the elephant, Troop Leader? Oh, there he is! The big pig! No fancy cakes in Ephesos, and the baker said it would take all day to make one, so I bought this loaf. And now the polluted elephant goes aboard without awaiting it!"

The little man looked ready to weep. I said: "Well done, Elisas. You may eat the loaf yourself, or share it with Aias if you like."

Aias made himself at home in the pen, which formed a huge square hole in the main deck. So tall was the elephant that as he stood on the reinforced oar deck, his eyes were on a level with the main deck. A wooden parapet around the edges of the pen, however, kept him from actually looking out.

"Kanadas!" I said. "What said you to Aias to change his mind?"

Kanadas smiled a rare smile. "I said: Siladites and I go to Athens on this great ship. We happy to have you come too, but if you will not, then stay here in Ephesos and starve."

296

Now the four Dahas, who had also been paid off, said farewell. They wrung Vardanas' hand and mine and walked down the mole. They vaulted on their horses. Each whipped out an arrow and loosed it at the sky. Then they galloped off with wild Sakan whoops toward their distant homeland. One of the spare horses they took with them was Vardanas' Rakous, which they promised to deliver to the Persian's kin at Sousa.

Kanadas, watching from the rail, said: "I wish I go with them." A tear ran down his dark face. "It is against my religion to travel over sea."

"Everything's against your religion, laddie," I said.

"Of course. That shows it is very pure, moral religion." He wiped his eyes. "Miss wives and children, too." He glanced at Aias' pen. "Also worry about Mahankal."

"Why? D'you fear he'll be seasick?"

"That will be bad, but is not what I meant. Rutting time due, and if he have no lady elephant he becomes dangerous."

"I know not what to do about that. There's no female beast within ten thousand furlongs who'd fit his monstrous member."

Captain Polyphron blew a trumpet. The anchor weights were drawn up. A three-banker towed us slowly away from the mole, its oars thumping and splashing. The Ephesians cheered and waved.

The towrope was cast off. Polyphron winded his horn again. One by one the oars were thrust out through the oar holes in the ship's side and secured by sailors to the thole pins in the outrigger. Another trumpet blast set our oars in motion. Up they rose, then forward, then down with a splash, and then back. The beat of the coxswain's gavel, slow at first and then quickening, came up to us as we headed out into the blue Aegean under fair spring skies.

BOOK NINE

Attika

THE DESTROYER MOVED but slowly, as she had only half her normal complement of three hundred and twenty rowers. The place of the rest was taken by Aias' pen and food crib. As was most of the fleet at Ephesos, the *Destroyer* was manned by free hired rowers. Polyphron explained:

"It costs more in the short run, but you're in less danger of having them seize the ship, tear all the free men to pieces, and row off to become pirates, than with a shipful of slaves."

We crept across the angle of the Ikarian Sea toward Mount Mykale. As the morning passed and Samos rose higher out of the sea, we could see the opening of the strait that sunders this isle from the mainland.

The sky was fair, the breeze light. Nonetheless, the waves were big enough to give a slight but regular motion to the ship, like unto an easy single-foot. Vardanas and the Indians became violently seasick. The elephant grumbled.

Finding that I, too, had a slight headache, I took a walk about the deck. I passed Pyrron and Nirouphar in converse. Nirouphar looked pale, while Pyrron, leaning lazily against the rail, spoke:

"...now observe, my dear, and you will see an exemplification of one of the major arguments in favor of the sphericity of the earth.

Notice how, as time passes, Ephesos disappears below the curvature of the sea, while Samos rises out of it."

"Oh, for Mithras' sake, stop lecturing for once!" said Nirouphar. "I feel unwell."

I hid a smile and walked on. Later I returned, sat beside the lass, and held her hand without speaking. She smiled gratefully; for once my habit of long silences was appreciated.

In the middle of the day, the oars of the lower banks were shipped to release the rowers for their midday meal. When each group had eaten in turn, the short oars were put out again. During the afternoon we rowed around Poseidon Promontory, with its splendid temple of Poseidon, and entered the strait. Aias fell silent as the ship's motion quieted.

Soon the strait opened out again to the south. We crept past the Heraion, rising back from the beach, and saw Myron's colossal statues of Zeus, Athena, and Herakles standing about the shrine. As the sun was setting behind Mount Kerkis, we came into Samos Harbor and dropped our anchor weights behind the huge breakwater. The city is built on flat ground around the harbor, but tiers of white-plastered houses extend up the hillside like rows of marble benches in a theater.

The whole hundred and sixty sweating and stinking rowers swarmed out on deck, climbed down the bow, and plunged into the shallow water, splashing and yelling. Then they waded to shore and went into the town, their wet rags clinging to them. They shouted boasts of what they would do, and how many times, to the whores of Samos.

Small boats put out, some with merchandise, some merely offering to ferry folk to land. I went ashore with my friends. We toured the town, where Pyrron showed us the birthplace of Pythagoras. We also visited the temple of Hera, which we had seen from the ship, but we did not have time to climb the mountain to see the famous aqueduct bored by the tyrant Polykrates through the bowels of the hill.

The next day we headed westward. We coasted around the north of Ikaria and stopped for the night at the island's only town, Oinoë. This, however, is such a wretched little village that few of us went ashore at all.

We left the Sporades behind and drove west into the Aegean. Polyphron told me he meant to pass between Delos and Tenos.

Poseidon, however, had other ideas. Shortly before noon, clouds swept over the sky from the north, and Boreas howled in our ears. The waves, already choppy, rose still further. The ship broke into a hard trot, jerking and groaning. Presently the oars of the lower bank were pulled in so that the oar holes could be stopped up. Sailors formed a chain to hand bailing buckets up from the oar deck. To my anxious questions, Polyphron replied:

"I like it not. It looks like an Etesian storm."

The elephant squealed and moaned. The motion of the ship made him stagger about his pen, bumping against the sides. Every time he did so, the ship shuddered and tipped. The Indians were in the pen with him, shouting endearments over the roar of the wind to soothe him. They had to keep skipping about in the ankle-deep water to avoid being trampled.

Polyphron hastened to the pen. He said to me: "By Zeus, 'Ipparch, you'd better do something before that monster charges through the side of the ship and sinks us!"

Kanadas slipped on the watery floor of the pen and sat down. Aias made one of his lunges. I was sure the elephant would tread the Indian flat. But Kanadas, with a mighty wrench, threw himself to one side as the elephant's feet came down.

"Kanadas!" I shouted. "Can you make the elephant lie down?"

The Indians held a brief but hot discussion in their own tongue. Then they shouted: "*Leto!*"

The elephant knelt and lowered himself to the floor of his pen. There he lay with the water washing about him. He squealed and gurgled while the Indians petted and praised him.

The wind howled louder. Gusts of rain lashed the deck. My people huddled at the stem, where the cabins gave some protection. The women and children had been put into the cabins lest they be washed overboard. Vardanas, gray of face, clung to a piece of woodwork and muttered prayers to Auramasdas between retching spells.

The only one who seemed undisturbed was Pyrron. The philosopher clung to the rail, looking out into the raging seas with keen interest as the wind whipped his shirt and fluttered his hair and beard.

As I came up to him, clutching the rail to keep from being swept away, he said:

"A fascinating phenomenon, the sea. For instance, why does it stay the same depth, when so many rivers constantly augment its volume?"

"By all the gods, how keep you so calm?" I shouted. "Belike we're on our way to Poseidon's realm, elephant and all!"

Pyrron pointed to the pigpen. One of the pigs stood with its legs braced against the motion of the ship, eating sturdily into the pile of garbage that had been dumped in the pen.

"A wise man could take a lesson in serenity from that young fellow!" he shouted back.

Polyphron blew his trumpet. Naked sailors picked up the light jury mast that lay on the main deck and tried to step it in a small socket forward, abaft the forecastle. They staggered about, wrestling with the mast, screaming at one another, and hauling on ropes. Several times they almost had it in the hole, when a pitch of the ship threw their plan awry. More than once I looked to see the whole lot swept overboard as wave crests slashed across the deck, covering it with water several fingers deep.

Polyphron stood on the forecastle, shouting directions. At last the stick went home, and the sailors secured it by stays to posts on the deck. Then they began trying to hoist a small sail. There were many failures and tangles of ropes before they got the thing up. It was not much bigger than a cloak, but it seemed to suit Polyphron. And indeed, the ship's gait settled down to an easy canter as soon as the sail had filled with wind.

Then Polyphron hurried to the main deck and clambered down to the oar deck, where he shouted more orders. The rowing stopped. Pair by pair, the long oars of the upper bank were pulled in through the oar holes.

Curious, I risked a dash across the deck to the hatch to see how this was done. The stench and din in the oar deck were frightful, but there was a kind of mad order about it. For each group of five men to draw a thirty-cubit oar in through the oar hole took careful timing so as not to fall foul of their comrades. With the ship pitching so violently, this became difficult. A couple of oars had broken; rowers sprawled on the deck, adding their cries to the hubbub. Water raced back and forth along the low outer parts of the deck with each pitch of the ship.

Little by little the captain brought order out of the confusion. In time the last oar had been stowed and lashed down. Then Polyphron let rowers come on deck, a few at a time, for a breath of fresh air. They grinned and cracked jokes as they did so. I decided that professional rowers were all men of mighty thews and puny wits, without the sense to be frightened by their deadly peril.

I started for the stern. A monstrous wave washed right over the poop, drenching those huddled there. Water raced over the main deck. I clung to the rail and should have made out well enough, but Pyrron lost his grip and shot down the edge of the deck, knocking my feet from under me. I managed to keep my grasp on the rail, and clung with my legs dangling overside as water rushed over me. I thought my grip was weakening when a strong hand hauled me back to safety. It was Inaudos. As he led me back to the quarter-deck he bawled in my ear:

"See, I save your life, as I say!"

Up forward, Polyphron and a sailor caught Pyrron as he was being washed overboard and hauled him back by his ankles. They righted him and dragged him back to the quarter-deck. Polyphron bellowed:

"Now stay there, you two idiots! I've enough worries without 'aving to fish you out of the deep!"

When I got my wind back and saw that my friend was safe, I asked Inaudos: "Have you ever been on a ship before?"

"No. What of it? Kordians fear nought on land or sea."

Except your wives, methought. With the oar ports all blocked, the sailors bailing, and the small sail keeping our bow downwind, the ship steadied. Great seas raced up behind us; it looked as if each wave would overwhelm us. But the poop deck rode high; the wave passed under us, hissing and boiling; and the stern dropped into the trough that foreran the next.

Polyphron reeled aft to the quarter-deck to assure himself that the steersmen were holding hard to the tiller that worked the steering oars. Then he tumbled down the ladder again.

"How goes it?" I shouted.

"We shall live, I 'ope; but we may end up in Crete or Egypt. I told the admiral we should wait another ten-day."

With dusk, the clouds broke up and the wind fell, though the ship still labored under heavy swells. Shouts from the sailors brought the captain in haste to the forecastle. Before us loomed a mountainous mass.

Polyphron shouted orders. The rowers put out the oars of the upper bank. With short quick strokes and careful timing, we swung to the right and rowed past the thundering, rocky shore. More than once I thought the swell would sweep us on the rocks, but we crept out of their reach. For a time we rowed by starlight.

The sea calmed until I felt I could risk speaking to the captain. "What land is that?"

"Naxos."

Vardanas said: "Was that not a frightful storm, Captain?"

"Not too bad," said Polyphron. "This ship has lived through worse. One can expect such a blow crossing the Aegean almost any season but late summer and autumn."

"Auramasdas save me from a really bad one, then!"

At midnight, as the half moon rose over the peaks of Naxos, we rowed into the harbor. Though the ship was now steady, the elephant refused to rise, but lay groaning and squealing with seasickness. When we dropped the anchor weights, my seasick hipparchia raised a feeble cheer of, "*Iai* for Thessalia!"

The next day we spent repairing our battered ship. First, howsomever, all the folk—passengers, sailors, and rowers—made a procession to the temple of Dionysos, on an islet in the harbor, to offer money for a handsome votive tablet. Even Pyrron contributed, though he murmured to me:

"Perhaps the gods did save us. But then, what of all the crews they have failed to save?"

That evening we held a party in town and got drunk on the famous wine of the island. Even Kanadas showed a tiny trace of tipsiness. Aside from having to break up a few fights between rowers and townspeople, nought marred our gaiety. The Persians and Indians, though, swore never to set foot on a ship again if ever they survived this voyage.

Next day we rowed to Kynthos, where we put the rowers ashore for the night. Then we proceeded into the Saronic Gulf, past the rocky Paralian Peninsula, and so came at last to Peiraieus. We crept around the promontory of Akte, under the frowning fortress of Eëtioneia, through the sea gate in the breakwater, into Peiraieus Bay, and into the inner harbor of Kantharos. Here we dropped our anchor weights among many great ships of war.

And thus, on the twenty-fourth of Thargelion, in the eleventh year of Alexander's reign and the third year of the hundred and thirteenth Olympiad, the king's elephant expedition arrived in Attika. We had been ten months and twelve days on the road and had but one day more of travel ahead of us.

After a talk with my officers next morning, I decided not to deliver the elephant that day. There were too many other things to do first. When I proposed leaving Aias aboard the *Destroyer* an extra day, however, Polyphron objected.

"Look 'ere, 'Ipparch," he said. "I 'ave work to do on the ship, to ready her for the voyage back. I can't get at it while that 'ideous monster's in the pen."

"But it would be a fearful bother for us to take Aias off and stable him! It would cost silver, too."

"I can't 'elp that. 'Ere's your destination, so get yourself and your people and your creature ashore."

"Another day's delay won't slay you. You told me it was too early for safe voyaging anyway."

"A plague on this argument! What I say on my own ship stands. Get off, all of you!"

"Gentlemen," said a timid voice with a guttural accent. It was Elisas. "Can tell Captain Polyphron how to turn the elephant's being on his ship to advantage."

"Well?" growled the Milesian.

"You can make a profit from it, noble Captain. For half the taking, I will do it for you."

"What's this idea, man?"

"Do you agree to an even division?"

"Yes, yes. Out with it!"

"All right. You are my witness, Troop Leader Leon. See you those people?"

A small crowd of longshoremen and loafers had collected on the waterfront near the *Destroyer*. They pointed at our ship and exclaimed with more interest than one would expect a mere ship to arouse. Then I saw that they were looking at Aias' back and the top of his head, which showed above the main deck. The sun shone on the granite-colored hide as the elephant paced about his pen.

Elisas said: "We can send word to shore that men will be allowed aboard to see the elephant for—" He closed his eyes in thought. "Those are mostly poor men and slaves, are they not? I put the fee at four coppers."

"Done!" said Polyphron. "I'll 'ave her towed to a pier and set out the big gangplank."

I left Polyphron and Elisas to their plans and went about my other affairs. One task was to pay off the Thessalians. I did this in the captain's cabin to get away from the noise of sight-seers who trooped aboard at a half-obolos a head to see the elephant. Of the twenty Thessalians who had begun the journey from India, counting the officers, one had been left behind wounded, two had been slain, and one had deserted. I could not give an accurate reckoning of the women and children, for I had lost count of births, deaths, runaways, and new concubines picked up.

Thanks to the deaths, to the heavy fines I levied after the mutiny in Kilikia, and most of all to Prince Arivarates' generosity, I ended up better than I had feared. I was able to give everybody his due pay and his bonus and still have an adequate sum left over to maintain the Indians during their stay in Athens. The understanding was that they should stay with Aias until they had trained local men to take their places. I also had Xenokrates' fifty talents, but this I kept in sealed bags separate from the rest. There were five of these bags of gold pieces, each weighing fifty pounds.

When all had been paid, we went ashore. Our first task was to change our money into Athenian. Hitherto, we had used Alexandrine with little trouble. For years, Alexander's mints had been melting down Persian treasure and pouring out new coins. Hence, though much Persian coin was still current in the empire, everybody accepted the new coinage. In Greece, however, each state still clung to its own coinage.

We pushed our way through the chattering throng to the section of the colonnaded Deigma devoted to banks. At random, I got in the line before the change table of the firm of Dareios and Pamphylios. The bankers were a pair of stout middle-aged Anatolians, probably freedmen. Dareios, who handled the money-changing table, came from Armenia. His partner, who took care of loans and deposits at another table, was, as his name showed, a Pamphylian from the southern coast. No doubt his real name was too hard for Greek tongues and so had been lost in the course of his adventures. Both were surrounded by slave clerks with account tablets and abaci and sacks of coin.

When we had bought enough Athenian owls to keep us in food and shelter for several days, we ate our lunch and went to buy horses. I picked a stout chestnut stallion named Thunderbolt. "Snail" would have been a better name, but at least he bore my weight without complaint. Vardanas bought two, one for himself and one for Nirouphar. He remarked:

"We call these little things rabbits in Persia."

He also bought a slave, a lumpish, tattooed, infibulated Scythian with barely enough wit to keep from stepping off a roof. Vardanas paid three hundred drachmai for the man, which I thought much too high. But I had decided that it was hopeless to try to make a thrifty shopper of him.

I did not feel the need of a slave, as I had the faithful Inaudos at my elbow. From him I learned to prefer a willing paid worker to most slaves. For one thing, I do not like to tie up several pounds of my capital in a human being, who is more likely than a well-tended horse or cow to run away, or to be stabbed in a brawl, or even to murder his master. There are of course advantages the other way, too. For example, it is hard to find a really willing free worker; and, if they are unwilling, one cannot beat them much, lest they leave.

When we had found stable quarters for our new horses, we went back to the ship to ready ourselves for the day of delivery. I did not repeat my error of Persepolis, that of being careless of my appearance. Inaudos polished my helmet until I could see my face in it. Kanadas wrapped his head in a new length of colored cloth and gave his beard a new coating of blue dye and cleaned his silver bangles. Vardanas got out his best embroidered coat and trousers, curled his beard, and was stopped only by my earnest protests from painting his face.

My last task of the day was to write two letters. One was to King Alexander, telling him of our safe arrival and my discharge of the soldiers. Of course, I expressed my joy at his recovery and wrote that my next letter would probably be the last.

The other letter was to my parents, to be delivered by one of my homeward-bound Thessalians. After telling them somewhat of my adventures, I besought them to write me and promised to be home in a few months at most.

The reason I gave them for not going home sooner was that I now had a matchless chance, unlikely to befall again, to study under the philosophers, as I had planned to do long before as a beardless youth. This was true as far as it went, but I told them not that an even stronger motive was the presence of my longed-for Nirouphar. As Vardanas planned to stay in Athens for a time, his sister would naturally be there also.

Some of the Thessalians set off for home as soon as they were paid off. Others, learning that they could have free quarters for another night, stayed abo ard the ship. Klonios spent the afternoon in Athens finding the Thessalian consul, an Athenian named Epikerdes, to arrange quarters for those Thessalians who wished to remain in the city.

When, next morning, we were ready to take Aias ashore, most of the Thessalians had gone about their business. Some had struck out for home; some were sight-seeing; some were looking for investments for their money. Four spent the night in such violent carousal that the Scythian archers had to be called to arrest them. They had to pay several pounds of silver in damages.

Five Thessalians, including Klonios, were still around when the time arrived to leave the ship. I persuaded them to come with us to find Aristoteles. It would, I told them, be a historic occasion.

Thirteen of us thus marched down the gangplank soon after Helios, rising over Mount Hymettos, gilded the bronze helm of

Pheidias' colossal Athena on the Akropolis of Athens. There were, forbye, porters carrying Aristoteles' specimens and Xenokrates' gold. I invited Elisas, too, to attend, but he begged off on the ground that he had to sell his Lydian carpets.

As we tramped through the straight, right-angled streets of Peiraieus, slave girls bringing the day's water to their masters' houses dropped their jugs and ran screaming at the sight of the elephant. Aias was fractious. Several times he balked or tried to go up the wrong street, and squealed angrily when made to obey.

At the stables we found that not everybody had a horse. So we rented three to fill out the total, as well as a cart to carry the specimens and the gold. Then we clattered out of Peiraieus on the Hamaxitos.

The horses, unused to elephants, snorted, rolled their eyes, and tried to bolt. Pyrron's nag did get away and carried the Eleian almost out of sight before he got it under control.

We splashed through the muddy Kephisos and rode across the flat Attic plain, broken by clumps of olive and fig trees, where the wet-harvest was just being reaped. On our right rose the famous long walls from Peiraieus to Athens. They may have been a formidable defense in the days of Themistokles, or even in those of Perikles, but now any able general could breach them with modern siege machinery.

An hour's ride brought us to the Peiraic Gate of Athens. I had ready my royal seal and my letters in case the guardians of the gate tried to deny us entry, but the Scythian archers were too astonished by the elephant even to speak to us.

Pyrron was the only one among us who had ever been in Athens before, and his memory of streets was none too good. Twice he led us astray. At last we followed the avenue from the Peiraic Gate until it opened out into the market place with its many fine statues and monuments. This we crossed to a street that runs along the bank of the Eridanos, and so we came to the Gate of Diochares on the eastern side of the city.

Having heard so much about Athens, I must confess to some slight disappointment. True, the Akropolis, rising from its great ship-shaped hill of tawny rock on our right, has as fine a lot of buildings, monuments, and statues as any city in the world. But after the broad, beautiful avenues of Sousa and Babylon, the city of Athens struck me as small and squalid—a jumble of little, crooked, unpaved streets, deep in mud and stinking refuse, winding amid buildings set at all angles. Although the city is of but modest size, traffic is a frightful tangle because of the crookedness of the streets and because no effort is made to control it.

As we left the Gate of Diochares and entered the eastern suburbs, I said to Vardanas and Pyrron: "Lads, Aristoteles is deemed by many the greatest thinker in the world. I hope he'll befriend us or at least let us listen to his wisdom. Now, if we burst in on him with the elephant and all, he'll be startled and put out of countenance. Therefore, I think we ought to gallop on ahead, give him the king's letter, and warn him of the coming of Aias. Thus he'll have time to compose himself."

Vardanas agreed, but Pyrron said: "You two go ahead. You know me; if I try to gallop, I shall fall off before I've proceeded a furlong."

Vardanas and I rode ahead. Five furlongs from the city, on the Marathon road, we came to Lykeion Park. The Scythian at the entrance made difficulties about letting us in, since we were not citizens, until I showed him my letters and seal.

"Where is Aristoteles' school?" I asked.

"That way, that way, then turn that way," he said with gestures. "You find, easy."

We passed the athletic grounds, where naked youths jumped, ran, and wrestled. The school was a group of small brick houses around a statue of Apollon, with rows of outdoor benches shaded by plane trees. As it was a fine spring day, classes were held out of doors. Two classes were now in session, at opposite ends of the school grounds. Lecturing one group of young Hellenes was a good-looking man in his forties. He was clean-shaven, a fashion just becoming common in Athens. In his hand he held an herb, on which he was discoursing; others lay at his feet.

I dismounted, leaving Vardanas to hold Thunderbolt, and walked toward this man. I almost hailed him when the thought struck me that he was too young to be Aristoteles. I therefore continued on to the other class.

The second lecturer was a slender man of medium height, with a close-cut iron-gray beard and graying hair carefully arranged by the barber to cover his bald spot. He looked about a decade older than the first one, with sharp, severe features and close-set little black eyes. He was wrapped in a billowing cloak of striking saffron and purple hue, and his fingers shone with rings. He spoke Attic with a slight Kalchidian accent, a lisp, and a quick, sharp, emphatic delivery, while he paced nervously about a large platform. As I came up, he was saying:

"...problem in organizing a viable state is the avoidance of thithms and theditions. For instance, heterogeneity of stocks may lead to thedition, at least until the component racial elements have had time to athimilate. A viable state cannot be constructed from any chance body of persons, or in any chance period of time, notwithstanding that dreamers and idealists thometimes think..."

Standing behind the last of the benches, I raised my hand and tried to catch the lecturer's eye. His glance glided over me as if I were not there. His voice went on:

"...states which have admitted perthons of another stock, either at the time of their foundation or later, have been troubled by thedition..."

I waved my hand, snapped my fingers, and whistled.

"...There are many instances. Thus the Achaians joined with thettlers from Troizen in founding Sybaris, but expelled them when their own numbers increased..."

"O Aristoteles!" I called. "Aristoteles of Stageira!"

The lecture broke off at last. The lecturer stared coldly at me and said: "Young man, the topic of my discourse may be of no interest to you. This is not surprising, as you have evidently been thubject to foreign influences in your travels. However, this topic is of moment to me and to my hearers. You will therefore oblige me by either taking your theat and remaining quiet until I have finished, or taking yourthelf elsewhere."

His hearers tittered. I could feel myself blushing. I did a military about-face and walked back to where Vardanas held our horses, raging at my loss of dignity.

"I'll pull that self-conceited old cull off his high horse!" I fumed, and vaulted on Thunderbolt's back. "We'll go back to the elephant and make a grand entrance."

310

We met Aias and the rest of our escort at the gate of the Lykeion and led them back to the school. This time Aristoteles halted his lecture without my having to whistle at him. He stopped in the middle of a long word with his mouth hanging open. A sheet of papyrus fluttered from his hand to the ground.

I dismounted, marched forward between the files of benches to the dais, banged my heels together in Macedonian drill sergeant's fashion, and whipped the king's letter to Aristoteles from under my arm. Holding it out, I cried in parade-ground tones:

"O Aristoteles son of Nikomachos, know that I am Leon of Atrax, troop leader to King Alexander of Macedonia and Asia. The king, my master, in consideration of your services to philosophy, sends you this elephant, late the property of King Poros of India, as a gift. I present the king's letter to you."

I stood rigidly, holding out the letter, for at least a hundred heartbeats. Aristoteles opened and shut his mouth several times silently, like a fish. For a moment he looked as if he would swoon.

At last he pulled himself together and read the letter. By the time he had finished, he had regained his composure. He walked around the elephant, looking Aias up and down.

"O Earth and the gods!" he breathed. "Is this all? The beast and this letter?"

"Not quite," I said. "The man atop the elephant is Kanadas of Paurava, the elephant's master, and the man on his neck is Kanadas' helper, Siladites. There is also a collection of inanimate specimens from India. Let's have the chest, lads."

When Inaudos and Pyrron heaved the chest of specimens out of the cart, Pyrron opened it and showed Aristoteles the specimens. Aristoteles said:

"I feel like the man who cast his line for a herring and caught a whale. It's true I once said thomething to the king about wishing to examine an elephant in the flesh, but—tell me, Hipparch. There's nothing in the letter about feeding and caring for the beast. How am I thupposed to do that?"

"The pay of the Indians is provided for until they can train Hellenes to take their places. As for food, the king has paid that up to now, but he said nought about any provision for it after I delivered the beast to you. I also ought to warn you that Aias is now in his rutting season and hence dangerous. He must be kept securely chained up."

Aristoteles stood with his chin in his hand. Then he said: "Methinks I detect traces of the royal thense of humor. I shall force each of my students to pay for one day's feeding of the beast until thome permanent arrangement is made." He smiled wryly. "I wronged you by snubbing you earlier, young man. You meant to warn me before this—ah—problem dethended on me. Pray do not hold it against me. Who are these other people?"

I presented my dozen. When I came to Pyrron, the clean-shaven assistant cried: "Pyrron of Elis! I've 'eard of you. I'm Theophrastos of Eresos."

Theophrastos was holding hands with a younger man who looked like Aristoteles and who, in fact, turned out to be his son Nikomachos. Theophrastos and Pyrron fell into low conversation about mutual friends in the philosophical profession.

Aristoteles said: "What are your plans now, Leon of Atrax? Back to the wars?"

"Nay. I have one more commission to execute, and then I shall be a civilian again. I hope to hear some philosophy ere I go home."

"You were better advised to listen to me and my colleagues rather than fall into the clutches of an aged charlatan I could name. I hope you'll soon be back; for, frankly, I need your help in disposing of this organism. As things stand I cannot feed it long, and it were thinful to slaughter it after you've conveyed it such a distance. Come back when you've finished your work for the king, and I think we can find ways to therve each other. Incidentally," he said, tapping the king's letter, "this is not the story I heard of the demise of my unfortunate if rashly self-athertive great-nephew. Do you know aught authentic of Kallisthenes' death?"

"Nay, good sir; only what the letter says." And, in sooth, I knew no more from firsthand knowledge; though I, too, had heard rumors that the king had fed Kallisthenes to a lion, or stretched him on a rack, or otherwise put him to an interesting death.

"Farewell for now, then," said Aristoteles. He turned to Kanadas, who had clambered down from his perch. "O Kanadas, do you speak Greek?"

"Little," said the Indian.

"Then see to it that the elephant is thecurely tethered in the park and arrange for its feeding. Dealers in fodder will trust you if you give them my name. Try to prevent the beast from consuming our shade trees. By the way, has the elephant articulations in its legs?"

"What?"

"You know, joints."

"Sorry, do not understand."

"Can it kneel? Like this." Aristoteles knelt.

"Oh yes." Kanadas said to the elephant: "*Baitbait!*" Aias knelt.

"Away goes another old wives' tale!" said Aristoteles. "I must make a note of that."

The philosopher stepped back to his dais, picked up the sheet of papyrus he had dropped, and scanned it, holding it at arm's length. "Where were we? Ah yes. Heterogeneity of territory is also an occasion of thedition. This happens in states not naturally adapted to political unity..."

Xenokrates conducted the Platonic school in a park, too, but in a direction opposite from Athens. We rode out the Dipylon Gate on the Sacred Way to Eleusis but soon took a fork to the right and traveled seven furlongs northwest to the Grove of Akademe. Here we found the school of Platon, with benches and a professor and his assistants, as we had in the Lykeion.

The professor, Xenokrates, was a heavy-set old man with an enormous white beard. He was lecturing in a slow sonorous drone on cosmogony. Quoth he:

"...agree with the divine Platon that almighty Zeus created matter in the form of four elements, to wit: fire, earth, air, and water, which are symbolized by the tetrahedron, the cube, the octahedron, and the icosahedron respectively. To those, we moderns add a fifth element, the sublime ether of which the vault of heaven is made. This addition is mine, working on a suggestion by my distinguished predecessor Speusippos. I cannot help it if a certain scrawny sophist on the other side of the city, notorious for claiming to know everything, arrogates this discovery to himself.

313

"But let us go back to the divine Platon, to see by what sublime train of irrefragable logic he establishes this elemental organization of the cosmos. I quote: If the body of the All had had to come into existence as a plane surface, having no depth, one middle term would have sufficed to bind together both itself and its fellow terms; but— How now, young man?"

I came forward and presented the king's letter, saying: "O Xenokrates, I am Leon of Atrax, an officer of King Alexander. The king sends you this letter, together with the sum of fifty talents. Give him the money, Inaudos."

The Kordian heaved the five fifty-pound bags out of the cart. One after another they fell to the ground with a musical jingle. Xenokrates opened one and pulled out a fistful of staters. His pupils clustered round. One tried to lift a moneybag and grunted in surprise at the weight, for it does not take a large bag to hold fifty pounds of gold.

"Herakles!" said the philosopher. "How much money said you?"

"'Tis the equivalent of fifty talents of silver," I said.

The old man gave a long whistle and fell silent while he read the king's letter. At last he said: "Let's go inside to discuss this matter."

When we were seated on a bench in his indoor classroom, and the money had been hauled in, too, he said: "With all due respect, O Leon, your king must be—ah—mad. I have done nothing to earn such a sum."

"I know nought of that, Xenokrates. I do but carry out my orders."

"Dear me! What could I do with so much money? I am comfortably off, between my own small patrimony and the fees of my pupils. This vast fortune would, I am sure, only involve me in scandals and swindles. Take it back to Alexander."

"What!" I cried. "Are you daft?"

"Take it back. I want it not."

"But I canna! I was commanded to give you this gold and get receipts. Taking it back would mean setting out on another ten months' journey, through the same toils and perils I thought to have escaped. Furthermore, when I've made delivery and sent off my final report, my commission will end. I shall no longer be a servant of the king."

Xenokrates spread his hands. "I know not what to say. Then keep it yourself, or drop it into Phaleron Bay. It's no concern of mine."

"I dare not. The king has a long reach. Take the money and give it away yourself, if that's how you feel. As Aisopos says, we oft despise that which is most useful to us."

"Not I! If—ah—word got around that I was giving away a fortune, every rogue and sponger in Attika would be on my trail overnight. I should have no peace to think. I might have my throat cut." Xenokrates looked at me sharply. "Are you he who led the elephant ashore at Peiraieus this morning? My slave brought me some such tale, but I didn't believe him."

"Aye."

"What has become of the elephant?"

"As the king commanded, I delivered him to Aristoteles."

"To that saucy braggart! O Zeus, is there no justice? Why sent the king not the elephant to Xenokrates, and this mass of trash"—he kicked a bag of gold—"to Aristoteles?"

"You must ask the king. But such being the case, surely you'll now take this gold! You would not have the Stageirite get ahead of you, would you?"

Xenokrates stroked his beard. "I will—ah—here is what I'll do. You say there's the equivalent of fifty talents of silver here?"

"Aye."

"And these bags are of equal weight?"

"Aye, or very nearly."

"That is"—Xenokrates closed his eyes while he did sums in his head—"thirty thousand drachmai. Well, I'll take one tenth of that, or three thousand drachmai." He put his head out the door and called to one of his students. "Myronides!"

When the youth came in, Xenokrates said: "Count the gold pieces in one of these bags into two equal piles. Take the rest back to the king, O Leon, and tell him I return it because he has many more folk in his service than I have, and so needs more money to pay them."

"But that leaves me as badly off as before!"

"I'm sorry, my dear young man, but what concern is that of mine? I accept this three thousand only because the school needs new books, and to keep ahead of the needle-nosed quibbler."

I continued the argument while Myronides sorted the staters, but to no avail. At last I said: "How about my receipt? I was told to get three copies."

"Ah—yes, of course." Xenokrates fumbled with his writing supplies. "Dear me, where did I put those sheets? Ah, here we are. I, Xenokrates son of Agathenor, of Kalchedon, hereby acknowledge receipt of the sum of three thousand drachmai, in gold, from Leon of Atrax. Done in the Akademeia in Attika on the fifth day from the end of Thargelion, in the archonship of Chremes."

Vardanas spoke: "Now I know the Hellenes are a mad folk. Most of you can smell a drachma at ten leagues and will tunnel through a mountain with your bare hands to get one. But lo! Here is a man who will not take them when they are honorably offered to him."

When the laugh died down he continued: "O philosopher, my friend here needs a receipt for the whole amount before he will be free of this millstone about his neck. If you want not the money, why not accept it, give him a receipt, and make him a gift of the part you will not keep? He can use it. So, for that matter, could I."

Xenokrates chuckled but tossed his head. "No, that would not be honest. I'll give a receipt only for the money I truly mean to keep. He must make his own arrangements with the king for the rest."

Vardanas' scheme seemed so reasonable that I, too, besought Xenokrates to change his mind, but the old fellow turned mulish. In the end, we rode back to Athens defeated, with Inaudos driving the cart containing gold worth twenty-seven thousand drachmai. Vardanas found my plight amusing.

"Your honesty does you credit, though," he said. "Most of your countrymen would simply hire some guards and a ship and set out for some western land, money and all."

"Basely won gains are the same as losses, but 'tis not wholly a matter of honesty. I've served Alexander many years and know how long he can hold a grudge. Suppose I fled to Syracuse, let's say? If my own guards did not murder me for the treasure, a year or so later some mysterious strangers would arrive in Syracuse. Presently, I should be found with my throat well cut, and what was left of the money would be on its way back to the king."

"Wellaway!" he said. "I suppose I must go back to Sousa some time. I shall be glad to go with you that far on your long road to India."

"Fornicate the long road to India! I'll find a way to get Xenokrates to take this money if I must needs turn Athens upside down!"

Epikerdes, the Thessalian consul, told me: "My own house is full of visiting Thessalians, but I can get you quarters in the house of Syloson of Mylai. My appropriation will cover seven nights' free board and lodging at Syloson's, but after that you'll have to pay him."

"How much does he want?"

"You must ask him, old boy, but I should think three oboloi a day for yourself and your servant would cover it."

"Has he room for anybody else?"

"I think he has. It's a big house in which he rattles around since his children left home. Why?"

"'Tis my Persian friends here. As they're well born, I am not eager to inflict the bugs and cutpurses of the usual Athenian inn upon them."

The consul pursed his lips. "The Persians have never kept a consul here, but, with Alexander uniting the world, who knows what strange things may not happen? You could ask Syloson, though I warn you he may be horrified by the idea of taking in foreigners."

Syloson, a bony, pock-marked, gray-bearded Thessalian with a missing ear, welcomed me at the door of his house in the Skambonidai.

"Rejoice, O Leon!" he said. His face fell when he saw the Persians behind me. "Who are these?"

"Merely friends, come to see me settled." I presented the pair.

Syloson acknowledged the introduction gruffly and led me to my room. There was some difficulty over Inaudos, who as a free man objected to being put in with the slaves. As I had become fond of the swaggering Kordian, I settled matters by bedding him in my own room, albeit it crowded me.

Meanwhile Vardanas went to work on my host with a skill that has been my lifelong envy. First he said: "O Syloson, proud though I be of my Persian heritage, at such times I am tempted to doff my trousers and pass myself off as a Hellene."

"What mean you?" said Syloson with a suspicious frown.

"Why, to have the benefits of knowing another Thessalian gentleman! In our months on the road, I have found Leon the bravest and truest man of my acquaintance. So I wish to test whether all men of that nation and class are so noble. You at least, if I be judge of character, are not behind him in these virtues."

"Whisht, you oriental flatterer!" said Syloson, trying to hide his pleasure.

"No, I am sincere, as Leon will tell you…" Soon they were deep in a warm discussion of horse-training methods. Syloson, like all Thessalians above the serf class, was devoted to the cult of the horse.

"But I canna ride the now," he said sadly. "A fall seven years syne hurt my back, so riding gars it ache…"

By the time I was settled, Vardanas was making his farewells at the front door. "Alas!" he said. "My sister has a horror of bugs, for we are cleanly folk in Sousa. But without a Persian consul to find us rooms, I suppose we are doomed to fight the battle of the blanket at the nearest inn."

"Losh, man," said Syloson. "Why can you no stay here? There's a plenty of room, and I can put the lass in the gynaikeion. 'Twill give my wife a body to talk to."

"Oh, my dear sir, I could not think of imposing on you! After all, we are foreigners, ignorant of your ways and manners…"

In the end, of course, Vardanas and Nirouphar moved into Syloson's house.

After dinner there came a knock at the front door and a cry of "Boy!" The porter opened to admit Pyrron, Kanadas, Theophrastos, and Nikomachos son of Aristoteles. Pyrron said:

"We're eaten with curiosity to know how you made out with Xenokrates, and we have a problem to talk about."

"You think you have a problem! By the Dog of Egypt, wait till you hear mine! See you that?" I kicked one of the five bags of golden coins and told them of Xenokrates' rejection of nine-tenths of the fortune proffered.

They marveled at the stiffness of principle that would make a man turn down good money. As none could suggest a way to get Xenokrates to take the rest of the gold, I asked:

"What's your problem, lads?"

Theophrastos, sitting with his arm about young Nikomachos, spoke in his Lesbian accent: "It's the polluted elephant. First, one of the stupid athletes teased him. In a rage, 'e pulled up his stake and chased everybody out of the Lykeion before the Indians brought him under control."

"Herakles!" I exclaimed. "Did he kill anybody?"

"No, but it was a near thing. I wonder you didn't 'ear the screams of Aias and his intended victims clear out to the Akademeia."

"I warned he was in rut," growled Kanadas. "Must get bigger stake."

"How did the people escape?" I asked. "Aias can make an amazing speed when he stirs those long legs."

"They ran! Some of the athletes ran faster than they ever 'ad in a race, and you should have seen my colleague Herakleides. 'E's almost too fat to walk, but he fled from the park like a doe from the 'ounds."

I said: "The gods be praised that no worse befell! When I left Aristoteles, he seemed to have things under control. For a man who had just been startled out of his wits, he made a quick recovery."

"That's 'e, 'whose little body lodged a mighty mind,' as says the Poet. 'E likes to cite the tale of Thales, who became tired of being asked: 'If you're so wise, why aren't you rich?' So Thales cornered the olive market, made a fortune, and went back to what really interested him—philosophy.

"'Owever, that doesn't get this monster fed. Your Indian friends collected a day's supply of 'ay, but when we left the Lykeion the beast had eaten most of it and was looking 'ungrily at our shade trees."

"We cannot suffer our park to be eaten up," said Nikomachos. "It belongs to Athens, and they let us use it only so long as we don't harm it."

Vardanas asked: "Are there no wastelands near the park where Aias could be grazed?"

"Yes," said Theophrastos. "Kanadas could drive him out the Brauron Road to the slopes of Mount 'Ymettos. There's lots of well-grassed public land there."

"But that means getting a grazing permit," said Nikomachos, "like any other stock raiser. And later in the year the grass will be so dry and sparse I don't think the beast could live on it."

Kanadas added: "Do not graze him for yet another ten-day. Too dangerous."

"Let's face the issue," said Theophrastos. "Whether we graze the beast at times or not, keeping it will cost money—more than the school can afford. For one thing, we shall 'ave to pay a keeper or two after the Indians go 'ome, or at least buy slaves to do their work. For another, we must needs stable the brute and feed it cut fodder through the winter months."

Vardanas said: "Why not put the elephant in an enclosure and charge the Athenians to look at him, as the sutler did on the ship? Or take them for rides?"

Theophrastos said: "I suggested something of the sort to Aristoteles, but he was 'orrified by such crass commercialism. 'E'd never let such an enterprise be connected with his school."

"Meseems Aristoteles' difficulties are of his own making," I said. "There are many things he can do: graze the elephant, commercialize it, give it away, kill it and sell the meat," (Kanadas scowled blackly at this suggestion) "or write the king begging for money to maintain it. Or he can rent Aias to a bathhouse, to squirt the bathers with his trunk. Till he's tried some of these courses, he has no cause to waul. I'm the one with the problem. I'm fain to quit the polluted army and go about my private business, but I cannot while I have this gold in my care."

Pyrron said: "The king surely has a sense of irony, to give the elephant but no money to one philosopher, and money to another who declines to accept it."

"*Papai!*" I said. "Why could we not get Xenokrates to give the money to Aristoteles for the maintenance of the elephant?"

The others cried out in praise of the proposal, but Theophrastos said: "You don't know our philosophers, Leon."

"What mean you?"

"Those two 'ate each other too much for any sensible compromise."

"Why is this so?"

"It's a long story, old boy, but I'll tell you. Twenty-five years ago they were fast friends, studying in Athens under the divine Platon. Then Platon died. Aristoteles expected, as Platon's most brilliant pupil, to succeed him. Instead, the faculty elected Platon's nephew Speusippos, a man of violent temper and unbridled lusts."

"Why chose they such a wight? They must have known what he was like."

"He had his virtues. He faithfully taught his master's doctrines and had a good practical mind for running the school. Moreover, a few years before, Aristoteles had quarreled with Platon and tried to set up a separate school. The school failed and the two were soon reconciled, but some of Platon's other followers never forgave Aristoteles.

"Disgusted with the ways of Fate, Aristoteles crossed the Aegean to live at Assos in Troyland. Xenokrates went with him and even stayed with him while he 'oneymooned on Lesbos with his first wife. I was with them much of this time, too. Later Aristoteles went to Macedonia to tutor Alexander, while Xenokrates returned to Athens. When Speusippos fell deathly sick, he resigned his post and urged that Xenokrates be chosen in his place.

"Aristoteles was then in Stageira, which he was rebuilding with money from King Philip. 'Earing from me of Speusippos' resignation, he started at once for Athens but found Xenokrates already in command of the school. 'E 'id his disappointment and a few years later removed to Athens to start his own school.

"For a time, 'e and Xenokrates kept on a friendly footing, though some of their followers fanned the growing rivalry between them. Not I; I love everybody. Then—well, Xenokrates is a dear old chap, but he is a bit of a bore, and Aristoteles has a razor-edged tongue and a waspish sense of 'umor. One day Xenokrates cornered Aristoteles in the market place and droned in his ears for hours. At the end he said: 'Oh, I do hope I haven't bored you to death with my chatter!' 'No indeed,' said Aristoteles, as polite as a Persian, 'for I haven't been listening to you.'

"So ended a beautiful friendship. Since then, neither's been able to find anything too bad to say about the other."

I said: "Theophrastos, setting aside the fact that you're Aristoteles' viceroy in the school, and assuming that this pair of proud pedants could be made to agree, what think you of my idea of having Xenokrates pay for the elephant's upkeep with Alexander's gold?"

"Splendid but impractical."

I pondered for a moment. "In confidence, are you so taken with the idea that you'd enter into a little plot to force them to submit to such a plan?"

Theophrastos looked astonished. "Force Aristoteles or Xenokrates? You're a bold man, Leon. They are the most independent-minded men on earth."

"That may be, but necessity knows no law but success. Would you help me in this plot? No harm shall come to either philosopher."

"Let me ask Pyrron. O Pyrron, you know Leon well. What think you of his proposal?"

"He'll do what he says or die trying," said Pyrron. "A stubborn and conscientious chap, kind and well-meaning under that gruff, soldierly bearing."

"All right," said Theophrastos. "'Not vain the weakest, if their force unite.' But 'Erakles 'elp us if your plan go awry!"

"What about you, Nikomachos?" I asked. "Will you too enter a plot against your own father—for his own good, of course?"

"I'll do as my darling Theophrastos tells me," said the youth with a fatuous smile.

I thought my landlord might be impressed by my distinguished guests and so inclined to use me with greater respect. Howsomever, when I cast a casual remark about them, Syloson grumbled: "Na, laddie; 'tis a shame to see a sound young body like you get into the clutches of these sophists."

"They're no sophists; they're philosophers," I said.

"'Tis all one. They teach sons to defy their fathers, debtors to cheat their creditors, and pious men to doubt their gods. Gin you'd lead ane honest life, keep clear of them."

Two nights later, Aristoteles came to Syloson's house with Nikomachos and Theophrastos and Pyrron and Kanadas. Ignoring Syloson's scowl, I presented Aristoteles to Amyntas of Ichnai, King Alexander's agent in Athens. I had persuaded Amyntas to play his part in my little comedy by offering him a talent's worth of Alexander's gold, provided the scheme went through.

Aristoteles, it soon became plain, had required much urging to come and was in no pleasant mood. "What's this I hear," he said, "of King Alexander's adopting Persian ways, even to dreth and manners?"

I said: "As I understand it, experience showed him that, as king of many nations, he must needs adopt some of their ways. Only thus could he make them love and revere him."

"And after all my teachings! What need of love and reverence from slavish Asiatics?" snapped Aristoteles. "A touch of the whip is all they require. As I have demonstrated in my lectures, they are the slaves of the Hellenes by nature."

Vardanas looked ready to burst with fury, but I motioned him to silence and said: "That may be your opinion. As one who has fought both with and against Persians and other Asiatics for many years, I must say they differ from Hellenes but little in matters of spirit. That is, some are brave and some cowardly, some honest and some dishonest, and so on through all the vices and virtues."

"As I remarked at our first meeting, you've been under foreign influence and so are not a trustworthy witneth."

Now I was about to fly into soldierly curses at this sneering sophist. But Vardanas rose, motioned me to silence, and addressed Aristoteles. He said:

"O Aristoteles, would you meet a mere foreigner like myself in the Sokratic mode of disputation?"

"Thertainly, my dear young man. I will encounter anybody in any kind of dispute."

"Then would you say that a fair definition of justice was: to treat each man according to his deserts?"

"Yes; without committing mythelf, that thounds fair enough."

"Now, have I ever wronged you?"

"Of course not. I've never theen you before, thave the day you arrived with Leon and the elephant."

"Then would it be just for you to whip me?"

"Ah, I see the trend of your reasoning. You hope to trap me by confusing the general with the particular. When I spoke of whipping Asiatics, I spoke generally, as touching on the issue of the Hellenes as a mass against the Persians as a mass. My opinions on this question wouldn't prevent my treating you as an individual with kindneth and generothity, did you prove to deserve them."

"Then why think you that Hellenes in the mass should be so hostile to Persians?"

"Why, there's the long record of aggressions against and oppressions of Hellenes, especially the Ionians, by the Persian Empire."

"But now the Persians are conquered in turn. So that debt is canceled, is it not?"

"It's not a matter of balancing one debt against another," said Aristoteles, "or we should have to go back to the Trojan War. It's a matter of national character, as shown by the long contacts of Hellenes with Persians."

"Such as the execution of your father-in-law?"

"Do you know about that?"

"Yes. Is it?"

"Since you're candid, I might as well be also. Yes, that's one reason I hate Persia and all it stands for."

"Even though Prince Hermeias was intriguing with King Philip for the overthrow of the Persian Empire?"

"By Zeus and all the gods, you are an acute young foreigner! Say rather that the noble Hermeias had striven by such means as were available to him to free Ionia from the Persian yoke."

"As Sokrates would have said, one man's liberation is another man's subversive plot. By the way, Aristoteles, did you ever know Dorymachos of Acharnai?"

Now, this shows the difference between Vardanas and myself. Meseemed he had a perfect logical opening to tax Aristoteles with confusing, in his turn, the general with the particular, by blaming all Persians for the death of his father-in-law Hermeias. Had I been Aristoteles' opponent, I should have gone for that point hammer and tongs. Vardanas, however, ignored the gap in his foe's defenses to go off on an irrelevant tangent.

"Let's see," said Aristoteles. "Why, yes, I was well acquainted with him, thirty years ago, when we were young men studying under the divine Platon. How in Hera's name do you know about him?"

"He was my teacher! He came wandering through the Persian cities, picking up a living by teaching and lecturing, and so came to

Sousa. My mother persuaded my father to hire him to teach my older brother and myself. Why, I owe him all the Hellenism I have!"

Aristoteles got up and grasped Vardanas' wrists, his teeth showing in a grin through his short beard. In a trice the pair were gabbling like old cronies reunited. No more talk of Hellene against foreigner; no more fencing with swords of logic; just a pair of dear friends united by a common acquaintance! I saw then that Vardanas was really cleverer than I in such matters.

This new friendship, however, was interrupted by a bang at the door. In came Xenokrates. He and Aristoteles stiffened at the sight of one another like a pair of hostile dogs. Xenokrates said:

"Rejoice, Aristoteles! I trust you have not lately let the vile passions of jealousy and disappointment swerve you from the search for truth?"

"Jealouthy? Dithappointment?" said Aristoteles. "What have I to be jealouth or dithappointed about? I have created a fine school from nothing, while others, who have inherited splendid schools, have let them run to seed."

"Gentlemen!" I said. "'Tis late, so let's to our business. It concerns five bags of golden coins..."

I went over the tale of Alexander's joke on the two professors, letting a fistful of staters rattle through my hands as I did so.

"Now," I said, "I have thought long on this matter and have concluded that drastic action is needed. Certainly we cannot let the king's benevolence and generosity to science be thwarted by petty human motives. If need be, I shall—"

"Good Leon!" cried Amyntas, as he had been coached to do. "Do not carry out your threat! Destroy not the glory of Athens!"

The Macedonian sank to one knee, giving an appearance of tenor. Vardanas, Pyrron, and Theophrastos joined in with pleas that I spare the city. The two senior philosophers looked bewildered.

"What can this vulgar young ape accomplish?" said Aristoteles.

Amyntas said: "You little know your peril, O Aristoteles. Have you heard of the Eyes and Ears of the Persian Kings?"

"Thertainly. Do you take me for an ignoramus?"

"Well, Troop Leader Leon is the Eyes and Ears of Alexander. The king, you know, has kept and even strengthened the security organization of the Persian kings. A harsh word in one of Leon's reports to Alexander were enough to snatch me from Athens, haul me off to Babylon in chains, and crucify me."

"Ah!" said Aristoteles, glaring defiantly at me. "When I hang on the croth at Babylon, O Leon, I trust you will be there to observe. It will make it easier, to thee a familiar face."

"I dinna threaten you personally," I said. "Nor Xenokrates. First, let me explain my plan. I have here gold pieces worth twenty-seven thousand drachmai, consigned to Xenokrates, who, however, refuses them. Aristoteles has an elephant that will, to put it gently, prove dear to keep.

"I propose that Xenokrates use this money to set up a fund for the elephant's keep. As so much gold would be unsafe to keep in anybody's house, I propose that the money be deposited with the banking firm of Dareios and Pamphylios. My inquiries show them to be trustworthy, and Aristoteles can draw on this deposit as needed. Then, as even elephants live not forever, you two can agree on some worthy cause on which to spend the balance of the money after Aias departs this life."

"Preposterous!" said Xenokrates.

"Utter rubbish!" said Aristoteles.

"Preposterous rubbish, perhaps," I said. "But hear what will happen if you agree not. I shall inform King Alexander that the schools of Athens are hotbeds of subversive anti-Macedonian agitation and conspiracy. I shall advise him to close down all philosophical schools anywhere in Hellas or in his empire. If you think of removing to Sicily, know that Alexander is on his way back from India. Soon, no doubt, he will gobble up Magna Graecia and Carthage as he has all other nations in his path. So much for philosophy!"

"My dear young man!" cried Xenokrates. "Do be—ah—reasonable!"

"I will not be reasonable! You two have placed me in an absurd and undignified position, and I'll do whatever I must to get out of it.

"Now, gentlemen, if you wish to discuss this proposal in private, yonder's my room. The rest of us will take a pull at this excellent Thasian while you settle the future of human thought betwixt you."

Aristoteles said: "A hundred years ago, Thessalian, none would have dared to make such a threat in Athens. You would have been knocked on the head and thrown into the Barathron for conspiring against the right of free Hellenes to freedom of thought. I fear, however, that the Light of Hellas flickered out at Chaironeia. As Sophokles says:

> *"Of all the ills that plague the human kind,*
> *None harsher is than stark Necessity.*

"Come, Xenokrates."

The professors withdrew: The rest of us drank and talked of trivial matters. Soon the two godlike intellects came out. Aristoteles said:

"So be it. Draw up your contracts. The barbarians have vanquished us after all, eh, Xenokrates?"

The signing took place in the Deigma at Peiraieus the following afternoon. The money was counted out and handed over to the bankers. Afterwards, as I walked out into the sunlight from the colonnade with Aristoteles, I noted that his bitterness and sarcasm of the night before had vanished. He said with a wry grin:

"I don't think you could have done as you threatened, young fellow. At worst, I could have written the king a letter that would have caused you more trouble than you caused us."

"Then why did you agree?"

He lowered his voice. "I thought so ingenious a plot deserved to succeed. Besides, old Xenokrates can't endure forever, and he ought not to carry his feud with me to his grave. And the money will, I confeth, be jolly convenient for keeping Aias in hay and cabbages." He chuckled. "My previous offer still stands. If you'll remain in Athens, answering all my thilly questions about the mysterious East, the school will permit you to attend the thummer term gratis. How say you?"

"Will you include my friend Vardanas? He can answer many questions that I cannot."

"A foreigner in *my* school? That were unheard of!"

"Doubtless you're right, O best one. I'll send him to the Akademeia instead; there he can perform the same office for Xenokrates that I do for you."

327

"Wait. On second thought, it were more expedient to bring him to my school. We cannot let foreigners acquire erroneous ideas of Greek thought as a result of dear old Xenokrates' fumbling attempts to elucidate it. Be at the Lykeion at thunrise tomorrow. You have your choice of my lecture on advanced political thience and Theophrastos' lecture on elementary natural history. In the afternoon, Herkleides will talk on the Pythagorean theorem. Bring a tablet for notes, and don't be late. We have no patience with slugabed scholars!"

That night I wrote the king my last report. I gave him a final accounting of his money, enclosed copies of Xenokrates' receipts, and tendered the resignation of Vardanas' and my commissions.

Let me note a curious thing about the two rival philosophers. Despite Aristoteles' patronizing remarks about poor old Xenokrates' short remaining life, Aristoteles died only three years later in exile in Chalkis, while Xenokrates survived eleven years after I met him and reached his eighties.

As even Aristoteles admitted, Xenokrates was a dear old chap and an earnest if humdrum interpreter of the divine Platon. But he was, in my opinion, no very deep or original thinker. He had none of Aristoteles' godlike brilliance and breadth of view of the workings of the universe. It would not surprise me if, a hundred years from now, men still remember the name of Aristoteles of Stageira.

Now began one of the happiest times of my life. Were human memory more trustworthy, I could fill another book with my discussions with Aristoteles. Although I clearly recall the opinions he expressed, after so many years I can no longer separate one discussion from another, let abee set them in proper order with correct dates. So any Aristotelian dialogues I wrote would be like those imaginary speeches historians put into the mouths of the men of yore: true in a higher sense, perhaps, but not literally and exactly true to what had befallen. And I prefer the literal, exact kind of truth, leaving loftier kinds to loftier minds. Forbye, Aristoteles' opinions are clearly set forth in his dialogues, of which most leading scholars and royal libraries have copies. I soon found, however, that while I could follow the philosophers when they spoke of commonplace things like the organs of animals and the politics of states, I soon went in over my head when they talked of logic or mathematics, or explained why Zeus put the earth at the center of the universe with the planets going round it. In fact, I could then make no sense of their talk at all. When I confessed this to Aristoteles, he said:

"Don't distreth yourself about it, Leon. There are people with abstract minds, and people with practical minds, and the unthinking mass with virtually no minds at all. You possess a practical mind, although of course the abstract mind is the noblest kind."

"Your kind of mind, you mean?"

"Thertainly. Shall I demonstrate it by logic?"

"I'll accept your word for it, wise one."

There were tense moments when Aristoteles uttered scornful opinions of foreigners, especially Persians, and Vardanas bristled. But, as Aristoteles came to know the Persian better, these outbursts came fewer and farther between.

I also discovered that I had somewhat to learn about being a gentleman in the Athenian sense. The well-bred Athenian, I found, prides himself on never walking fast and never raising his voice. My years in the field had given me a swift, active stride and voice trained to be heard above the roar of battle. It was to these qualities, I learned, that Aristoteles referred when he called me a vulgar young ape, as well as to my unfortunate lack of beauty. To impress my new colleagues, I tried to slow my step and soften my voice, though I fear with no great success. Mighty is the empire of habit.

Howsomever, my plainness of feature was not extreme enough to keep all the men of Athens at bay. Every few days I had to fend off an amorous proposal from one or another of them.

Shortly after I had begun my courses, Elisas came to bid us farewell. He had obtained a bottomry loan from Dareios and Pamphylios, which he had invested in a cargo of oil to sell in Egypt.

"You see me again in the autumn, if the sea god allow," he said. "I am taking oil to Egypt and fetching back Egyptian wheat, fancy furniture, ornaments, and jewelry."

Then, about the middle of Skirophorion, Pyrron said: "Dear friends, I must be off for home tomorrow. My sister is frantic to see me, and I must organize my classes."

We were sitting on the steps of the little temple of Athena Nike on the Akropolis, watching the sunset. I was happy to see that Nirouphar, who was with us, took Pyrron's utterance with perfect calm.

Vardanas had told me the poor lass was having a dull time in Athens. Aristoteles would not hear of admitting a woman to his classes, so she had to spend most of her time with Syloson's elderly wife, listening to her foolish chatter and helping her spin and weave. This was hard on Nirouphar, because free Persian women deem it a disgrace to make cloth, and it took all Vardanas' powers of persuasion to get her to submit to Hellenic ways in this regard. And the Athenians clap up their women so closely that she had no chance to meet other maids of her own age and class.

Theophrastos said: "You must see Diogenes on your way through Corinth, Pyrron."

"Is he still alive?"

"Yes, though perhaps not for long."

"Did his owner ever free him?"

"No. Xeniades offered to emancipate him long ago, but he refused. 'E said he was too old for travel, so he preferred to eat Xeniades' food and lord it over his 'ousehold for the rest of his days."

Pyrron said: "I heard you finding excuses for slavery the other day, Aristoteles. Surely the enslavement of Diogenes refutes all your claims as to the justice of the institution!"

"If you'd attended closely, my dear Pyrron," said Aristoteles, "you would have heard that I carefully qualified my approval. I pointed out that, while thome like Vardanas' stupid Scythian are natural-born slaves, the folk who are actually enslaved are often chosen more by luck than by merit."

Pyrron rejoined: "Then the only way to terminate this injustice is to abolish slavery. If you had ever experienced enslavement yourself, as did Platon and Diogenes, you would openly confess that I'm right."

"And stir up all Athens against him as a dangerous revolutionary?" said Theophrastos with a chuckle. "'E's not so simple."

"Viper!" said Aristoteles. "As if I had ever trimmed my opinions to the prejudices of the unthinking mob! Theriously, though, while dreamers may prate of a classless society, we have to make do with the societies we actually possess. As things stand, civilization would collapse without slavery."

"Why?" said Pyrron. "One can always hire free men to do the work."

"But not so cheaply. And think what would happen if, for example, the slaves of Athens were all liberated simultaneously! The majority are foreign adult males: cowardly Egyptians, grasping Syrians, dull Anatolians, milk-drinking Scythians, and bloodthirsty blue-eyed Celts. Free these creatures, and overnight they'd have the rings cut from their phalli to enjoy the pleasures of love. Next they'd demand the right to espouse Athenian women, and they'd be too many and too strong to be easily gainsaid. Before they finished, they'd force the Athenians to admit them to citizenship. Our Greek blood would be mongrelized, and our thuperior culture would perish with our racial purity."

"Don't be sure they'd stay," said Pyrron. "I'll wager that most, given a choice, would go haring back to their homelands like bullets from a sling."

"How would one prove that athertion?"

"I suppose one could inquire of the slaves."

"That were impractical, on two counts," said Aristoteles. "First, everyone knows that a slave can be counted upon to tell the truth only under torture. Second, if anybody, given a free choice, really preferred some barbarous foreign land to Athens as a place to dwell, he would thereby prove himself an inferior, whom it were natural and right for Hellenes to enslave."

"All I can say is," said Pyrron, "that you should try enslavement yourself before you talk so glibly of its being right and natural. Experience often changes the point of view, and for a group of slaveholders to talk solemnly of justice is like a congress of rabbits discussing lion hunting."

"I will concede it's a difficult question," said Aristoteles. "But, practically speaking, men will never succeed in abolishing slavery, unjust though it be at times, until they invent machines to perform the labor of the slaves."

"Why don't you invent such a machine?" said Pyrron. "If anybody could, you could."

"I?" said Aristoteles. "Tinker with mechanical devices? After all, old boy, I am a gentleman!"

"Well, that leaves the situation hopeless," said Pyrron. "For, while I'm not too proud to use my hands, I cannot drive a nail without mashing my thumb. Perhaps the remedy for slavery lies in the other direction: establishing ideal communities like those proposed by the divine Platon, where all shall be free and equal."

"Platon was not so egalitarian as all that," said Aristoteles, "and I shall believe that thuch schemes are practicable when I see one in operation."

Theophrastos said: "Do you remember that son of the Macedonian regent who studied with us last year? 'E had some such plan in mind."

"Yes," said Aristoteles. "Alexarchos Antipatrou was determined to establish, with funds from the Macedonian treasury, a complete Platonic community, with communistic ownership of property. He even had a scheme for an artificial international language."

"What said you to that?" I asked.

"I advised him to proceed, but to omit communism of women and children."

"Why?" said Vardanas. "It sounds exciting."

"Perhaps," said Aristoteles, "but there was a fatal objection to it. Under such an arrangement, nobody would know his own father. Hence men, in their homothexual love affairs, might unwittingly have intercourse with their own sons or brothers. And that, I told Alexarchos, would be a shocking indecency!"

The next one of our little band to depart was Kanadas. When the tall Indian came to settle some small money matters with me, he said: "Leon, you must do something about Siladites!"

"Do what about him?"

"He says he will not come back to India! He lives in sin with Egyptian woman. He says he will become a registered foreigner, stay in Athens, never obey caste rules any more."

"What of it?"

"That is wicked! He must stop sinful life, go back home, take up caste duties! Otherwise the gods degrade him further in next life."

"Look here, laddie, Siladites works for Aristoteles the now, not for me or for King Alexander. So what he does is his own affair."

"Oh, you are just another immoral Hellene!" he snorted, and stormed out. Next day, however, he bade us a courteous farewell, placing his palms together and bowing over them.

"Ship sails for Sidon tomorrow," he said. "There I buy horses, ride back to India."

"Can you manage alone?" I asked. "Shouldn't you buy a slave or hire a traveling merchant like Elisas as your guide?"

"Me, throw away good money? Anyhow, I do not approve of slavery. Do not worry about me. I am a seasoned traveler now. Wait till I tell friends in Paurava of adventures. Those poor clods would fear to cross the sea in ship!"

I thought it tactful not to mention the fuss Kanadas had made about his first sea voyage. He swaggered off, the huge sword hanging down his back, on his way to Peiraieus. Though not an easy man to know, he was brave and honest and true in his own dour way. I hope he made it home.

Thus Siladites became Aristoteles' head elephant keeper. His Greek, though still frightful, was good enough to order around his helper, a trembling Nubian slave whom Aristoteles bought with money from the king's fund. Without Kanadas to keep him in the narrow path of caste rules, Siladites blossomed into a man of some character and consequence. In later years, though his Greek remained foul, he became chief elephantarch to Antipatros and his son Kassandros when they ruled Macedonia.

As the year of Antikles' archonship began and the heat of summer came on, my Persian friends suffered in the warm woolen coats and trousers they had brought from Sousa the previous winter. They found that, while they could buy thin stuffs for summer suits, nobody in Athens could do the elaborate tailoring needed to make garments of the Persian style.

I therefore persuaded Nirouphar to try on a Greek woman's chiton. When she walked out from Syloson's gynaikeion, Vardanas gave a shriek. "Cover yourself, hussy!" he cried.

"Oh, hush your shouting!" said Nirouphar. "Anybody would think you my maiden aunt!"

Syloson's wife had given Nirouphar a Dorian chiton, open on the right side from the shoulder down. I found the sight of my loved one's bare flank charming, but Persian modesty won out.

"Now," said I, when Nirouphar had been pinned together, "our next step, buckie, is to get you out of those flapping trousers."

Vardanas said: "Oh no! Not for me to walk the streets waving my private parts in the breeze as you do!"

"You are an old fuss-budget like Father," said Nirouphar. "Rheon—I mean Leon—has sense. In trouser country he wears trousers, and in this bare-breeked land he goes without. Whom fear you to shock? Having seen Athenians strolling about their town stert-naked, I am no longer surprised by such things."

"You do not understand these things," said Vardanas. "It is a matter of honor with me to protect your purity and innocence."

"Rubbish!" said Nirouphar. "Either you try Greek garb, or I will forth without these safety pins."

"Mithras, do not do that!" he cried. At last we got him into one of my shirts, a little short for him but perfectly proper. But, at the next lecture, he stood through the whole session, explaining afterwards: "I dared not sit for fear of indecent exposure."

What with the lectures to hear and the beautiful monuments of Athens to see, I felt I needed only to be joined to Nirouphar for my happiness to be complete. I hinted as much to Vardanas, hoping that time and his sister's growing regard for me would dispose him more kindly to such a marriage. But Vardanas looked squarely at me and said:

"Dear Leon, betimes you have twitted me for acting impulsively and without enough forethought."

"So I have. But what has that to do—"

"A moment, please. I shall demonstrate by irrefragable logic, as Aristoteles would say, that you are now so acting yourself."

"How so?"

"First, passing by the question of racial purity, it is your Greek custom for the parents of a bride to give the couple a sum of money and property called a dowry. In Persia the girls do not have dowries.

Instead, the groom, or his parents, give the dowry. To put it crudely, Hellenes buy husbands; Persians buy wives. Would you wed a Persian woman under those conditions?"

"This is no matter of vulgar money," I said, though not so forcefully as I might have. I confess that this news had shaken me.

"Hear the rich young lordling! Which brings up a second point: to wit, what would your parents say about such a match? Unless you are minded to defy them—a course on the imprudence of which, if I remember aright, you once lectured me." Vardanas smiled a little grimly.

This silenced me, for I had not thought about the matter at all. Or, to be truthful, I had thought about it but quickly pushed the thought to the back of my mind because of the discomfort it caused me. I knew my parents would make an uproar when they heard of the proposal, and I was not prepared to defy them. Despite the usual petty squabbles that occur in most families, we were a close-knit group who dearly loved one another. Moreover, there were property rights involved, which a serious quarrel would jeopardize.

"Thirdly," continued the Persian implacably, "I know something of your Greek customs: how a man wed to a poor woman, given a chance to marry one with a large marriage portion, thinks nothing whatever of divorcing the first wife to take the second. I would not have my sister so used."

"That's Athens, not Thessalia," said I feebly.

"It is the general opinion in Hellas, north and south, east and west, that to marry for love, rather than for property and posterity, is foolish and uncivilized conduct. If you insist, I will get Aristoteles to testify to this effect. And fourthly, what says your law about marriage to foreigners?"

"I know not," I said miserably. "I never thought of such a thing ere I left home, and of course there was nobody to ask about such matters in Persia and India."

"Well, the other day Aristoteles was talking about the methods that Greek states use to preserve their—what is that long word he uses?—their homogeneity, thus to keep down schisms and seditions. One method is to forbid marriages between citizens and strangers. If an Athenian wed an alien and live here, the alien shall be sold into slavery. Now, I do not know what the rules are in Thessalia, but the matter were worth looking into ere you do aught rash."

Crushed, I gave up for the time being and pined after Nirouphar more desperately than ever from afar. When my lusts became intolerable I sought relief in the brothel, pretending it was Nirouphar I rode.

I was cheered by another letter, reading as follows:

EUMENES OF KARDIA WISHES LEON ARISTOU WELL

King Alexander asks me to convey to you his unstinted praise and admiration for the glorious feat you have accomplished, and to request you to pass on to your lieutenant, Vardanas of Sousa, his thanks for the loyal support that Vardanas has afforded you in this enterprise.

The king notes with regret that you and Vardanas have tendered your resignations from the armies of Macedonia and Asia. He has instructed me to enter your names in the roll of honorably discharged soldiers with ranks one grade higher than those you last had: Leon of Atrax to be squadron leader, and Vardanas of Sousa to be troop leader. If ever you or Vardanas decide to re-enlist, those ranks shall be yours for the asking.

We are at the mouth of the Indus, preparing for an overland march westward along the shores of the Ocean. Rumor says that the march will be through difficult deserts; but, with Alexander to lead them, there is nothing our soldiers cannot do.

BOOK TEN

Thessalia

AT FIRST I MEANT to end my book here, as Eumenes' letter severed my official tie to Aristoteles and to the elephant. True, I saw Aias years later at the Macedonian court, and he remembered me and hugged me with his trunk. But I was no longer responsible for him thenceforth.

The rest of my life's history, while full enough of lively adventures, is that of a mere private man, not of the agent of the greatest king of his age on a strange and wonderful mission. Whereas that mission was now completed, this seemed a likely place to rein in my galloping pen.

Howsomever, when I read the manuscript to an audience of my friends and my children, they set up an outcry that I should go on, tell what betided next, and explain how I came to be where and what I now am. And so, for a short space, I continue my tale.

Time flew. The month of Pyanepsion had come, the weather had cooled, and the mountains stood brown from the summer's drouth, when one of Aristoteles' slaves, Pyrraios, brought a strange tale from Peiraieus. Harpalos, Alexander's treasurer, had suddenly appeared at the tip of the Paralian peninsula with thirty warships bristling with soldiers. All but one of these ships anchored in the lee of Sounion Promontory. The men went ashore, set up a rude fortification, and rested.

Meanwhile Harpalos came on to Peiraieus with a single ship and urged the Athenians to let his whole fleet into the principal harbor. He held a shouted conference with Philokles, the Athenian general in command of Fort Eëtoneia, Harpalos standing on the forecastle of his ship and Philokles on one of the chain towers of the sea gate.

"Are you here as King Alexander's man?" said Philokles.

Harpalos shouted back: "Nay. I am my own master."

"Then what do you want with us? We don't let strange war fleets into our harbor."

"I have come to save you from Alexander's insatiable ambition!"

"We are at peace with Alexander. If you have aught to say to the people of Athens, say it through proper channels."

"Let me in, ere it be too late! Alexander is returning from India, burning to reduce Athens to slavery."

"Begone or I'll open on you with the catapults!"

The argument went on all day. Philokles sent a runner to Athens for advice. The prytaneis called the generals and politicians to a hurried consultation. Demosthenes advised against admitting Harpalos and persuaded the rest. So in the end Harpalos had to row away, as the chain was up and he could not enter the harbor without a fight.

The market place seethed with the excitement of the volatile Athenians, each asking the other what this visitation meant and shouting in a thousand voices for war, peace, attack, defense, retreat, surrender, alliance, isolation, and any other policies that the mind of man could conceive. After I had spent a while there, picking up wild and contradictory rumors, I went to see Alexander's resident minister Amyntas. Although I was no longer a servant of the king, Amyntas had kept on a friendly footing with me, no doubt in hope of another bribe. He told me:

"I had not expected Harpalos to come here, but it does not astonish me. I have had letters lately from the king himself. Alexander is returning from India. He had passed through the deadly deserts of Gedrosia and is now in Persia. He has already begun to chop off the heads of governors who proved unworthy. No doubt Harpalos got word of this, too, and fled while his head was still affixed to his body."

Next day it became known that Harpalos' fleet had rowed away. The excitement died, save for speculation as to whither Harpalos had gone: to Syracuse, Carthage, or even farther.

Half a month later, as the season's first rain drizzled down upon Athens, word came by a trading ship that Harpalos had not gone far. He coasted south and west until he turned the promontory of Tainaron, the middlemost of the three prongs of Lakedaimonia. He rounded the promontory and beached at the village of Tainaron. As the peninsula is rocky and sparsely settled, it was unlikely the Spartans could expel him. The Spartan spirit had been broken at Megalopolis, when King Agis fell before Antipatros' Macedonians, even as had the Athenian spirit at Chaironeia.

Now veered the winds of politics in Athens. Several leaders who had loudly demanded that Harpalos be kept off the sacred soil of Attika began speaking well of the man. Some argued that nought had been proved against him; some said any foe of Alexander was a friend of Athens.

I asked Aristoteles about this, one evening as we were walking home from the Lykeion with Theophrastos, Vardanas, some other members of the faculty, and our servants. Ordinarily I should have ridden the distance. But Aristoteles was a great walker, so that, if one wanted an extra half-hour of his company, one had to walk, too. He said:

"Harpalos has let it be known that he possesses thousands of talents, and that his friends in Athens shan't go unrewarded. He has probably sprinkled a few talents among them already as bait. If you wish to see what I mean by the tendency of democrathy to degenerate into anarchy, behold our demagogues."

Vardanas said: "Do you remember, Leon, our argument in the wilds of Assyria about democracy? See how Aristoteles supports me in that!"

"What's this?" said Aristoteles. Vardanas gave the gist of his argument against democracy.

"There's something in what you say," said Aristoteles, "but you forget that all other forms of government become corrupted as well. Thus monarchy decays into tyranny, and aristocrathy into oligarchy. However, it takes an exceptional degree of culture and thivic spirit, such as Athens had at her best, to practice democrathy at all. I've never heard of democrathy among foreigners."

"It exists," I said. "Some Indian states are democratically ruled, and so are some of the Gandarian tribes."

"Come, my good Leon, that cannot be real democrathy. I can prove that Hellenes are the only folk…"

Off we went on another argument. We came to the crossing in the Skambonidai where we usually broke up, going to our several dwellings. Instead of parting, however, we stood jabbering while the sun set. In the twilight, a man stepped out of the shadows and said:

"Pardon, gentlemen, but is not one of you Leon of Atrax?"

"I am," I said. I thought the man was a traveler with a letter from home for me. (I had long since delivered, or arranged for delivery of, the letters my comrades-in-arms had entrusted to me in India.) I was reckoning how much to tip him when he drew a dirk and lunged.

Luckily, I was trained in the art of fighting without a shield. Many soldiers, even experienced ones, do not know it. As the man thrust at my breast, I brought my left fist down upon his wrist, knocking his arm aside. The blade ripped my cloak and shirt but did not touch my skin. I struck at his face with my right fist, but he rolled his head so that the blow glanced from his scalp. He drew back his arm for another stab.

I stepped back, starting to whip off my cloak as a shield, while my friends stood in amaze with their mouths open. Then Inaudos, my lusty manservant, seized my attacker from behind. They scuffled for the space of a couple of heartbeats. The Kordian hurled the stranger to the ground. However, ere anybody could leap upon the latter to pin him, he squirmed free, leaped up, and dashed off, leaving his cloak in Theophrastos' grasp. Vardanas and I gave chase but soon lost him in the dark, winding alleys.

We came back to find Inaudos nursing a bleeding forearm and the others looking over the attacker's dirk and wallet.

"Did he cut you?" I asked Inaudos. "Let me see."

"He never cut me! Villain bit me!" roared the hillman.

The dirk had nought distinctive about it, but the wallet contained a fistful of shiny new staters. I held one of these up in the fading light and said:

"This looks fresh from the mint at Tarsos."

"Which means," said Theophrastos, "that our assassin was 'ired by 'Arpalos to make way with you. Now why should he do that? I remember 'ow you escaped him, but that's not enough to make him send murderers after you."

"I also reported his misdeeds to Alexander," I said. "I suppose Harpalos heard of this, perhaps through his brother Philippos in India."

Theophrastos said: "It's a shame the fellow is such a scoundrel; 'e really knows something of botany. I've 'ad letters from him about the plants of the East."

"Well," said I, "in any case, my guardian spirit tells me I'd better get along home to Thessalia, ere worse befall. Next time he'll hire a whole gang of ready-for-aughts to screed me."

"Methinks you need not leave so precipitately," said Aristoteles. "We'll take the matter up with the magistrates. Harpalos is unlikely to try another attempt soon. Besides, I haven't finished my notes on the animals of Persia and India."

As Aristoteles seemed to me only a little lower than Zeus himself, I let him talk me into staying on against my better judgment. Looking back, it now seems as though he cared little what became of me or anybody else so long as he collected his scientific data.

I reported the attack to the Board of Eleven, but the magistrates only raised their eyebrows and spoke of the rise of crime that resulted from having so many foreigners in the city. The president of the board said:

"After all, man of Thessalia, nobody knows who your attacker is, and this Harpalos person is out of our jurisdiction. But most important, you are not even a citizen, are you?"

"Nay; I'm a citizen of the Thessalian Federation, and thus a subject of King Alexander."

"Then are you registered as a resident alien?"

"Nay."

"How long have you been in Athens?"

"Since last Thargelion."

"Oh dear me! Then you are liable to arrest, imprisonment, and a fine."

"Say you so?" said I, rising. "What for, fellow?"

"You should have registered and paid the alien tax long ago!"

"Bugger that talk! I'm an officer of King Alexander, at present on inactive duty, but still carried on his rolls. I have a letter at my landlord's house to prove it. So it were better not to speak of imprisonment."

"Oh well, that's different, blessed one. Nevertheless you cannot bring suit save through a patron."

"How does one acquire a patron?"

"Go to the Thessalian consul. He can either act as your patron or find you somebody who will."

So I went to the consul. "Yes," said Epikerdes, "I could act as your patron. It would cost you money, though. The Thessalian assembly doesn't pay me for this, and I'm entitled to a return for time spent representing foreigners."

"How much?"

"Let's say a hundred drachmai as a retainer. Then there'll be your alien registration fee of twelve drachmai, and legal work will of course be more."

I gulped and said: "I'll let you know." I suspected that the consul knew of my discharge bonus and hoped to dig his claws into it.

I went back to Aristoteles, who said: "I fear you waste your time, Leon. What this individual doesn't extract from you, Demosthenes and the other speech writers will."

"Can these Scythian archers do nought?"

"You can try their commander, but I doubt if it will help. He's responsible only to the Board of Eleven, and the slave watchmen are good only for patrolling the streets at night and keeping order at meetings and festivals. You'd have to apprehend your attacker yourself."

"An he's still in Attika, I'll find him!"

"Ah, but he's probably far from Attika by now. Even if you caught him, you would still have to prosecute him, and that's no light matter. Nothing is less predictable than an Athenian board of judges. They're nought but common men, chosen by lot, and as stupid and capricious as such people normally are. You'd better abandon this chase, old boy, but go armed henceforth."

* * *

Elisas returned to Athens with a pile of Egyptian wares from his voyage. He came to me, purring with success, carrying a bag and a wicker basket with a lid. I asked him for news.

"Very good journey," he said. "Made good profits and paid off Dareios and Pamphylios. We were chased by a pirate ship off Crete, but a warship frightened the pirate away."

"Did you see the pyramids?"

"No, I had no time for sight-seeing—"

The basket gave a sudden yowl. "What in Hera's name have you in there, man?" I asked.

"You leave soon for Thessalia, yes?"

"As things are going, I may. But the basket—"

"When I was in Egypt, I thought, my old friend Leon will want some nice gifts for his family. So I bring some things. Very reasonable prices; hardly any profit to me. Here in the basket is an Egyptian cat, for your mother."

He brought out the animal, which I could see was a high-bred pussy. These creatures are popular with the Athenians, who say they catch mice, but the only cats we have in Thessalia are the wild kind.

"And here are bracelets and other jewelry for the ladies of your house; a fancy walking stick for your father..."

"Elisas, you'll be the death of me!" I reached over to pat the cat, which scratched the back of my hand and drew blood.

"*Pheu!* Off goes half the price of this villainous beast," I said. "Now let's get down to prices."

In the end, he got nearly a hundred drachmai from me. He probably swindled me on some items; but, if he had not come around with these goods just then, I should never have thought to buy homecoming presents at all.

A few days later, our calm was shattered again by the news that Harpalos was back. He had arrived at Peiraieus with two triremes and demanded admission as a suppliant.

Aristoteles excused his classes to go down to Peiraieus to see the sight. It was a cool, windy morning, and the wharves of Peiraieus were crowded. Philokles had lowered the chain to let the ship bearing the treasurer into the Kantharos. The ship anchored a plethron from shore, Harpalos on the forecastle. A plain brown cloak flapped about his gross body as he spoke slowly, gasping and wheezing with the effort of making himself heard by thousands.

"Athenians!" he bellowed. "Men of the violet-crowned city, star in the crown of Hellas! Behold me, a poor suppliant, a fugitive from the wrath of the terrible Alexander! Ah—the Macedonian monster is now marching westward, covered with gore from his Eastern conquests. All who have tried to protect the rights of the conquered are slain without mercy, Hellenes and foreigner alike! The small degree of freedom that Alexander has left you will not long remain you, do you not halt this all-depraved blood drinker ere he reach your holy city. Now comes the great, perhaps the last chance for Hellas to throw off the barbarous Macedonian yoke. Remain supine, and—ah—you will be ground into the mire; rise, and all Asia, now groaning under Alexander's despotism, will rise with you!

"Ah—join me ere it be too late! Though a fugitive, I am no beggar. I bring—ah—material help. Eight thousand stout soldiers, thirty warships, and five thousand talents' worth of money!"

He spoke for two hours, then went back to his cabin. The Athenians dispersed, chattering like magpies. The prytaneis called a special assembly for the next day. On my way to the Lykeion next morn, I heard their trumpets winding in all the towns of Attika.

At the school, Aristoteles looked sharply at Vardanas and me and spoke one word: "Pack!"

"Will they vote to let that scoundrel in?"

"Perhaps. You'd better be ready in any cathe. Once he's in, his bribes will range the magistrates against you, no matter what violence he undertakes."

"Can I attend the assembly?"

"No; not even I may attend, not being a citizen. I'll send Pyrraios to the entrance. As soon as the vote is tallied, he'll athertain from the Scythians how it went and run to your house with the news."

"Are you coming too?" I asked Vardanas. "I should love for you and Nirouphar to put up your horses at my home, but you're a free man."

"Of course I shall come," he said. "Philosophy is fine, but a friend like you is of greater value. Besides, I must pass through Thessalia on my way to Pella to seek a commission from Antipatros. I only beseech that I be not asked to sleep with your pet serpent."

I threw my arms about him. "Thank the gods for that! A congenial companion on the road, they say, is as good as a carriage."

To Aristoteles I said: "O sage, this may be farewell, as we shall ride northward when we go. Suffer me to say how much these months of study with you have meant to me—"

"Oh, rubbish, boy!" he snapped. "Consider the formal farewells all said, and get along with you. If you can return thafely, do so; if not, my thanks for the data. Now, where were we? Ah yes. Today we shall discuth the methods by which tyrants retain their illegal power. There are, in general, two courses of action by which the tyrant can keep his position...."

We tore ourselves away from the lecture, embraced Siladites (who burst into tears), patted Aias' trunk, and departed. And thus it came to pass that, as late in the afternoon a wreath-crowned Harpalos made a triumphal entrance into Athens through the Sacred Gate, Leon, Vardanas, Nirouphar, and their two menservants rode through the Dipylon Gate and galloped at reckless speed along the Sacred Way toward Eleusis and Thebes.

By pressing on after dark, we reached Thria that night. For want of other quarters, we slept on the benches and floor of the inn, which had but few beds and those occupied.

Next morn we were on the road ere the dawn of a cold, wet, windy day. We galloped across the Thriasian Plain with the wind whipping our mantles and fluttering the horses' streaming manes. We broke our fast at Oea and followed the winding western Kephisos through the Parnes range. There was little traffic, as most of the peddlers had packed away their stocks for the winter.

We climbed the pine-covered slopes of Kithairon, where Aktaion was changed to a stag and Pentheus was screeded by the Bacchantes, to the pass of Dryoskephalai. Here a border patrol of epheboi stopped us, but a flourish of my papers got us through. The folk the militia were seeking were runaway slaves, and we were patently not these unfortunates.

At the crest of the pass, we entered Boiotia. Down the long slope on the north flank of Kithairon we rode, where Oidipous of Thebes was exposed as an infant, while a wan winter sun cast long shadows through the oaks. And thus a day of hard riding brought us at dusk to Boiotian Thebes.

Ah, woe! No more did proud Thebes of the Seven Gates overlook the Ismenian Plain, for Alexander had razed the city ten years before. I had heard he left standing only the temples and the house of Pindaros. The descendants of the poet who dwelt in this house were almost the only Thebans neither slain nor sold.

Now, however, quite a few houses stood among the ruins besides the temples. Some were dwellings that the soldiers had not utterly demolished and which had been patched up again. Others were hovels which squatters had put up. Life stirred in Thebes, but there was no sign of welcome for travelers.

I knocked on a door. A great barking arose. The door opened a crack, and a voice said in broad Boiotian: "Who be you?"

"Travelers. We wondered—"

"Ain't got no room. Don't like strangers nohow."

"Then could you tell me—"

"Ain't no other place, neither."

"Do you ken the house of Pindaros?"

"Never heard of it. Now get, or I'll set the dogs on you!"

I turned away, saying: "If the Thebans be all such churls, no wonder Alexander destroyed them!"

We found shelter in the half-ruined temple of Herakles, south of the Kadmea. The temple, I think, had been left standing at the time of the sack, but, with the desolation of Thebes, not enough offerings had come in to keep it up. So the priests abandoned it. Now a part of one side wall had crumbled away.

Having been softened by our months of comfort in Athens, we found sleep on cold limestone hard to come by. Toward midnight I got up to stretch my legs and found Nirouphar also awake. She was leaning against the edge of the gap in the wall and looking out at the setting moon, which cast black shadows of the slender columns outside across the floor of the temple.

"Rhe—Leon," she said, "I am frightened."

346

I put my arm around her. "Fear not the Boiotians, dear one."

"It is not they, but your family I fear."

"By the! What's amiss with my folk? They dinna devour the neighbors' bairns for dinner!"

"Of course not, darling. But they are the first real Greek family I shall have visited, for Syloson and his wife scarcely count. I fear to offend unwittingly by my ignorance of your ways and manners."

"If a Hellene can visit a Persian family without disaster, the reverse should be easy. You Persians have far more formal manners than we. All I ask is that you curb your ribald jests. They bother me not, but I'm a soldier; my people feel differently about such things."

"I will. Now tell me more about your people, for I am not sure I remember all their names and relationships."

I went through the roster again, adding a little about our position in the district: how we were the only branch of the Aleuadai in the Atrax district not slain or driven out when the Perraiboi rose against their Larissan overlords, following King Philip's conquest of Thessalia, because we had intermarried with the Perraiboi and were three quarters of their blood.

"It sounds like us and the Houzans," she said, "though, thanks to Auramasdas, they have not attacked us. If that befall, we can make no plea of Houzan blood. We are pure Persian, as you have heard."

"That I have, all too oft. But, with Alexander mixing up the whole world, purity of lineage may cease to be a virtue. Suppose, likein, I were to wed a well-born Persian lass?"

"You would have a true and loving wife, albeit more spirited than these poor downtrodden Greek girls."

She turned her face up to me, and the next instant we were embracing, kissing, murmuring foolishness, and acting as lovers have since the gods first molded men.

There is no telling whither our ardor might have swept us (or rather, it were a simple telling) had not a cough made us turn. There stood Vardanas, fists clenched in the moonlight, and still blinking the sleep from his eyes.

"Leon," said he in a heavy voice, "how far has this gone?"

"No further than you've seen. We did but discover our love the now."

Nirouphar said: "You must see reason, Vardanas. With Alexander mixing up the world, purity of descent no longer matters. And the wise Pyrron told us that such prejudices are unworthy of a truly civilized—"

"Silence, wench," said Vardanas. "My friend, have you forgotten all the obstacles to such a union?"

"For the moment I'd forgotten all but your sister's nearness," I said, still holding her. "But surely these obstacles can be overcome, with resolution and ingenuity."

"Well, I am no world-thinker like Aristoteles, but even I see that the walls of custom between nations are mighty barriers that change but slowly, century by century."

"Let's be plain, Vardanas. Do you deny me the lass, now and forever?"

A tear glistened on the Persian's face in the moonlight. "Were it not for these obstacles, there is no man I had rather give her to than you. But, until she can wed with the honor due our house, I must refuse."

"What mean you, wed with honor? I would not use her otherwise, either. What can I do to gain your blessing?"

"Let us take the first obstacle first: your family. Do you gain their approval and then come to me again; otherwise I will not yield a finger of my opposition."

I saw that my friend, though in some ways light-minded, was deadly serious in this matter. In the end we all three wept and embraced each other and swore eternal loyalty, whatever betided. Then I tried, quite in vain, to go back to sleep.

We rode westward through the foggy fenlands south of Lake Kopaïs. Through rolling farm land we passed Koroneia, and Lebadea, and Chaironeia with its great stone lion in memory of the Boiotians who fell fighting against King Philip. We entered Phokis and crossed yet another River Kephisos at Potamoi. Mount Parnassos, rising hugely on our left, already bore its wintry snowcap.

Nirouphar and I, like any young couple in love, rode side by side and talked all the time, largely about things of no importance. Vardanas, usually so gay, was sunk in one of his glooms and said little.

Elatea, our next large town, stands on a hill, a spur of Kallidromos that cuts across northern Phokis. We reached it on a cold, clear afternoon after a day of rain. After a long uphill ride we drew rein at an inn on the south side of the city, outside the wall. The road stretched off to southward in a straight line. We were handing over our horses to the grooms when Inaudos said:

"Hipparch, look at those riders!"

I looked southwards along the road and saw, several furlongs distant, a small dark spot that might have been a group of horsemen.

"What make you of them?" I said.

The Kordian's blue eyes seemed to bulge with the effort of seeing at the limits of vision. "Five—no, six riders, galloping, and some led horses," he said.

"What of it? We're no the only travelers in Hellas."

"Ah, but I think those are same men I saw on the road between Chaironeia and Potamoi! You remember, there was a place with long view there, too."

"Why spoke you not then?"

"Because I said to myself, like you, we are not only travelers. But now I see them again, and that is different."

"In others words, you think they're pursuing us. *Ea*, Vardanas!"

With groans for the warm beds we durst not stop to enjoy, we pressed on, riding so hard that we wind-broke one horse and had to abandon it. In the dark we stumbled through the passes between Mounts Knemis and Kallidromos. We arrived at the coast of Lokris-below-Knemis half frozen and half falling from horses whose weary heads hung nigh to the ground. Vardanas said:

"If we fain would keep ahead of those men, Leon, we must needs buy spare horses."

The village of Thronion was asleep when we arrived. The innkeeper gave us room in his bugsome dormitory. Ere cockcrow we were off again. At Skarphea we picked up two horses, and another at Nikaia. Each successive horse seemed to cost us more and be of lesser worth than the last. Although it shames me to confess it, I paid over seven hundred drachmai for those three nags, though the lot were not worth four hundred.

In midmorning we passed the hot spring of Thermopylai, where stood the pillars reared to the men who fell fighting Xerxes' Persians. As we had not yet broken fast, we dismounted to snatch a bite and let the horses graze on the narrow strip, a bare sixteen paces wide, between the Trachinian Cliffs and the sea. While we munched, Vardanas read the inscriptions. On reading the one to the Spartans:

> Go, stranger, and to Lakedaimon tell
> That here, obeying her commands, we fell

he broke into tears—not for pity at the Spartans, who had after all been fighting his own forebears, but at the poetic elegance of the couplet. "They come still," said Inaudos, shading his eyes to look back along the shore road.

"I hope your eyesight is as good as it seems," I said, clasping my hands to give Nirouphar a leg up. "Get up, all!"

We reached Lamia ere nightfall in the midst of an anxious discussion of our best route. The main wagon road continues on around the north side of the Malian Gulf and follows the shore all the way to the head of the Pagasaian Gulf, with many turns and twists. A lesser road, not suitable for wheels but much shorter, runs north from Lamia over the Achaian mountains into Phthiotis and thence into Thessalia. I held that our horses were failing, even with the spares; that the quicker we reached my own land the easier it would be to summon help; that we must leave the road to hide overnight in hope our pursuers would pass us by; and that this would be more feasible in the Achaian mountains than on the shore road.

So we took the track north from Lamia instead of the main road eastward. Nightfall found us plodding on panting beasts into the Achaian hills. Our pursuers dropped behind at Lamia, no doubt to ask which way we had gone. But, ere the sun had set, Inaudos, looking back from the top of a long rise, said they were on our trail again.

When we neared the crest of the Achaians, which divide Ainania from Achaia Phthiotis, I cast about for a hiding place. As this range is well forested with oak and pine, such a haven was not hard to find. With a quick look back to make sure our pursuers were not in sight, I waved my people off the road and up the course of a brook. A furlong from the road we found a well-hidden hollow with plenty of browse for the horses.

Leaving Nirouphar, Inaudos, and the Scythian in the hollow, Vardanas and I returned to the road on foot and lay behind some ferns, watching. I said:

"Take that polluted bucket off your head, laddie. They'll see it a league away."

Vardanas doffed his tall Persian hat. We must have waited half an hour before the pursuing party appeared. Like us, they were alternately cantering and walking. Now they were walking, strung out in a long line, two horses abreast, because of the narrowness of the track. It was some comfort to see that they and their beasts looked nigh as tired as we. Vardanas whispered:

"I could nail two or three with arrows ere they knew what had befallen them."

"Nay. We know not yet if they be Harpalos' men."

"How will you learn? By standing up and asking?"

"I'll tell you anon. Now hush!"

We lay while the twelve horses plodded past, with men on the backs of six. Although it was too dark to make out the men's faces, they wore rough plain clothing and carried both swords and spears. When they had gone, Vardanas asked:

"Perhaps you know what you do. Meseems you have let slip a chance that will not soon come again."

"I told you I should find out if they're Harpalos' men, did I not? Now hear this. If they be pursuers, they've been stopping at towns along the way to ask for tidings of us, thus making sure we had not left the road. Now, if they be but harmless fellow travelers, they'll go on about their business, and we shall never see them more. But if they seek us, they'll ask at the first towns in Phthiotis. When they learn we've not passed that way, they'll wheel around and come pelting back through these mountains, looking for side trails by which we might have left the road. So a watch and wait of a day or two, at this point, ought to settle the question."

"Mithras!" he said. "You are a tactician second only to Alexander himself. I think you err in leaving the army."

"'Tis nought so wonderful," I said.

"But what shall we do then?" quoth he. "Take up our journey again on this road? Or try to give them the slip in the forest?"

"We might try either. But I fear these slopes are too steep for horses. Besides, they know I'm bound for Atrax, and so would soon be on our trail again."

"What then? An ambuscade?"

"My thought exactly, buckie. Yonder's a fine place for fell work."

We took stock of our weapons. Everybody but the Scythian had a knife. I had a sword. Vardanas was much the best armed, having a sword, a spiked club, a bow, and his Persian kamynda of braided leather. I said: "If this rope were stretched across the road at a height of two or three feet just before the foe arrived, they'd trip over it and fall in a fine heap." We talked of methods of stretching the rope. Then Vardanas said: "We do not need a man on each end. If we fasten the noose around a tree, it will be enough for one man on the other end, across the road, to stretch it taut and give a quick turn around another tree to hold it."

"Good," I said. "Inaudos, as the biggest man here, you shall pull the rope taut. When they pile up, we'll rush in on them and slay all that are not killed in the wreck. Vardanas, your bow is our fellest weapon. Sit your horse among the trees until they pass, then swing into the road behind them and start shooting as they strike the rope. The Scythian and I shall charge down from the sides."

"How about me?" said Inaudos. "If I have to untie horse and mount without help, the fight will be over before I come. I cannot vault on horse as you do."

"You'd best attack on foot. There'll be others dismounted, too, and in such a rough-and-tumble you may do more good that way."

"What shall I fight with? This little thing?" said Inaudos, showing his dagger.

"Take my sword," said Vardanas. "But treat it well; my grandsire wielded it at Kounaxa."

"What will you use besides your bow?" I said.

"The mace," said Vardanas. "It is good only for cracking skulls. Easier it is for a mounted man to crack the skull of a foeman afoot than the contrary."

"They still have the advantage," said Inaudos. "They have spears, while we have none, nor shields either."

"We shall have spears of a sort," I said. "As for shields, let each of us, ere he close with the foe, wrap his mantle around his left arm."

Nirouphar said: "Although I am no warrior, I burn to take part in this battle, too. Can I not hold horses or something?"

We all shouted her down and insisted that a woman's place was well to the rear, where she would not get in the way.

It was a little after noon on the second day of our watch when Inaudos trotted back to us from his lookout. "They come," he said.

"Are you sure they're the same lot?"

"Oh yes. Same number, same dress, same weapons."

"How long ere they reach us?"

He tried to tell me, but the Kordian was not used to dividing the day into hours. He finally said: "If you get ready right now, you have some time before they arrive."

He dismounted, and Nirouphar led his horse back to the hollow. Vardanas, wearing his coat of iron scales and his Greek helmet, walked his horse up the road for twenty paces and then turned into the trees. The rope lay slack across the road, here three paces wide, with dust and leaves heaped upon it to hide it. Inaudos lay down behind a tree, holding the free end.

The Scythian and I mounted and pulled our horses up among the trees opposite Inaudos. Each of us grasped a crude wooden lance that I had whittled out of a pair of saplings. They were mere sharpened poles, with the points hardened by charring and scraping, like those the Assakenians used in Gandaria. Such a weapon is of little use against armor, but an unarmored man can be pushed off his horse with it, and a lucky thrust that pierces the torso will slay a man as dead as if he had been run through with tempered steel.

After a long wait, the sound of hooves came to us through the trees. Then my heart sank, for the sound was that of horses walking, not cantering. If they went past us at a walk, we could not trip them with the rope. As it had not occurred to me that they might do this,

Inaudos had no orders to cover the case. I hoped he would have sense enough to let them go past without discovering us.

Nearer and nearer they came. Then came a command, and the hoofbeats quickened to a gallop, louder and louder.

A shadow fell on the road before us. I saw a flash of movement beyond as Inaudos tautened the rope. There was a mingled scream of horses and their riders. The air was full of hurtling bodies and flailing limbs.

"Come," I said to the Scythian, leveling my lance and spurring Thunderbolt. "Get up!"

But I spoke to empty air. At the first crash, the Scythian dropped his lance, wheeled his mount, and galloped off into the woods.

I heard the snap of Vardanas' bow and his cry of, "Verethragnas aid me!"

Though the Scythian's desertion reduced our odds to one to two, there was no time to chase the dastard and give him his deserts. I had to help my friends quickly or they would be beyond help.

With a prayer to Ares I charged into the road. Two horses with riders had tripped over the rope and fallen. The rider of one lay still; that of the other was rising groggily. A third horse had blundered into the tangle, half fallen, and recovered, but had thrown its rider. A fourth rider had swerved to one side and jumped his mount over the rope. The two others had pulled up in time, but one of these riders was now down with a Persian arrow through him. The other was fighting his horse, which reared and bucked with the pain of another of Vardanas' arrows.

A couple of the led horses had fallen but were scrambling up again, while the rest milled wildly about, kicking and biting at anything that moved within reach.

The most dangerous man I judged to be the one who had jumped the rope. He was just turning his mount to charge back. I spurred Thunderbolt until even that sluggish mass of fat bestirred himself to an honest gallop. I dodged past some of the led horses and clutched my mount's mane to affix myself firmly in my seat against the shock of collision.

The rider was still turning when my lance caught him in the side below the armpit. It was one of my best lance thrusts, for it drove deeply into the man's body and hurled him from his seat. His weight dragged down the point of the lance, whose shaft broke across his horse's back.

I wheeled. Something struck my helmet with a clang, but I heeded it not. Seeing the man on the wounded horse still mounted, I made for him, swinging the stump of my lance like a cudgel. Riderless horses got between me and my quarry, so that no matter how many I dodged or drove away with blows, there always seemed to be more.

I had at last forced Thunderbolt within reach of the mounted man and had swung back the staff for a mighty blow, when two of the dismounted men ran at me from opposite sides. Thunderbolt screamed as one slashed at his hock while the other thrust a spear into his shoulder.

Hamstrung, the horse fell back and then on its side, pinning my right leg. The beast kicked and thrashed, rolling back and forth on my tortured leg. The led horses milled about us, almost stepping on me, until at last most of them ran off down the road.

Hopelessly, I fumbled for my sword as my two attackers stepped forward to finish me. Then I saw one become locked in a grapple with Inaudos. The other poised his spear for a thrust at my heart. I raised my sword in a futile effort to parry the lunge.

The man above me suddenly dropped his spear and clawed at his head, which seemed to be enveloped in a yellow fur cap. When the cap sprang away with a screech, the man stood dazedly feeling his scratched and bleeding face. Vardanas rode past him, looking furlongs high, and brought his spiked club down with a crunch. A thrown spear glanced off Vardanas' armor ere he passed from my sight.

Presently Inaudos and Vardanas returned together. Inaudos looked at my horse and cut its throat. The two dragged the carcass off me and helped me up. My leg was unbroken, but so badly bruised that I could not stand on it.

All six pursuers lay dead. One of their horses was dead also; the rest had run away. Inaudos had a brace of flesh wounds. Vardanas, thanks to his coat of lizard mail, had come through without a scratch.

Nirouphar rushed up and covered me with kisses.

"What befell?" I asked, hobbling back toward the hollow with my arms about my comrades' necks. "The lout was about to skewer me—"

Then I saw the empty cat basket at the edge of the forest. The cat had vanished. "Did you throw that cat at him?"

"Yes indeed, darling," said Nirouphar. "It was all I could think of, having neither sword nor spear to hand."

"A lucky cast, forsooth! I owe my life to it, though my mother must needs do without her Egyptian kitten. We shall have to rely on our dear old snake to keep the mice at bay." I sat down with a groan in the hollow.

"Whither has my slave gone?" said Vardanas.

"Fled at the first onset," I said. "If I be any soothsayer, he'll be halfway to Macedonia the morn. Thence he'll press on to Scythia, robbing hen roosts, unless he join a robber band. You'll never see him again. Now for Hera's sake give me some wine to lessen the pain!"

"The Scythian tried to take me with him," said Nirouphar, handing me a wineskin.

"Mithras smite the viper!" cried Vardanas. "What did the knave?"

"Hardly had the sound of the ambush come to my ears, when the slave galloped back to the hollow. He shouted something about my coming, caught my wrist, and tried to drag me across his horse's back. I pricked the horse with my dagger; it reared and nearly threw him. He cast a curse at me and rode on."

Vardanas cursed the Scythian with frightful curses. Calming, he said: "Why should the abandoned scoundrel do that, Leon? A woman's no use to him with his infibulation. At least, so the slave dealer told me."

"Nay; but, if he win to his own land, he'll soon have the ring snipped from his prong. After a few days' soreness he'll be as doughty a spearman as ever."

"Castration is better," growled Vardanas, cursing some more.

I said: "Come, my friend, would you not seize a chance to escape, were you a slave in Scythia?"

"Arimanes take such talk! Our philosophical friends in Athens have addled your mind with their foolish ideas of the equality of all men."

"Equal or not, he's free," I said, "and on two legs, which I am not. Now let's look to our own future. We've lost two horses—not that they were any kin to Pegasos—but we have captured no beasts to take their place."

"How stupid of me!" cried Vardanas, fumbling with the lacings of his mail coat. "Help me out of this crab's shell, Inaudos. I go to fetch a horse."

When free of his armor, Vardanas retrieved the kamynda from the dust, coiled it, and vaulted upon his steed. Off he went. Inaudos dragged the corpses off the road and buried them, while Nirouphar comforted me.

"At least," I said, "your brother need not worry about your virtue the now. While I'm in this sorry state, Aphrodite herself could get no pleasure from me. Though, of course, you are fully as beautiful as she," I hastily added.

As my injuries were of the kind that only time would mend, I resigned myself to sitting in the hollow for a few days. Late that afternoon, when Inaudos was broiling a steak from one of the slaughtered beasts, Vardanas brought in a horse he had caught with his noose.

"The kamynda is not meant for forests," he said. "I readily found the horses, but most of my casts were fouled by branches."

He rode off once more and at dusk returned with another. The next day he fetched two more, but on the following hunt failed to find the masterless remnant, which had now scattered too widely. Still, we were now two horses better off than when we set out.

Vardanas was vastly impressed by the grassy plains of Thessalia, even in their dreary winter guise. "What horse country!" he cried. "But alas, my friend, I see no horses; only herds of these oversized hares you falsely call by the noble name of 'horse.'"

I said: "True, we could do with some of your Median monsters. Belike, when our personal problems are settled, we could devise a scheme for fetching horses of the royal breed from your land to mine."

"We have a herd of them already," he said. "At my family's estate, that is. There were ten to begin with, but now they've doubled under my brother Kambouzias' loving care."

"Let us speak of this again," I said. "My parents would be outraged did I go into general trading, albeit I have some bent in that direction.

Luckily, horse trading is the one business a Thessalian knight may engage in without dishonor."

To reach Atrax, one goes sixty furlongs up the winding valley of the Peneios from Larissa. As we came unto the demesnes of my family, I began excitedly to point out landmarks.

"Over yonder lies my elder cousin Demonax's land, as far as you can see up the river," I babbled. "This parcel we rent to Yeoman Abas; that patch about his house he owns in qualified fee simple. Yon kine I think are ours...."

We entered our own holdings and rode several furlongs to the manor house. I saw that my brother Demonax had at last effected one of his favorite projects: that of putting gravel on the road to make it less muddy in winter and dusty in summer.

I meant at first to ride straight to the door of the manor, but as we passed by the farmyard it struck me that most of my family would be there at this time of day. And so it proved.

Tears started to my eyes as there unfolded before me the dear familiar scenes of my childhood, but little changed by time: my elder brother Demonax training a horse, the old pigpen removed to make way for a fountain, my sister Phila and a serving wench carrying between them a great basket of laundry from the washhouse, a new stable, my brother Aristos beating a serf, a cock chasing a hen around the dunghill, my father in heated dispute with the chief groom....

They all saw me at once. My sister dropped her wash in the mud with a screech that must have been heard in Larissa. My brothers ran toward me, bellowing a welcome until our horses danced uneasily. I dismounted, still limping, and was soon engulfed in family, retainers, and servants, all of whom rushed out to hug and kiss me. My mother heard the noise, came out from the manor house, and plowed through the crowd like a ship through the waves to add her embraces. She was a tall large-boned woman, and it secretly grieved me to see how much older she appeared than I remembered.

After greeting me, my father (who had put on weight and lost his hair since I saw him last) looked Vardanas over and whispered to me: "Is this the young Persian callant I've been hearing about, Leon?

Should I cast mysel down in the muck afore him, or what? Persians are a terrible polite folk, I'm told."

"He's a brother to me, so use him as such," I said. "And the lady is his sister Nirouphar."

Then they embraced and kissed Vardanas and Nirouphar, who took it with good grace. I opened my saddlebags and handed out my homecoming gifts amid shrieks from the women and affectionate roars from the men.

As we walked toward the manor, my father said: "I suppose you've come home full of grand Athenian ideas of how to play the gentleman. You'll be wanting us to eat lying down the now, and keep the women locked up in the benmost part of the house, eh?"

"Nought of the kind, Goodsire! I've seen men and their customs from Athens to India, and, by Zeus and all the gods, it does my heart good to be where I can act natural again!"

"Good lad!"

"As for my Persian friends, the more you entreat them like kinfolk, the happier 'twill make me. There's but one small matter. Is old Typhon still with us?"

"Aye; I saw him in the barn but yestreen."

"Then I ask that he be kept out of the house while they're here. Like many foreigners, they have a foolish fear of snakes."

"Losh, what queer folk foreigners maun be! But it shall be as you say. Tell me, do Persians dine mixed, or men and women separate? I ask because your good mother would hate to be parted from her bairn at your first repast at home."

"Mixed," I said. As we came to the door of the manor house, my mother said:

"I hope you've no forgotten how to wipe your feet, Leon darling!"

The torches and lamps burnt past midnight as we sat in the hall and told our adventures. My grandmother dozed through most of it. After sleeping the morning through, I forgathered with my parents to talk serious business. I showed them the money I had brought home.

"No vast Persian treasure?" said my father mockingly.

"Dinna bait the lad," said my mother. "Seeing all the temptations to fling one's silver away that there be in a soldier's life, he's done well to save as muckle as he has. But now, sweet Leon, there's another matter we maun speak of. How old are you? Twenty-six?"

"I entered my twenty-eighth year last month," I said.

"And still unwed. Sin you've left the king's service, you'll be settling down here, is it no?"

"What are you ettling after, Mother?"

My father interrupted: "When we got your letter from Athens— did you receive mine, by the bye?"

"Na, I didna."

"That oft befalls. As I wrote, your mother and I have taken thought on finding you a proper goodwife. I've put out inquiries among the knightly families of the region, and methinks I've found one."

"Who?" I gulped.

"Manto, daughter of Ion of Argoura."

I tried to recall Ion's family. He had several daughters, but the lass would have grown beyond recognition, anyway.

"She's fifteen," said my mother, "and well brought up. At no rate ugly, albeit her teeth might be better. But that's of less weight than her portion. Ion's offering two and a half talents! With your bonus you'll be a rich young couple. Besides, they're a branch of the Skopadai, so we shall have a connection with ilk of the best families of southern Thessalia."

I grunted. My father said: "The lad's no listening. What's agley?"

"Nought. Only—well—ah—"

"Is your mind bent another way?" asked my father suspiciously.

When I did not answer, Mother burst out: "'Tis the foreign cutty! Is it no true? I thought I saw him rolling ox eyes at her yesternight! Answer me, Leon!"

"Rhoda, my dear," said my father, "let's no—"

"Is it no true, Leon?" she cried. "The Persian strumpet—"

"I'll no have you speak on her in sic words!" I said, rising. "An you persist, I'll forth into the world again, talent and all."

"Leon! You darena speak thus till your own mother—"

"Pray, pray!" said my father. "Let's be keeping our tempers. Tell us about the kimmer, Leon."

"She's a well-born Persian lady, of a landowning family in Sousa muckle like ours. Aside from that, she's the brawest, purest, bonniest lass I've met in Hellas or Persia."

My mother said: "These foreign wenches can easily fool a wean like you. Too late you find they're temple whores or the like."

"I said I wudna bear sic talk!" I shouted.

"Now, now," said my father. "Do curb your tongue, Rhoda. You're but making matters waur. Now, Leon, let's speak of the little matter of property. Some Persians are said to be unco rich—"

"'Tis no for her property I love her, for she has none. She quarreled with her goodsire and ran away with her brother. And even gif she be reconciled, the Persians dinna give their daughters dowries. The man's family pays, instead."

My father's eyes bulged, and he sat down heavily. "By the gods!" he gasped. "I wudna have believed it. A foreigner is bad enough, let abee a dowerless wench—why son, you're fair, dune daft! I have never heard the like!"

"There was my grandfather Leon," I said.

"Aye, but that's long syne. Look you, Leon, take the besom to concubine if you maun. We all ken how strong are the lusts of youth—"

"Dinna speak on her so! Persians of good class are as jealous of their women's virtue as we, and I'll warrant she's a virgin still."

"Virgin or no," said my mother, "I might put up with a lass of small dowry, were she of well-known respectable local folk. But a filthy foreigner! Why, son, you'd even lose your franchise! 'Twere a disgrace to us all! I durstna see my friends again, but would shut mysel up like Danaë in her tower. Well, one thing's sure: the hussy maun be out of my house the night."

"An she go, I go, too," I said.

My mother raged at me, but my father asserted himself for once. "Hold your tongue, Rhoda. He has all your stubbornness; press him too far and he'll go as he says. Whereas, while he stays, there's a chance he'll somegate be brought to see reason. Forbye, 'twould smirch our repute for hospitality to ask our guests to leave over a matter in which, as far as we ken, they're blameless."

After some further argument, my father and I wrung a grudging agreement from my mother that there should be no more talk of sending my friends away.

"More by token," I said, "the lass shall be used with all our wonted courtesy. The erst I hear to the contrary—out I go!"

That night my father bid a number of his knightly friends and relations to the hall for a man's banquet. By next day, our quarrel had simmered down for the nonce. That morning I met Nirouphar in the courtyard and asked her how things went.

"They're as kind as they could be," she said. "Especially your dear mother, whom I love already as my own. But—oh, Rheon, she was telling me of your marriage customs! I fear it is hopeless for us."

I saw what Mother was up to, but short of leaving home I knew not what I could do about it. Despite my heated speech of the previous day, I was loath to leave, so soon at any rate after so long an absence. Besides, I had no definite plans for earning my bread, aside from hazy thoughts of re-enlisting in Alexander's armies.

In the afternoon, Vardanas came in from showing my brother Aristos tricks with his kamynda. The downy-bearded young Aristos was ever the difficult one of our family, dour and self-willed, but he was like putty in the Persian's hands. Next, Vardanas borrowed Aristos' lyre. When I came upon them, Vardanas was sitting in the courtyard, singing sad Persian love songs in a high quavery voice. When Aristos got bored and went off to practice with the noose, Vardanas struck a final chord and said:

"Have you spoken to your parents about the matter that concerns us all, Leon?"

"Aye. And the violence of their protests all but blew the roof off."

"As I expected," he said, striking another sad chord.

"Are you no pleased?"

"Nay, my friend. For I bid fair to join you in your misery."

"What mean you, laddie?"

"It is your fair sister Phila."

"Herakles! What see you in her?" I blurted. To me Phila was simply a snub-nosed brat with reddish hair who had grown up into a snub-nosed sixteen-year-old maid with reddish hair—a good fishing companion, perhaps, but not the sort any man in search of wife or mistress would look at twice.

"She has my heart in her keeping, though she know it not."

"O deathless gods! Eros has tied a knot more snarled than that of Gordios, and we have no sword wherewith to cleave it. Belike 'twere better not to bring this condition of yours before my parents yet; they've had one shock already."

Vardanas gave a deep sigh. "Alas, dearest friend! Would we were Athenians, who fall in love only with those of their own sex!" He began another melancholy Persian love song.

This was serious enough, but that night Phila stopped me in the house to ask me all about Vardanas.

"Oh," said she, closing her eyes, "is he no grand, though?"

Things quieted down for the nonce. There was always so much to be done on the estate that a man suffering from frustrated love could thus work off his feelings.

But in the month of Gamelion, when a sudden snowstorm had driven us in for the day and our guests were occupied elsewhere, our problem blew up into another domestic storm. I threatened to leave home, Phila threatened to slay herself if Vardanas departed, and my parents threatened all sorts of dire things.

Into this battle of words came my brother Demonax, shaking the snow from the folds of his cloak and thus further displeasing Mother, who hated wet floors. Everybody appealed to him, for he was by general consent deemed the wisest and justest of us all, and he had of late been taking over more and more of the management of the manor from my father.

Demonax, howsomever, kept a judicial silence, seeming more amused than appalled by our various plights. When the rest of us had shouted ourselves hoarse, he smiled his slow smile and said mildly:

"Hellenes give dowries; Persians give bride payments. What for no suffer these customs to cancel out? Let Vardanas give his bride payment to his sister to be her dowry; and, sin he'll then no have muckle left to live on, let you give Phila her marriage portion to set up housekeeping with the Persian, though he dinna expect it."

My mother cried: "Would you really let your own flesh and blood marry on these strangers from ayont the seas, where they practice the gods know what abominations?"

"What for no? Gin the king can do it, we can. As for Vardanas, from what I've seen of him, I call him a braw chappie. He and I have just ridden into town and back."

"But, Demonax!" protested my father. "'Tis clean illegal! 'Twould cost Leon his citizenship, let abee social standing!"

Now Demonax grinned broadly. "That may have been true last month, but 'tis so no longer," said he, relishing every word. "Have you no heard of the notice on the news board in the market place in Atrax?"

"Na!" we all cried. "What says it?"

"'Tis a proclamation by the king, which arrived by royal post a few days syne. Alas, that we were no in town to hear it read by the crier! 'Twould have saved a muckle havering. But what it says is this: Alexander, to cement a lasting bond of love atween the noblest peoples of his realm, namely the Hellenes and the Persians, has adopted a policy of intermarriage. He will this very month, at Sousa, celebrate a marriage atween himself and his Macedonian generals on one hand, and ane equal number of Persian ladies on the other. Soldiers who have taken Persian concubines shall have their unions made legal unless previous marriages prevent. All laws again such interracial marriages, throughout his empire, are repealed; and all penalties sic as loss of citizenship shall be remitted."

"Why said you no so, long syne?" I cried. "'Tis a cause for me to rejoice!"

"Alexander will never persuade the southern Greeks to swallow that doctrine," said my father.

Phila, her eyes red from weeping, said: "Please, Father, let him go on."

Demonax continued: "Such marriages shall be deemed as noble and legitimate as any other, and aught to the contrary shall incur the king's displeasure. To give the new unions ane auspicious start, all soldiers and former soldiers taking part shall receive a dowry of one year's pay from the royal treasury. What was your pay, Leon?"

"Eh?" So turbulent were my thoughts that he had to repeat his question.

I said: "I'm carried on the rolls as squadron leader the now. That would make—let me think—about sixteen pounds of silver." In sooth, the question of money interested me much less than the fact that the last legal obstacle to an honorable union had been blown away by the king's decree, like a scrap of papyrus in a gale.

While my parents sat with stunned demeanor, Demonax went on: "So all you maun do is wed your Persian lass, ride to Larissa with witnesses or depositions, and file a claim with the governor again the Macedonian treasury. Gin all go well, you should be getting a bonny nest egg in a month or two."

I muttered my thanks and started for the door to find my sweetling, but my brother caught my arm. "One moment, Leon. Vardanas and I talked business on our ride, and he has a thought that might make this union gey profitable to us."

"Aye?" said my father, rousing himself from his stupor. "Profit? Say on, son."

"You ken the giant cavalry chargers of Media, the royal breed? Well, it seems that horse thieves broke up the great herd at the fall of Dareios, and some of these horses came into the hands of Vardanas' family. Vardanas thinks we could fetch the increase of this herd hither from Sousa. They'll command fabulous prices in Hellas."

My father looked at Phila and me. "Children," he said, "I yield to the manifest will of the gods. Wed your Persians with my blessing!"

There was much to be done ere all these high-sounding plans could be executed. We sent Getas, a trusted slave who had refused emancipation, to Sousa with letters to Vardanas' family. While awaiting a reply, we busied ourselves with the myriad chores: delivering calves and foals, building a new hay cart, mending the horse trough, and visiting sick serfs.

My mother, to give her due credit, did all she could to make up for her early hostility by being good to our guests. On closer acquaintance she came to love them even as I had.

In the spring, Getas returned. He brought news that old Thraitau-nas had grown feeble and was confined to his bed. Young Kambou-zias, who now held the reins of the household, wrote that his sire longed to see his runaway son and daughter again. If they came home ere he died, they might wed black Ethiops for aught he cared. As for the royal horses, the herd was waxing, and the proposal for an export trade was excellent. When could we begin?

So, one fine day in Mounychion, Vardanas was joined to Phila and I to Nirouphar. We borrowed my uncle Leon's house so that there should be the proper wedding processions both ways.

Ere she would wed me, however, Nirouphar exacted one extraordinary promise: namely, that I should teach her to read and write Greek proficiently. At the time, I thought this a mere womanish whim, but it turned out well. If my readers detect in this memoir a touch of literary art beyond what would be expected of an old soldier and horse trader, the credit should go to the merciless prodding, criticism, and revision of my dear wife, who seems to have a natural literary gift.

Her one regret is that she did not learn to read and write the Greek tongue in childhood. She is sure that if she had, she would have surpassed Sappho as a poet, Thoukydides as a historian, and the divine Homer himself as a spinner of tales of adventure. Who knows? Belike she would have, at that.

It were not decent to go into the details of my married life. I will only say that if, like most married couples, we have had our ups and downs, I would repeat those marriage vows without hesitation.

After the wedding feast, we set forth once more upon our travels. We traveled in comparative comfort, with slaves and my burly Kord-ian to tend us. One pleasure of this merry journey was to show Phila, who had never even been to Larissa, the sights of distant lands. We reached Sousa at the beginning of Skirophorion, in time to receive the onset of the terrible summer heat. But business is business, as we say in Thessalia.

Our horse trade went through appalling vicissitudes, but in the end it flourished. We have had the patronage of Seleukos the Victorious, king of Syria and Persia. He alone of the Successors kept the Persian wife whom Alexander thrust upon him, the princess

Apama; and he therefore looked with favor upon Vardanas and me because of our mixed marriages. We have also had the good will of the younger Arivarates of Kappadokia, through whose land the roads to Hellas run.

I bought a house at Alexandreia-by-Issos from that same Syrian stonemason who sought to sell me one when I went there with the elephant, thus placing myself in an advantageous position in the middle of our horse-trading route. I also bought enough land to provide grazing for the beasts on their way through. My children are as proud of this patch of Syrian seacoast as I was aforetime of our broad Thessalian plethra.

On the whole, I have done well. I have seen the pyramids of Egypt, the snows of Scythia, and the bustle of Syracuse, greatest of Greek cities. I have outlived many of those who played leading roles in this tale. For, after Alexander's death, the philosopher Aristoteles was forced to leave Athens because of his Macedonian connections, and the next year he died in Euboia. My brother Aristos, alas, perished in the Lamian War, which broke out at this time.

That fat rascal Harpalos, who had tried so diligently to have me slain, for a time had all Athens dancing to the tune of his bribes. The great windbag Demosthenes succumbed easily. Even grim old Phokion, the general-in-chief, was drawn into the circle of corruption by a commission to his son-in-law to build a huge monument to the treasurer's first wife.

Then the Athenians changed their minds—whether from a rush of conscience, or fear of Alexander, or sheer fickleness—and drove Harpalos out. He fled to Crete, where his follower Thimbron murdered him and in his turn perished adventuring in Africa. As they say, no tears are shed when an enemy dies.

Vardanas and my brother Demonax, praise to the gods, survive hale and whole and will leave many children and grandchildren to make offerings to their shades. Assuming, as Pyrron of Elis would say, that such things as shades exist.

Speaking of Pyrron and of the gods, I have become, like him, very skeptical about supernatural matters. But here I shall thank any gods there be, that, in a world so lavishly supplied with fools and knaves, they chose for me such stout and worthy comrades on that long and perilous journey which I made with Aias the elephant. Never shall I forget the faithful and practical soldier Thyestes, the sober and earnest Indian elephantarch Kanadas, the wise and cheerful philosopher Pyrron, the shrewd and foresighted Syrian trader Elisas, and most of all, the gallant Persian gentleman Vardanas. If any gods do in fact exist, I wish them to know I am grateful; if they exist not, no harm is done.

Finished at Alexandreia-by-Issos,
on the tenth day of Metageitnion,
in the fourth year of the hundred and twentieth Olympiad,
and the archonship of Antiphates

Postscript

THE FOLLOWING PERSONS appearing or mentioned in this story were real persons; alternative forms of their names are given in parentheses: Aboulites, Agathon, Agis, Aischylos (Aeschylus), Alexander (Alexandras), Alexarchos, Anaximandros (Anaximander), Antigonos, Antipatros (Antipater), Apollodoros, Archelaos, Aristoteles (Aristotle), Arivarates (Ariarathes, Ariwarat, the name of two kings), Artaxerxes (Ardashir, Arfakhshathra, Artaxšaçah, the name of three kings), Asandros (Asander), Baiton, Bas, Boupares, Charidemos, Dareios (Darayavauš, Darius, the name of three kings), Dareios (banker), Deinokrates, Demetrios, Demosthenes, Eumenes, Euripides, Harpalos, Hephaistion, Herakleides, Kalas, Kallikrates, Kallisthenes, Kephisodotos, Krateros, Kroisos (Croesus), Kyros (Cyrus, Kuruš, the name of a king and a pretender), Masdais (Mazaeus, Mazdai), Masdaros (Mazarus), Menes (Maniš), Menon, Nabarzanes, Naboukodreusor (Nebuchadnezzar, Naboukodonosoros, Nabu-kudurri-ushur), Nikomachos, Ombis (Omphis, Ambhi), Oneskritos, Pamphylios, Peithagoras, Philip (Philippos, king), Philippos (brother of Harpalos), Philokles, Philoxenos, Phokion, Phratapharnas (Fratafarnah, Phrataphernes), Phrashavartes (Frašavartiš, Phrasaortes), Platon (Plato, Aristokles), Polykleitos, Poros (Puru), Praxiteles, Psammon, Ptolemaios (Ptolemaeus, Ptolemy), Pyrraios (Pyrrhaeus), Pyrron (Pyrrho), Pythagoras, Sabiktas (Sabistamenes), Sangaios (Sangaeus), Sasigouptas (Sasigupta, Sisicottus), Seleukos (Seleucus), Sokrates, Sophokles, Stamenes (Stamaniš), Stasanor, Theophrastos (Tyrtamos), Thimbron, Tissaphernes (Chithrafarna, Ciçafarnah), Vaukas (Ochos, Vahaukah),

Vaxathras (Oxathres, Vaxšaθrah), Vaxouvartas (Oxyartes, Vaxšuvartah), Xenokrates, Xerxes (Khshayarsha, Xšayaršah, the name of two kings), Zarathoushtras (Zarathustra, Zaraθuštrah, Zardusht, Zoroaster), Zenophilos. So were a number of well-known characters from earlier times, such as Thales and Solon, mentioned by the people in the story.

It is not known whether Alexander really sent an elephant to Aristotle, but he may well have. It is known that he gave subsidies (including the gift to Xenokrates) to various philosophers, that Kallisthenes sent astronomical data to Aristotle from Babylon, and that Aristotle wrote an accurate description of an elephant that reads as if he had seen one. The story is based on the strong possibility that Alexander did send an elephant.

Approximate modern equivalents of weights and measures mentioned in the story are as follows:

Pound *(mna)*	1.1	pounds
Talent *(talanton)*	66	pounds
Finger *(daktylos)*	¾	inch
Palm *(palaistē)*	3	inches
Foot *(pous)*	1	foot"
Cubit *(pēchys)*	18	inches
Pace *(bēma)*	30	inches
Plethron	100	feet; 10,000 square feet
Furlong *(stadiōn)*	⅛	mile
League *(parasangē)*	3.5	miles
Quart *(choinix)*	1	(dry) quart
Medimnos	1.5	bushels

Attic units of weight were less than the Babylonian units used in the Persian and Alexandrine empires. The Attic pound = .95 English pounds.

In money, 8 chalkoi ("coppers") = 1 obolos; 6 oboloi = 1 drachma; 100 drachmai = 1 mna ("pound"); 60 mnai = 1 talent of silver. All these units were originally weights of silver, not coins; the mna and talent were never coins. There were about fifteen common denominations of bronze and silver coins, ranging up to the dekadrachmon (ten drachmai) more than half again as heavy as a silver dollar. The commonest larger silver coins were the drachma (about the size of a dime but heavier) and the tetradrachmon (four drachmai, about the size of a half dollar). The Athenian drachma was called an "owl" from the design on the reverse. The drachma's purchasing power was equivalent to several dollars, though exact comparisons are impossible because we have so many things to spend our money on that did not exist in ancient times. The main golden coins were the Persian daric *(dareikos)* and the stater, worth about twenty-three and twenty-eight drachmai respectively, though the ratio fluctuated.

In Leon's time, most Greek cavalry was organized in troops, each troop *(ilē)* comprising about fifty to seventy-five men. Typically, two troops made a squadron *(telos);* two squadrons a battalion *(taxis);* two battalions a regiment *(tagma);* and two regiments a brigade *(phylē).*

However, as with measures and coinage, the sizes and names of the units varied widely from time to time and place to place. *Hipparchia* was a general term for a cavalry command, unit, or detachment. All horses except the Median cavalry chargers were mere ponies by modern standards, and neither stirrups nor horseshoes existed.

The Attic year, used by Leon, began on the day of the first new moon following the summer solstice; hence it might begin any day from June 23 to July 22. The exact date of the battle of the Hydaspes, which opens the story, is not known, but it took place in the spring or early summer of 326 B.C.

Leon's "mountain mouse" is the bobac or Asiatic marmot, a cousin of our woodchuck. His "unicorn" is the Indian rhinoceros. His "tree wool" and "tree grass" are cotton and bamboo respectively. The "Chattians" are the Hittites.

Some peculiarities of Leon's spelling of foreign names may be noted. Unlike most Greeks, he distinguishes between *b*—and *v*—sounds, spelling the former with *beta* and the latter with the obsolete *digamma (ϝ)* which was used in writing dialects though it had long disappeared from standard Attic. He uses the obsolete *san (ϱ)* to indicate the common *sh*-sounds of Asiatic tongues, though not consistently. Another idiosyncrasy is his indication of *h*-sounds in the middle of foreign names, like *Daha*. This too, was not done in standard Attic, but was in some Greek dialects.

Here follows a table of geographical names in the story, with approximate modern equivalents. In some cases the location of the ancient city is doubtful or is some miles from the modern one. Names marked (*) are fictional names formed by analogy with known names.

Old	**Modern**
Adana	Seyhan, Sihun
Aigaiai (Aegaeae)	Ceyhan, Jihun
Alexandreia Archotion (see Gazaka)	
Alexandreia-by-Issos	Alexandretta, Iskanderum
Alexandropolis (see Kandacha)	
Amida	Diyarbekir
Arachotia (Arachosia, Harauvatish, Hauravatish)	Kandahar Prov.
Arachotis Lake	Ab-i-Istáda
Arachotos R., east branch	Tarnak R.
Arachotos R., west branch	Arghand-Ab
Arados	Arwad, Rouad
Areia (Haraiva)	Herat Prov.
Areios (Haraiva, Harauvatish, etc.) L.	Hamun-i-Helmand
Areios R.	Adraskand Rud
Mt. Argaios (Argaeus)	Erciyas Daği
Ariana	Iran
Asagartia (Sagartia)	Southern Khurasan
Assakenia (Souastene)	Swat
Athens (Athenai)	Athenai or Athena
Attika	Attiki
Babylon (Babilu)	Kweiresh
Boiotia (Boeotia)	Voiotia
Byblos (Gebel)	Djebeïl
Chaarena (Chaarene)*	Kharan

Chaboras (Araxes) R.	Khabur or Khabour R.
Chaibara* Pass	Khaibar or Khyber Pass
Chasis* R.	Khash Rud
Chattysas* (Hattusas)	Boğazkale, formerly Boğazköy or Boghaz Keui
Chavaspes* (Choaspes) R.	Kunar R.
Chavaspes* (Choaspes) R.	Kherkah R.
Dahai* (Daai, Dahae), Land of the	Turkmen Rep.
Dida* (Koprates, Itite, Idide) R.	Ab-i-Diz
Doura (Dura)	Dour
Ephesos	Ayasolük
Eulaios (Ulai) R.	Upper Karun R.
Europos (Karchemish)	Djerablous
Gandaria (Gandara, Gandhara)	Kabul Prov.
Garis* (Gari, Harakhraiti)	Girishk
Gaugamela	Tell Gomel
Gazaka (Alexandreia Arachotion?)	Ghazni
Gorva* (Gorouaia, Goryene)	Bajaur
Hagmatana (Agbatana, Ecbatana)	Hamadan
Haitoumans* (Etymandros, Haetumant) R.	Helmand R.
Haravatis* (Harauvatish, Arachotia City?)	Kalat-i-Ghilzai?
Hydaspes (Visasta) R.	Jhelam R.
Hyrkania (Varkana, Gurgan)	Mazanderan + Asterabad Provs.
Ikonion (Iconium)	Konya
India (Hindush, Sindhu)	Panjab
Ipsos (Kaystros)	Çay
Issos	Dörtyol
Istros (Ister) R.	Danube R.

373

Kaboura (Cabura, Orthospana)	Kabul
Kandacha* (Kandach, Alexandropolis?)	Kandahar
Kapisa	Bulola
Karmana	Kerman C.
Karmania	Kerman Prov.
Karrai (Carrhae)	Haran
Kasipapoura* (Kaspatyros, Caspapyrus, Kasyapapura)	Jalalabad
Keramon–agora	Usak
Kithairon (Cithaeron) Mts.	Kathairon or Elatea Mts.
Kophen (Cophes) R.	Kabul R.
Kophen R., south branch	Logar R.
Kordavana* (Gordyene, Corduëne)	Kurdistan
Kybistra (Herakleia)	Eregli
Kydnos (Cydnus) R.	Tersous Chai
Kyros (Cyrus, Araxes) R.	Kur or Bandamir R.
Kyrros (Cyrrhus)	Kilis
Laranda	Karaman
Lebadeia	Levadeia
Mazaka (Caesarea)	Kayseri
Mopsou–hestia	Misis
Nia (Nië)	Neh, Nikh
Ninos (Ninua, Nineveh)	Mosul
Nisaia (Nisaya, Nesaion)	Kazvin + Tehran Provs.
Nisibis	Nusaybin
Opis (Upi)	Balad
Parin	Pir-Zada?
Parsagarda (Pasargadae)	Murghab
Parthia (Parthava)	Shaman-Damghan Prov.
Peneios (Peneus) R.	Salambria R.
Persepolis (Parsa)	Takht-i-Jamshid
Persia	variously Fars, Iran, or the Persian Empire

Persis (Parsa)	Fars Prov.
Peukala (Peucelaotis, Pushkalavati)	Charsadda
Phrada (Phra)	Farah
Phrada (Phra) R.	Farah Rud
Pinaros R.	Deli R.
Pasitigris (Positigris) R.	Lower Karun R.
Prymnessos	Afyon Karahisar
Pteria	Alaca Hüyük
Pyramos R.	Ceyhan or Jihun R.
Rhesaina	Resülayn, Ras-el-Ain
Sakai (Sacae, Sacians, Min), Land of the	Turkestan
Saros R.	Seyhan or Sihun R.
Scythia	Ukraine
Sousa (Susa, Shushan)	Shush
Sousiana, Houza* (Elam, Elymais,	Khuzistan
Hūja, Uvja, Kissia, Goution)	
Soustara*	Shushtar, Shuster
Tabara* (Tiberus) R.	Tabra or Tamra R.
Tarsos (Tarsus)	Tersous
Lake Tatta	Tuz Gölü
Taurus Mts.	Toros Dağları
Taxasila* (Taxila, Takshaçila)	Rawalpindi
Thatagous* (Thatagush, Sattagydia,	Logar Dist.?
Kophene)	
Thebes (Thebai)	Thevai
Tyana	Kiz Hisar
Tyre (Tyros, Zor)	Sour
Zabatos R.	Zab R.
Zarangiana (Drangiana, Zranka)	Seistan

Lightning Source UK Ltd.
Milton Keynes UK
UKHW010409270620
365636UK00001B/96